How could the face of a soldier drive his fellows desert by the dozen? Find out in Ed Gorman's ''The Face'' . . .

In Thomas Thompson's ''Gun Job,'' Jeff Anderson wants to give up the dangerous life of a lawman for his family's sake, but in the eyes of his townspeople, he will always be a marshal . . .

A newcomer to the Yukon thinks a real man can brave anything alone—even eighty-degrees-below-freezing cold—in Jack London's ''To Build a Fire'' . . .

Chosen by the Western Writers of America and edited by Dale L. Walker, these stories—including four that have been brought to the screen as Western classics such as *High Noon* and *3:10 to Yuma*—represent a wide-ranging showcase of talent . . . and serve as an example of everything that great Western fiction can be: dramatic, romantic, and a true adventure of the human spirit.

THE WESTERN HALL OF FAME ANTHOLOGY

THE WESTERN HALL OF FAME ANTHOLOGY

STORIES BY
Louis L'Amour, Elmore Leonard,
Elmer Kelton, Jack London,
Loren D. Estleman,
and others

EDITED BY
DALE L. WALKER

BERKLEY BOOKS, NEW YORK

THE WESTERN HALL OF FAME ANTHOLOGY

A Berkley Book / published by arrangement with
Tekno-Books and Dale L. Walker

PRINTING HISTORY
Berkley edition / December 1997

All rights reserved.
Copyright © 1997 by Tekno-Books and Dale L. Walker.
A continuation of copyright credits appears on page 267.
This book may not be reproduced in whole or in part,
by mimeograph or any other means, without permission.
For information address: The Berkley Publishing Group,
a member of Penguin Putnam Inc.,
200 Madison Avenue, New York, New York 10016.

The Putnam Berkley World Wide Web site address is
http://www.berkley.com

ISBN: 0-425-15906-X

BERKLEY®
Berkley Books are published by The Berkley Publishing Group,
a member of Penguin Putnam Inc.,
200 Madison Avenue, New York, New York 10016.
BERKLEY and the "B" design
are trademarks belonging to Berkley Publishing Corporation.

PRINTED IN THE UNITED STATES OF AMERICA

10 9 8 7 6 5 4 3 2 1

CONTENTS

INTRODUCTION

The span of time covered by the stories in *The Western Hall of Fame Anthology* is 150 years—from Bret Harte's California Gold Rush tale "The Luck of Roaring Camp" to Max Evans's allegorical "Candles in the Bottom of the Pool," set in the contemporary Southwest.

But I hope you'll read the timeless "Gun Job" before you read the others.

There are good reasons to start with it. First, it is an archetypal Western yarn, set in a town named Alkali, with an underlying sodbuster-vs.-cattleman plot and involving a retired lawman called back to duty. Second, it is instructive to read it as a "Golden Age" (1930s–1950s) Western story and contrast it with works by such modern-day masters of the genre as Max Evans, Loren D. Estleman, Bill Pronzini, and Ed Gorman to see not only how far the Western has come, but how far it can go.

And there is a third reason.

"Gun Job" connects with the origin of this book: it was written by a founder of the organization responsible for selecting these Hall of Fame stories, a writer who had no idea his old *Collier's* story would be regarded as one of the best short Westerns of all time.

In the summer of 1952, a one-time Texas cowboy and New Mexico quarter-horse ranch owner who had studied at the Cincinnati Art Academy received a letter from a California friend who had been a merchant sailor, furniture salesman, and nightclub singer.

Despite their miscellaneous backgrounds, the two men had something significant in common: between them they had published thirty-five Western novels and a lot of stories for the Western pulp magazines. And now the pulps were dead or dying and the two writers felt they were being set adrift. They knew a lot of others who felt the same way, and wondered what they could do about the situation.

Nelson Coral Nye, the former cowboy, and Thomas Thompson, the former sailor, talked by letter about the sad state of Westerns and after some weeks of postal hand-wringing, decided the least they could do would be to organize—bring together a number of professional Western writers, have a meeting, maybe publish a newsletter.

Nye and Thompson pulled it all together and in less than a year, after enlisting the help of four other veteran writers—Harry Sinclair Drago, Norman A. Fox, Dwight B. Newton, and Wayne D. Overholser—launched Western Writers of America, Inc., with a constitution, a president (Nye), vice-president (Drago), a secretary-treasurer (Newton), and a mimeographed publication they called *The Roundup*, the first issue of which, edited by Nye, appeared in April 1953.

The original members of WWA formed a cadre of giants of Western storytelling: Frederick D. Glidden (Luke Short), William McLeod Raine, Steve Frazee, Bill Gulick, Lew Holmes, Noel Loomis, Walker Thompkins, Garland Roark, Lewis B. Patten, Roe Richmond, Giff Cheshire, Leslie Ernenwein, and Frank C. Robertson, and agents, editors, and publishers Gus Lenniger, Don Ward, Raymond T. Bond (of Dodd, Mead), Charles Heckelmann (of Popular Library), Clarkson N. Potter, and Ian Ballantine.

Tommy Thompson, who became membership chairman of the fledgling organization also took command of somebody's idea to give awards for the best Western novels and stories of the year. Les Ernenwein suggested the awards be called "Ernies" in memory of everybody's idea of the "classic" Western writer, Ernest Haycox, who had died in 1950; Norman Fox wanted them called "Charlies" after Western artist and author Charles M. Russell. Others had other ideas.

"In the middle of the night a thought struck me," Thompson recalled. "Why not call them 'Spurs'? A spur is definitely Western and if you win one it would spur you on the way to bigger and better things . . .''

The first Spur Awards were given out at WWA's first convention in Denver in 1954. The ''Best Novel'' Spur went to Lee Leighton (Wayne D. Overholser) for *Lawman*, the ''Best Short Story'' to Thomas Thompson for ''Gun Job,'' published the year before in *Collier's*.

With publication of this collection of Western short story classics, forty-five years had passed since the founding of Western Writers of America, Inc. There were twenty-nine men in that original group and to be an ''active'' member you had to have published at least three novels. Magazine writers had a separate membership category and no nonfiction writers, poets, screen, television or juvenile writers need apply.

In 1996, WWA had over 600 members in forty-three states, Canada, Germany, and Norway. About half of the ''active'' (professional writer) membership is made up of nonfiction writers; the ''associate'' (non-writer) members include literary agents, editors, publishers, critics, librarians, and booksellers.

The organization still meets annually (always the last week in June) in a Western city; the convention is open to non-members and stages panels, seminars, speeches, and a Spur Award banquet, to celebrate ''the Western'' in all its forms—short story and novel, magazine article and nonfiction book, screen and teleplay.

In 1995, a year-long survey was conducted among members of Western Writers of America to determine the members' choice of the all-time best Westerns—Westerns worthy of a Hall of Fame.

A 121-title list of short stories was produced by 100 Active members of WWA and the stories herein were selected from that list.

—Dale L. Walker
President, WWA (1992–1994)
El Paso, Texas

AUTHOR NOTES

Louis L'Amour was the Stephen King of Westerns. Nobody before or since has had his luck in selling Western novels.

Born in 1908, L'Amour started out as a two-fisted pulp writer, filling many pulps with his rugged, if primitive, tales. He was one of those writers who consciously improved his craft. He got a lot better, so much so that his fiction began appearing in the occasional slick as well as the pulps.

Early on, L'Amour became a staple in the production of paperback originals, writing several for Ace Double Books as Jim Mayo. He also did many Westerns under his own name for Fawcett Gold Medal, where he was published quite successfully.

But it was not until the late fifties, when Bantam began publishing him, that he became a phenomenon. He ultimately sold more than 100,000,000 copies.

L'Amour was frequently a much better writer than his critics were willing to admit. His stories had pulp muscle and a kind of melancholy spirit rarely seen in best-sellerdom. He wrote action tales, true, but was able to give his stories theme and subtext. He will likely remain in print well into the next century.

Thomas Thompson's career was the sort that most of his contemporaries looked upon with great admiration and at least a bit of envy. Born in 1913, graduated from high school in 1930, Thompson embarked on a career that included being a sailor, working as a nightclub entertainer, and selling furniture. But by 1940, he was working as a full-time writer, his fiction leading him to such great positions as associate producer and writer of the *Bonanza* TV series and the story consultant for the *Temple Houston* crime dramas.

Thompson's writing displays genre virtues at their best—his stories and books are tight, precise, and laid out with maximum drama, all these being virtues he no doubt learned by writing for motion pictures and television.

As author Bill Pronzini has noted, "Once the highest paid short-story writer in America, **Bret Harte** [1836–1902] wrote perhaps the finest fictional accounts of the lusty and sometimes violent life in the mining camps and boomtowns during the great California Gold Rush of the 1850s."

Equally celebrated was his literary feud with Mark Twain, who seemed to feel threatened and intimidated by Harte. Or perhaps it was simply jealousy. For a long stretch of time, Harte was the more successful of the two writers. Hard as it is to imagine, writers do get jealous of each other.

In the long run, Twain proved to be the deeper writer but Harte was nonetheless a wonderful entertainer, one almost as cynical in his own way as his erstwhile rival Twain.

Hollywood recently re-released John Ford's unedited *The Red Badge of Courage* to extremely favorable reviews. As Ford said just before his death, "I only got a tenth of the novel's power on film." While Ford was being uncharacteristically modest, his notion is probably correct: Nobody could ever "film" *The Red Badge of Courage*. Despite its short length, it is simply too rich and ripe in symbolism to ever translate to any other medium.

Stephen Crane was as good with the short story as he was with the novel. "The Blue Hotel" is one of the landmarks in American literature. One can certainly see its influence on later generations of writers. Both Hemingway and Steinbeck talked about its great influence on their own work.

Jack London was born in 1876 and came of age just as America was discovering its real power and influence. He was prototypical of his generation—inquisitive, adventurous, impatient, a wee bit arrogant, and filled with the notion of manifest destiny.

He was so reckless and prolific as a writer that the establishment of literary critics rarely found his work noteworthy. But he didn't write for them. He wrote for his vast public, taking them, through his fiction, to such exotic locales as the South Seas and the Klondike.

His revenge on the literary establishment was like Poe's: He confounded his critics by remaining popular long after his death.

To dismiss London as "an adventure writer," as so many have, is to miss the underpinnings of despair and fear found in so many of his stories. His best stories speak not only of physical adventure . . . but of spiritual adventure as well. His stories have endured because they speak to the eternal theme of loneliness . . . all his heroes rushing about trying to find the real purpose of existence . . . and never quite finding it at all.

To names such as Owen Wister, Jack Schaefer, and Elmore Leonard, one must add the name **Elmer Kelton.** Like those other men, he took the raw material of the Western novel and shaped it into a means of expression that was wholly his own.

Some of his titles alone tell you how different and special his books are: *The Day the Cowboys Quit, After the Bugles, The Time It Never Rained.*

Born in Texas in 1926, Kelton brought realism and naturalism to the Western novel. Like other serious writers of his generation, including John Steinbeck, Kelton wanted to show the world what the real old West had been like . . . and, in some of his later novels, what the real West is like today.

There is a hard-bitten lyricism to be found in the sentences of Kelton. The land of Texas seems to especially inspire him. He is one of the few writers able to demonstrate the relationship of man to land . . . and how the land itself shapes and changes mankind.

• • •

Loren D. Estleman is probably the most innovative Western writer of his generation. He has worked in virtually every sub-genre—from the historical Western to the hard-boiled fusion of crime and Western—and reinvented each form he's worked with.

In addition to his skills with plot, Estleman is one of the two or three best stylists the genre has ever produced. His prose is flat-out magnificent but never pretentious or portentous.

Though Estleman was born in 1952, and is thus a baby boomer, his themes reflect an older and more conservative America, the pioneering spirit, if you will.

What is particularly notable about Loren's career is that he has accomplished so much well before his fiftieth birthday. Few others can make the same claim.

Glendon Swarthout wrote a number of highly successful novels that also became highly successful movies. But he also wrote a number of novels that, while less successful commercially, secured his lasting place in the Western Writers Hall of Fame.

The Shootist is one of the most important Western novels ever published. It completely destroys—then carefully rebuilds—the myth of the Western gunfighter. The prose is impeccable, as it is in such other Swarthout novels as *They Came to Cordura* and *Skeletons*. An educated man, a professor in fact, he seemed to have a first-rate understanding of the gears and mechanisms of American popular fiction. With *The Shootist,* he demonstrated that he could successfully write literature, as well.

Swarthout was born in 1918 and his books reflect the concerns and obsessions of his generation, culminating in the sentimental but well-written novel *Luck and Pluck.*

Ed Gorman is a Midwesterner, born in Iowa in 1941, growing up in Minneapolis, Minnesota; Marion, Iowa; and finally Cedar Rapids, Iowa. While primarily a suspense novelist, he has written half a dozen Western novels and published a collection of Western stories. His novel *Wolf*

Moon was a Spur nominee for Best Paperback Original. About his Western novels, *Publishers Weekly* said, "Gorman writes Westerns for grown-ups," which the author says he took as a high compliment, and was indeed his goal in writing his books.

Rodeo performer, rancher, miner, **Max Evans,** who was born in 1925, was able to experience life as it was frequently lived in the old West . . . and to write about it.

Evans is one of the genre's superstars, a 100 percent original talent. Nobody is foolish enough to try and imitate him. He is his own man in every respect.

Evans works in the most difficult yet most rewarding of all literary forms, the tragi-comedy. He's as good at making you cry as he is at making you laugh.

He is also, in his own sly way, a fine reporter, setting down with no false romance the West as it really was, and really is.

He is also one of Western fiction's real stylists. His sentences bark, roll over, wag their tails, and leave you begging for more.

Bill Gulick was born in Missouri in 1916. He notes, in a biographical sketch, "I write books that are set in the West—not Westerns."

In such fully realized novels as *Bend of the Snake* and *Liveliest Town in the West*, one sees the distinction Gulick makes. His books are character studies as well as plot-driven stories, and his take on frontier America is almost always as exciting as his story lines.

Gulick has continued to write, and write well, into the present day. He is one of those writers whose love of the craft is apparent in each and every sentence.

Bill Pronzini is another suspense writer who also writes Westerns. He brings his distinct narrative voice, and formidable literary skills, to each book and story. His characters are especially haunting, being the driven and often lonely men who were definitely a part of the old West landscape. Many of his stories have an Old Testament feel, timeless and classic people playing out their roles in timeless and classic situations.

Readers should also sample Pronzini's crime work, which is among the best being written today. Such novels as *Blue Lonesome*, which was a *New York Times* Notable Book of the Year, is already considered a classic. Pronzini was born in 1943.

It seems that each generation produces a number of excellent writers who are never quite given their proper due or recognition.

This is certainly the case with **Peggy Simson Curry**. Her slight body of work, a great deal of which appeared in such slick magazines as *Saturday Evening Post* and *Collier's*, fell somewhere between traditional Western fiction and mainstream literature. Her literary influences seemed to run more to Willa Cather and Katherine Anne Porter than to any Western writers. Curry was born in Ayshire, Scotland, in 1911, and this influence can also be felt in her work.

Readers are encouraged to read any of her fourteen or so other stories, especially "In the Silence," which is one of the true masterpieces of American literature.

Elmore Leonard has written some of the best Western novels and stories of the century. But, generally speaking, Hollywood discovered him before the reading public did. Films such as *The Tall T* and *Hombre* brought his name to the mainstream public, even though his books (this was in the early sixties) were still unknown outside the genre.

Leonard, who was born in 1925, spent his early years in advertising. He wrote for the Western pulps at night.

Even today, there are critics who prefer his Westerns to his widely read and influential best-selling crime novels.

If Leonard's greatest gift as a crime novelist is his humor, his greatest gift as a Western writer is his ability to create real human beings out of the stereotypes of "cowboy fiction."

Leonard sees the eternal in his Western situations. He

writes of honor and shame and love and hate. He understands what William Faulkner meant by "the human heart in conflict with itself." This is what his stories are about. And that's why his characters remain so vital and familiar to us.

John M. Cunningham's most famous story is "The Tin Star," which moviegoers around the globe know better as the legendary Western film *High Noon*.

As with most of his stories and novels, "The Tin Star" takes a familiar situation and gives it new life. Cunningham has always been careful to give us real people, and carefully drawn backdrops for his stories. He has a reporter's eye for the one right detail that brings a setting to vivid life.

Cunningham has lately returned to writing Western novels after a long absence, and demonstrated that he has lost none of his wiles as a chronicler of the old West.

THE DEFENSE OF SENTINEL

Louis L'Amour

When the morning came, Finn McGraw awakened into a silent world. His eyes opened to the wide and wondering sky where a solitary cloud wandered reluctantly across the endless blue.

At first he did not notice the silence. He had awakened, his mouth tasted like a rain-soaked cathide, he wanted a drink, and he needed a shave. This was not an unusual situation.

He heaved himself to a sitting position, yawned widely, scratching his ribs—and became aware of the silence.

No sound . . . No movement. No rattling of well buckets, no cackling of hens, no slamming of doors. Sentinel was a town of silence.

Slowly, his mind filling with wonder, Finn McGraw climbed to his feet. With fifty wasted years behind him, he had believed the world held no more surprises. But Sentinel was empty.

Sentinel, where for six months Finn McGraw had held the unenvied position of official town drunk. He had been the tramp, the vagabond, the useless, the dirty, dusty, un-

1

shaven, whisky-sodden drunk. He slept in alleys. He slept in barns—wherever he happened to be when he passed out.

Finn McGraw was a man without a home. Without a job. Without a dime. And now he was a man without a town.

What can be more pitiful than a townless town drunk?

Carefully, McGraw got to his feet. The world tipped edgewise and he balanced delicately and managed to maintain his equilibrium. Negotiating the placing of his feet with extreme caution, he succeeded in crossing the wash and stumbling up the bank on the town side. Again, more apprehensively, he listened.

Silence.

No smoke rising from chimneys, no barking dogs, no horses. The street lay empty before him, like a street in a town of ghosts.

Finn McGraw paused and stared at the phenomenon. Had he, like Rip van Winkle, slept for twenty years?

Yet he hesitated, for well he knew the extreme lengths that Western men would go for a good practical joke. The thought came as a relief. That was it, of course, this was a joke. They had all gotten together to play a joke on him.

His footsteps echoed hollowly on the boardwalk. Tentatively, he tried the door of the saloon. It gave inward, and he pushed by the inner, batwing doors and looked around. The odor of stale whisky mingled with cigar smoke lingered, lonesomely, in the air. Poker chips and cards were scattered on the table, but there was nobody. . . . Nobody at all!

The back bar was lined with bottles. His face brightened. Whisky! Good whisky, and his for the taking! At least, if they had deserted him they had left the whisky behind.

Caution intervened. He walked to the back office and pushed open the door. It creaked on a rusty hinge and gave inward, to emptiness.

"Hey?" His voice found only an echo for company. "Where is everybody?"

No answer. He walked to the door and looked out upon the street. Suddenly the desire for human companionship blossomed into a vast yearning.

He rushed outside. He shouted. His voice rang empty in the street against the false-fronted buildings. Wildly, he rushed from door to door. The blacksmith shop, the livery stable, the saddle shop, the bootmaker, the general store, the jail—all were empty, deserted.

He was alone.

Alone! What had *happened*? Where *was* everybody? Saloons full of whisky, stores filled with food, blankets, clothing. All these things had been left unguarded.

Half-frightened, Finn McGraw made his way to the restaurant. Everything there was as it had been left. A meal half-eaten on the table, dishes unwashed. But the stove was cold.

Aware suddenly of a need for strength that whisky could not provide, Finn McGraw kindled a fire in the stove. From a huge ham he cut several thick slices. He went out back and rummaged through the nests and found a few scattered eggs. He carried these inside and prepared a meal.

With a good breakfast under his belt, he refilled his coffee cup and rummaged around until he found a box of cigars. He struck a match and lighted a good Havana, pocketing several more. Then he leaned back and began to consider the situation.

Despite the excellent meal and the cigar, he was uneasy. The heavy silence worried him, and he got up and went cautiously to the door. Suppose there was something here, something malign and evil? Suppose— Angrily, he pushed the door open. He was going to stop supposing. For the first time in his life he had a town full of everything, and he was going to make the most of it.

Sauntering carelessly down the empty street to the Elite General Store, he entered and coolly began examining the clothing. He found a hand-me-down gray suit and changed his clothes. He selected new boots and donned them as well as a white cambric shirt, a black string tie, and a new black hat. He pocketed a fine linen handkerchief. Next he lighted another cigar, spat into the brass spittoon, and looked upon life with favor.

On his right as he turned to leave the store was a long rack of rifles, shotguns and pistols. Thoughtfully, he studied them. In his day—that was thirty years or so ago—he had been a sharpshooter in the Army.

He got down a Winchester '73, an excellent weapon, and loaded it with seventeen bullets. He appropriated a fine pair of Colts, loaded them, and belted them on, filling the loops with cartridges. Taking down a shotgun, he loaded both barrels with buckshot, then he sauntered down to the saloon, rummaged under the bar until he came up with Dennis Magoon's excellent Irish whisky, and poured three fingers into a glass.

Admiring the brown, beautiful color, the somber amber, as he liked to call it, he studied the sunlight through the glass, then tasted it.

Ah! Now that was something like it! There was a taste of bog in that! He tossed off his drink, then refilled his glass.

The town was his—the whole town—full of whisky, food, clothing—almost everything a man could want.

But *why*? Where *was* everybody?

Thoughtfully, he walked outside. The silence held sway. A lonely dust devil danced on the prairie outside of town, and the sun was warm.

At the edge of town he looked out over the prairie toward the mountains. Nothing met his eye save a vast, unbelievable stretch of grassy plain. His eyes dropped to the dust and with a kind of shock he remembered that he could read sign. Here were the tracks of a half-dozen rigs, buckboards, wagons and carts. From the horse tracks all were headed the same direction—east.

He scowled and, turning thoughtfully, he walked back to the livery barn.

Not a horse remained. Bits of harness were dropped on the ground—a spare saddle. Everything showed evidence of a sudden and hasty departure.

An hour later, having made the rounds, Finn McGraw returned to the saloon. He poured another glass of the Irish, lighted another Havana, but now he had a problem.

The people of the town had not vanished into thin air, they had made a sudden, frightened, panic-stricken rush to get away from the place.

That implied there was, in the town itself, some evil.

Finn McGraw tasted the whisky and looked over his shoulder uncomfortably. He tiptoed to the door, looked one way, then suddenly the other way.

Nothing unusual met his gaze.

He tasted his whisky again and then, crawling from the dusty and cobwebbed convolutions of his brain, long befuddled by alcohol, came realization.

Indians!

He remembered some talk the night before while he was trying to bum a drink. The Ladder Five ranch had been raided and the hands had been murdered. Victorio was on the warpath, burning, killing, maiming. *Apaches!*

The Fort was east of here! Some message must have come, some word, and the inhabitants had fled like sheep and left him behind.

Like a breath of icy air he realized that he was alone in the town, there was no means of escape, no place to hide. And the Apaches were coming!

Thrusting the bottle of Irish into his pocket, Finn McGraw made a break for the door. Outside, he rushed down to the Elite General Store. This building was of stone, low and squat, and built for defense, as it had been a trading post and stage station before the town grew up around it. Hastily, he took stock.

Moving flour barrels, he rolled them to the door to block it. Atop the barrels he placed sacks, bales and boxes. He barred the heavy back door, then blocked the windows. In the center of the floor he built a circular parapet of more sacks and barrels for a last defense. He got down an armful of shotguns and proceeded to load ten of them. These he scattered around at various loopholes, with a stack of shells by each.

Then he loaded several rifles. Three Spencer .56's, a Sharps .50 and seven Winchester '73's.

He loaded a dozen of the Colts and opened boxes of ammunition. Then he lighted another Havana and settled down to wait.

The morning was well nigh gone. There was food enough in the store, and the position was a commanding one. The store was thrust out from the line of buildings in such a way that it commanded the approaches of the street in both directions, yet it was long enough so that he could command the rear of the buildings as well, by running to the back.

The more he studied his position the more he wondered why Sentinel inhabitants had left the town undefended. Only blind, unreasoning panic could have caused such a flight.

At noon he prepared himself a meal from what he found in the store, and waited. It was shortly after high sun when the Indians came.

The Apaches might have been scouting the place for hours; Finn had not seen them. Now they came cautiously down the street, creeping hesitantly along.

From a window that commanded the street, old Finn Mc-Graw waited. On the windowsill he had four shotguns, each with two barrels loaded with buckshot. And he waited . . .

The Apaches, suspecting a trap, approached cautiously. They peered into empty buildings, flattened their faces against windows, then came on. The looting would follow later. Now the Indians were suspicious, anxious to know if the town was deserted. They crept forward.

Six of them bunched to talk some forty yards away. Beyond them a half dozen more Apaches were scattered in the next twenty yards. Sighting two of his shotguns, Finn McGraw rested a hand on each. The guns were carefully held in place by sacks weighting them down, and he was ready. He squeezed all four triggers at once!

The concussion was terrific! With a frightful roar, the four barrels blasted death into the little groups of Indians, and instantly, McGraw sprang to the next two guns, swung one of them slightly, and fired again.

Then he grabbed up a heavy Spencer and began firing

as fast as he could aim, getting off four shots before the street was empty. Empty, but for the dead.

Five Apaches lay stretched in the street. Another, dragging himself with his hands, was attempting to escape.

McGraw lunged to his feet and raced to the back of the building. He caught a glimpse of an Indian and snapped a quick shot. The Apache dropped, stumbled to his feet, then fell again and lay still.

That was the beginning. All through the long, hot afternoon the battle waged. Finn McGraw drank whisky and swore. He loaded and reloaded his battery of guns. The air in the store was stifling. The heat increased, the store smells thickened, and over it all hung the acrid smell of gunpowder.

Apaches came to recover their dead and died beside them. Two naked warriors tried to cross the rooftops to his building, and he dropped them both. One lay on the blistering roof, the other rolled off and fell heavily.

Sweat trickled into McGraw's eyes, and his face became swollen from the kick of the guns. From the front of the store he could watch three ways, and a glance down the length of the store allowed him to see a very limited range outside. Occasionally he took a shot from the back window, hoping to keep them guessing.

Night came at last, bringing a blessed coolness, and old Finn McGraw relaxed and put aside his guns.

Who can say that he knows the soul of the Indian? Who can say what dark superstitions churn inside his skull? For no Apache will fight at night, since he believes the souls of men killed in darkness must forever wander, homeless and alone. Was it fear that prevented an attack now? Or was it some fear of this strange, many-weaponed man—if man he was—who occupied the dark stone building?

And who can say with what strange expressions they stared at each other as they heard from their fires outside the town the weird thunder of the old piano in the saloon, and the old man's whisky-bass rolling out the words of "The Wearing of the Green"; "Drill, Ye Tarriers, Drill";

"Come Where My Love Lies Dreaming" and "Shenandoah."

Day came and found Finn McGraw in the store, ready for battle. The old lust for battle that is the birthright of the Irish had risen within him. Never, from the moment he realized that he was alone in a town about to be raided by Apaches, had he given himself a chance for survival. Yet it was the way of the Irish to fight, and the way even of old, whisky-soaked Finn.

An hour after dawn, a bullet struck him in the side. He spun half-around, fell against the flour barrels and slid to the floor. Blood flowed from the slash, and he caught up a handful of flour and slapped it against the wound. Promptly he fired a shot from the door, an aimless shot, to let them know he was still there. Then he bandaged his wound.

It was a flesh wound, and would have bled badly but for the flour. Sweat trickled into his eyes, grime and powder smoke streaked his face. But he moved and moved again, and his shotguns and rifles stopped every attempt to approach the building. Even looting was at a minimum, for he controlled most of the entrances, and the Apaches soon found they must dispose of their enemy before they could profit from the town.

Sometime in the afternoon, a bullet knocked him out, cutting a furrow in his scalp, and it was nearing dusk when his eyes opened. His head throbbed with enormous pain, his mouth was dry. He rolled to a sitting position and took a long pull at the Irish, feeling for a shotgun. An Apache was even then fumbling at the door.

He steadied the gun against the corner of a box. His eyes blinked. He squeezed off both barrels and, hit in the belly, the Apache staggered back.

At high noon on the fourth day, Major Magruder with a troop of cavalry, rode into the streets of Sentinel. Behind him were sixty men of the town, all armed with rifles.

At the edge of town, Major Magruder lifted a hand. Jake Carter and Dennis Magoon moved up beside him. "I thought you said the town was deserted?"

His extended finger indicated a dead Apache.

Their horses walked slowly forward. Another Apache sprawled there dead . . . and then they found another.

Before the store four Apaches lay in a tight cluster, another savage was stretched at the side of the walk. Windows of the store were shattered and broken, a great hole had been blasted in the door. At the Major's order, the troops scattered to search the town. Magruder swung down before the store.

"I'd take an oath nobody was left behind," Carter said.

Magruder shoved open the store. The floor inside was littered with blackened cartridge cases and strewn with empty bottles. "No one man could fire that many shells or drink that much whisky," Magruder said positively.

He stooped, looking at the floor and some flour on the floor. "Blood," he said.

In the saloon they found another empty bottle and an empty box of cigars.

Magoon stared dismally at the empty bottle. He had been keeping count, and all but three of the bottles of his best Irish glory was gone. "Whoever it was," he said sorrowfully, "drank up some of the best whisky ever brewed."

Carter looked at the piano. Suddenly he grabbed Magoon's arm. "McGraw!" he yelled. " 'Twas Finn McGraw!"

They looked at each other. It couldn't be! And yet—who had seen him? Where was he now?

"Who," Magruder asked, "is McGraw?"

They explained, and the search continued. Bullets had clipped the corners of buildings, bullets had smashed water barrels along the street. Windows were broken, and there were nineteen dead Indians—but no sign of McGraw.

Then a soldier yelled from outside of town, and they went that way and gathered around. Under the edge of a mesquite bush, a shotgun beside him, his new suit torn and bloodstained, they found Finn McGraw.

Beside him lay two empty bottles of the Irish. Another, partly gone, lay near his hand. A rifle was propped in the forks of the bush, and a pistol had fallen from his holster.

There was blood on his side and blood on his head and face.

"Dead!" Carter said. "But what a battle!"

Magruder bent over the old man, then he looked up, a faint twinkle breaking the gravity of his face. "Dead, all right," he said. "Dead *drunk*!"

GUN JOB

▼

Thomas Thompson

He was married in June, and he gave up his job as town marshal the following September, giving himself time to get settled on the little ranch he bought before the snows set in. That first winter was mild, and now, with summer in the air, he walked down the main street of the town and thought of his own calf crop and of his own problems, a fine feeling after fifteen years of thinking of the problems of others. He wasn't Marshal Jeff Anderson any more. He was Jeff Anderson, private citizen, beholden to no man, and that was the way he wanted it.

He gave the town his quick appraisal, a tall, well-built man who was nearing forty and beginning to think about it, and every building and every alley held a memory for him, some amusing, some tragic. The town had a Sunday morning peacefulness on it, a peacefulness Jeff Anderson had worked for. It hadn't always been this way. He inhaled deeply, a contented man, and he caught the scent of freshly sprinkled dust that came from the dampened square of street in front of the ice cream parlor. There was a promise of heat in the air and already the thick, warm scent of the tar weed was drifting down from the yellow slopes in back of the town. He kept to the middle of the street, enjoying his freedom, not yet free of old habits, and he headed for the marshal's office, where the door was closed, the shade drawn.

This was his Sunday morning pleasure, this brief tour of the town that had claimed him so long. It was the same tour he had made every Sunday morning for fifteen years; but now he could enjoy the luxury of knowing he was making it because he wanted to, not because it was his job. A man who had built a bridge or a building could sit back and look at his finished work, remembering the fun and the heartache that had gone into it, but he didn't need to chip away personally at its rust or take a pot of paint to its scars.

In front of the marshal's office Anderson paused, remembering it all, not missing it, just remembering; then he turned and pushed open the door, the familiarity of the action momentarily strong on him. The floor was worn and his own boot heels had helped wear it; the desk was scarred and some of those spur marks were as much his own as his own initials would have been. He grinned at the new marshal and said, "Caught any criminals lately?"

The man behind the desk glanced up, his face drawn, expressionless, his eyes worried. He tried to joke. "How could I?" he said. "You ain't been in town since last Sunday." He took one foot off the desk and kicked a straight chair toward Jeff. "How's the cow business?"

"Good," Jeff said. "Mighty good." He sat down heavily and stretched his long legs, pushed his battered felt hat back on his thinning, weather-bleached hair, and made himself a cigarette. He saw the papers piled on the desk, and glancing at the clock, he knew it was nearly time to let the two or three prisoners exercise in the jail corridor. A feeling of well-being engulfed him. These things were another man's responsibility now, not Jeff Anderson's. "How's it with you, Billy?" he asked.

The answer came too quickly, the answer of a man who was nervous or angry, or possibly both. "You ought to know, Jeff. The mayor and the council came to see you, didn't they?''

Annoyance clouded Jeff Anderson's gray eyes. He hadn't liked the idea of the city fathers going behind the new marshal's back. If they didn't like the job Billy was doing, they should have gone to Billy, not to Jeff. But that was typical of the city council. Jeff had known three mayors and three different councils during his long term in office, and they usually ran to a pattern. A few complaints and they got panicky and started going off in seven directions at once. They seemed to think that because Jeff had recommended Billy for this job, the job was still Jeff's responsibility—. ''They made the trip for nothing, Billy,'' Jeff said. ''If you're worried about me wanting your job, you can forget it. I told them that plain.''

''They'll keep asking you, Jeff.''

''They'll keep getting no for an answer,'' Jeff said.

Billy Lang sat at his desk and stared at the drawn shade of the front window, the thumb of his left hand toying nervously with the badge on his calfskin vest. He was a small man with eternally pink cheeks and pale blue eyes. He wore a full white mustache, and there was a cleft in his chin. He was married and had five children, and most of his life he had clerked in a store. When Jeff Anderson recommended him for this job Billy took it because it paid more and because the town was quiet. But now there was trouble, and Billy was sorry he had ever heard of the job. He said, ''You can't blame them for wanting you back, Jeff. You did a good job.''

There was no false modesty in Jeff Anderson. He had done a good job here and he knew it. He had handled his job exactly the way he felt it should be handled and he had backed down to no one. But it hadn't been all roses, either. He grinned. ''Regardless of what a man does, there's some who won't like it.''

''Like Hank Fetterman?''

Jeff shrugged. Hank Fetterman was a cattleman. Sometimes Hank got the idea that he ought to take this town over and run it the way he once had. Hank hadn't gotten away with it when Jeff was marshal. Thinking about it now, it didn't seem to matter much to Jeff one way or the other, and it was hard to remember that his fight with Hank Fetterman had once been important. It had been a long time ago and things had changed—. "Hank's not a bad sort," Jeff said.

"He's in town," Billy Lang said. "Did you know that?"

Jeff felt that old, familiar tightening of his stomach muscles, the signal of trouble ahead. He inhaled deeply, let the smoke trickle from his nostrils, and the feeling went away. Hank Fetterman was Jeff Anderson's neighbor now, and Jeff was a rancher, not a marshal. "I'm in town too," he said. "So are fifty other people. There's no law against it."

"You know what I mean, Jeff," Billy Lang said. "You talked to Rudy Svitac's boy."

Jeff moved uneasily in his chair. Billy Lang was accusing him of meddling, and Jeff didn't like it. Jeff had never had anything to do with the marshal's job since his retirement, and he had promised himself he never would. It was Billy's job, and Billy was free to run it his own way. But when a twelve-year-old kid who thought you were something special asked you a straight question you gave him a straight answer. It had nothing to do with the fact that you had once been a marshal—

"Sure, Billy," Jeff said. "I talked to Rudy's boy. He came to see me about it just the way he's been coming to see me about things ever since he was big enough to walk. The kid needs somebody to talk to, I guess, so he comes to me. He's not old country like his folks. He was born here; he thinks American. I guess it's hard for the boy to understand them. I told him to have his dad see you, Billy."

"He took your advice," Billy Lang said. "Three days ago." He turned over a paper. "Rudy Svitac came in and swore out a warrant against Hank Fetterman for trespassing. He said his boy told him it was the thing to do."

Jeff had a strange feeling that he was suddenly two people. One was Jeff Anderson, ex-marshal, the man who had recommended Billy Lang for this job. As such, he should offer Billy some advice right here and now. The other person was Jeff Anderson, private citizen, a man with a small ranch and a fine wife and a right to live his own life. And that was the Jeff Anderson that was important. Jeff Anderson, the rancher, grinned. "Hank pawin' and bellerin' about it, is he?"

"I don't know, Jeff," Billy Lang said. "I haven't talked to Hank about it. I'm not sure I'm going to."

Jeff glanced quickly at the new marshal, surprised, only half believing what he had heard. He had recommended Billy for this job because he figured he and Billy thought along the same lines. Surely Billy knew that if you gave Hank Fetterman an inch, he would take a mile. . . .

He caught himself quickly, realizing suddenly that it was none of his business how Billy Lang thought. There were plenty of businessmen in town who had argued loudly and openly that Jeff Anderson's methods of law enforcement had been bad for their cash registers. They had liked the old days when Hank Fetterman was running things and the town was wide open. Maybe they wanted it that way again. Every man was entitled to his own opinion, and Billy Lang was entitled to handle his job in his own way. This freedom of thought and action that Jeff prized so highly had to work for everyone. He stood up and clapped a hand affectionately on Billy Lang's shoulder, anxious to change the conversation. "That's up to you, Billy," he said. "It's sure none of my affair." His grin widened. "Come on over to the saloon and I'll buy you a drink."

Billy Lang stared at the drawn shade, and he thought of Hank Fetterman, a man who was big in this country, waiting over at the saloon. Hank Fetterman knew there was a warrant out for his arrest; the whole town knew it by now. You didn't need to tell a thing like that. It just got around. And before long, people would know who the law was in this town, Hank Fetterman or Billy Lang. Billy colored slightly, and there was perspiration on his forehead. "You go ahead and have your drink, Jeff," he said. "I've got some paperwork to do—." He didn't look up.

Jeff went outside and the gathering heat of the day struck the west side of the street and brought a resinous smell from

the old boards of the false-fronted buildings. He glanced at
the little church, seeing Rudy Svitac's spring wagon there,
remembering that the church hadn't always been here; then
he crossed over toward the saloon, the first business building this town had erected. He had been in a dozen such
towns, and it was always the same. The saloons and the
deadfalls came first, the churches and the schools later.
Maybe that proved something. He didn't know. He had
just stepped onto the board sidewalk when he saw the
druggist coming toward him. The druggist was also the
mayor, a sanctimonious little man, dried up by his own
smallness. "Jeff, I talked to Billy Lang," the mayor said.
His voice was thin and reedy. "I wondered if you might
reconsider—"

"No," Jeff Anderson said. He didn't break his stride. He
walked by the mayor and went into the saloon. Two of
Hank Fetterman's riders were standing by the piano, leaning on it, and one of them was fumbling out a one-finger
tune, cursing when he missed a note. Hank Fetterman was
at the far end of the bar, and Jeff went and joined him. A
little cow talk was good of a Sunday morning, and Hank
Fetterman knew cows. The two men at the piano started to
sing.

Hank Fetterman's glance drifted lazily to Jeff Anderson
and then away. His smile was fleeting. "How are you,
Jeff?"

"Good enough," Jeff said. "Can I buy you a drink?"

"You twisted my arm," Hank Fetterman said.

Hank Fetterman was a well-built man with a weathered
face. His brows were heavy and they pinched together toward the top, forming a perfect diamond of clean, hairless
skin between his deep-set eyes. His voice was quiet, his
manner calm. Jeff thought of the times he had crossed this
man, enforcing the no-gun ordinance, keeping Hank's riders in jail overnight to cool them off—. He had no regrets
over the way he had handled Hank in the past. It had nothing to do with his feeling toward Hank now or in the future.
He saw that Hank was wearing a gun and he smiled inwardly. That was like Hank. Tell him he couldn't do some-

thing and that was exactly what he wanted to do. "Didn't figure on seeing you in town," Jeff said. "Thought you and the boys were on roundup."

"I had a little personal business come up," Hank Fetterman said. "You know about it?"

Jeff shrugged. "Depends on what it is."

The pale smile left Hank Fetterman's eyes but not his lips. "Rudy Svitac is telling it around that I ran a bunch of my cows through his corn. He claims I'm trying to run him out of the country."

Jeff had no trouble concealing his feelings. It was a trick he had learned a long time ago. He leaned his elbows on the bar and turned his shot glass slowly in its own wet circle. Behind him Hank Fetterman's two cowboys broke into a boisterous ribald song. The bartender wiped his face with his apron and glanced out the front window across toward the marshal's office. Jeff Anderson downed his drink, tossed the shot glass in the air and caught it with a down sweep of his hand. "You're used to that kind of talk, Hank." He set the shot glass on the bar.

"You're pretty friendly with the Svitacs, aren't you, Jeff?" Hank Fetterman asked. He was leaning with his back to the bar, his elbows behind him. His position made the holstered gun he wore obvious.

Again, just for a moment, Jeff Anderson was two people. He remembered the man he wanted to be. "I don't reckon anybody's very friendly with the Svitacs," he said. "They're hard to know. I think a lot of their boy. He's a nice kid."

Slowly the smile came back into Hank Fetterman's amber eyes. He turned around and took the bottle and poured a drink for himself and one for Jeff. "That forty acres of bottom land you were asking me about for a calf pasture," he said. "I've been thinking about it. I guess I could lease it to you all right."

"That's fine, Hank," Jeff Anderson said. "I can use it." He doffed his glass to Hank and downed his drink. It didn't taste right, but he downed it anyway. The two cowboys started to scuffle and one of them collided with a table. It overturned with a crash.

"Please, Hank," the bartender said. "They're gonna get me in trouble—." His voice trailed off and his eyes widened. A man had come through the door. He stood there, blinking the bright sun out of his eyes. Jeff Anderson felt his heart start to pump heavily, slowly, high in his chest. "Morning, Mr. Svitac," the bartender mumbled.

Rudy Svitac stood in the doorway, a thick, dull man with black hair and brows that met across the bridge of his nose and a forehead that sloped. Jeff saw the rusty suit the man wore on Sundays, the suit that had faint soil stains on the knees because this man could not leave the soil alone, even on Sundays. He had to kneel down and feel the soil with his fingers, feeling the warmth and the life of it; for the soil was his book and his life and it was the only thing he understood completely and perhaps the only thing that understood him. He looked at Jeff, not at Hank Fetterman. "Is no good," Rudy Svitac said. "My son says I must talk to Billy Lang. I talk to Billy Lang, but he does nothing. Is no good."

A thick silence settled in the room and the two cowboys who had been scuffling quit it now and stood there looking at the farmer. Hank Fetterman said, "Say what's on your mind, Svitac."

"You broke my fence," Rudy Svitac said. "You drive your cows in my corn and spoil my crop. All winter I wait to plant my crop and now is grow fine and you drive your cows in."

"Maybe you're mistaken, Svitac," Hank Fetterman said.

"My boy says is for judge to decide," Rudy Svitac said. "My boy tell me to go to Billy Lang and he will make a paper and judge will decide. My boy says is fair. Is America." Rudy Svitac stared unblinkingly. He shook his head slowly. "Is not so. I want my money. You broke my fence."

"You're a liar, Svitac," Hank Fetterman said. He moved away from the bar, slowly. He looked steadily at Jeff Anderson, then he glanced across the street toward the marshal's office. The door was still closed, the shade still drawn. Hank Fetterman smiled. He walked forward and gripped Rudy Svitac by the shirt front. For a moment he held the man that way, pulling him close, then he shoved, and Rudy Svitac stumbled backward, out through the door, and his heel caught on a loose board in the sidewalk. He fell hard and for a long time he lay there, his dull, steady eyes staring at Jeff Anderson; then he turned and pushed himself up and he stood there looking at the dust on his old suit. He dropped his head and looked at the dust and he reached with his fingers and touched it. One of Hank Fetterman's cowboys started to laugh.

Across the street Jeff Anderson saw the blind on the window of the marshal's office move aside and then drop back into place, and immediately the door opened and Billy Lang was hurrying across the street. He came directly to Rudy Svitac and put his hand on Svitac's arm and jerked him around. "What's going on here?" Billy Lang demanded.

"Svitac came in looking for trouble," Hank Fetterman said. "I threw him out." Hank was standing in the doorway, directly alongside Jeff. For a brief moment Hank Fetterman's amber eyes met Jeff's gaze and Jeff saw the challenge. If you don't like it, do something about it, Hank Fetterman was saying. I want to know how you stand in this thing and I want to know now.

There was a dryness in Jeff Anderson's mouth. He had backed Hank Fetterman down before; he could do it again. But for what? One hundred and fifty dollars a month and a chance to get killed? Jeff had had fifteen years of that. A man had a right to live his own life. He looked up toward the church and the doors were just opening and people were coming out to stand on the porch, a small block of humanity suddenly aware of trouble. Jeff saw his wife Elaine, and he knew her hand was at her throat, twisting the fabric of her dress the way she did. He thought of the little ranch and of the things he and Elaine had planned for the future, and then he looked at Billy Lang and he knew Billy wasn't going to buck Hank Fetterman. So Jeff could make a stand,

and it would be his own stand and he would be right back into it again just the way he had been for fifteen years. There was a thick line of perspiration on Jeff's upper lip. "That's the way it was, Billy," Jeff said.

He saw the quick smile cross Hank Fetterman's face, the dull acceptance and relief in Billy Lang's eyes. "Get out of town, Svitac," Billy Lang said. "I'm tired of your troublemaking. If Hank's cows got in your corn, it was an accident."

"Is no accident," Rudy Svitac said stubbornly. "Is for judge to decide. My son says—"

"It was an accident," Billy Lang said. "Make your fences stronger." He didn't look at Jeff. He glanced at Hank Fetterman and made his final capitulation. "Sorry it happened, Hank."

For a long moment Rudy Svitac stared at Billy Lang, at the star on Billy's vest, remembering that this star somehow had a connection with the stars in the flag. His son Anton had explained it, saying that Jeff Anderson said it was so, so it must be so. But it wasn't so. Hank Fetterman wasn't in jail. They weren't going to do anything about the ruined corn. The skin wrinkled between Rudy Svitac's eyes, and there was perspiration on his face and his lips moved thickly but no sound came out. He could not understand. Thirteen years he had lived in this America, but still he could not understand. His son had tried to tell him the things they taught in the schools and the things Jeff Anderson said were so; but Rudy had his soil to work and his crops to plant, and when a man's back was tired his head did not work so good. Rudy Svitac knew only that if the jimson weed grew in the potato patch, you cut it out. And the wild morning-glory must be pulled out by the roots. No one came to do these things for a man. A man did these chores himself. He turned and walked solidly up the street toward where he had left his spring wagon by the church.

His wife Mary was there, a thick, tired woman who never smiled nor ever complained, and watching them, Jeff saw Anton, their son, a boy of twelve with an old man's face, a boy who had always believed every word Jeff Anderson said. Jeff saw young Anton looking down the street toward him, and he remembered the boy's serious brown eyes and the thick, black hair that always stood out above his ears and lay rebelliously far down his neck. He remembered the hundred times he had talked to young Anton, patiently explaining things so Anton would understand, learning his own beliefs from the process of explaining them in simple words. And Anton would listen and then repeat to his parents in Bohemian, telling them this was so because Jeff Anderson said it was so. A bright boy with an unlimited belief in the future, in a household where there was no future. At times it seemed to Jeff almost as if God had looked upon Rudy and Mary Svitac and wanted to compensate in some way, so he had given them Anton.

Jeff saw Rudy reaching into the bed of the wagon. He saw Mary protest once; then Mary stood there, resigned, and now the boy had his father's arm and there was a brief struggle. The father shook the boy off, and now Rudy had a rifle and he was coming back down the street, walking slowly, down the middle of the street, the rifle in the crook of his arm.

Billy Lang moved. He met Rudy halfway, and he held out his hand. Jeff saw Rudy hesitate, take two more steps; and now Billy was saying something and Rudy dropped his head and let his chin lie on his chest. The boy came running up, and he took the rifle out of his father's hand and the crowd in front of the saloon expelled its breath. Jeff felt the triumph come into Hank Fetterman. He didn't need to look at the man. He could feel it.

The slow, wicked anger was inside Hank Fetterman, goaded by his ambition, his sense of power, and the catlike eagerness was in his eyes. "No Bohunk tells lies about me and gets away with it," he murmured. "No Bohunk comes after me with a gun and gets a second chance." His hand dropped and rested on the butt of his holstered six-shooter, and then the thumb of his left hand touched Jeff Anderson's arm. "Have a drink with me, Jeff?"

Jeff saw Elaine standing in front of the church, and he could feel her anxiety reaching through the hot, troubled

air. And he saw the boy there in the street, the gun in his
hands, his eyes, bewildered, searching Jeff Anderson's face.
"I reckon I won't have time, Hank," Jeff said. He walked
up the street, and now the feeling of being two people was
strong in him, and there was a responsibility to Billy Lang
that he couldn't deny. He had talked Billy into taking this
job. It was a lonely job, and there was never a lonelier time
than when a man was by himself in the middle of the street.
He came close to Billy and he said, "Look, Billy, if you
can take a gun away from one man, you can take a gun
away from another."

Billy looked at him. Billy's hands were shaking, and
there was sweat on his face. "A two-year-old kid could
have taken that gun away from Rudy, and you know it,"
he said. He reached up swiftly and unpinned the badge from
his vest. He handed it across. "You want it?"

Jeff looked at that familiar piece of metal, and he could
feel the boy's eyes on him; and then he looked up and he
saw Elaine there on the church porch, and he thought of
his own dreams and of the plans he and Elaine had made
for the future. "No, Billy," he said. "I don't want it."

"Then let it lay there," Billy Lang said. He dropped the
badge into the dust of the street and hurried off, a man who
had met defeat and accepted it, a man who could now go
back to the clothing store and sell shirts and suits and over-
alls because that was the job he could do best. There was
no indignity in Billy Lang's defeat. He had taken a role
that he wasn't equipped to handle, and he was admitting it.

The boy said, "Mr. Jeff, I don't understand. You told
me once—"

"We'll talk about it later, Anton," Jeff said. "Tell your
dad to go home." He walked swiftly toward Elaine, swal-
lowing against the sourness in his throat.

They drove out of town, Jeff and Elaine Anderson, toward their own home and their own life; and now the full
heat of the day lay on the yellow slopes, and the dry air
crackled with the smell of dust and the cured grass, and the
leather seat of the buggy was hot to the touch. A mile out
of town Jeff stopped in the shade of a sycamore, and put

up the top. He moved with dull efficiency, pausing momentarily to glance up as Hank Fetterman and his two riders passed on their way back to the ranch. He got back into the buggy and unwrapped the lines from the whipstock, and Elaine said, "If there's anything you want to say, Jeff—"

How could he say it? He couldn't, for the thing that was most in his mind had nothing to do with the matter at hand, and yet it had everything to do with it and it couldn't be explained. For he was thinking not of Hank Fetterman nor of Rudy Svitac, but of a colored lithograph, a town promotion picture that had once hung on every wall in this town. It showed wide tree-lined streets, a tremendous townhouse with a flag half as large as the building flying from a mast, and lesser pennants, all mammoth, rippling from every building. Tiny men in cutaway coats and top hats leisurely strolled the avenues, and high-wheeled bicycles rolled elegantly past gleaming black victorias on the street of exclusive shops, while three sleek trains chuffed impatiently at the station. The railroad had put on a large land promotion around here when the road was first built. They had offered excursion trips free so that people could see the charms of New Canaan. They had handed out these lithos of the proposed town by the bushel. For a while New Canaan bustled with activity, and men bought town lots staked out in buffalo grass. And then the bubble burst, and New Canaan settled back to what it was before—a place called Alkali at the edge of open cattle range. And young Anton Svitac had come to see Marshal Jeff Anderson for the first time and he had come about that picture—

Jeff remembered how the boy had looked that day, no more than six years old, his eyes too large for his old-man's face, his voice a mirror of the seriousness of thought that was so much a part of him. He had come to Jeff Anderson because Jeff Anderson was authority, and already young Anton had learned that in America authority was for everyone. "My father and mother do not understand," he said. "They do not speak English." He unrolled the lithograph and put his finger on it, and then indicated the town of

Alkali with a spread hand. "Is not the same," he said. "Is not so."

There were dreams in that boy's eyes, and they were about to be snuffed out; and Jeff Anderson didn't want it to happen. "Sure it's so, Anton," he heard himself saying. "It's not what it is today, it's what's going to be tomorrow, see?" He remembered the trouble he had with the words, and then it was all there and he was telling it to Anton, telling it so this boy could go home and tell it to a work-bent man and a tired woman. "It's like America, see? Some of the things aren't right where you can touch them. Maybe some of the things you see are ugly. But the picture is always there to look at, and you keep thinking about the picture, and you keep working and making things better all the time, see? America isn't something you cut off like a piece of cake and say there it is. You keep on looking ahead to what it's going to be, and you keep working hard for it all the time, and you keep right on knowing it's going to be good because you've got the picture there to look at. You never stop working and say, 'Now the job is done,' because it never is. You see that, Anton?"

The boy hadn't smiled. This was a big thing and a boy didn't smile about big things. He rolled the lithograph carefully. "I see," he said. "Is good. I will tell my father. We will keep the picture—"

Those were Jeff Anderson's thoughts, and how could he tell them, even to Elaine; for they had so little to do with the matter at hand and yet they had everything to do with it.

And Elaine, looking at her husband now, respected his silence. She remembered the three long years she was engaged to this man before they were married, years in which she had come to know him so well because she loved him so well. She knew him even better now. He was a man who was born to handle trouble, and a piece of tin on his vest or a wife at his side couldn't change the man he was born to be. She knew that and she didn't want to change him, but a woman couldn't help being what she was either and a woman could be afraid, especially at a time like this when there was so much ahead. She wanted to help him. "Maybe the Svitacs would be better off some place else," she said. "They never have made the place pay."

And that was exactly the same argument he had used on himself; but now, hearing it put into words, he didn't like the sound of it and he wanted to argue back. His voice was rough. "I reckon they look on it as home," he said. "The boy was born there. I reckon it sort of ties you to a place if your first one is born there."

She closed her eyes tightly, knowing that she was no longer one person but three, knowing the past was gone and the future would always be ahead, and it was her job to help secure that future as much as it was Jeff's job. She opened her eyes and looked at her husband, still afraid, for that was her way; but somehow prouder and older now. She folded her hands in her lap and the nervousness was gone. "I suppose we'll feel that way too, Jeff," she said. "It will always be our town after our baby is born here. I talked to the doctor yesterday—"

He felt the hard knot in the pit of his stomach. Then the coldness ran up his spine, and it was surprise and fear and a great swelling pride; and the feeling crawled up his neck, and every hair on his head was an individual hair, and the hard lump was in his throat—. He moved on the seat, suddenly concerned for her comfort. "You feel all right, honey? Is there anything I can do?"

She didn't laugh at him any more than Anton had laughed at him that day in the office. She reached over and put her hand on his hand, and she smiled. As they drove down the lane the great pride was inside him, swelling against him until he felt that the seat of the buggy was no longer large enough to contain him. He helped her out of the buggy, his motions exaggerated in their kindness; and he took her arm and helped her up the front steps.

The coolness of the night still lingered in the little ranch house, for she had left the shades drawn; and now she went to the west windows and lifted the shades slightly, and she could see down the lane and across the small calf pasture where a thin drift of dust from their buggy wheels still lingered. There was a loneliness to Sunday after church, a stillness on the ranch. She glanced toward the barn, and Jeff was unharnessing the mare and turning her into the corral, his back broad, his movements deliberate; and she saw him stand for a moment and look down the creek toward where Rudy Svitac's place cornered on Hank Fetterman's huge, unfenced range.

He came into the house later, into the cool living room, and he sat down in his big chair with a gusty sigh, and pulled off his boots and stretched his legs. "Good to be home," he said. "Good to have nothing to do." He raised his eyes to meet hers and they both knew he was lying. There was always something to do.

The moment he was sure, she knew it was easier for him, but he still had to be positive that she understood that now it was different. Once he made this move there would be no turning back. She had to see that. An hour ago the town had been a town, nothing more; and if certain merchants felt business would be better with Hank Fetterman running things, that was their business; and if Billy Lang wanted to go along with that thinking or go back to the clothing store, that was his business. Jeff Anderson hadn't needed the town. It was a place to shop and nothing more, and a man could shop as well with Hank Fetterman running things as he could with Jeff Anderson running things. But now, suddenly, that had changed, and there was tomorrow to think about, and it was exactly as he had explained it to Anton. Now, one day soon, Jeff Anderson might be explaining the same things to his own son; and a man had to show his son that he believed what he said, for if he didn't, there was nothing left—. "I was wrong about Billy Lang," Jeff Anderson said. "He's not going to stand up to Hank Fetterman."

She looked into his eyes and saw the deep seriousness and knew his every thought, and in this moment they were closer than they had ever been before; and she remembered thinking so many times of men and women who had been married for fifty years or more and of how they always looked alike. She said, "I have some curtains I promised

Mary Svitac. Will you take them to her when you go?"

She didn't trust herself to say more, and she didn't give him a lingering embrace as a woman might who was watching her man go off to danger; but she pretended to be busy and turned her head so that his lips just brushed her temple, and it was as casual as if he were only going to his regular day's work. "And thank her for the pickles," she said.

He stalked out of the house as if he didn't like having his Sunday disturbed by such woman nonsense, but when he was halfway to the barn his stride lengthened and she saw the stiffness of his back and the set of his shoulders. She sat down then and cried.

Anton, the boy, was pouring sour milk into a trough for the pigs when Jeff rode into the Svitac yard. The world could collapse, but pigs had to be fed, and the boy was busy with his thoughts and did not see Jeff ride up. The door of the little house that was half soddy, half dugout, opened, and Mary Svitac called something in Bohemian. The boy looked up, startled, and Jeff smiled. "Will you ride my horse over and tie him in the shade, Anton?"

The flood of hope that filled the boy's eyes was embarrassing to a man, and Jeff dismounted quickly, keeping his head turned. He took the bundle of curtains from behind the saddle, and handed the reins to the boy; then walked on to the sod house where Mary Svitac stood, the shawl tied under her chin framing her round, expressionless face. He handed her the curtains. "Those pickles you gave us were fine, Mrs. Svitac. Elaine wanted me to bring these curtains over."

Mary Svitac let her rough fingers caress the curtain material. "I will give you all the pickles," she said. "We don't need the curtains. We don't stay here no more."

Rudy's thick voice came from the dark interior of the sod house; and now Jeff could see him there, sitting in a chair, a man dulled with work and disappointments, a man with a limited knowledge of English who had come to a new country with a dream, and found grasshoppers and drought and blizzards and neighbors who tried to drive him out. He looked up. "We don't stay," he said.

"Can I come in for a minute, Mrs. Svitac?" Jeff asked.

"I make coffee," she said.

He stooped to pass through the low door, and he took off his hat and sat down. Now that his eyes were accustomed to the darkness of the room, he saw the big lithograph there on the wall, the only decoration. Rudy Svitac stared unblinkingly at the floor, and a tear ran unashamed down the side of his nose. "We don't stay," he said.

"Sure, Rudy," Jeff Anderson said softly. "You stay."

Mary Svitac started to cry. There were no tears, for the land had taken even that away from her. There were just sobs—dry, choking sounds as she made the coffee—but they were woman sounds, made for her man; and she was willing to give up fifteen years of work if her man would be safe. "They will fight with us," she said. "They put cows in my Rudolph's corn. They tear down our fence. Soon they come to break my house. Is too much. Rudolph does not know fight. Rudolph is for plant the ground and play wiolin—"

"You stay, Rudy," Jeff Anderson said. "The law will take care of you. I promise you that."

Rudy Svitac shook his ponderous head. "Law is for Hank Fetterman," he said. "Is not for me."

"It's not so, Rudy," Jeff said. "You ask Anton. He knows."

"I ask Anton," Rudy Svitac said. "He says I am right. Law is for Hank Fetterman."

The boy came to the door and stood there, peering inside the room. His face was white, drawn with worry; but the hope was still in his eyes and a confidence was there. He didn't say anything. He didn't need to. Jeff could hear the sound of horses approaching—Jeff stood up and the feeling that was in him was an old and familiar feeling—a tightening of all his muscles. He went to the corner of the room and took Rudy Svitac's rifle from its place, and he levered in a shell, leaving the rifle at full cock. He stepped through the door then, and he put his hand on the boy's head. "You explain again to your father about the law," he said. "You know, Anton, like we talked before."

"I know," Anton Svitac said.

Jeff stepped swiftly through the door into the sunlight, and he saw Hank Fetterman and the same two riders who had been with him at the saloon coming toward the soddy. Only Hank was armed, and this could be handy later, when Hank talked to the judge. If we had expected trouble, all three of us would have been armed, Judge, Hank Fetterman could say—. They rode stiffly, holding their horses in. Jeff Anderson stood the cocked rifle by the fencepost, placing it carefully. He pushed his hat back on his head and felt the sun on his back as he leaned there, one foot on a fence rail, watching the pigs eat the sour milk.

He knew when the riders were directly beside him, and he turned, his elbows leaning on the top rail of the fence behind him. His hat was pushed back, but his face was in shade, for he had moved to where he was between the sun and the riders. Hank Fetterman said, "We're seeing a lot of each other, neighbor."

"Looks that way," Jeff said.

Hank Fetterman quieted his horse with a steady hand. His eyes never left Jeff Anderson's face. "I asked you once today if you was a friend of the Bohunks," he said. "Maybe I better ask it again."

"Maybe it depends on what you've got on your mind, Hank."

"The Bohunk's been eating my beef," Fetterman said. "I'm sick of it."

"You sure that's it, Hank?" Jeff asked quietly. "Or is it just that there's something that eats on you and makes you want to tear down things other folks have taken years to build up?"

There were small white patches on either side of Hank Fetterman's mouth. "I said the Bohunk was eating my beef," Hank Fetterman said. His lips didn't move. "You doubting my word?"

"No," Jeff said. "I'm calling you a liar."

He saw the smoldering anger in Hank Fetterman, the sore, whisky-nursed anger, and then the cattleman felt the full shock as the flat insult in Jeff's voice reached through to him. He cursed and half twisted in the saddle, blinking directly into the sun. "You forgetting you ain't a lawman any more?" he demanded.

"You decide, Hank," Jeff said.

They looked at each other, two men who had killed before and knew the meaning of it, two men who respected a gun and understood a gun. They said nothing and yet they spoke a silent language, and the man who had been a lawman said, I'm telling you to back down, Fetterman; and the man who wanted to be king said, You'll have to be big enough to make me. No actual words, and yet they knew; and they faced each other with muscles tense and faces drawn, and appeared at ease. Jeff Anderson had dealt himself into the game, and he had checked the bet.

Hank Fetterman saw the rifle by the post. He knew it was cocked and loaded. He wondered if Jeff Anderson was actually as quick and as accurate as men said he was; and because he was Hank Fetterman, he had to know, because if he backed down now, it was over for him and he knew it. He jerked his horse around, trying to avoid that direct glare of the sun, and he made his decision. His hand went for his gun.

Jeff Anderson saw the move coming. It seemed to him that he had plenty of time. He had placed the rifle carefully and now he held it, hip high, gripping it with one hand, tilting it up and pulling the trigger all at the same time. He didn't hear the sound of the rifle's explosion. You never did, he remembered; but he saw the thin film of gunsmoke, and he saw Hank Fetterman's mouth drop open, saw the man clawing at his chest. He didn't feel the sickness. Not yet—

Time passed as if through a film of haze, and nothing was real. Then they were gone and a canvas was stretched over the still form of Hank Fetterman, and Rudy Svitac was whipping his team toward town to get the coroner. Now the sickness came to Jeff Anderson. He stood by the barn, trembling, and he heard the boy come up behind him. The boy said, "This was in the street in town, Mr. Anderson." The boy held out the tin star. "I told my father how the law was for everybody in America. Now he knows.''

Jeff Anderson took the tin star and dropped it into his pocket.

Elaine saw him through the front window. She had been watching a long time, and she had been praying, silently; and now she said, ''Thank God,'' and she went and sat down, and she was like that when he came into the room. She wanted to ask him about it, but her throat kept choking; and then he was kneeling there, his head in her lap, and he was crying deep inside, not making a sound. ''It's all right, Jeff,'' she said. ''It's all right.''

For that was the thing he had to know—that it was all right with her. He had to know that she loved him for the man he was and not for the man he had tried to become. He couldn't change any more than Billy Lang could change. She had never told him to take off his gun—not in words—but she had wanted him to, and he had understood, and he had tried. No woman could ask for greater love than that a man try to change himself. And no woman need be afraid when she had such love. She thought of young Anton Svitac and of her own son who was to be, and she was calm and sure.

A long time later she picked up Jeff's coat and laid it across her arm. The tin star fell to the floor. For a long time she looked at it, then she bent her knees and reached down and picked it up and put it back into the coat pocket. She went into the bedroom then and hung the coat carefully. From the bureau drawer she took a clean white pleated-front shirt and laid it out where he could see it. Marshal Jeff Anderson had worn a clean white pleated-front shirt to the office on Monday morning for as long back as she could remember. She didn't expect him to change his habits now.

THE LUCK OF ROARING CAMP

▼▼

Bret Harte

There was commotion in Roaring Camp. It could not have been a fight, for in 1850 that was not novel enough to have called together the entire settlement. The ditches and claims were not only deserted, but "Tuttle's grocery" had contributed its gamblers, who, it will be remembered, calmly continued their game the day that French Pete and Kanaka Joe shot each other to death over the bar in the front room. The whole camp was collected before a rude cabin on the outer edge of the clearing. Conversation was carried on in a low tone, but the name of a woman was frequently repeated. It was a name familiar enough in the camp—"Cherokee Sal."

Perhaps the less said of her the better. She was a coarse and, it is to be feared, very sinful woman. But at that time she was the only woman in Roaring Camp, and was just then lying in sore extremity, when she most needed the ministration of her own sex. Dissolute, abandoned, and irreclaimable, she was yet suffering a martyrdom hard enough to bear even when veiled by sympathizing womanhood, but now terrible in her loneliness. The primal curse had come to her in that original isolation which must have made the punishment of the first transgression so dreadful. It was, perhaps, part of the expiation of her sin that, at a moment when she most lacked her sex's intuitive tenderness and care, she met only the half-contemptuous faces of her masculine associates. Yet a few of the spectators were, I think, touched by her sufferings. Sandy Tipton thought it was "rough on Sal," and in the contemplation of her condition, for a moment rose superior to the fact that he had an ace and two bowers in his sleeve.

It will be seen also that the situation was novel. Deaths were by no means uncommon in Roaring Camp, but a birth was a new thing. People had been dismissed from the camp effectively, finally, and with no possibility of return; but this was the first time that anybody had been introduced *ab initio*. Hence the excitement.

"You go in there, Stumpy," said a prominent citizen known as "Kentuck," addressing one of the loungers. "Go in there, and see what you kin do. You've had experience in them things."

Perhaps there was a fitness in the selection. Stumpy, in other climes, had been the putative head of two families; in fact, it was owing to some legal informality in these proceedings that Roaring Camp—a city of refuge—was indebted to his company. The crowd approved the choice, and Stumpy was wise enough to bow to the majority. The door closed on the extempore surgeon and midwife, and Roaring Camp sat down outside, smoked its pipe, and awaited the issue.

The assemblage numbered about a hundred men. One or two of these were actual fugitives from justice, some were criminal, and all were reckless. Physically they exhibited no indication of their past lives and character. The greatest scamp had a Raphael face, with a profusion of blond hair; Oakhurst, a gambler, had the melancholy air and intellectual abstraction of a Hamlet; the coolest and most courageous man was scarcely over five feet in height, with a soft voice and an embarrassed, timid manner. The term "roughs" applied to them was a distinction rather than a definition. Perhaps in the minor details of fingers, toes, ears, etc., the camp may have been deficient, but these slight omissions did not detract from their aggregate force. The strongest man had but three fingers on his right hand; the best shot had but one eye.

Such was the physical aspect of the men that were dispersed around the cabin. The camp lay in a triangular valley between two hills and a river. The only outlet was a steep trail over the summit of a hill that faced the cabin, now illuminated by the rising moon. The suffering woman might have seen it from the rude bunk whereon she lay—seen it winding like a silver thread until it was lost in the stars above.

A fire of withered pine boughs added sociability to the gathering. By degrees the natural levity of Roaring Camp returned. Bets were freely offered and taken regarding the result. Three to five that "Sal would get through with it"; even that the child would survive; side bets as to the sex and complexion of the coming stranger. In the midst of an excited discussion an exclamation came from those nearest the door, and the camp stopped to listen. Above the swaying and moaning of the pines, the swift rush of the river, and the crackling of the fire rose a sharp, querulous cry— a cry unlike anything heard before in the camp. The pines stopped moaning, the river ceased to rush, and the fire to crackle. It seemed as if Nature had stopped to listen too.

The camp rose to its feet as one man! It was proposed to explode a barrel of gunpowder; but in consideration of the situation of the mother, better counsels prevailed, and only a few revolvers were discharged; for whether owing to the rude surgery of the camp, or some other reason, Cherokee Sal was sinking fast. Within an hour she had climbed, as it were, that rugged road that led to the stars, and so passed out of Roaring Camp, its sin and shame, forever. I do not think that the announcement disturbed them much, except in speculation as to the fate of the child.

"Can he live now?" was asked of Stumpy. The answer was doubtful. The only other being of Cherokee Sal's sex and maternal condition in the settlement was an ass. There was some conjecture as to fitness, but the experiment was tried. It was less problematical than the ancient treatment of Romulus and Remus, and apparently as successful.

When these details were completed, which exhausted another hour, the door was opened, and the anxious crowd of men, who had already formed themselves into a queue, entered in single file. Beside the low bunk or shelf, on which the figure of the mother was starkly outlined below the blankets, stood a pine table. On this a candlebox was placed, and within it, swathed in staring red flannel, lay the last arrival at Roaring Camp. Beside the candlebox was placed a hat. Its use was soon indicated. "Gentlemen," said Stumpy, with a singular mixture of authority and *ex officio* complacency—"gentlemen will please pass in at the front door, round the table, and out at the back door. Them as wishes to contribute anything toward the orphan will find a hat handy." The first man entered with his hat on; he uncovered, however, as he looked about him, and so unconsciously set an example to the next. In such communities good and bad actions are catching. As the procession filed in comments were audible—criticisms addressed perhaps rather to Stumpy in the character of showman: "Is that him?" "Mighty small specimen;" "Hasn't more'n got the color;" "Ain't bigger nor a derringer." The contributions were as characteristic: A silver tobacco box; a doubloon; a navy revolver, silver mounted; a gold specimen; a very beautifully embroidered lady's handkerchief (from Oakhurst the gambler); a diamond breastpin; a diamond ring (suggested by the pin with the remark from the giver that he "saw that pin and went two diamonds better"); a slung shot; a Bible (contributor not detected); a golden spur; a silver teaspoon (the initials, I regret to say, were not the giver's); a pair of surgeon's shears; a lancet; a Bank of England note for £5; and about $200 in loose gold and silver coin. During these proceedings Stumpy maintained a silence as impassive as the dead on his left, a gravity as inscrutable as that of the newly born on his right. Only one incident occurred to break the monotony of the curious procession. As Kentuck bent over the candlebox half curiously, the child turned, and, in a spasm of pain, caught at his groping finger and held it fast for a moment. Kentuck looked foolish and embarrassed. Something like a blush tried to assert itself in his weather-beaten cheek. "The d—d little cuss!" he said, as he extricated his finger, with perhaps more tenderness and care than he might have been deemed capable of showing. He held that finger a little apart from its fellows as he went out, and examined it curiously. The examination provoked the same original remark in regard to the child. In fact, he seemed to enjoy repeating it. "He rastled with my finger," he remarked to Tipton, holding up the member, "the d—d little cuss!"

It was four o'clock before the camp sought repose. A light burnt in the cabin where the watchers sat, for Stumpy did not go to bed that night. Nor did Kentuck. He drank quite freely, and related with great gusto his experience, invariably ending with his characteristic condemnation of the newcomer. It seemed to relieve him of any unjust implication of sentiment, and Kentuck had the weaknesses of the nobler sex. When everybody else had gone to bed, he walked down to the river and whistled reflectingly. Then he walked up the gulch past the cabin, still whistling with demonstrative unconcern. At a large redwood tree he paused and retraced his steps, and again passed the cabin. Halfway down to the river's bank he again paused, and then returned and knocked at the door. It was opened by Stumpy. "How goes it?" said Kentuck, looking past Stumpy toward the candlebox. "All serene!" replied Stumpy. "Anything up?" "Nothing." There was a pause—an embarrassing one— Stumpy still holding the door. Then Kentuck had recourse to his finger, which he held up to Stumpy. "Rastled with it— the d—d little cuss," he said, and retired.

The next day Cherokee Sal had such rude sepulture as Roaring Camp afforded. After her body had been committed to the hillside, there was a formal meeting of the camp

to discuss what should be done with her infant. A resolution
to adopt it was unanimous and enthusiastic. But an ani-
mated discussion in regard to the manner and feasibility of
providing for its wants at once sprang up. It was remarkable
that the argument partook of none of those fierce person-
alities with which discussions were usually conducted at
Roaring Camp. Tipton proposed that they should send the
child to Red Dog—a distance of forty miles—where female
attention could be procured. But the unlucky suggestion
met with fierce and unanimous opposition. It was evident
that no plan which entailed parting from their new acqui-
sition would for a moment be entertained. "Besides," said
Tom Ryder, "them fellows at Red Dog would swap it, and
ring in somebody else on us." A disbelief in the honesty
of other camps prevailed at Roaring Camp, as in other
places.

The introduction of a female nurse in the camp also met
with objection. It was argued that no decent woman could
be prevailed to accept Roaring Camp as her home, and the
speaker urged that "they didn't want any more of the other
kind." This unkind allusion to the defunct mother, harsh
as it may seem, was the first spasm of propriety—the first
symptom of the camp's regeneration. Stumpy advanced
nothing. Perhaps he felt a certain delicacy in interfering
with the selection of a possible successor in office. But
when questioned, he averred stoutly that he and "Jinny"—
the mammal before alluded to—could manage to rear the
child. There was something original, independent, and heroic about the plan that pleased the camp. Stumpy was re-
tained. Certain articles were sent for to Sacramento.
"Mind," said the treasurer, as he pressed a bag of gold
dust into the expressman's hand, "the best that can be
got—lace, you know, and filigree work and frills—d—n
the cost!"

Strange to say, the child thrived. Perhaps the invigorating
climate of the mountain camp was compensation for material deficiencies. Nature took the foundling to her broader
breast. In that rare atmosphere of the Sierra foothills—that
air pungent with balsamic odor, that ethereal cordial at once

bracing and exhilarating—he may have found food and nourishment, or a subtle chemistry that transmuted ass's milk to lime and phosphorus. Stumpy inclined to the belief that it was the latter and good nursing. "Me and that ass," he would say, "has been father and mother to him! Don't you," he would add, apostrophizing the helpless bundle before him, "never go back on us."

By the time he was a month old the necessity of giving him a name became apparent. He had generally been known as "The Kid," "Stumpy's Boy," "The Coyote" (an illusion to his vocal powers), and even by Kentuck's endearing diminutive of "The d—d little cuss." But these were felt to be vague and unsatisfactory, and were at last dismissed under another influence. Gamblers and adventurers are generally superstitious, and Oakhurst one day declared that the baby had brought "the luck" to Roaring Camp. It was certain that of late they had been successful. "Luck" was the name agreed upon, with the prefix of Tommy for greater convenience. No allusion was made to the mother, and the father was unknown. "It's better," said the philosophical Oakhurst, "to take a fresh deal all round. Call him Luck, and start him fair." A day was accordingly set apart for the christening. What was meant by this ceremony the reader may imagine who has already gathered some idea of the reckless irreverence of Roaring Camp. The master of ceremonies was one "Boston," a noted wag, and the occasion seemed to promise the greatest facetiousness. This ingenious satirist had spent two days in preparing a burlesque of the Church service, with pointed local allusions. The choir was properly trained, and Sandy Tipton was to stand godfather. But after the procession had marched to the grove with music and banners, and the child had been deposited before a mock altar, Stumpy stepped before the expectant crowd. "It ain't my style to spoil fun, boys," said the little man, stoutly eyeing the faces around him, "but it strikes me that this thing ain't exactly on the squar. It's playing it pretty low down on this yer baby to ring in fun on him that he ain't goin' to understand. And ef there's goin' to be any godfathers round, I'd like to see

who's got any better rights than me." A silence followed
Stumpy's speech. To the credit of all humorists be it said
that the first man to acknowledge its justice was the satirist
thus stopped of his fun. "But," said Stumpy, quickly following up his advantage, "we're here for a christening, and
we'll have it. I proclaim you Thomas Luck, according to
the laws of the United States and the State of California,
so help me God." It was the first time that the name of the
Deity had been otherwise uttered than profanely in the
camp. The form of christening was perhaps even more ludicrous than the satirist had conceived; but strangely
enough, nobody saw it and nobody laughed. "Tommy"
was christened as seriously as he would have been under a
Christian roof, and cried and was comforted in as orthodox
fashion.

And so the work of regeneration began in Roaring Camp.
Almost imperceptibly a change came over the settlement.
The cabin assigned to "Tommy Luck"—or "The Luck,"
as he was more frequently called—first showed signs of
improvement. It was kept scrupulously clean and white-
washed. Then it was boarded, clothed, and papered. The
rosewood cradle, packed eighty miles by mule, had, in
Stumpy's way of putting it, "sorter killed the rest of the
furniture." So the rehabilitation of the camp became a necessity. The men who were in the habit of lounging in at
Stumpy's to see "how 'The Luck' got on" seemed to ap-
preciate the change, and in self-defense the rival establishment of "Tuttle's grocery" bestirred itself and imported a
carpet and mirrors. The reflections of the latter on the appearance of Roaring Camp tended to produce stricter habits
of personal cleanliness. Again Stumpy imposed a kind of
quarantine upon those who aspired to the honor and privilege of holding The Luck. It was a cruel mortification to
Kentuck—who, in the carelessness of a large nature and
the habits of frontier life, had begun to regard all garments
as a second cuticle, which, like a snake's, only sloughed
off through decay—to be debarred this privilege from certain prudential reasons. Yet such was the subtle influence
of innovation that he thereafter appeared regularly every

afternoon in a clean shirt and face still shining from his ablutions. Nor were moral and social sanitary laws neglected. "Tommy," who was supposed to spend his whole existence in a persistent attempt to repose, must not be disturbed by noise. The shouting and yelling, which had gained the camp its infelicitous title, were not permitted within hearing distance of Stumpy's. The men conversed in whispers or smoked with Indian gravity. Profanity was tacitly given up in these sacred precincts, and throughout the camp a popular form of expletive known as "D—n the luck!" and "Curse the luck!" was abandoned, as having a new personal bearing. Vocal music was not interdicted, being supposed to have a soothing, tranquilizing quality; and one song, sung by "Man-o'-War Jack," an English sailor from her Majesty's Australian colonies, was quite popular as a lullaby. It was a lugubrious recital of the exploits of "the Arethusa, Seventy-four," in a muffled minor, ending with a prolonged dying fall at the burden of each verse, "On b-oo-o-ard of the Arethusa." It was a fine sight to see Jack holding The Luck, rocking from side to side as if with the motion of a ship, and crooning forth this naval ditty. Either through the peculiar rocking of Jack or the length of his song—it contained ninety stanzas, and was continued with conscientious deliberation to the bitter end—the lullaby generally had the desired effect. At such times the men would lie at full length under the trees in the soft summer twilight, smoking their pipes and drinking in the melodious utterances. An indistinct idea that this was pastoral happiness pervaded the camp. "This 'ere kind o' think," said the Cockney Simmons, meditatively reclining on his elbow, "is 'evingly." It reminded him of Greenwich.

On the long summer days The Luck was usually carried to the gulch from whence the golden store of Roaring Camp was taken. There, on a blanket spread over pine boughs, he would lie while the men were working in the ditches below. Latterly there was a rude attempt to decorate this bower with flowers and sweet-smelling shrubs, and generally someone would bring him a cluster of wild honeysuckles, azaleas, or the painted blossoms of Las Mariposas. The men had suddenly awakened to the fact that there were beauty and significance in these trifles, which they had so long trodden carelessly beneath their feet. A flake of glittering mica, a fragment of variegated quartz, a bright pebble from the bed of the creek, became beautiful to eyes thus cleared and strengthened, and were invariably put aside for The Luck. It was wonderful how many treasures the woods and hillsides yielded that "would do for Tommy." Surrounded by playthings such as never child out of fairyland had before, it is to be hoped that Tommy was content. He appeared to be serenely happy, albeit there was an infantine gravity about him, a contemplative light in his round gray eyes, that sometimes worried Stumpy. He was always tractable and quiet, and it is recorded that once, having crept beyond his "corral"—a hedge of tessellated pine boughs, which surrounded his bed—he dropped over the bank on his head in the soft earth, and remained with his mottled legs in the air in that position for at least five minutes with unflinching gravity. He was extricated without a murmur. I hesitate to record the many other instances of his sagacity, which rest, unfortunately, upon the statements of prejudiced friends. Some of them were not without a tinge of superstition. "I crep' up the bank just now," said Kentuck one day, in a breathless state of excitement, "and dern my skin if he wasn't a-talking to a jay bird as was a-sittin' on his lap. There they was, just as free and sociable as anything you please, a-jawin' at each other just like two cherrybums." Howbeit, whether creeping over the pine boughs or lying lazily on his back blinking at the leaves above him, to him the birds sang, the squirrels chattered, and the flowers bloomed. Nature was his nurse and playfellow. For him she would let slip between the leaves golden shafts of sunlight that fell just within his grasp; she would send wandering breezes to visit him with the balm of bay and resinous gum; to him the tall redwoods nodded familiarly and sleepily, the bumblebees buzzed, and the rooks cawed a slumbrous accompaniment.

Such was the golden summer of Roaring Camp. They were "flush times," and the luck was with them. The claims had yielded enormously. The camp was jealous of its privileges and looked suspiciously on strangers. No encouragement was given to immigration, and, to make their seclusion more perfect, the land on either side of the mountain wall that surrounded the camp they duly preempted. This, and a reputation for singular proficiency with the revolver, kept the reserve of Roaring Camp inviolate. The expressman—their only connecting link with the surrounding world—sometimes told wonderful stories of the camp. He would say, "They've a street up there in 'Roaring' that would lay over any street in Red Dog. They've got vines and flowers round their houses, and they wash themselves twice a day. But they're mighty rough on strangers, and they worship an Ingin baby."

With the prosperity of the camp came a desire for further improvement. It was proposed to build a hotel in the following spring, and to invite one or two decent families to reside there for the sake of The Luck, who might perhaps profit by female companionship. The sacrifice that this concession to the sex cost these men, who were fiercely skeptical in regard to its general virtue and usefulness, can only be accounted for by their affection for Tommy. A few still held out. But the resolve could not be carried into effect for three months, and the minority meekly yielded in the hope that something might turn up to prevent it. And it did.

The winter of 1851 will long be remembered in the foothills. The snow lay deep on the Sierras, and every mountain creek became a river, and every river a lake. Each gorge and gulch was transformed into a tumultuous watercourse that descended the hillsides, tearing down giant trees and scattering its drift and debris along the plain. Red Dog had been twice under water, and Roaring Camp had been forewarned. "Water put the gold into them gulches," said Stumpy. "It's been here once and will be here again!" And that night the North Fork suddenly leaped over its banks and swept up the triangular valley of Roaring Camp.

In the confusion of rushing water, crashing trees, and crackling timber, and the darkness which seemed to flow with the water and blot out the fair valley, but little could be done to collect the scattered camp. When the morning broke, the cabin of Stumpy, nearest the riverbank, was gone. Higher up the gulch they found the body of its unlucky owner; but the pride, the hope, the joy, The Luck, of Roaring Camp had disappeared. They were returning with sad hearts when a shout from the bank recalled them.

It was a relief-boat from down the river. They had picked up, they said, a man and an infant, nearly exhausted, about two miles below. Did anybody know them, and did they belong here?

It needed but a glance to show them Kentuck lying there, cruelly crushed and bruised, but still holding The Luck of Roaring Camp in his arms. As they bent over the strangely assorted pair, they saw that the child was cold and pulseless. "He is dead," said one. Kentuck opened his eyes. "Dead?" he repeated feebly. "Yes, my man, and you are dying too." A smile lit the eyes of the expiring Kentuck. "Dying!" he repeated; "he's a-taking me with him. Tell the boys I've got The Luck with me now;" and the strong man, clinging to the frail babe as a drowning man is said to cling to a straw, drifted away into the shadowy river that flows forever to the unknown sea.

THE BLUE HOTEL

▼

Stephen Crane

I

The Palace Hotel at Fort Romper was painted a light blue, a shade that is on the legs of a kind of heron, causing the bird to declare its position against any background. The Palace Hotel, then, was always screaming and howling in a way that made the dazzling winter landscape of Nebraska seem only a gray swampish hush. It stood alone on the prairie, and when the snow was falling, the town two hundred yards away was not visible. But when the traveler alighted at the railway station, he was obliged to pass the Palace Hotel before he could come upon the company of low clapboard houses which composed Fort Romper, and it was not to be thought that any traveler could pass the Palace Hotel without looking at it. Pat Scully, the proprietor, had proved himself a master of strategy when he chose his paints. It is true that on clear days, when the great transcontinental expresses, long lines of swaying Pullmans, swept through Fort Romper, passengers were overcome at the sight, and the cult that knows the brown reds and the subdivisions of the dark greens of the East expressed shame, pity, horror, in a laugh. But to the citizens of this prairie town and to the people who would naturally stop there, Pat Scully had performed a feat. With this opulence and splendor, these creeds, classes, egotisms, that streamed through Romper on the rails day after day, they had no color in common.

As if the displayed delights of such a blue hotel were not sufficiently enticing, it was Scully's habit to go every morning and evening to meet the leisurely trains that stopped at Romper and work his seductions upon any man that he might see wavering, gripsack in hand.

One morning, when a snow-crusted engine dragged its long string of freight cars and its one passenger coach to the station, Scully performed the marvel of catching three men. One was a shaky and quick-eyed Swede, with a great shining cheap valise; one was a tall bronzed cowboy, who was on his way to a ranch near the Dakota line; one was a little silent man from the East, who didn't look it and didn't announce it. Scully practically made them prisoners. He was so nimble and merry and kindly that each probably felt it would be the height of brutality to try to escape. They trudged off over the creaking board sidewalks in the wake of the eager little Irishman. He wore a heavy fur cap squeezed tightly down on his head. It caused his two red ears to stick out stiffly, as if they were made of tin.

At last, Scully, elaborately, with boisterous hospitality, conducted them through the portals of the blue hotel. The room which they entered was small. It seemed to be merely a proper temple for an enormous stove, which, in the center, was humming with godlike violence. At various points on its surface, the iron had become luminous and glowed yellow from the heat. Beside the stove Scully's son Johnnie was playing high-five with an old farmer who had whiskers both gray and sandy. They were quarreling. Frequently the old farmer turned his face toward a box of sawdust—colored brown from tobacco juice—that was behind the stove, and spat with an air of great impatience and irritation. With a loud flourish of words, Scully destroyed the game of cards and bustled his son upstairs with part of the baggage of the new guests. He himself conducted them to three basins of the coldest water in the world. The cowboy and the Easterner burnished themselves fiery red with this water, until it seemed to be some kind of metal polish. The Swede, however, merely dipped his fingers gingerly and with trepidation. It was notable that throughout this series of small ceremonies, the three travelers were made to feel that Scully was very benevolent. He was conferring great favors upon them. He handed the towel from one to another with an air of philanthropic impulse.

Afterward they went to the first room, and, sitting about the stove, listened to Scully's officious clamor at his daughters, who were preparing the midday meal. They reflected in the silence of experienced men who tread carefully amid new people. Nevertheless, the old farmer, stationary, invincible in his chair near the warmest part of the stove, turned his face from the sawdust box frequently and addressed a glowing commonplace to the strangers. Usually he was answered in short but adequate sentences by either the cowboy or the Easterner. The Swede said nothing. He seemed to be occupied in making furtive estimates of each man in the room. One might have thought that he had the sense of silly suspicion which comes to guilt. He resembled a badly frightened man.

Later, at dinner, he spoke a little, addressing his conversation entirely to Scully. He volunteered that he had come from New York where for ten years he had worked as a tailor. These facts seemed to strike Scully as fascinating, and afterward he volunteered that he had lived at Romper for fourteen years. The Swede asked about the crops and the price of labor. He seemed barely to listen to Scully's extended replies. His eyes continued to rove from man to man.

Finally, with a laugh and a wink, he said that some of these Western communities were very dangerous; and after his statement he straightened his legs under the table, tilted his head and laughed again, loudly. It was plain that the demonstration had no meaning to the others. They looked at him wondering and in silence.

II

As the men trooped heavily back into the front room, the two little windows presented views of a turmoiling sea of snow. The huge arms of the wind were making attempts—mighty, circular, futile—to embrace the flakes as they sped. A gatepost like a still man with a blanched face stood aghast amid this profligate fury. In a hearty voice Scully announced the presence of a blizzard. The guests of the blue hotel, lighting their pipes, assented with grunts of lazy masculine contentment. No island of the sea could be exempt in the degree of this little room with its humming stove. Johnnie, son of Scully, in a tone which defined his opinion of his ability as a cardplayer, challenged the old farmer of both gray and sandy whiskers to a game of high-five. The farmer agreed with a contemptuous and bitter scoff. They sat close to the stove, and squared their knees under a wide board. The cowboy and the Easterner watched the game with interest. The Swede remained near the window, aloof, but with a countenance that showed signs of an inexplicable excitement.

The play of Johnnie and the graybeard was suddenly ended by another quarrel. The old man arose while casting a look of heated scorn at his adversary. He slowly buttoned his coat, and then stalked with fabulous dignity from the room. In the discreet silence of all the other men, the Swede laughed. His laughter rang somehow childish. Men by this time had begun to look at him askance, as if they wished to inquire what ailed him.

A new game was formed jocosely. The cowboy volunteered to become the partner of Johnnie, and they all then turned to ask the Swede to throw in his lot with the little Easterner. He asked some questions about the game, and, learning that it wore many names, and that he had played it when it was under an alias, he accepted the invitation. He strode toward the men nervously, as if he expected to be assaulted. Finally, seated, he gazed from face to face and laughed shrilly. This laugh was so strange that the Easterner looked up quickly, the cowboy sat intent and with his mouth open, and Johnnie paused, holding the cards with still fingers.

Afterward there was a short silence. Then Johnnie said, "Well, let's get at it. Come on, now!" They pulled their chairs forward until their knees were bunched under the board. They began to play, and their interest in the game caused the others to forget the manner of the Swede.

The cowboy was a board-whacker. Each time that he held superior cards he whanged them, one by one, with exceeding force, down upon the improvised table, and took the tricks with a glowing air of prowess and ride that sent thrills of indignation into the hearts of his opponents. A game with a board-whacker in it is sure to become intense. The countenances of the Easterner and the Swede were miserable whenever the cowboy thundered down his aces and kings, while Johnnie, his eyes gleaming with joy, chuckled and chuckled.

Because of the absorbing play none considered the strange ways of the Swede. They paid strict heed to the game. Finally, during a lull caused by a new deal, the Swede suddenly addressed Johnnie. "I suppose there have been a good many men killed in this room." The jaws of the others dropped and they looked at him.

"What in hell are you talking about?" said Johnnie.

The Swede laughed again his blatant laugh, full of a kind of false courage and defiance. "Oh, you know what I mean all right," he answered.

"I'm a liar if I do!" Johnnie protested. The card was halted, and the men stared at the Swede. Johnnie evidently felt that as the son of the proprietor he should make a direct inquiry. "Now, what might you be drivin' at, mister?" he asked. The Swede winked at him. It was a wink full of cunning. His fingers shook on the edge of the board. "Oh, maybe you think I have been to nowheres. Maybe you think I'm a tenderfoot?''

''I don't know nothin' about you,'' answered Johnnie, ''and I don't give a damn where you've been. All I got to say is that I don't know what you're driving at. There hain't never been nobody killed in this room.''

The cowboy, who had been steadily gazing at the Swede, then spoke. ''What's wrong with you, mister?''

Apparently it seemed to the Swede that he was formidably menaced. He shivered and turned white near the corners of his mouth. He sent an appealing glance in the direction of the little Easterner. During these moments he did not forget to wear his air of advanced pot-valor. ''They say they don't know what I mean,'' he remarked mockingly to the Easterner.

The latter answered after prolonged and cautious reflection. ''I don't understand you,'' he said impassively.

The Swede made a movement then which announced that he thought he had encountered treachery from the only quarter where he had expected sympathy, if not help. ''Oh, I see you are all against me. I see—''

The cowboy was in a state of deep stupefaction. ''Say,'' he cried, as he tumbled the deck violently down upon the board, ''say, what are you gittin' at, hey?''

The Swede sprang up with the celerity of a man escaping from a snake on the floor. ''I don't want to fight!'' he shouted. ''I don't want to fight!''

The cowboy stretched his long legs indolently and deliberately. His hands were in his pockets. He spat into the sawdust box. ''Well, who the hell thought you did?'' he inquired.

The Swede backed rapidly toward a corner of the room. His hands were out protectingly in front of his chest, but he was making an obvious struggle to control his fright. ''Gentlemen,'' he quavered, ''I suppose I am going to be killed before I can leave this house! I suppose I am going to be killed before I can leave this house!'' In his eyes was the dying-swan look. Through the windows could be seen the snow turning blue in the shadow of dusk. The wind tore at the house, and some loose thing beat regularly against the clapboards like a spirit tapping.

A door opened, and Scully himself entered. He paused in surprise as he noted the tragic attitude of the Swede. Then he said, "What's the matter here?"

The Swede answered him swiftly and eagerly, "These men are going to kill me."

"Kill you!" ejaculated Scully. "Kill you! What are you talkin'?"

The Swede made the gesture of a martyr.

Scully wheeled sternly upon his son. "What is this, Johnnie?"

The lad had grown sullen. "Damned if I know," he answered. "I can't make no sense to it." He began to shuffle the cards, fluttering them together with an angry snap. "He says a good many men have been killed in this room, or something like that. And he says he's goin' to be killed here too. I don't know what ails him. He's crazy, I shouldn't wonder."

Scully then looked for explanation to the cowboy, but the cowboy simply shrugged his shoulders.

"Kill you?" said Scully again to the Swede. "Kill you? Man, you're off your nut."

"Oh, I know," burst out the Swede. "I know what will happen. Yes, I'm crazy—yes. Yes, of course, I'm crazy—yes. But I know one thing—" There was a sort of sweat of misery and terror upon his face. "I know I won't get out of here alive."

The cowboy drew a deep breath, as if his mind was passing into the last stages of dissolution. "Well, I'm doggoned," he whispered to himself.

Scully wheeled suddenly and faced his son. "You've been troublin' this man!"

Johnnie's voice was loud with its burden of grievance. "Why, good Gawd, I ain't done nothin' to 'im."

The Swede broke in. "Gentlemen, do not disturb yourselves. I will leave this house. I will go away, because"—he accused them dramatically with his glance—"because I do not want to be killed."

Scully was furious with his son. "Will you tell me what is the matter, you young devil? What's the matter, anyhow? Speak out!"

"Blame it!" cried Johnnie in despair, "don't I tell you I don't know? He—he says we want to kill him, and that's all I know. I can't tell what ails him."

The Swede continued to repeat, "Never mind, Mr. Scully; never mind. I will leave this house. I will go away, because I do not wish to be killed. Yes, of course, I am crazy—yes. But I know one thing! I will go away. I will leave this house. Never mind, Mr. Scully; never mind. I will go away."

"You will not go 'way," said Scully. "You will not go 'way until I hear the reason of this business. If anybody has troubled you, I will take care of him. This is my house. You are under my roof, and I will not allow any peaceable man to be troubled here." He cast a terrible eye upon Johnnie, the cowboy and the Easterner.

"Never mind, Mr. Scully; never mind. I will go away. I do not wish to be killed." The Swede moved toward the door which opened upon the stairs. It was evidently his intention to go at once for his baggage.

"No, no," shouted Scully peremptorily; but the white-faced man slid by him and disappeared. "Now," said Scully severely, "what does this mean?"

Johnnie and the cowboy cried together, "Why, we didn't do nothin' to 'im!"

Scully's eyes were cold. "No," he said, "you didn't?"

Johnnie swore a deep oath. "Why, this is the wildest loon I ever see. We didn't do nothin' at all. We were just sittin' here playin' cards, and he—"

The father suddenly spoke to the Easterner. "Mr. Blanc," he asked, "what has these boys been doin'?"

The Easterner reflected again. "I didn't see anything wrong at all," he said at last slowly.

Scully began to howl. "But what does it mane?" He stared ferociously at his son. "I have a mind to lather you for this, me boy."

Johnnie was frantic. "Well, what have I done?" he bawled at his father.

III

"I think you are tongue-tied," said Scully finally to his son, the cowboy and the Easterner; and at the end of this scornful sentence, he left the room.

Upstairs the Swede was swiftly fastening the straps of his great valise. Once his back happened to be half turned toward the door, and, hearing a noise there, he wheeled and sprang up, uttering a loud cry. Scully's wrinkled visage showed grimly in the light of the small lamp he carried. This yellow effulgence, streaming upward, colored only his prominent features, and left his eyes, for instance, in mysterious shadow. He resembled a murderer.

"Man! man!" he exclaimed. "Have you gone daffy?"

"Oh, no! Oh, no!" rejoined the other. "There are people in this world who know pretty nearly as much as you do—understand?"

For a moment they stood gazing at each other. Upon the Swede's deathly pale cheeks were two spots brightly crimson and sharply edged, as if they had been carefully painted. Scully placed the light on the table and sat himself on the edge of the bed. He spoke ruminatively. "By cracky, I never heard of such a thing in my life. It's a complete muddle. I can't, for the soul of me, think how you ever got this idea into your head." Presently he lifted his eyes and asked, "And did you sure think they were going to kill you?"

The Swede scanned the old man as if he wished to see into his mind. "I did," he said at last. He obviously suspected that this answer might precipitate an outbreak. As he pulled on a strap his whole arm shook, the elbow wavering like a bit of paper.

Scully banged his hand impressively on the footboard of the bed. "Why, man, we're goin' to have a line of ilictric streetcars in this town next spring."

" 'A line of electric streetcars,' " repeated the Swede stupidly.

"And," said Scully, "there's a new railroad goin' to be built down from Broken Arm to here. Not to mention the four churches and the smashin' big brick schoolhouse. Then there's the big factory, too. Why, in two years Romper'll be a met-tro-*pol*-is."

Having finished the preparation of his baggage, the Swede straightened himself. "Mr. Scully," he said, with sudden hardihood, "how much do I owe you?"

"You don't owe me anythin'," said the old man, angrily.

"Yes, I do," retorted the Swede. He took seventy-five cents from his pocket and tendered it to Scully; but the latter snapped his fingers in disdainful refusal. However, it happened that they both stood gazing in a strange fashion at three silver pieces on the Swede's open palm.

"I'll not take your money," said Scully at last. "Not after what's been goin' on here." Then a plan seemed to strike him. "Here," he cried, picking up his lamp and moving toward the door. "Here! Come with me a minute."

"No," said the Swede, in overwhelming alarm.

"Yes," urged the old man. "Come on! I want you to come and see a picter—just across the hall—in my room."

The Swede must have concluded that his hour was come. His jaw dropped and his teeth showed like a dead man's. He ultimately followed Scully across the corridor, but he had the step of one hung in chains.

Scully flashed the light high on the wall of his own chamber. There was revealed a ridiculous photograph of a little girl. She was leaning against a balustrade of gorgeous decoration, and the formidable bang to her hair was prominent. The figure was as graceful as an upright sled-stake, and, withal, it was of the hue of lead. "There," said Scully, tenderly, "that's the picter of my little girl that died. Her name was Carrie. She had the purtiest hair you ever saw. I was that fond of her, she—"

Turning then, he saw that the Swede was not contemplating the picture at all, but, instead, was keeping keen watch on the gloom in the rear.

"Look, man!" cried Scully, heartily. "That's the picter of my little gal that died. Her name was Carrie. And then here's the picter of my oldest boy, Michael. He's a lawyer in Lincoln, an' doin' well. I gave that boy a grand eddication, and I'm glad for it now. He's a fine boy. Look at 'im now. Ain't he bold as blazes, him there in Lincoln, an honored an' respicted gintleman! An honored and re-spicted gintleman," concluded Scully with a flourish. And, so saying, he smote the Swede jovially on the back.

The Swede faintly smiled.

"Now," said the old man, "there's only one more thing." He dropped suddenly to the floor and thrust his hand beneath the bed. The Swede could hear his muffled voice. "I'd keep it under me piller if it wasn't for that boy Johnnie. Then there's the old woman— Where is it now? I never put it twice in the same place. Ah, now come out with you!"

Presently he backed clumsily from under the bed, drag-ging with him an old coat rolled into a bundle. "I've fetched him," he muttered. Kneeling on the floor, he un-rolled the coat and extracted from its heart a large yellow brown whisky bottle.

His first maneuver was to hold the bottle up to the light. Reassured, apparently, that nobody had been tampering with it, he thrust it with a generous movement toward the Swede.

The weak-kneed Swede was about to eagerly clutch this element of strength, but he suddenly jerked his hand away and cast a look of horror upon Scully.

"Drink," said the old man affectionately. He had risen to his feet, and now stood facing the Swede.

There was a silence. Then again Scully said, "Drink!"

The Swede laughed wildly. He grabbed the bottle, put it to his mouth; and as his lips curled absurdly around the opening and his throat worked, he kept his glance, burning with hatred, upon the old man's face.

IV

After the departure of Scully the three men, with the cardboard still upon their knees, preserved for a long time an astounded silence. Then Johnnie said, "That's the daddangedest Swede I ever see."

"He ain't no Swede," said the cowboy scornfully.

"Well, what is he then?" cried Johnnie. "What is he then?"

"It's my opinion," replied the cowboy deliberately, "he's some kind of a Dutchman." It was a venerable custom of the country to entitle as Swedes all light-haired men who spoke with a heavy tongue. In consequence the idea of the cowboy was not without its daring. "Yes, sir," he repeated. "It's my opinion this feller is some kind of a Dutchman."

"Well, he says he's a Swede, anyhow," muttered Johnnie, sulkily. He turned to the Easterner. "What do you think, Mr. Blanc?"

"Oh, I don't know," replied the Easterner.

"Well, what do you think makes him act that way?" asked the cowboy.

"Why, he's frightened." The Easterner knocked his pipe against a rim of the stove. "He's clear frightened out of his boots."

"What at?" cried Johnnie and the cowboy together.

The Easterner reflected over his answer.

"What at?" cried the others again.

"Oh, I don't know, but it seems to me this man has been reading dime novels, and he thinks he's right out in the middle of it—the shootin' and stabbin' and all."

"But," said the cowboy, deeply scandalized, "this ain't Wyoming, ner none of them places. This is Nebrasker."

"Yes," added Johnnie, "an' why don't he wait till he gits *out West*?"

The traveled Easterner laughed. "It isn't different there even—not in these days. But he thinks he's right in the middle of hell."

Johnnie and the cowboy mused long.

"It's awful funny," remarked Johnnie at last.

"Yes," said the cowboy. "This is a queer game. I hope we don't git snowed in, because then we'd have to stand this here man bein' around with us all the time. That wouldn't be no good."

"I wish Pop would throw him out," said Johnnie.

Presently they heard a loud stamping on the stairs, accompanied by ringing jokes in the voice of old Scully, and laughter, evidently from the Swede. The men around the stove stared vacantly at each other. "Gosh!" said the cowboy. The door flew open, and old Scully, flushed and anecdotal, came into the room. He was jabbering at the Swede, who followed him, laughing bravely. It was the entry of two roisterers from a banquet hall.

"Come now," said Scully sharply to the three seated men, "move up and give us a chance at the stove." The cowboy and the Easterner obediently sidled their chairs to make room for the newcomers. Johnnie, however, simply arranged himself in a more indolent attitude, and then remained motionless.

"Come! Git over there," said Scully.

"Plenty of room on the other side of the stove," said Johnnie.

"Do you think we want to sit in the draught?" roared the father.

But the Swede here interposed with a grandeur of confidence. "No, no. Let the boy sit where he likes," he cried in a bullying voice to the father.

"All right! All right!" said Scully, deferentially. The cowboy and the Easterner exchanged glances of wonder.

The five chairs were formed in a crescent about one side of the stove. The Swede began to talk; he talked arrogantly, profanely, angrily. Johnnie, the cowboy and the Easterner maintained a morose silence, while old Scully appeared to be receptive and eager, breaking in constantly with sympathetic ejaculations.

Finally the Swede announced that he was thirsty. He moved in his chair, and said that he would go for a drink of water.

"I'll git it for you," cried Scully at once.

"No," said the Swede, contemptuously. "I'll get it for myself." He arose and stalked with the air of an owner off into the executive parts of the hotel.

As soon as the Swede was out of hearing, Scully sprang to his feet and whispered intensely to the others, "Upstairs he thought I was tryin' to poison 'im."

"Say," said Johnnie, "this makes me sick. Why don't you throw 'im out in the snow?"

"Why, he's all right now," declared Scully. "It was only that he was from the East, and he thought this was a tough place. That's all. He's all right now."

The cowboy looked with admiration upon the Easterner. "You were straight," he said. "You were on to that there Dutchman."

"Well," said Johnnie to his father, "he may be all right now, but I don't see it. Other time he was scared, but now he's too fresh."

Scully's speech was always a combination of Irish brogue and idiom, Western twang and idiom, and scraps of curiously formal diction taken from the storybooks and newspapers. He now hurled a strange mass of language at the head of his son. "What do I keep? What do I keep? What do I keep?" he demanded, in a voice of thunder. He slapped his knee impressively, to indicate that he himself was going to make reply, and that all should heed. "I keep a hotel," he shouted. "A hotel, do you mind? A guest under my roof has sacred privileges. He is to be intimidated by none. Not one word shall he hear that would prijudice him in favor of goin' away. I'll not have it. There's no place in this here town where they can say they iver took in a guest of mine because he was afraid to stay here." He wheeled suddenly upon the cowboy and the Easterner. "Am I right?"

"Yes, Mr. Scully," said the cowboy, "I think you're right."

"Yes, Mr. Scully," said the Easterner, "I think you're right."

V

At six o'clock supper, the Swede fizzed like a fire wheel. He sometimes seemed on the point of bursting into riotous song, and in all his madness he was encouraged by old Scully. The Easterner was encased in reserve; the cowboy sat in wide-mouthed amazement, forgetting to eat, while Johnnie wrathily demolished great plates of food. The daughters of the house, when they were obliged to replenish the biscuits, approached as warily as Indians, and, having succeeded in their purpose, fled with ill-concealed trepidation. The Swede domineered the whole feast, and he gave it the appearance of a cruel bacchanal. He seemed to have grown suddenly taller; he gazed, brutally disdainful, into every face. His voice rang through the room. Once when he jabbed out harpoon-fashion with his fork to pinion a biscuit, the weapon nearly impaled the hand of the Easterner, which had been stretched quietly out for the same biscuit.

After supper, as the men filed toward the other room, the Swede smote Scully ruthlessly on the shoulder. "Well, old boy, that was a good, square meal." Johnnie looked hopefully at his father; he knew that shoulder was tender from an old fall; and, indeed, it appeared for a moment as if Scully was going to flame out over the matter, but in the end he smiled a sickly smile and remained silent. The others understood from his manner that he was admitting his responsibility for the Swede's new viewpoint.

Johnnie, however, addressed his parent in an aside. "Why don't you license somebody to kick you downstairs?" Scully scowled darkly by way of reply.

When they were gathered about the stove, the Swede insisted on another game of high-five. Scully gently deprecated the plan at first, but the Swede turned a wolfish glare upon him. The old man subsided, and the Swede canvased the others. In his tone there was always a great threat. The cowboy and the Easterner both remarked indifferently that they would play. Scully said that he would presently have to go to meet the 6:58 train, and so the Swede turned menacingly upon Johnnie. For a moment their glances crossed like blades, and then Johnnie smiled and said, ''Yes, I'll play.''

They formed a square, with the little board on their knees. The Easterner and the Swede were again partners. As the play went on, it was noticeable that the cowboy was not board-whacking as usual. Meanwhile, Scully, near the lamp, had put on his spectacles and, with an appearance curiously like an old priest, was reading a newspaper. In time he went out to meet the 6:58 train, and, despite his precautions, a gust of polar wind whirled into the room as he opened the door. Besides scattering the cards, it chilled the players to the marrow. The Swede cursed frightfully. When Scully returned, his entrance disturbed a cozy and friendly scene. The Swede again cursed. But presently they were once more intent, their heads bent forward and their hands moving swiftly. The Swede had adopted the fashion of board-whacking.

Scully took up his paper and for a long time remained immersed in matters which were extraordinarily remote from him. The lamp burned badly, and once he stopped to adjust the wick. The newspaper, as he turned from page to page, rustled with a slow and comfortable sound. Then suddenly he heard three terrible words. ''You are cheatin'!''

Such scenes often prove that there can be little of dramatic import in environment. Any room can present a tragic front; any room can be comic. This little den was now hideous as a torture chamber. The new faces of the men themselves had changed it upon the instant the Swede held a huge fist in front of Johnnie's face, while the latter looked steadily over it into the blazing orbs of his accuser. The Easterner had grown pallid; the cowboy's jaw had dropped in that expression of bovine amazement which was one of his important mannerisms. After the three words, the first sound in the room was made by Scully's paper as it floated forgotten to his feet. His spectacles had also fallen from his nose, but by a clutch he had saved them in air. His hand, grasping the spectacles, now remained poised awkwardly and near his shoulder. He stared at the cardplayers.

Probably the silence was while a second elapsed. Then, if the floor had been suddenly twitched out from under the men, they could not have moved quicker. The five had projected themselves headlong toward a common point. It happened that Johnnie, in rising to hurl himself upon the Swede, had stumbled slightly because of his curiously instinctive care for the cards and the board. The loss of the moment allowed time for the arrival of Scully, and also allowed the cowboy time to give the Swede a great push which sent him staggering back. The men found tongue together, and hoarse shouts of rage, appeal or fear burst from every throat. The cowboy pushed and jostled feverishly at the Swede, and the Easterner and Scully clung wildly to Johnnie; but through the smoky air, above the swaying bodies of the peace-compellers, the eyes of the two warriors ever sought each other in glances of challenge that were at once hot and steely.

Of course the board had been overturned, and now the whole company of cards was scattered over the floor, where the boots of the men trampled the fat and painted kings and queens as they gazed with their silly eyes at the war that was waging above them.

Scully's voice was dominating the yells. "Stop now! Stop, I say! Stop, now—"

Johnnie, as he struggled to burst through the rank formed by Scully and the Easterner, was crying, "Well, he says I cheated! He says I cheated! I won't allow no man to say I cheated! If he says I cheated, he's a————!"

The cowboy was telling the Swede, "Quit, now! Quit, d'ye hear—"

The screams of the Swede never ceased. "He did cheat! I saw him! I saw him—"

As for the Easterner, he was importuning in a voice that was not heeded, "Wait a moment, can't you? Oh, wait a moment. What's the good of a fight over a game of cards? Wait a moment—"

In this tumult no complete sentences were clear. "Cheat"—"quit"—"he says"—these fragments pierced the uproar and rang out sharply. It was remarkable that, whereas Scully undoubtedly made the most noise, he was the least heard of any of the riotous band.

Then suddenly there was a great cessation. It was as if each man had paused for breath; and although the room was still lighted with the anger of men, it could be seen that there was no danger of immediate conflict, and at once Johnnie, shouldering his way forward, almost succeeded in confronting the Swede. "What did you say I cheated for? What did you say I cheated for? I don't cheat, and I won't let no man say I do!"

The Swede said, "I saw you! I saw you!"

"Well," cried Johnnie, "I'll fight any man what says I cheat!"

"No, you won't," said the cowboy. "Not here."

"Ah, be still, can't you?" said Scully, coming between them.

The quiet was sufficient to allow the Easterner's voice to be heard. He was repeating, "Oh, wait a moment, can't you? What's the good of a fight over a game of cards? Wait a moment!"

Johnnie, his red face appearing above his father's shoulder, hailed the Swede again. "Did you say I cheated?"

The Swede showed his teeth. "Yes."

"Then," said Johnnie, "we must fight."

"Yes, fight," roared the Swede. He was like a demoniac. "Yes, fight! I'll show you what kind of a man I am! I'll show you who you want to fight! Maybe you think I can't fight! Maybe you think I can't! I'll show you, you skin, you cardsharp. Yes, you cheated! You cheated! You cheated!"

"Well, let's go at it, then, mister," said Johnnie coolly.

The cowboy's brow was beaded with sweat from his efforts in intercepting all sorts of raids. He turned in despair to Scully. "What are you goin' to do now?"

A change had come over the Celtic visage of the old man. He now seemed all eagerness; his eyes glowed.

"We'll let them fight," he answered, stalwartly. "I can't put up with it any longer. I've stood this damned Swede till I'm sick. We'll let them fight."

VI

The men prepared to go out-of-doors. The Easterner was so nervous that he had great difficulty in getting his arms into the sleeves of his new leather coat. As the cowboy drew his fur cap down over his ears, his hands trembled. In fact, Johnnie and old Scully were the only ones who displayed no agitation. These preliminaries were conducted without words.

Scully threw open the door. "Well, come on," he said. Instantly a terrific wind caused the flame of the lamp to struggle at its wick, while a puff of black smoke sprang from the chimney top. The stove was in mid-current of the blast, and its voice swelled to equal the roar of the storm. Some of the scarred and bedabbled cards were caught up from the floor and dashed helplessly against the farther wall. The men lowered their heads and plunged into the tempest as into a sea.

No snow was falling, but great whirls and clouds of flakes, swept up from the ground by the frantic winds, were streaming southward with the speed of bullets. The covered land was blue with the sheen of an unearthly satin, and there was no other hue save where, at the low black railway station—which seemed incredibly distant—one light gleamed like a tiny jewel. As the men floundered into a thigh-deep drift, it was known that the Swede was bawling out something. Scully went to him, put a hand on his shoulder and projected an ear. "What's that you say?" he shouted.

"I say," bawled the Swede again, "I won't stand much show against this gang. I know you'll all pitch on me."

Scully smote him reproachfully on the arm. "Tut, man!" he yelled. The wind tore the words from Scully's lips and scattered them far alee.

"You are all a gang of—" boomed the Swede, but the storm also seized the remainder of this sentence.

Immediately turning their backs upon the wind, the men had swung around a corner to the sheltered side of the hotel. It was the function of the little house to preserve here, amid this great devastation of snow, an irregular V-shape of heavily encrusted grass, which crackled beneath the feet. One could imagine the great drifts piled against the windward side. When the party reached the comparative peace of this spot, it was found that the Swede was still bellowing.

"Oh, I know what kind of a thing this is! I know you'll all pitch on me. I can't lick you all!"

Scully turned upon him panther-fashion. "You'll not have to whip all of us. You'll have to whip my son Johnnie. An' the man what troubles you durin' that time will have me to deal with."

The arrangements were swiftly made. The two men faced each other, obedient to the harsh commands of Scully, whose face, in the subtly luminous gloom, could be seen set in the austere impersonal lines that are pictured on the countenances of the Roman veterans. The Easterner's teeth were chattering, and he was hopping up and down like a mechanical toy. The cowboy stood rocklike.

The contestants had not stripped off any clothing. Each was in his ordinary attire. Their fists were up, and they eyed each other in a calm that had the elements of leonine cruelty in it.

During this pause, the Easterner's mind, like a film, took lasting impressions of three men—the iron-nerved master of the ceremony; the Swede, pale, motionless, terrible; and Johnnie, serene yet ferocious, brutish yet heroic. The entire prelude had in it a tragedy greater than the tragedy of action, and this aspect was accentuated by the long, mellow cry of the blizzard as it sped the tumbling and wailing flakes into the black abyss of the south.

"Now!" said Scully.

The two combatants leaped forward and crashed together like bullocks. There was heard the cushioned sound of blows, and of a curse squeezing out from between the tight teeth of one.

As for the spectators, the Easterner's pent-up breath exploded from him with a pop of relief, absolute relief from the tension of the preliminaries. The cowboy bounded into the air with a yowl. Scully was immovable as from supreme amazement and fear at the fury of the fight which he himself had permitted and arranged.

For a time the encounter in the darkness was such a perplexity of flying arms that it presented no more detail than would a swiftly revolving wheel. Occasionally, a face, as if illumined by a flash of light, would shine out, ghastly and marked with pink spots. A moment later, the men might have been known as shadows if it were not for the involuntary utterance of oaths that came from them in whispers.

Suddenly a holocaust of warlike desire caught the cowboy, and he bolted forward with the speed of a bronco. "Go it, Johnnie! Go it! Kill him! Kill him!"

Scully confronted him. "Kape back," he said; and by his glance the cowboy could tell that this man was Johnnie's father.

To the Easterner there was a monotony of unchangeable fighting that was an abomination. This confused mingling was eternal to his sense, which was concentrated in a longing for the end, the priceless end. Once the fighters lurched near him, and as he scrambled hastily backward he heard them breathe like men on the rack.

"Kill him, Johnnie! Kill him! Kill him! Kill him!" The cowboy's face was contorted like one of those agony masks in museums.

"Keep still," said Scully icily.

Then there was a sudden loud grunt, incomplete, cut short, and Johnnie's body swung away from the Swede and fell with sickening heaviness to the grass. The cowboy was barely in time to prevent the mad Swede from flinging himself upon his prone adversary. "No, you don't," said the cowboy, interposing an arm. "Wait a second."

Scully was at his son's side. "Johnnie! Johnnie, me boy!" His voice had a quality of melancholy tenderness. "Johnnie! Can you go on with it?" He looked anxiously down into the bloody, pulpy face of his son.

There was a moment of silence, and then Johnnie answered in his ordinary voice. "Yes, I—it—yes."

Assisted by his father he struggled to his feet. "Wait a

bit now till you git your wind," said the old man.

A few paces away the cowboy was lecturing the Swede. "No, you don't! Wait a second!"

The Easterner was plucking at Scully's sleeve. "Oh, this is enough," he pleaded. "This is enough! Let it go as it stands. This is enough!"

"Bill," said Scully, "git out of the road." The cowboy stepped aside. "Now." The combatants were actuated by a new caution as they advanced toward collision. They glared at each other, and then the Swede aimed a lightning blow that carried with it his entire weight. Johnnie was evidently half stupid from weakness, but he miraculously dodged, and his fist sent the overbalanced Swede sprawling.

The cowboy, Scully and the Easterner burst into a cheer that was like a chorus of triumphant soldiery, but before its conclusion the Swede had scuffed agilely to his feet and come in berserk abandon at his foe. There was another perplexity of flying arms, and Johnnie's body again swung away and fell, even as a bundle might fall from a roof. The Swede instantly staggered to a little wind-waved tree and leaned upon it, breathing like an engine, while his savage and flame-lit eyes roamed from face to face as the men bent over Johnnie. There was a splendor of isolation in his situation at this time which the Easterner felt once when, lifting his eyes from the man on the ground, he beheld that mysterious and lonely figure, waiting.

"Are you any good yet, Johnnie?" asked Scully in a broken voice.

The son gasped and opened his eyes languidly. After a moment he answered, "No—I ain't—any good—any—more." Then from shame and bodily ill, he began to weep, the tears furrowing down through the bloodstains on his face. "He was too—too—heavy for me."

Scully straightened and addressed the waiting figure. "Stranger," he said, evenly, "it's all up with our side." Then his voice changed into that vibrant huskiness which is commonly the tone of the most simple and deadly announcements. "Johnnie is whipped."

Without replying, the victor moved off on the route to the front door of the hotel.

The cowboy was formulating new and unspellable blasphemies. The Easterner was startled to find that they were out in a wind that seemed to come direct from the shadowed arctic floes. He heard again the wail of the snow as it was flung to its grave in the south. He knew now that all this time the cold had been sinking into him deeper and deeper, and he wondered that he had not perished. He felt indifferent to the condition of the vanquished man.

"Johnnie, can you walk?" asked Scully.

"Did I hurt—hurt him any?" asked the son.

"Can you walk, boy? Can you walk?"

Johnnie's voice was suddenly strong. There was a robust impatience in it. "I asked you whether I hurt him any!"

"Yes, yes, Johnnie," answered the cowboy, consolingly, "he's hurt a good deal."

They raised him from the ground, and as soon as he was on his feet, he went tottering off, rebuffing all attempts at assistance. When the party rounded the corner, they were fairly blinded by the pelting of the snow. It burned their faces like fire. The cowboy carried Johnnie through the drift to the door. As they entered, some cards rose from the floor and beat against the wall.

The Easterner rushed to the stove. He was so profoundly chilled that he almost dared to embrace the glowing iron. The Swede was not in the room. Johnnie sank into a chair and, folding his arms on his knees, buried his face in them. Scully, warming one foot and then the other at the rim of the stove, muttered to himself with Celtic mournfulness. The cowboy had removed his fur cap, and with a dazed and rueful air he was running one hand through his tousled locks. From overhead they could hear the creaking of boards as the Swede tramped here and there in his room.

The sad quiet was broken by the sudden flinging open of a door that led toward the kitchen. It was instantly followed by an onrush of women. They precipitated themselves upon Johnnie amid a chorus of lamentation. Before they carried their prey off to the kitchen, there to be bathed

and harangued with that mixture of sympathy and abuse
which is a feat of their sex, the mother straightened herself
and fixed old Scully with an eye of stern reproach. "Shame
be upon you, Patrick Scully!" she cried. "Your own son,
too. Shame be upon you!"

"There, now! Be quiet, now!" said the old man weakly
to this slogan, sniffed disdainfully in the direction of those
trembling accomplices, the cowboy and the Easterner. Presently they bore Johnnie away, and left the three men to
dismal reflection.

VII

"I'd like to fight this here Dutchman myself," said the
cowboy, breaking a long silence.

Scully wagged his head sadly. "No, that wouldn't do. It
wouldn't be right. It wouldn't be right."

"Well, why wouldn't it?" argued the cowboy. "I don't
see no harm in it."

"No," answered Scully, with mournful heroism. "It
wouldn't be right. It was Johnnie's fight, and now we
mustn't whip the man just because he whipped Johnnie."

"Yes, that's true enough," said the cowboy, "but—he
better not get fresh with me, because I couldn't stand no
more of it."

"You'll not say a word to him," commanded Scully,
and even then they heard the tread of the Swede on the
stairs. His entrance was made theatric. He swept the door
back with a bang and swaggered to the middle of the room.
No one looked at him. "Well," he cried, insolently, at
Scully, "I s'pose you'll tell me now how much I owe
you?"

The old man remained stolid. "You don't owe me
nothin'."

"Huh!" said the Swede. "Huh! Don't owe 'im nothin'."

The cowboy addressed the Swede. "Stranger, I don't see
how you come to be so gay around here."

Old Scully was instantly alert. "Stop!" he shouted, holding his hand forth, fingers upward. "Bill, you shut up!"

The cowboy spat carelessly into the sawdust box. "I didn't say a word, did I?" he asked.

"Mr. Scully," called the Swede, "how much do I owe you?" It was seen that he was attired for departure, and that he had his valise in his hand.

"You don't owe me nothin'," repeated Scully in the same imperturbable way.

"Huh!" said the Swede. "I guess you're right. I guess if it was any way at all, you'd owe me somethin'. That's what I guess." He turned to the cowboy. " 'Kill him! Kill him! Kill him!' " he mimicked, and then guffawed victoriously. " 'Kill him!' " He was convulsed with ironical humor.

But he might have been jeering the dead. The three men were immovable and silent, staring with glassy eyes at the stove.

The Swede opened the door and passed into the storm, giving one derisive glance backward at the still group.

As soon as the door was closed, Scully and the cowboy leaped to their feet and began to curse. They trampled to and fro, waving their arms and smashing into the air with their fists. "Oh, but that was a hard minute!" wailed Scully. "That was a hard minute! Him there leerin' and scoffin'! One bang at his nose was worth forty dollars to me that minute! How did you stand it, Bill?"

"How did I stand it?" cried the cowboy in a quivering voice. "How did I stand it? Oh!"

The old man burst into sudden brogue. "I'd loike to take that Swade," he wailed, "and hould 'im down on a shtone flure and bate 'im to a jelly wid a shtick!"

The cowboy groaned in sympathy. "I'd like to git him by the neck and ha-ammer him"—he brought his hand down on a chair with a noise like a pistol shot—"hammer that there Dutchman until he couldn't tell himself from a dead coyote!"

"I'd bate 'im until he—"

"I'd show *him* some things—"

And then together they raised a yearning, fantastic cry—
"Oh-o-oh! If we only could—"

"Yes!"

"Yes!"

"And then I'd—"

"O-o-oh!"

VIII

The Swede, tightly gripping his valise, tacked across the face of the storm as if he carried sails. He was following a line of little naked, grasping trees which, he knew, must mark the way of the road. His face, fresh from the pounding of Johnnie's fists, felt more pleasure than pain in the wind and the driving snow. A number of square shapes loomed upon him finally, and he knew them as the houses of the main body of the town. He found a street and made travel along it, leaning heavily upon the wind whenever, at a corner, a terrific blast caught him.

He might have been in a deserted village. We picture the world as thick with conquering and elate humanity, but here, with the bugles of the tempest pealing, it was hard to imagine a peopled earth. One viewed the existence of man then as a marvel, and conceded a glamour of wonder to these lice which were caused to cling to a whirling, fire-smitten, ice-locked, disease-stricken, space-lost bulb. The conceit of man was explained by this storm to be the very engine of life. One was a coxcomb not to die in it. However, the Swede found a saloon.

In front of it an indomitable red light was burning, and the snowflakes were made blood color as they flew through the circumscribed territory of the lamp's shining. The Swede pushed open the door of the saloon and entered. A sanded expanse was before him, and at the end of it four men sat about a table drinking. Down one side of the room extended a radiant bar, and its guardian was leaning upon his elbows listening to the talk of the men at the table. The

Swede dropped his valise upon the floor and, smiling fraternally upon the barkeeper, said, "Gimme some whisky, will you?" The man placed a bottle, a whisky glass, and a glass of ice-thick water upon the bar. The Swede poured himself an abnormal portion of whisky and drank it in three gulps. "Pretty bad night," remarked the bartender indifferently. He was making the pretension of blindness which is usually a distinction of his class; but it could have been seen that he was furtively studying the half-erased bloodstains on the face of the Swede. "Bad night," he said again.

"Oh, it's good enough for me," replied the Swede hardily as he poured himself some more whisky. The barkeeper took his coin and maneuvered it through its reception by a highly nickeled cash-machine. A bell rang; a card labeled "20 cts." had appeared.

"No," continued the Swede, "this isn't too bad weather. It's good enough for me."

"So?" murmured the barkeeper languidly.

The copious drams made the Swede's eyes swim, and he breathed a trifle heavier. "Yes, I like this weather. I like it. It suits me." It was apparently his design to impart a deep significance to these words.

"So?" murmured the bartender again. He turned to gaze dreamily at the scroll-like birds and birdlike scrolls which had been drawn with soap upon the mirrors in back of the bar.

"Well, I guess I'll take another drink," said the Swede presently. "Have something?"

"No, thanks; I'm not drinkin'," answered the bartender. Afterward he asked, "How did you hurt your face?"

The Swede immediately began to boast loudly. "Why, in a fight. I thumped the soul out of a man down here at Scully's hotel."

The interest of the four men at the table was at last aroused.

"Who was it?" said one.

"Johnnie Scully," blustered the Swede. "Son of the man what runs it. He will be pretty near dead for some weeks, I can tell you. I made a nice thing of him, I did. He couldn't get up. They carried him in the house. Have a drink?''

Instantly the men in some subtle way encased themselves in reserve. ''No, thanks,'' said one. The group was of curious formation. Two were prominent local business men; one was the district attorney; and one was a professional gambler of the kind known as ''square.'' But a scrutiny of the group would not have enabled an observer to pick the gambler from the men of more reputable pursuits. He was, in fact, a man so delicate in manner when among people of fair class, and so judicious in his choice of victims, that in the strictly masculine part of the town's life he had come to be explicitly trusted and admired. People called him a thoroughbred. The fear and contempt with which his craft was regarded were undoubtedly the reason why his quiet dignity shone conspicuous above the quiet dignity of men who might be merely hatters, billiard markers or grocery clerks. Beyond an occasionally unwary traveler who came by rail, this gambler was supposed to prey solely upon reckless and senile farmers, who, when flush with good crops, drove into town in all the pride and confidence of an absolutely invulnerable stupidity. Hearing at times in circuitous fashion of the despoilment of such a farmer, the important men of Romper invariably laughed in contempt of the victim, and if they thought of the wolf at all, it was with a kind of pride at the knowledge that he would never dare think of attacking their wisdom and courage. Besides, it was popular that this gambler had a real wife and two real children in a neat cottage in a suburb, where he led an exemplary home life; and when any one even suggested a discrepancy in his character, the crowd immediately vociferated descriptions of this virtuous family circle. Then men who led exemplary home lives, and men who did not lead exemplary home lives, all subsided in a bunch, remarking that there was nothing more to be said.

However, when a restriction was placed upon him—as, for instance, when a strong clique of members of the new Polywog Club refused to permit him, even as a spectator, to appear in the rooms of the organization—the candor and gentleness with which he accepted the judgment disarmed many of his foes and made his friends more desperately partisan. He invariably distinguished between himself and a respectable Romper man so quickly and frankly that his manner actually appeared to be a continual broadcast compliment.

And one must not forget to declare the fundamental fact of his entire position in Romper. It is irrefutable that in all affairs outside his business, in all matters that occur eternally and commonly between man and man, this thieving cardplayer was so generous, so just, so moral, that in a contest he could have put to flight the consciences of nine-tenths of the citizens of Romper.

And so it happened that he was seated in this saloon with the two prominent local merchants and the district attorney.

The Swede continued to drink raw whisky, meanwhile babbling at the barkeeper and trying to induce him to indulge in potations. "Come on. Have a drink. Come on. What—no? Well, have a little one, then. By gawd, I've whipped a man tonight, and I want to celebrate. I whipped him good, too. Gentlemen," the Swede cried to the men at the table. "Have a drink?"

"Ssh!" said the barkeeper.

The group at the table, although furtively attentive, had been pretending to be deep in talk, but now a man lifted his eyes toward the Swede and said shortly, "Thanks. We don't want any more."

At this reply the Swede ruffled out his chest like a rooster. "Well," he exploded, "it seems I can't get anybody to drink with me in this town. Seems so, don't it? Well!"

"Ssh!" said the barkeeper.

"Say," snarled the Swede, "don't you try to shut me up. I won't have it. I'm a gentleman, and I want people to drink with me. And I want 'em to drink with me now. *Now*—do you understand?" He rapped the bar with his knuckles.

Years of experience had calloused the bartender. He merely grew sulky. "I hear you," he answered.

"Well," cried the Swede, "listen hard then. See those

men over there? Well, they're going to drink with me, and don't you forget it. Now you watch.''

"Hi!'' yelled the barkeeper. "This won't do!''

"Why won't it?'' demanded the Swede. He stalked over to the table, and by chance laid his hand upon the shoulder of the gambler. "How about this?'' he asked wrathfully. "I asked you to drink with me.''

The gambler simply twisted his head and spoke over his shoulder. "My friend, I don't know you.''

"Oh, hell!'' answered the Swede. "Come and have a drink.''

"Now, my boy,'' advised the gambler kindly, "take your hand off my shoulder and go 'way and mind your own business.'' He was a little, slim man, and it seemed strange to hear him use this tone of heroic patronage to the burly Swede. The other men at the table said nothing.

"What! You won't drink with me, you little dude? I'll make you, then! I'll make you!'' The Swede had grasped the gambler frenziedly at the throat, and was dragging him from his chair. The other men sprang up. The barkeeper dashed around the corner of his bar. There was a great tumult, and then was seen a long blade in the hand of the gambler. It shot forward, and a human body, this citadel of virtue, wisdom, power, was pierced as easily as if it had been a melon. The Swede fell with a cry of supreme astonishment.

The prominent merchants and the district attorney must have at once tumbled out of the place backward. The bartender found himself hanging limply to the arm of a chair and gazing into the eyes of a murderer.

"Henry,'' said the latter as he wiped his knife on one of the towels that hung beneath the bar rail, "you tell 'em where to find me. I'll be home, waiting for 'em.'' Then he vanished. A moment afterward the barkeeper was in the street, dinning through the storm for help and, moreover, companionship.

The corpse of the Swede, alone in the saloon, had its eyes fixed upon a dreadful legend that dwelt atop of the cash-machine: "This registers the amount of your purchase."

IX

Months later the cowboy was frying pork over the stove of a little ranch near the Dakota line when there was a quick thud of hoofs outside, and presently the Easterner entered with the letters and the papers.

"Well," said the Easterner at once, "the chap that killed the Swede has got three years. Wasn't much, was it?"

"He has? Three years?" The cowboy poised his pan of pork while he ruminated upon the news. "Three years. That ain't much."

"No. It was a light sentence," replied the Easterner as he unbuckled his spurs. "Seems there was a good deal of sympathy for him in Romper."

"If the bartender had been any good," observed the cowboy thoughtfully, "he would have gone in and cracked that there Dutchman on the head with a bottle in the beginnin' of it and stopped all this here murderin'."

"Yes, a thousand things might have happened," said the Easterner tartly.

The cowboy returned his pan of pork to the fire, but his philosophy continued. "It's funny, ain't it? If he hadn't said Johnnie was cheatin', he'd be alive this minute. He was an awful fool. Game played for fun, too. Not for money. I believe he was crazy."

"I feel sorry for that gambler," said the Easterner.

"Oh, so do I," said the cowboy. "He don't deserve none of it for killin' who he did."

"The Swede might not have been killed if everything had been square."

"Might not have been killed?" exclaimed the cowboy. "Everythin' square? Why, when he said that Johnnie was cheatin' and acted like such a jackass? And then in the saloon he fairly walked up to git hurt?" With these arguments the cowboy browbeat the Easterner and reduced him to rage.

"You're a fool!" cried the Easterner, viciously. "You're a bigger jackass than the Swede by a million majority. Now let me tell you one thing. Let me tell you something. Listen! Johnnie *was* cheating!"

"Johnnie," said the cowboy, blankly. There was a minute of silence, and then he said, robustly, "Why, no. The game was only for fun."

"Fun or not," said the Easterner, "Johnnie was cheating. I saw him. I know it. I saw him. And I refused to stand up and be a man. I let the Swede fight it out alone. And you— you were simply puffing around the place and wanting to fight. And then old Scully himself! We are all in it! This poor gambler isn't even a noun. He is kind of an adverb. Every sin is the result of a collaboration. We, five of us, have collaborated in the murder of this Swede. Usually there are from a dozen to forty women really involved in every murder, but in this case it seems to be only men— you, I, Johnnie, old Scully and that fool of an unfortunate gambler came merely as a culmination, the apex of a human movement, and gets all the punishment."

The cowboy, injured and rebellious, cried out blindly into this fog of mysterious theory, "Well, I didn't do anythin', did I?"

TO BUILD A FIRE

▼

Jack London

Day had broken cold and gray, exceedingly cold and gray, when the man turned aside from the main Yukon trail and climbed the high earth bank, where a dim and little-traveled trail led eastward through the fat spruce timberland. It was a steep bank, and he paused for breath at the top, excusing the act to himself by looking at his watch. It was nine o'clock. There was no sun nor hint of sun, though there was not a cloud in the sky. It was a clear day, and yet there seemed an intangible pall over the face of things, a subtle gloom that made the day dark, and that was due to the absence of sun. This fact did not worry the man. He was used to the lack of sun. It had been days since he had seen the sun, and he knew that a few more days must pass before that cheerful orb, due south, would just peep above the skyline and dip immediately from view.

The man flung a look back along the way he had come. The Yukon lay a mile wide and hidden under three feet of ice. On top of this ice were as many feet of snow. It was all pure white, rolling in gentle undulations where the ice jams of the freeze-up had formed. North and south, as far as his eye could see, it was unbroken white, save for a dark hairline that curved and twisted from around the spruce-covered island to the south, and that curved and twisted away into the north, where it disappeared behind another spruce-covered island. This dark hairline was the trail—the main trail—that led south five hundred miles to the Chilcoot Pass, Dyea, and salt water; and that led north seventy miles to Dawson, and still on to the north a thousand miles to Nulato, and finally to St. Michael on Bering Sea, a thousand miles and half a thousand more.

But all this—the mysterious, far-reaching hairline trail, the absence of sun from the sky, the tremendous cold, and the strangeness and weirdness of it all—made no impression on the man. It was not because he was long used to it. He was a newcomer in the land, a *chechaquo*, and this was his first winter. The trouble with him was that he was without imagination. He was quick and alert in the things of life, but only in the things, and not in the significances. Fifty degrees below zero meant eighty-odd degrees of frost. Such fact impressed him as being cold and uncomfortable, and that was all. It did not lead him to meditate upon his frailty as a creature of temperature, and upon man's frailty in general, able only to live within certain narrow limits of heat and cold; and from there on it did not lead him to the conjectural field of immortality and man's place in the universe. Fifty degrees below zero stood for a bite of frost that hurt and that must be guarded against by the use of mittens, earflaps, warm moccasins, and thick socks. Fifty degrees below zero was to him just precisely fifty degrees below zero. That there should be anything more to it than that was a thought that never entered his head.

As he turned to go on, he spat speculatively. There was a sharp, explosive crackle that startled him. He spat again. And again, in the air, before it could fall to the snow, the spittle crackled. He knew that at fifty below spittle crackled on the snow, but this spittle had crackled in the air. Undoubtedly it was colder than fifty below—how much colder he did not know. But the temperature did not matter. He was bound for the old claim on the left fork of Henderson

Creek, where the boys were already. They had come over across the divide from the Indian Creek country, while he had come the roundabout way to take a look at the possibilities of getting out logs in the spring from the islands in the Yukon. He would be into camp by six o'clock; a bit after dark, it was true, but the boys would be there, a fire would be going, and a hot supper would be ready. As for lunch, he pressed his hand against the protruding bundle under his jacket. It was also under his shirt, wrapped up in a handkerchief and lying against the naked skin. It was the only way to keep the biscuits from freezing. He smiled agreeably to himself as he thought of those biscuits, each cut open and sopped in bacon grease, and each enclosing a generous slice of fried bacon.

He plunged in among the big spruce trees. The trail was faint. A foot of snow had fallen since the last sled had passed over, and he was glad he was without a sled, traveling light. In fact, he carried nothing but the lunch wrapped in the handkerchief. He was surprised, however, at the cold. It certainly was cold, he concluded, as he rubbed his numb nose and cheekbones with his mittened hand. He was a warm-whiskered man, but the hair on his face did not protect the high cheekbones and the eager nose that thrust itself aggressively into the frosty air.

At the man's heels trotted a dog, a big native husky, the proper wolf dog, gray-coated and without any visible or temperamental difference from its brother, the wild wolf. The animal was depressed by the tremendous cold. It knew that it was no time for traveling. Its instinct told a truer tale than was told to the man by the man's judgment. In reality, it was not merely colder than fifty below zero; it was colder than sixty below, than seventy below. It was seventy-five below zero. Since the freezing point is thirty-two above zero, it meant that one hundred and seven degrees of frost obtained. The dog did not know anything about thermometers. Possibly in its brain there was no sharp consciousness of a condition of very cold such as was in the man's brain. But the brute had its instinct. It experienced a vague but menacing apprehension that subdued it and made it slink along at the man's heels, and that made it question eagerly every unwonted movement of the man as if expecting him to go into camp or to seek shelter somewhere and build a fire. The dog had learned fire, and it wanted fire, or else to burrow under the snow and cuddle its warmth away from the air.

The frozen moisture of its breathing had settled on its fur in a fine powder of frost, and especially were its jowls, muzzle, and eyelashes whitened by its crystalled breath. The man's red beard and mustache were likewise frosted, but more solidly, the deposit taking the form of ice and increasing with every warm, moist breath he exhaled. Also, the man was chewing tobacco, and the muzzle of ice held his lips so rigidly that he was unable to clear his chin when he expelled the juice. The result was that a crystal beard of the color and solidity of amber was increasing its length on his chin. If he fell down it would shatter itself, like glass, into brittle fragments. But he did not mind the appendage. It was the penalty all tobacco chewers paid in that country, and he had been out before in two cold snaps. They had not been so cold as this, he knew, but by the spirit thermometer at Sixty Mile he knew they had been registered at fifty below and at fifty-five.

He held on through the level stretch of woods for several miles, crossed a wide flat of niggerheads, and dropped down a bank to the frozen bed of a small stream. This was Henderson Creek, and he knew he was ten miles from the forks. He looked at his watch. It was ten o'clock. He was making four miles an hour, and he calculated that he would arrive at the forks at half-past twelve. He decided to celebrate that event by eating his lunch there.

The dog dropped in again at his heels, with a tail drooping discouragement, as the man swung along the creek bed. The furrow of the old sled trail was plainly visible, but a dozen inches of snow covered the marks of the last runners. In a month no man had come up or down that silent creek. The man held steadily on. He was not much given to thinking, and just then particularly he had nothing to think about save that he would eat lunch at the forks and that at six o'clock he would be in camp with the boys. There was nobody to talk to; and, had there been, speech would have been impossible because of the ice muzzle on his mouth. So he continued monotonously to chew tobacco and to increase the length of his amber beard.

Once in a while the thought reiterated itself that it was very cold and that he had never experienced such cold. As he walked along he rubbed his cheekbones and nose with the back of his mittened hand. He did this automatically, now and again changing hands. But rub as he would, the instant he stopped, his cheekbones went numb, and the following instant the end of his nose went numb. He was sure to frost his cheeks; he knew that, and experienced a pang of regret that he had not devised a nose strap of the sort Bud wore in cold snaps. Such a strap passed across the cheeks, as well, and saved them. But it didn't matter much, after all. What were frosted cheeks? A bit painful, that was all; they were never serious.

Empty as the man's mind was of thoughts, he was keenly observant, and he noticed the changes in the creek, the curves and bends and timber jams, and always he sharply noted where he placed his feet. Once, coming around a bend, he shied abruptly, like a startled horse, curved away from the place where he had been walking, and retreated several paces back along the trail. The creek he knew was frozen clear to the bottom—no creek could contain water in that arctic winter—but he knew also that there were springs that bubbled out from the hillsides and ran along under the snow and on top of the ice of the creek. He knew that the coldest snaps never froze these springs, and he knew likewise their danger. They were traps. They hid pools of water under the snow that might be three inches deep, or three feet. Sometimes a skin of ice half an inch thick covered them, and in turn was covered by the snow. Sometimes there were alternate layers of water and ice skin, so that when one broke through he kept on breaking through for a while, sometimes wetting himself to the waist.

That was why he had shied in such panic. He had felt the give under his feet and heard the crackle of a snow-hidden ice skin. And to get his feet wet in such a temperature meant trouble and danger. At the very least it meant delay, for he would be forced to stop and build a fire, and under its protection to bare his feet while he dried his socks and moccasins. He stood and studied the creek bed and its banks, and decided that the flow of water came from the right. He reflected awhile, rubbing his nose and cheeks, then skirted to the left, stepping gingerly and testing the footing for each step. Once clear of the danger, he took a fresh chew of tobacco and swung along at his four-mile gait.

In the course of the next two hours he came upon several similar traps. Usually the snow above the hidden pools had a sunken, candied appearance that advertised the danger. Once again, however, he had a close call; and once, suspecting danger, he compelled the dog to go on in front. The dog did not want to go. It hung back until the man shoved it forward, and then it went quickly across the white, unbroken surface. Suddenly it broke through, floundered to one side, and got away to firmer footing. It had wet its forefeet and legs, and almost immediately the water that clung to it turned to ice. It made quick efforts to lick the ice off its legs, then dropped down in the snow and began to bite out the ice that had formed between the toes. This was a matter of instinct. To permit the ice to remain would mean sore feet. It did not know this. It merely obeyed the mysterious prompting that arose from the deep crypts of its being. But the man knew, having achieved a judgment on the subject, and he removed the mitten from his right hand and helped tear out the ice particles. He did not expose his fingers more than a minute, and was astonished at the swift numbness that smote them. It certainly was cold. He pulled on the mitten hastily, and beat the hand savagely across his chest.

At twelve o'clock the day was at its brightest. Yet the sun was too far south on its winter journey to clear the horizon. The bulge of the earth intervened between it and Henderson Creek, where the man walked under a clear sky at noon and cast no shadow. At half-past twelve, to the minute, he arrived at the forks of the creek. He was pleased at the speed he had made. If he kept it up, he would certainly be with the boys by six. He unbuttoned his jacket and shirt and drew forth his lunch. The action consumed no more than a quarter of a minute, yet in that brief moment the numbness laid hold of the exposed fingers. He did not put the mitten on, but, instead, struck the fingers a dozen sharp smashes against his leg. Then he sat down on a snow-covered log to eat. The sting that followed upon the striking of his fingers against his leg ceased so quickly that he was startled. He had had no chance to take a bite of biscuit. He struck the fingers repeatedly and returned them to the mitten, baring the other hand for the purpose of eating. He tried to take a mouthful, but the ice muzzle prevented. He had forgotten to build a fire and thaw out. He chuckled at his foolishness, and as he chuckled he noted the numbness creeping into the exposed fingers. Also, he noted that the stinging which had first come to his toes when he sat down was already passing away. He wondered whether the toes were warm or numb. He moved them inside the moccasins and decided they were numb.

He pulled the mitten on hurriedly and stood up. He was a bit frightened. He stamped up and down until the stinging returned into the feet. It certainly was cold, was his thought. That man from Sulphur Creek had spoken the truth when telling how cold it sometimes got in the country. And he had laughed at him at the time! That showed one must not be too sure of things. There was no mistake about it, it *was* cold. He strode up and down, stamping his feet and threshing his arms, until reassured by the returning warmth. Then he got out matches and proceeded to make a fire. From the undergrowth, where high water of the previous spring had lodged a supply of seasoned twigs, he got his firewood. Working carefully from a small beginning, he soon had a roaring fire, over which he thawed the ice from his face and in the protection of which he ate his biscuits. For the moment the cold of space was outwitted. The dog took satisfaction in the fire, stretching out close enough for warmth and far enough away to escape being singed.

When the man had finished, he filled his pipe and took his comfortable time over a smoke. Then he pulled on his mittens, settled the earflaps of his cap firmly about his ears, and took the creek trail up the left fork. The dog was disappointed and yearned back toward the fire. This man did not know cold. Possibly all the generations of his ancestry had been ignorant of cold, of real cold, of cold one hundred and seven degrees below freezing point. But the dog knew; all its ancestry knew, and it had inherited the knowledge. And it knew that it was not good to walk abroad in such fearful cold. It was the time to lie snug in a hole in the snow and wait for a curtain of cloud to be drawn across the face of outer space whence this cold came. On the other hand, there was no keen intimacy between the dog and the man. The one was the toil slave of the other, and the only caresses it had ever received were the caresses of the whiplash and of harsh and menacing throat sounds that threatened the whiplash. So the dog made no effort to communicate its apprehension to the man. It was not concerned in the welfare of the man; it was for its own sake that it yearned back toward the fire. But the man whistled, and spoke to it with the sound of whiplashes, and the dog swung in at the man's heels and followed after.

The man took a chew of tobacco and proceeded to start a new amber beard. Also, his moist breath quickly powdered with white his mustache, eyebrows, and lashes. There did not seem to be so many springs on the left fork of the Henderson, and for half an hour the man saw no signs of any. And then it happened. At a place where there were no signs, where the soft, unbroken snow seemed to advertise solidity beneath, the man broke through. It was not deep. He wet himself halfway to the knees before he floundered out to the firm crust.

He was angry, and cursed his luck aloud. He had hoped to get into camp with the boys at six o'clock, and this would delay him an hour, for he would have to build a fire and dry out his footgear. This was imperative at that low temperature—he knew that much; and he turned aside to the bank, which he climbed. On top, tangled in the underbrush about the trunks of several small spruce trees, was a high-water deposit of dry firewood—sticks and twigs, principally, but also larger portions of seasoned branches and fine, dry, last year's grasses. He threw down several large pieces on top of the snow. This served for a foundation and prevented the young flame from drowning itself in the snow it otherwise would melt. The flame he got by touching a match to a small shred of birchbark that he took from his pocket. This burned even more readily than paper. Placing it on the foundation, he fed the young flame with wisps of dry grass and with the tiniest dry twigs.

He worked slowly and carefully, keenly aware of his danger. Gradually, as the flame grew stronger, he increased the size of the twigs with which he fed it. He squatted in the snow, pulling the twigs out from their entanglement in the brush and feeding directly to the flame. He knew there must be no failure. When it is seventy-five below zero, a man must not fail in his first attempt to build a fire—that is, if his feet are wet. If his feet are dry, and he fails, he can run along the trail for half a mile and restore his circulation. But the circulation of wet and freezing feet cannot be restored by running when it is seventy-five below. No matter how fast he runs, the wet feet will freeze the harder.

All this the man knew. The old-timer on Sulphur Creek had told him about it the previous fall, and now he was appreciating the advice. Already all sensation had gone out of his feet. To build the fire he had been forced to remove his mittens, and the fingers had quickly gone numb. His pace of four miles an hour had kept his heart pumping blood to the surface of his body and to all the extremities. But the instant he stopped, the action of the pump eased down. The cold of space smote the unprotected tip of the planet, and he, being on that unprotected tip, received the full force of the blow. The blood of his body recoiled before it. The blood was alive, like the dog, and like the dog it wanted to hide away and cover itself up from the fearful cold. So long as he walked four miles an hour, he pumped that blood, willy-nilly, to the surface; but now it ebbed away and sank down into the recesses of his body. The extremities were the first to feel its absence. His wet feet froze the faster, and his exposed fingers numbed the faster, though they had not yet begun to freeze. Nose and cheeks were already freezing, while the skin of all his body chilled as it lost its blood.

But he was safe. Toes and nose and cheeks would be only touched by the frost, for the fire was beginning to burn with strength. He was feeding it with twigs the size of his finger. In another minute he would be able to feed it with branches the size of his wrist, and then he could remove his wet footgear, and, while it dried, he could keep his naked feet warm by the fire, rubbing them at first, of course, with snow. The fire was a success. He was safe. He remembered the advice of the old-timer on Sulphur Creek, and smiled. The old-timer had been very serious in laying down the law that no man must travel alone in the Klondike after fifty below. Well, here he was; he had had the accident; he was alone; and he had saved himself. Those old-timers were rather womanish, some of them, he thought. All a man had to do was to keep his head, and he was all right. Any man who was a man could travel alone. But it was surprising, the rapidity with which his cheeks and nose were freezing. And he had not thought his fingers could go lifeless in so short a time. Lifeless they were, for he could scarcely make them move together to grip a twig, and they seemed remote from his body and from him. When he touched a twig, he had to look and see whether or not he had hold of it. The wires were pretty well down between him and his finger ends.

All of which counted for little. There was the fire, snapping and crackling and promising life with every dancing flame. He started to untie his moccasins. They were coated with ice; the thick German socks were like sheaths of iron halfway to the knees; and the moccasin strings were like rods of steel all twisted and knotted as by some conflagration. For a moment he tugged with his numb fingers, then, realizing the folly of it, he drew his sheath knife.

But before he could cut the strings, it happened. It was his own fault or, rather, his mistake. He should not have built the fire under the spruce tree. He should have built it in the open. But it had been easier to pull the twigs from the brush and drop them directly on the fire. Now the tree under which he had done this carried a weight of snow on its boughs. No wind had blown for weeks, and each bough was fully freighted. Each time he had pulled a twig he had communicated a slight agitation to the tree—an imperceptible agitation, so far as he was concerned, but an agitation sufficient to bring about the disaster. High up in the tree one bough capsized its load of snow. This fell on the boughs beneath, capsizing them. This process continued, spreading out and involving the whole tree. It grew like an avalanche, and it descended without warning upon the man and the fire, and the fire was blotted out! Where it had burned was a mantle of fresh and disordered snow.

The man was shocked. It was as though he had just heard his own sentence of death. For a moment he sat and stared at the spot where the fire had been. Then he grew very calm. Perhaps the old-timer on Sulphur Creek was right. If he had only had a trail mate he would have been in no danger now. The trail mate could have built the fire. Well, it was up to him to build the fire over again, and this second time there must be no failure. Even if he succeeded, he would most likely lose some toes. His feet must be badly frozen by now, and there would be some time before the second fire was ready.

Such were his thoughts, but he did not sit and think them. He was busy all the time they were passing through his mind. He made a new foundation for a fire, this time in the open, where no treacherous tree could blot it out. Next, he gathered dry grasses and tiny twigs from the high-water flotsam. He could not bring his fingers together to pull them out, but he was able to gather them by the handful. In this way he got many rotten twigs and bits of green moss that were undesirable, but it was the best he could do. He worked methodically, even collecting an armful of the larger branches to be used later when the fire gathered strength. And all the while the dog sat and watched him, a certain yearning wistfulness in its eyes, for it looked upon him as the fire provider, and the fire was slow in coming.

When all was ready, the man reached in his pocket for a second piece of birchbark. He knew the bark was there, and, though he could not feel it with his fingers, he could hear its crisp rustling as he fumbled for it. Try as he would, he could not clutch hold of it. And all the time, in his consciousness, was the knowledge that each instant his feet were freezing. This thought tended to put him in a panic, but he fought against it and kept calm. He pulled on his mittens with his teeth, and threshed his arms back and forth, beating his hands with all his might against his sides. He did this sitting down, and he stood up to do it; and all the while the dog sat in the snow, its wolf brush of a tail curled around warmly over its forefeet, its sharp wolf ears pricked forward intently as it watched the man. And the man, as he beat and threshed with his arms and hands, felt a great surge of envy as he regarded the creature that was warm and secure in its natural covering.

After a time he was aware of the first faraway signals of sensation in his beaten fingers. The faint tingling grew stronger till it evolved into a stinging ache that was excruciating, but which the man hailed with satisfaction. He stripped the mitten from his right hand and fetched forth the birchbark. The exposed fingers were quickly going numb again. Next he brought out his bunch of sulphur matches. But the tremendous cold had already driven the life out of his fingers. In his effort to separate one match from the others, the whole bunch fell in the snow. He tried to pick it out of the snow, but failed. The dead fingers could neither touch nor clutch. He was very careful. He drove the thought of his freezing feet, and nose, and cheeks, out of his mind, devoting his whole soul to the matches. He watched, using the sense of vision in place of that of touch, and when he saw his fingers on each side of the bunch, he closed them—that is, he willed to close them, for the wires were down, and the fingers did not obey. He pulled the mitten on the right hand, and beat it fiercely against his knee. Then, with both mittened hands, he scooped the bunch of matches, along with much snow, into his lap. Yet he was no better off.

After some manipulation he managed to get the bunch between the heels of his mittened hands. In this fashion he carried it to his mouth. The ice crackled and snapped when by a violent effort he opened his mouth. He drew the lower jaw in, curled the upper lip out of the way, and scraped the bunch with his upper teeth in order to separate a match. He succeeded in getting one, which he dropped on his lap. He was no better off. He could not pick it up. Then he devised a way. He picked it up in his teeth and scratched it on his leg. Twenty times he scratched before he succeeded in lighting it. As it flamed he held it with his teeth to the birchbark. The burning brimstone went up his nostrils and into his lungs, causing him to cough spasmodically. The match fell into the snow and went out.

The old-timer on Sulphur Creek was right, he thought in the moment of controlled despair that ensued: after fifty below, a man should travel with a partner. He beat his hands, but failed in exciting any sensation. Suddenly he bared both hands, removing the mittens with his teeth. He caught the whole bunch between the heels of his hands. His arm muscles not being frozen enabled him to press the hand heels tightly against the matches. Then he scratched the bunch along his leg. It flared into flame, seventy sulphur matches at once! There was no wind to blow them out. He kept his head to one side to escape the strangling fumes, and held the blazing bunch to the birchbark. As he so held it, he became aware of sensation in his hand. His flesh was burning. He could smell it. Deep down below the surface he could feel it. The sensation developed into pain that grew acute. And still he endured it, holding the flame of the matches clumsily to the bark that would not light readily because his own burning hands were in the way, absorbing most of the flame.

At last, when he could endure no more, he jerked his hands apart. The blazing matches fell sizzling into the snow, but the birchbark was alight. He began laying dry grasses and the tiniest twigs on the flame. He could not pick and choose, for he had to lift the fuel between the heels of his hands. Small pieces of rotten wood and green moss clung to the twigs, and he bit them off as well as he could with his teeth. He cherished the flame carefully and awkwardly. It meant life, and it must not perish. The withdrawal of blood from the surface of his body now made him begin to shiver, and he grew more awkward. A large piece of green moss fell squarely on the little fire. He tried to poke it out with his fingers, but his shivering frame made him poke too far, and he disrupted the nucleus of the little fire, the burning grasses and tiny twigs separating and scattering. He tried to poke them together again, but in spite of the tenseness of the effort, his shivering got away with him, and the twigs were hopelessly scattered. Each twig gushed a puff of smoke and went out. The fire provider had failed. As he looked apathetically about him, his eyes chanced on the dog, sitting across the ruins of the fire from him, in the snow, making restless, hunching movements, slightly lifting one forefoot and then the other, shifting its weight back and forth on them with wistful eagerness.

The sight of the dog put a wild idea into his head. He remembered the tale of the man, caught in a blizzard, who killed a steer and crawled inside the carcass, and so was saved. He would kill the dog and bury his hands in the warm body until the numbness went out of them. Then he could build another fire. He spoke to the dog, calling it to him; but in his voice was a strange note of fear that frightened the animal, who had never known the man to speak in such way before. Something was the matter, and its suspicious nature sensed danger—it knew not what danger, but somewhere, somehow, in its brain arose an apprehension of the man. It flattened its ears down at the sound of the man's voice, and its restless, hunching movements and the liftings and shiftings of its forefeet became more pronounced; but it would not come to the man. He got on his hands and knees and crawled toward the dog. This unusual posture again excited suspicion, and the animal sidled mincingly away.

The man sat up in the snow for a moment and struggled

for calmness. Then he pulled on his mittens, by means of his teeth, and got up on his feet. He glanced down at first in order to assure himself that he was really standing up, for the absence of sensation in his feet left him unrelated to the earth. His erect position in itself started to drive the webs of suspicion from the dog's mind; and when he spoke peremptorily, with the sound of whiplashes in his voice, the dog rendered its customary allegiance and came to him. As it came within reaching distance, the man lost his control. His arms flashed out to the dog, and he experienced genuine surprise when he discovered that his hands could not clutch, that there was neither bend nor feeling in the fingers. He had forgotten for the moment that they were frozen and that they were freezing more and more. All this happened quickly, and before the animal could get away, he encircled its body with his arms. He sat down in the snow, and in this fashion held the dog, while it snarled and whined and struggled.

But it was all he could do, hold its body encircled in his arms and sit there. He realized that he could not kill the dog. There was no way to do it. With his helpless hands he could neither draw nor hold his sheath knife nor throttle the animal. He released it, and it plunged wildly away, with tail between its legs, and still snarling. It halted forty feet away and surveyed him curiously, with ears sharply pricked forward. The man looked down at his hands in order to locate them, and found them hanging on the ends of his arms. It struck him as curious that one should have to use his eyes in order to find out where his hands were. He began threshing his arms back and forth, beating the mittened hands against his sides. He did this for five minutes, violently, and his heart pumped enough blood up to the surface to put a stop to his shivering. But no sensation was aroused in the hands. He had an impression that they hung like weights on the ends of his arms, but when he tried to run the impression down, he could not find it.

A certain fear of death, dull and oppressive, came to him. This fear quickly became poignant as he realized that it was no longer a mere matter of freezing his fingers and toes, or of losing his hands and feet, but that it was a matter of life and death with the chances against him. This threw him into a panic, and he turned and ran up the creek bed along the old, dim trail. The dog joined in behind and kept up with him. He ran blindly, without intention, in fear such as he had never known in his life. Slowly, as he ploughed and floundered through the snow, he began to see things again—the banks of the creek, the old timber jams, the leafless aspens, and the sky. The running made him feel better. He did not shiver. Maybe, if he ran on, his feet would thaw out; and, anyway, if he ran far enough, he would reach camp and the boys. Without doubt he would lose some fingers and toes and some of his face; but the boys would take care of him, and save the rest of him when he got there. And at the same time there was another thought in his mind that said he would never get to the camp and the boys; that it was too many miles away, that the freezing had too great a start on him, and that he would soon be stiff and dead. This thought he kept in the background and refused to consider. Sometimes it pushed itself forward and demanded to be heard, but he thrust it back and strove to think of other things.

It struck him as curious that he could run at all on feet so frozen that he could not feel them when they struck the earth and took the weight of his body. He seemed to himself to skim along above the surface, and to have no connection with the earth. Somewhere he had once seen a winged Mercury, and he wondered if Mercury felt as he felt when skimming over the earth.

His theory of running until he reached camp and the boys had one flaw in it: he lacked the endurance. Several times he stumbled, and finally he tottered, crumpled up, and fell. When he tried to rise, he failed. He must sit and rest, he decided, and next time he would merely walk and keep on going. As he sat and regained his breath, he noted that he was feeling quite warm and comfortable. He was not shivering, and it even seemed that a warm glow had come to his chest and trunk. And yet, when he touched his nose or cheeks, there was no sensation. Running would not thaw them out. Nor would it thaw out his hands and feet. Then the thought came to him that the frozen portions of his body must be extending. He tried to keep this thought down, to forget it, to think of something else; he was aware of the panicky feeling that it caused, and he was afraid of the panic. But the thought asserted itself, and persisted, until it produced a vision of his body totally frozen. This was too much, and he made another wild run along the trail. Once he slowed down to a walk, but the thought of the freezing extending itself made him run again.

And all the time the dog ran with him, at his heels. When he fell down a second time, it curled its tail over its forefeet and sat in front of him, facing him, curiously eager and intent. The warmth and security of the animal angered him, and he cursed it till it flattened down its ears appeasingly. This time the shivering came more quickly upon the man. He was losing in his battle with the frost. It was creeping into his body from all sides. The thought of it drove him on, but he ran no more than a hundred feet, when he staggered and pitched headlong. It was his last panic. When he had recovered his breath and control, he sat up and entertained in his mind the conception of meeting death with dignity. However, the conception did not come to him in such terms. His idea of it was that he had been making a fool of himself, running around like a chicken with its head cut off—such was the simile that occurred to him. Well, he was bound to freeze anyway, and he might as well take it decently. With this newfound peace of mind came the first glimmerings of drowsiness. A good idea, he thought, to sleep off to death. It was like taking an anaesthetic. Freezing was not so bad as people thought. There were lots worse ways to die.

He pictured the boys finding his body the next day. Suddenly he found himself with them, coming along the trail and looking for himself. And, still with them, he came around a turn in the trail and found himself lying in the snow. He did not belong with himself anymore, for even then he was out of himself, standing with the boys and looking at himself, standing with the boys and looking at himself in the snow. It certainly was cold, was his thought. When he got back to the States he could tell the folks what real cold was. He drifted on from this to a vision of the old-timer on Sulphur Creek. He could see him quite clearly, warm and comfortable, and smoking a pipe.

"You were right, old hoss; you were right," the man mumbled to the old-timer of Sulphur Creek.

Then the man drowsed off into what seemed to him the most comfortable and satisfying sleep he had ever known. The dog sat facing him and waiting. The brief day drew to a close in a long, slow twilight. There were no signs of a fire to be made, and, besides, never in the dog's experience had it known a man to sit like that in the snow and make no fire. As the twilight drew on, its eager yearning for the fire mastered it, and with a great lifting and shifting of forefeet, it whined softly, then flattened its ears down in anticipation of being chidden by the man. But the man remained silent. Later, the dog whined loudly. And still later it crept close to the man and caught the scent of death. This made the animal bristle and back away. A little longer it delayed, howling under the stars that leaped and danced and shone brightly in the cold sky. Then it turned and trotted up the trail in the direction of the camp it knew, where there were the other food providers and fire providers.

THE BURIAL OF
LETTY STRAYHORN

▼
▼

Elmer Kelton

Greenleaf Strayhorn frowned as he rode beyond the dense liveoak motte and got his first clear look at Prosperity. The dry west wind, which had been blowing almost unbroken for a week, picked up dust from the silent streets and lifted it over the frame buildings to lose it against a cloudless blue sky. He turned toward the brown packhorse that trailed the young sorrel he was riding. His feeling of distaste deepened the wrinkles which had resulted from long years of labor in the sun.

"Wasn't much of a town when we left here, Letty, and I can't see that it's got any better. But you wanted to come back."

Prosperity had a courthouse square but no courthouse. Even after voting some of its horses and dogs, it had lost the county-seat election to rival Paradise Forks, a larger town which could rustle up more horses and dogs. Greenleaf hoped the dramshop was still operating. He had paused

95

in Paradise Forks only long enough to buy a meal cooked by someone other than himself, and that had been yesterday. He was pleased to see the front door open. If the sign out front had been repainted during his twelve-year absence, he could not tell it.

"*Finest in liquors, wines and bitters,*" he read aloud. "*Cold beer and billiards.* Our kind of a place. Mine, anyway. You never was one for self-indulgence."

The sorrel's ears poked forward distrustfully as a yellow dog sauntered out to inspect the procession. Greenleaf tightened his knee grip, for the young horse was still prone to regard with great suspicion such things as dogs, chickens and flying scraps of paper. It had pitched him off once already on this trip. Greenleaf was getting to an age when rodeoing was meant to be a spectator sport, not for personal participation. The dog quickly lost interest in rider and horses and angled off toward the liveoak motte to try and worry a rabbit or two.

Greenleaf tied up the horses in front of the saloon, loosening the girth so his saddlehorse could breathe easier. He checked the pack on the brown horse and found it still snug. Seeing no others tied nearby, he knew the saloon was enjoying another in a long succession of slow days.

He stepped up onto the board sidewalk, taking an extra-long stride to skip over a spot where two planks had been removed. Somebody had evidently fallen through in the relatively distant past. The rest of the boards were badly weathered, splintered and worn. It was only a matter of time until they, too, caused someone embarrassment, and probably skinned shins.

The whole place looked like the tag end of a hot, dry summer. Whoever had named this town Prosperity was a terrible prophet or had a wicked sense of humor, he thought.

A black cat lay curled in the shade near the front door. It opened one eye in response to Greenleaf's approach, then closed the eye with minimum compromise to its rest.

The bartender sat on a stool, his head upon his arms atop

the bar. He stirred to the jingling of spurs and looked up, sleepy-eyed.

"Beer," Greenleaf said. "A cold one if you've got it."

The man delivered it to him in a mug and gave him a squinting appraisal. "Ain't your name Greenleaf Shoehorn?"

"Strayhorn."

"A name like Greenleaf ain't easily forgot. The rest of it . . ." He shrugged. "Didn't you used to work on Old Man Hopkins' place?"

"And married his daughter Letty."

Memory made the bartender smile. "Anybody who ever met Letty would remember her. A mighty strong-willed woman. Where's she at?"

"Outside, on a horse."

The bartender frowned. "You'd leave her in the hot sun while you come in here for a cool drink?" He walked to the door. "All I see is two horses."

"She's under the tarp on the packhorse, in a lard can. Her ashes, I mean."

The bartender's face fell. "She's dead?"

"Took by a fever two weeks ago. Last thing she asked me was to bring her back here and bury her on the homeplace alongside her mama and papa. It was so far, the only way I could do it was to bring her ashes."

Soberly the bartender refilled the mug Greenleaf had drained. "Sorry about Letty. Everybody liked her. Everybody except Luther Quinton. He hated all the Hopkinses, and everybody that neighbored them."

"It always makes it easier when you hate the people you set out to rob. Less troublin' on the conscience."

"He still owns the old Hopkins place. He may not take it kindly, you buryin' Letty there. Asked him yet?"

"Wasn't figurin' on askin' him. Just figured on doin' it."

The bartender's attention was drawn to the front window. "If you *was* thinkin' about askin' him, this'd be the time. That's him comin' yonder."

Greenleaf carried his beer to the door, where he watched as the black cat raised up from its nap, stretched itself luxuriously, and meandered out into the windy street, crossing Quinton's path. Quinton stopped abruptly, turning back and taking a path that led him far around the cat. It stopped in the middle of the deserted street to lick itself.

The bartender remarked, "Superstitious, Luther is. Won't buy anything by the dozen because he's afraid they may throw in an extra one on him. They say he won't even keep a mirror in his house because he's afraid he might break it."

"He probably just doesn't like to look at himself. I never liked lookin' at him either." Quinton had long legs and a short neck. He had always reminded Greenleaf of a frog.

Quinton came to the door, looking back to be sure the cat had not moved. He demanded of the bartender, "How many more lives has that tomcat got? I've been hopin' a wagon might run over him in the street."

"She ain't a tomcat, and there ain't enough traffic. She's liable to live for twenty years."

"I'd haul her off and dump her, but I know she'd come back."

Quinton's attention shifted to Greenleaf, and his eyes narrowed with recognition. "Speakin' of comin' back . . ." He pointed a thick, hairy finger. "Ain't you the hired hand that married the Hopkins girl?"

"Letty. Yep, I'm the one."

"There's no accountin' for some people's judgment. Wonder she ain't killed and scalped you before now. Has Indian blood in her, don't she?"

"Her mama was half Choctaw."

"Probably some kind of a medicine woman. That Letty laid a curse on me the day I took over the Hopkins place. Cow market went to hell. Calf crop dropped to half. Rain quit and the springs dried up. I had nothin' but bad luck for over a year."

"Only a year? She must not've put her whole heart into it."

Dread was in Quinton's eyes. "She back to cause me more misery?"

"She died."

Relief washed over Quinton's round, furrowed face like sunshine breaking through a dark cloud. He was not one to smile easily, but he ventured dangerously near. "I'm mighty sorry to hear it." He gulped down a glass of whiskey in one long swallow. "Mighty sorry."

Greenleaf grunted. "I can see that." He turned to the bartender. "Old Brother Ratliff still doin' the preachin'?"

The bartender nodded. "You'll find him at the parsonage over by the church. My sympathies about Letty."

Greenleaf thanked him and walked out. He had not expected this to be a pleasant homecoming, and running into Luther Quinton had helped it live down to his expectations. Untying the two horses, he looked a moment at the pack on the second animal, and a catch came in his throat. He had worked his way through the darkest of his grief, but a lingering sadness still shadowed him. He wanted to fulfill his promise to Letty, then put this place behind him for once and all. His and Letty's leavetaking from here had created a residue of memories bitter to the taste.

Not all the fault had been Quinton's. Letty's father should have known he was dealing himself a busted flush when he tried farming on land where the average rainfall was only about fifteen inches a year, and half of that tended to come in one night if it came at all. Letty's stubborn nature was a natural heritage from both sides of her family. She had tried to keep on farming even though her father had accomplished four crop failures in a row. He had died of a seizure in the middle of a diatribe against the bank for letting him borrow himself so deeply into the hole and refusing to let him dig the hole any deeper.

All Quinton had done, really, was to buy the notes from the frustrated banker and foreclose on Letty. Quinton had acquired several other properties the same way. He was not a hawk that kills its prey but rather a buzzard which feeds on whatever has died a natural death.

Greenleaf had not considered Brother Ratliff an old man when he had lived here, but like the town, the minister had aged a lot in a dozen years. Greenleaf had to knock on the door a third time before it swung inward and a tall, slightly

stooped gentleman peered down at him, cocking his head
a little to one side to present his best ear. From Ratliff's
gaunt appearance, Greenleaf judged that the Sunday offer-
ing plate had been coming back but little heavier than it
went out.

"May I be of service to you, friend?"

"I'm Greenleaf Strayhorn. You may not remember, but
you tied the knot for me and Letty Hopkins a long time
ago."

The minister smiled broadly and made a gesture that in-
vited him into the spare little house. "I do remember. Quite
a beautiful bride, she was. Have you brought her with
you?"

"In a manner of speakin', yes sir. I was wonderin' if
you'd be kind enough to say some fittin' words over her
so I can put her ashes in the ground?"

The minister's smile died. "The Lord calls all of us
home eventually, but it would seem He has called her much
too early. I hope she had a good life to compensate for its
shortness."

"We did tolerable well. Got us a nice little ranch up
north, though we wasn't blessed with kids. She just never
could shake loose from her old family homeplace. The
memory of it was always there, itchin' like a wool shirt.
She wanted me to bring her back."

"It's a sad thing to preach a funeral, but part of my
calling is to comfort the bereaved and commend the soul
to a better land. When would you want me to perform the
service?"

"Right now, if that's not too soon."

The minister put on his black coat and walked with
Greenleaf to the church next door. "Would you mind pulling the bell rope for me, son? The devil has afflicted my
shoulder with rheumatism."

Afterward, Greenleaf unwrapped the pack and fetched
the lard can containing all that was left in the world of
Letty Strayhorn. He placed it in front of the altar. A dozen
or so citizens came, curious about the reason for the bell
to ring in the middle of the week. Among them was the

bartender, who knew. He had removed his apron and put on a coat, though the church was oppressively warm. Its doors and windows had been kept shut because the wind would have brought in too much dust.

The sermon was brief, for Brother Ratliff did not know all that much to say about Letty's past, just that she had been a hard-working, God-fearing woman who held strong opinions about right and wrong and did not easily abide compromise.

At the end of the closing prayer he said, "Now, if any of you would like to accompany the deceased to her final resting place, you are welcome to go with us to the old Hopkins farm."

A loud voice boomed from the rear of the church. "No, you ain't! The place is mine, and that woman ain't fixin' to be buried in any ground that belongs to me!"

The minister was first surprised, then dismayed. "Brother Quinton, surely you would not deny that good soul the right to be buried amongst her own."

"Good soul? A witch, I'd call her. A medicine woman, somethin' from the Indian blood in her."

"She has passed on to another life. She can do you no harm now."

"I'm takin' no chances. You want her buried, bury her here in town. You ain't bringin' her out to my place."

Apologetically the minister looked back to Greenleaf. "I am sorry, Brother Strayhorn. I may argue with Brother Quinton's logic, but I cannot argue with his legal rights."

Greenleaf stood up and studied Quinton's physical stature. He decided he could probably whip the man, if it came to a contest. But he would no doubt end up in jail, and he still would not be able to carry out Letty's final wish.

"She's goin' to be disappointed," he said.

The town cemetery was a depressing place, the site picked for convenience rather than for beauty. His sleeves rolled up, Greenleaf worked with a pair of posthole diggers that belonged to the minister. Brother Ratliff, looking too frail to help in this kind of labor, sat on a marble gravestone and watched as the hole approached three feet in depth.

The length of the handles would limit Greenleaf's digging. The bartender had come to the cemetery but had left after a few minutes to reopen the saloon lest he miss out on any thirsty customers. Or perhaps he had feared he might be called upon to lend a hand with the diggers.

Ratliff said, "It matters not where the body lies."

"So the old song says," Greenleaf responded, turning into the wind. Though its breath was warm, it felt cool against his sweaty face and passing through his partially soaked shirt. "But I feel like I'm breakin' a promise. I never got to do everything I wanted to for Letty while she was livin', but at least I never broke a promise to her."

"You made your promise in good faith. Now for reasons beyond your control you cannot fulfill it. She would understand that. Anyway, you brought her back to her hometown. That's close."

"I remember a couple of times my stomach was growlin' awful loud at me, and I bore down on a whitetail deer for meat but missed. Close wasn't good enough. I was still hungry."

"You've done the best you could."

"No, I ain't." Greenleaf brought the diggers up out of the hole and leaned on their handles while he pondered. "Mind lendin' me these diggers a little longer, Preacher?"

Ratliff studied him quizzically. "You'd be welcome to keep them. Should I ask you what for?"

"A man in your profession ain't supposed to lie. If I don't tell you, you won't have to lie to anybody that might ask you."

Greenleaf used the diggers to rake dirt back into the hole and tamp it down. The lard can still sat where he had placed it beside a nearby gravestone. "We had a full moon last night. It ought to be just as bright tonight."

The minister looked up at the cloudless sky. "Unless it rains. I would say our chance for rain is about as remote as the chance of Luther Quinton donating money for a new church. Would you like for me to go with you?"

"You've got to live here afterward, Preacher. I don't." Greenleaf finished filling the hole. "If I was to leave you the money, would you see to it that a proper headstone is put up for her?''

''I would consider it a privilege.''

''Thanks.'' Greenleaf extended his hand. ''You don't just know the words, Preacher. You know the *Lord*.''

Even if the moon had not been bright, Greenleaf could have found the old Hopkins place without difficulty. He had ridden the road a hundred times in daylight and in darkness. Nothing had changed in the dozen years since he had last traveled this way. He rode by the deserted house where the Hopkins family had lived while they struggled futilely to extract a good living from a soil that seemed always thirsty. He stopped a moment to study the frame structure. The porch roof was sagging, one of its posts buckled out of place. He suspected the rest of the house looked as desolate. The wind, which had abated but little with moonrise, moaned through broken windows.

''Probably just as well we've come at night, Letty. I doubt you'd like the looks of the place in the daytime.''

Memories flooded his mind, memories of coming to work here as hired help, of first meeting Letty, of gradually falling in love with her. A tune ran through his brain, a tune she had taught him when they had first known one another and that they had often sung together. He dwelled at length upon the night he had brought her back here after their wedding in town. Life had seemed golden then . . . for a while. But reality had soon intruded. It always did, after so long. It intruded now.

''I'd best be gettin' about the business, Letty, just in case Luther Quinton is smarter than I think he is.''

The small family cemetery lay halfway up a gentle hillside some three hundred yards above the house. Rocks which the plow had turned up in the field had been hauled to the site to build a small protective fence. Greenleaf dismounted beside the gate and tied the saddlehorse to the latchpost. He let the packhorse's rein drop. The brown would not stray away from the sorrel. He untied the rope that bound the diggers to the pack, then unwrapped the pack.

Carefully he lifted down the lard can. He had been amazed at how little it weighed. Letty had never been a large woman, but it had seemed to him that her ashes should represent more weight than this. Carrying the can under one arm and the diggers under the other, he started through the gate.

He had never been of a superstitious nature, but his heart almost stopped when he saw three dark figures rise up from behind the gravestones that marked the resting places of Letty's mother and father. He gasped for breath.

The voice was not that of a ghost. It belonged to Luther Quinton. "Ain't it strange how you can tell some people *no* and they don't put up an argument? Tell others and it seems like they can't even hear you."

The shock lingered, and Greenleaf had trouble getting his voice back. "I guess it's because *no* doesn't always make much sense."

"It don't have to. All that counts is that this place belongs to me, and I don't want you on it, you or that woman of yours either. Lucky for me I set a man to watchin' you in town. He seen you fill that hole back up without puttin' anything in it but dirt."

"Look, Luther, you hurt her enough when she was livin'. At least you could let her rest in peace now. Like the preacher said, she's in no shape to do you any harm. She just wanted to be buried next to her folks. That don't seem like much to ask."

"But it is. You heard her when she laid that curse on me after I took this place. She named a dozen awful things that was fixin' to happen to me, and most of them did. Anybody that strong ain't goin' to quit just because they're dead." Quinton shook his head violently. "I'm tellin' you, she's some kind of an Indian medicine woman. If I was to let you bury her here, I'd never be shed of her. She'd be risin' up out of that grave and hauntin' my every move."

"That's a crazy notion. She never was a medicine

woman or anything like that. She wasn't but a quarter Indian in the first place. The rest was white.''

"All I know is what she done to me before. I don't aim to let her put a hex on me again.''

"You can't watch this place all the time. I can wait. Once she's in the ground, you wouldn't have the guts to dig her up.''

"I could find twenty men who'd do it for whiskey money. I'd have them carry her over into the next county and throw her in the river, can and all.''

Frustration began to gnaw at Greenleaf. Quinton had him blocked.

Quinton's voice brightened with a sense of victory. "So take her back to town, where you ought to've buried her in the first place. Since you seem to enjoy funerals, you can have another one for her.''

"I hope they let me know when *your* funeral takes place, Luther. I'd ride bareback two hundred miles to be here.''

Quinton spoke to the two men beside him. "I want you to ride to town with him and be sure he doesn't do anything with that can of ashes. I want him to carry it where you can watch it all the way.''

One of the men tied up Greenleaf's pack and lashed the diggers down tightly against it. The other held the can while Greenleaf mounted the sorrel horse, then handed it up to him.

Quinton said, "If I ever see you on my place again, I'm liable to mistake you for a coyote and shoot you. Now git!''

To underscore his order, he drew his pistol and fired a shot under the young sorrel's feet.

That was a bad mistake. The horse bawled in fright and jumped straight up, then alternated between a wild runaway and fits of frenzied pitching in a semicircle around the little cemetery. Greenleaf lost the reins at the second jump and grabbed at the saddlehorn with his left hand. He was handicapped by the lard can, which he tried to hold tightly under his right arm. He did not want to lose Letty.

It was a forlorn hope. The lid popped from the can, and the ashes began streaming out as the horse ran a few strides, then whipped about, pitched a few jumps and ran again. The west wind caught them and carried them away. At last Greenleaf felt himself losing his seat and his hold on the horn. He bumped the rim of the cantle and kicked his feet clear of the stirrups to keep from hanging up. He had the sensation of being suspended in midair for a second or two, then came down. His feet landed hard on the bare ground but did not stay beneath him. His rump hit next, and he went rolling, the can bending under his weight.

It took him a minute to regain his breath. In the moonlight he saw one of Quinton's men chasing after the sorrel horse. The packhorse stood where it had been all along, watching the show with only mild interest.

Quinton's second man came, finally, and helped Greenleaf to his feet. "You hurt?"

"Nothin' seems to be broke except my feelin's." Greenleaf bent down and picked up the can. Most of the ashes had spilled from it. He waited until Quinton approached, then poured out what remained. The wind carried part of them into Quinton's face.

The man sputtered and raged and tried desperately to brush away the ashes.

"Well, Luther," Greenleaf said, "you really done it now. If I'd buried her here, you'd've always known where she was. The way it is, you'll never know where she's at. The wind has scattered her all over the place."

Quinton seemed about to cry, still brushing wildly at his clothing. Greenleaf thrust the bent can into his hands. Quinton made some vague shrieking sound and hurled it away as if it were full of snakes.

The first Quinton man brought Greenleaf his horse. Greenleaf's hip hurt where he had fallen, and he knew it would be giving him unshirted hell tomorrow. But tonight it was almost a good pain. He felt strangely elated as he swung up into the saddle. He reached down for the packhorse's rein.

"This isn't what Letty asked for, but I have a feelin' she wouldn't mind. She'd've liked knowin' that no matter where you go on this place, she'll be there ahead of you.

And she won't let you forget it, not for a minute.''

Riding away, he remembered the old tune Letty had taught him a long time ago. Oddly, he felt like whistling it, so he did.

HELL ON THE DRAW

▼
▼

Loren D. Estleman

In the weeks to come there would be considerable debate
and some brandishing of weapons over who had been the
first to lay eyes on Mr. Nicholas Pitt of Providence; but the
fact of the matter is the honor belonged to Ekron Fast,
Persephone's only blacksmith. It was he, after all, who replaced the shoe the stranger's great black hammerhead had
thrown just outside town, and as everyone who lived there
knew, a traveler's first thought upon reaching water or civ-
ilization in that dry Huachuca country was his horse. Nor
was Pitt's a horse for a former cow man like Ekron to
forget.

"Red eyes," he declared to the gang at the Fallen Shaft
that Wednesday night in July. "Eighteen—hell, *twenty*
hands if he was one, that stud, with nary a speck of any
color but black on him except for them eyes. Like burning
pipeplugs they was. Feature that."

"Oklahoma Blood Eye." Gordy Wolf, bartender at the
Shaft, refilled Ekron's glass from a measured bottle, collected his coin, and made a note of the transaction in the
ledger with a gnawed stub of pencil. As a half-breed Crow

he couldn't drink, and so the owner required him to keep track of what came out of stock. "I seen it in McAlester. Thisyer dun mare just up and rolled over on the cavalry sergeant that was riding her, snapped his neck like dry rot. Your Mr. Pip better watch that don't happen to him."

"Fermented mash, more'n likely, both cases." This last came courtesy of Dick Wagner, who for the past eleven years had stopped off at the Shaft precisely at 6:45 for one beer on his way home from the emporium. He chewed sensen in prodigious amounts to keep his wife Lucy from detecting it on his breath.

"Pitt, not Pip," said Ekron. "Mr. Nicholas Pitt of Providence. Where's that?"

"East a ways," Wagner said. "Kansas I think."

"He didn't talk like no Jayhawker I ever heard. 'There's a good fellow,' says he, and gives me that there ten-cent piece."

"This ain't no ten-cent piece." Gordy Wolf was staring at the coin Ekron had given him for the drink. It had a wavy edge and had been stamped crooked with the likeness of nobody he recognized. He bit it.

"Might I see it?"

Gordy Wolf now focused his good eye on Professor the Doctor Webster Bennett, late of the New York University classical studies department, more lately of the Brimstone Saloon across the street. The bartender's hesitation did not mean he suspected that the coin would not be returned; he was just unaccustomed to having the good educator conscious at that hour. Professor the Doctor Bennett's white linen and carefully brushed broadcloth had long since failed to conceal from anyone in Persephone that beneath it, at any hour past noon, was a sizeable bag.

Handed the piece, Professor the Doctor Bennett stroked the edge with his thumb, then raised his chin from the bar and studied the coin on both sides, at one point holding it so close to his pinkish right eye he seemed about to screw it in like a monocle. Finally he returned it.

"Roman. Issued, I would say, sometime after the birth

of Christ, and not very long after. The profile belongs to Tiberius.''

''It cover Ekron's drink?''

''I rather think it will.'' He looked at Ekron. ''I would hear more of your Mr. Pitt.''

''He ain't *my* Mr. Pitt. Anyway I don't much look at folks, just the animals they ride in on. Seen his clothes; fine city ones they was, and a duster. Hogleg tied down on his hip like you read in the nickel novels. And there's something else.''

''Gunfighter?'' Wagner sat up straight. His greatest regret, aside from having chosen Lucy for his helpmeet, was that he had come West from Louisiana too late to see a real gunfight. The great pistoleers were all dead or gone East to act on the stage. All except one, of course, and he had proved frustrating.

''Or a dude,'' said Gordy Wolf. ''Tenderfoot comes out here, wants everyone to think he's Wild Bill.''

Ekron spat, missing the cuspidor by his standard margin. ''Forget the damn gun, it don't count. Leastwise not till it goes off. Gordy, you're injun. Man comes in off that desert country up North. Babocomari's dry till September, Tucson's a week's ride, gila and roadrunner's the only game twixt here and Iron Springs. What you figure he's got to have in provisions and truck?''

''Rifle, box of cartridges. Grain for the horse. Bacon for himself and maybe some tinned goods. Two canteens or a skin. That's if he's white. Apache'd do with the rifle and water.''

''Well, Mr. Nicholas Pitt of Providence didn't have none of that.''

''What you mean, just water?''

''I mean nothing. Not water nor food nor rifle nor even a blanket roll to keep the chill off his *cojones* in the desert at night. Man rides in with just his hip gun and saddle and nary a bead of sweat on man nor mount, and him with nothing behind him but a hunnert miles of sand and alkali.'' He jerked down his whiskey and looked around at his listeners. "Now, what would you call a man like that, if not the Devil his own self?"

Thus, in addition to having been first to spot the stranger who would mean so much to the town's fortunes, Ekron Fast settled upon him the appelation by which he would be commonly known when not directly addressed. From that time forward, His Own Self, uttered in silent but generally agreed-upon capitals, meant none other and required no illumination.

At the very moment that this unconscious christening was taking place, Guy Dante, manager at the Belial Hotel, was in the throes of a similar demonstration, albeit with somewhat less theater, for his wife. Angel Dante had come in perturbed to have found Dick Wagner gone and the emporium closed and therefore a trip wasted to purchase red ink with which to keep the books. As was his custom, Guy had been bleating on while she unpinned her hat and removed her gloves, and so went unheeded for the crucial first minute of his speech.

". . . registered with no mark like I ever saw, and him from his clothes and deportment a city gentleman who should certainly have enjoyed a considerable education," he finished.

"What mark? What gentleman? Oh, Mr. Dante, sometimes I believe you talk sideways just to increase my burden." She tugged on green velvet pen-wipers for another go at the books.

"Room six. He registered while you were out. I just sent Milton up with water for his bath. Weren't you listening?"

She didn't acknowledge the question. In truth she was slightly hard of hearing and preferred to have people think she was rude rather than advertise the fact that she was seven years older than her husband; a piece of enlightenment that would have surprised many of the town's citizens, who assumed that the difference was much greater. "I don't smell the stove," she said.

"He said cold water would be more than satisfactory. Here's his mark I was telling you about." He shoved the registration book at her.

She seated her spectacles in the dents alongside her nose and examined the two-pronged device scratched deeply into the creamy paper. She ran a finger over it. "It looks like some kind of brand. He must be a cattleman."

"He didn't look like one. What would a cattleman be doing in this country?"

"Perhaps he knows something. Perhaps the railroad is coming and he's here to check out the prospects for shipping beef. Oh, Mr. Dante, why did you give him six? Nine's the presidential."

"He asked for six."

"Land. I hope you had the presence to have Milton carry up his traps."

"He didn't have any. And he didn't talk like any cattleman either. He asked about the Brimstone. Wanted to know if it's for sale."

"An entrepreneur, in Persephone?" She cast a glance up the stairs, removing her spectacles as if the portly, diamond-stickpinned figure she associated with an entrepreneur might appear on the landing and see them. "Land. He must know something."

"If he does, this town sure isn't it. Nor Ned Harpy. He'd sell his sister before he'd let that saloon go. And for a smaller price to boot."

"Nevertheless we must make him comfortable. Prosperity may be involved."

Dante made that braying noise his wife found distressing. "I hope he tells us when it's fixed to start. Wait till you see what he gave me for the room."

Only the manager's familiar bray rose above the first floor, where Milton heard it on his way to room six. Inside he hung up the fine striped suit he had finished brushing and asked the man splashing behind the screen if he wanted his boots blacked as well. Milton made beds, served meals, and banished dirt and dust from the Belial with an industry that came naturally to the son of a stablehand.

"If you would, lad." The man's whispery voice barely rose above the lapping in the tub. It reminded Milton of a big old rattler shucking its skin. "There's something on the

bureau for you. Much obliged.'' Then he laughed, which
was worse than when he spoke.

Milton picked up the boots, handsome black ones with
butter-soft tops that flopped over and a curious two-pointed
design on each one that looked like a cow's hoofprint. They
were made of a wonderful kind of leather he had never
seen or felt before, as dark as his father's skin. His skin
was much lighter than his father's. He knew that some
mean folks around town said he wasn't Virgil's son at all,
sired as like as not by some unparticular plantation owner—
disregarding that Milton was only thirteen and born well
after Mr. Lincoln did his duty. Such folks could go to hell.

He got a chill then, in that close room in July in Arizona,
and took his mind off it by examining the strange coin he
had picked up from the dresser. Confederate pewter, most
like. No wonder Mr. Pitt had laughed.

Only he didn't think that was the reason. Damn little
about strangers made sense—those few that found their
way here after the last of the big silver interests had hauled
its wagon east—but this one less than most. Where were
his possibles? Why weren't his clothes caked and stinking
of man and horse, instead of just dusty? And how was it,
after Milton had filled the bathtub himself with buckets of
water ice-cold from the pump, that steam was rolling out
under the screen where the stranger was bathing?

Josh Marlowe rode up from Mexico in the middle of a
September rainstorm with water funneling off his hatbrim
fore and aft and shining on his black oilskin. Charon's
hoofs splashed mud up over his boots and made sucking
sounds when they pulled clear. The gray snorted its misery.

Josh concurred. In times past he had preferred entering
a town in weather that kept folks indoors. There were some
short fuses then who'd throw down on him the second they
recognized him but wouldn't later when they had a chance
to think of it, making arrivals the most dangerous time in
a gunman's experience. But that was before he'd given up
the road. Persephone was home, and now that there was no
danger he discovered he hated riding in the rain.

Peaceable though he was these days, he clung to his old custom of coming in the back way. He dismounted behind the livery, found the back door locked, stepped back, and kicked it until Virgil opened it from inside. He stood there like always with coal-oil light at his back and his old Colt's Dragoon gleaming in his big black fist.

"Virgil, how many times I tell you to snuff that lantern when a stranger comes?"

The stablehand's barn-door grin shone in the bad light. He stuck the big pistol under his belt. "Balls, Mr. Josh. You ain't no stranger."

Josh left the point short of argument and handed him the reins. "How's Milton?"

"Gettin' uppity. Hotel work's got him thinking he's town folks." He led the gray inside.

The barrel stove was glowing. Josh slung his saddle and pouches over an empty stall and warmed his hands. When he turned to put heat on his backside he spotted the black standing in its stall. He whistled. Reflection from the fire made its eyes look red.

"That there's Mr. Pitt's horse." Virgil began rubbing down Charon with burlap. "You stand clear of that animal, Mr. Josh. He's just plain evil."

"Who might Mr. Pitt be?"

"That's right, you been gone."

"Two months trailing grandee beef to Mexico City. This Pitt with the railroad? Credit won't acquire a mount like that."

"If he is, the railroad done bought the Brimstone. Mr. Pitt he runs the place now."

"Horseshit. Ned Harpy told me he'd die before he sold out."

"I reckon he wasn't pulling your leg."

Josh saw the stablehand wasn't smiling. "The hell you say."

The black horse reared, screamed, plunged, and kicked its stall. The hammering mingled with a long loud peal of thunder. Even Charon shied from it.

"You see what I mean about that animal," Virgil said,

when it had calmed down. "It happened real quick, Mr. Josh. Mr. Ned he got mad when that Mr. Pitt wouldn't take no as an answer and pulled on him right there in the game-room. Only Mr. Pitt filled his hand first and just drilled that man full of holes. He was dead when he hit the floor. Mrs. Harpy, she sold out and went back East."

"Ned was fast."

"Near as fast as you." Virgil was grave. "You stay out of the Brimstone, Mr. Josh."

He grinned. "Save that talk for your boy. I gave all that up years ago."

"I hopes so, Mr. Josh. I surely does. You can't beat that man. Nobody can."

From there Josh went to the Fallen Shaft, where he closed the door against the wind and rain and piano music clattering out of the Brimstone. Gordy Wolf was alone. He took his elbows off the bar.

"Josh Marlowe. Gouge out my eyes and pour vinegar in the holes if it ain't. What can I draw you, Josh?"

"Tanglefoot. Where is everybody?" He slapped water off his hat and hooked a heel over the rail.

Gordy Wolf shook his head, poured, and made a mark in the ledger. "You could touch off a Hotchkiss in here since they put the piano in across the street. Nobody'd mind."

"What about Professor the Doctor Webster Bennett? He'd never desert the Shaft."

"He's give up the Creature. Says it don't fit with teaching school."

"That's what the council said when they booted him for falling on his face during sums. Then they closed down the schoolhouse."

"Mr. Pitt bought it and opened it back up. Professor the Doctor ain't got but six pupils and one of them's near as old as him. Way he struts and fluffs his feathers you'd think he's still learning Eyetalian and Greek to them rich men's sons back home."

"This the same Pitt killed Ned Harpy?"

"If there's two I'd hear about it."

"From what Virgil said I didn't take him to be one for the community."

"Before the school he bought the Belial Hotel from Old Man Merry and deeded it to Guy and Angel Dante and then he bought the emporium from Dick Wagner and made him manager at the Brimstone."

"I can't feature Lucy Wagner sitting still for that."

"Lucy went back to New Orleans. She got on worse with Mr. Pitt than she did with Dick. You wouldn't know Dick now. He's got him a red vest and spats."

"What's Pitt's purpose? When the mines played out I gave Persephone five years."

"He told Ekron Fast there's future here. Then he bought him a new forge and an autymobile."

"Ain't no autymobiles twixt here and Phoenix."

"There's one now. 'Thisyer's the future I been telling you about,' he says to Ekron. 'Master it.' Ekron run it straight into an arroyo. But he fixed it with his new forge."

"I reckon he's one stranger who's made himself popular," Josh said.

"He's got him an eye for what every man he meets wants more'n anything, plus a pocket deep enough to get it for him."

"Except Ned Harpy."

"Nobody much liked Ned anyway. If Mr. Pitt was to run for mayor tomorrow I reckon he'd get everybody's vote but two."

"How is it he ain't throwed his loop over you and Virgil?"

The half-breed put an elbow on the bar and leaned in close enough for Josh to discover that his ledger-keeping had not prevented him from sampling the Shaft's stock. "On account of Virgil's a Christian man," he said. "And on account of I ain't. Mr. Pitt he gets what falls between."

"That's heathen talk."

"It ain't neither. Just because they threw me out of the mission school after a week don't mean I didn't hear what they had to teach."

Josh drank whiskey. "I got to meet this fellow."

"How long's it been since you wore a pistol?" Gordy Wolf kept his good eye on him.

"Three years."

"You'd best not."

"Talking's all I'm after."

"When your kind meet his kind it don't stop at talking."

"What kind's mine, Christian or Ain't?"

"I seen you struggling with both."

He stopped grinning and drained his glass. "It's a damn shame the mission school didn't keep you, Gordy. You'd of made a right smart preacher."

"Call me what you like. I'm just saying you'd best climb on that gray horse and ride out and forget all about Persephone. That Mr. Pitt is hell on the draw."

Thunder cracked.

Two months was hardly long enough for the Brimstone to change as much as it had since Josh's last visit. It was one thing to cover the knotty walls with scarlet cloth and take down the prizefighter prints behind the bar to make room for a gilt-framed painting of a reclining naked fat lady holding an apple and laughing; quite another to rip out the old pine bar and replace it with one made from gnarled black oak with what looked like horned evil children carved into the corners. Such items, like the enormous chandelier that now swung from the center rafter, its thousand candles filling the room with oppressive heat, required more time than that to order and deliver. Let alone make, for what catalogue house stocked statuary representing serpents amorously entwined with more naked femininity like the two Amazons thus engaged on either side of the batwing doors?

Mr. Pitt's tastes were apparently not excessive for Persephone's nightlife, however. The main room was packed. Under an awning of lazily turning smoke the drinkers' voices rose above the noise from the piano, where a thickish man in a striped suit and derby was playing something fit to raise blisters on a stump. The strange, fast melody was unknown to Josh, who decided he had been below the border a mite too long.

"Look what the wind blew up from Mexico!"

Gordy Wolf hadn't lied about the spats and red vest. They were accompanied by green silk sleeve garters, a platinum watch chain with a dyed rabbit's-foot fob, and an eastern straw hat tipped forward at such a steep angle the former merchant had to slant his head back to see in front of him.

"Howdy, Dick." Josh sentenced his hand to serious pumping by one heavy with rings.

"What you think of the old place?" Dick Wagner asked. His eyes looked wild and he was grinning to his molars.

"Talks up for itself, don't it?"

"Loud and proud. Lucy'd hate it to death." He roared and clapped a hand on Josh's shoulder. "Keep! Draw one on the house for my gunslinging friend here."

"After I talk to the owner. He around?"

"That's him banging the pianny."

Josh stared at the derbied piano player. He was built like a nailkeg and very fair—a fact that surprised Josh, though he could not own why—and wore jaunty reddish chin-whiskers that put the former gunman in mind of an elf he had seen carved on the door of Irish Mike's hospitable house in St. Louis. As Josh approached him he turned glass-blue eyes on the newcomer. "I'll warrant you're Marlowe." He went on playing the bizarre tune.

"I reckon news don't grow much grass in a town this size."

"Nor does your reputation. I am Nicholas Pitt, originally of Providence. You'll excuse me for not clasping hands."

"It sounds a difficult piece."

"A little composition of my own. But it's not the reason. I only touch flesh with someone when we've reached accord."

Something in Pitt's harsh whisper made Josh grateful for this eccentricity. "I admired your horse earlier this evening."

"Beelzebub? I've had him forever. Ah, thank you, Margaret. Can I interest you in a libation, Marlowe?" He quit playing and accepted a tall glass from a plump girl in a spangled corset. She looked to Josh like one of old Harry Bosch's daughters. He shook his head. Pitt shrugged and drank. A thread of steam rose from the liquid when he lowered it. "I watched you as you came in. You don't approve of the renovations." It was a statement.

"I ain't used to seeing the place so gussy."

"The gameroom is unoccupied. I'll show it to you if you'll mosey in there with me." Laughing oddly, he rose. His coat-frock swayed, exposing briefly the shiny black handle of a Colt's Peacemaker strapped to his hip.

The side room was similarly appointed, with the addition of faro and billiard tables covered in red felt. Milton, the black stablehand's son, sat in the dealer's chair polishing a cuspidor.

"That will be all, lad." Pitt tossed him a silver dollar.

Josh laid a hand on Milton's shoulder as he was headed for the door. "Your pa know you're here?"

"No sir. I get a whuppin'. But Mr. Pitt he pays better than the hotel." He lowered his voice. " 'Specially since he started paying real money." He left.

"Good lad. But I have hopes for him." Pitt took another sip and set his glass on the billiard table, where it boiled over.

"Who are you?" Josh asked.

"I am a speculator."

"Persephone's past speculating."

"That's where you're wrong, Marlowe. My commodity is most plentiful here."

"What's your commodity?"

"Something that is valued by only three in town at present. Milton's father Virgil, because he understands it. The half-breed Gordy Wolf, because he does not possess it. And I."

"What about me?"

"You have been a signal disappointment. When you came to this territory, that item which you are pleased to call yours was more than half mine. Since then you have begun to reclaim it."

"You came to take it back?"

Pitt laughed. It sounded like scales dragging over stone. "You exalt yourself. What is your soul against the soul of an entire town?"

"Then Virge and Gordy was right. You're him."

"Succinctly put. Gary Cooper would be proud."

"Who?"

"Perhaps I should explain myself. But where to start? Aha. Has it ever occurred to you in your wanderings that the people you meet are a tad too colorful, their behavior insufferably eccentric, their language over-folksy? That they themselves are rather—well, *broad*? Half-breed Crows tending bar, drunken college professors, henpecked merchants, gossipy blacksmiths, Negro liverymen who talk as if they just stepped off the plantation—really, where does one encounter these types outside of entertainment?"

"Keep cranking, Mr. Pitt. You ain't drawed a drop yet."

"There. That's just what I mean. Why can't you say simply that you don't follow? I don't suppose you'd understand the concept of alternate earths."

Josh said nothing.

"There is, if you will, a Master Earth, against which all the lesser alternate earths must be measured. Each earth has an equal number of time frames, and it's my privilege to move in and out of these frames among the Master and alternate earths. Now, on Master Earth, the American West within this frame is quite different from the one in which you and I find ourselves. *This* West, with its larger-than-life characters and chivalric codes of conduct, is but a mythology designed for escapist entertainment on Master Earth. That earth's West is a much drearier place. Are you still with me?"

"Sounds like clabber."

"How to put it." Pitt worried a whiskered lip between small ivory teeth. "You were a gunfighter. Were you ever struck by the absurdity of this notion that the faster man in a duel is the moral victor, when the smart way to settle a fatal difference would be to ambush your opponent or shoot him before he's ready?"

"We don't do things that way here."

"Of course not. But on Master Earth they do. Or did. I get my tenses tangled jumping between time frames. In any case being who and what I am, I thought it would be fine sport to do my speculating in this alternate West. The fact that I am mortal here lends a nice edge to those splendid fast-draw contests like the one I enjoyed with Ned Harpy. His soul was already mine when I came here, but I couldn't resist the challenge." He sighed heavily; Josh felt the heat. "I'm aggrieved to say I've found none to compare with it. I'd expected more opposition."

"You talk like you got the town sewed up."

"I bagged the entire council this very afternoon when I promised them they'd find oil if they drilled north of Cornelius Street. The rest is sweepings."

"What do you need with Milton?"

"The souls of children hold no interest for me. But his father's would be a prize. I'm certain a trade can be arranged. Virgil will make an excellent pair of boots when these wear out." He held up a glossy black toe and laughed. Wind and rain lashed the windows, howling like demons.

"You trade often?"

Pitt cocked an eyebrow under the derby. "When the bargain is sufficient. What are you proposing?"

"I hear you're fast against saloonkeepers. How are you with a genuine gunman?"

"Don't be ludicrous. You haven't been in a fight in years."

"You yellowing out?"

Pitt didn't draw; the Peacemaker was just in his hand. Lightning flashed, thunder roared, a windowpane blew in and rain and wind extinguished the lamps in the room. All at once they re-ignited. The Peacemaker was in its holster. Pitt smiled. "What will you use for a gun?"

"I'll get one."

"That won't be necessary." He opened a drawer in the faro table and took out a glistening gray leather gun belt with a slate-handled converted Navy Colt's in the holster. "I think you'll find this will fit your hand."

Josh accepted the rig and drew out the pistol. The cylinder was full. "I sold this set in Tucson. How'd you come by it?"

"I keep track of such things. What are the spoils?"

"Me and the town if you win. If I win you ride out on that red-eyed horse and don't come back. Leave the town and everybody in it the way you found them."

"That won't be necessary. In the latter event I'd be as dead as you in the former. In this world, anyway. What is hell for a gunfighter, Marlowe? Eternity on a dusty street where you take on all challengers, your gun hand growing swollen and bloody, never knowing which man you face is your last? I'll see you're kept interested."

"Stop jawing and go to fighting."

Smiling, Pitt backed up several paces, spread his feet, and swept his coat-frock behind the black-handled pistol, setting himself. Josh shot him.

The storm wailed. Pitt staggered back against the billiard table and slid to the floor. Black blood stained his striped vest. The glass-blue eyes were wide. "Your gun was already out! You didn't give me a chance!"

Josh shrugged. "Did you think you were the only one who could travel between worlds?"

A HORSE FOR MRS. CUSTER

▼

Glendon Swarthout

*Every man lives around the corner from history. Some pass
it every day and never make the turning. Others, on their
way, are detained by chance and cannot bear it witness.
One recalls the Roman who, granting himself the luxury of
a stay at Baiae, a resort on the Tyrrhenian coast, did not
attend the Senate on the day Gaius Julius Caesar was
struck down. One thinks nineteen centuries later of the gun-
ner, fallen ill at the last moment, who was replaced in the
ball turret of the B-29 that flew over Hiroshima. Yet the
stories of men who have missed one of the larger human
events are frequently as interesting as those who have par-
ticipated. One of the strangest of these has lately come to
light. It is remarkable in that history repeated itself, and
the person absent on the first occasion was afforded the
unique opportunity of being present at the second.*

The tale is told in a small volume entitled Dakota Days,
*one of several privately printed in 1928 and written by
Brigadier General Alexander Peddie, U.S.A., during the
years of his retirement. General Peddie's career was long
and distinguished and since his prose is that of a soldier,*

honest and direct, it is unfortunate that his reminiscences have not had wider circulation. Dakota Days *recounts his duty with the Seventh Cavalry Regiment beginning in the autumn of 1876, four months after its bloody stand, under George Armstrong Custer, on the Little Bighorn. It contains not only vivid descriptions of the Great Plains but the little-known episode mentioned above, the authenticity of which there can be no doubt.*

Permission has been granted by his granddaughter, Alice Peddie Wycomb, his only heir, to excerpt such passages as may serve the ends of unity.

Historians record that tidings of the Little Bighorn battle came as a dreadful shock to the nation. On 25 June 1876, the Seventh Cavalry was split in three formations by its commander in the face of twelve thousand Sioux, Oglala, and Cheyenne under Sitting Bull. Troops C, E, F, I, and L, those under Custer, were lost to the last man and horse, while other units, with Major Marcus Reno, were severely mauled. But the nation's grief changed soon to indignation as attempts were made in Congress and the press to fix the blame for the disaster. President Grant was personally assailed, but public attention was eventually concentrated on Custer himself. The country, as one pamphlet put it, "chose up sides." To the man in the street or the horse car or the saloon, General Custer became either hero or fool, martyr or murderer. Unfortunately, little heed was given to the effects such angry division would have upon the broken remnants of the now-famous Seventh.

It was at this juncture that young Alexander Peddie, newly commissioned a second lieutenant of cavalry from West Point, was ordered to Fort Abraham Lincoln in the Dakota Territory.

It was a long three days by train from St. Paul to Fargo and Bismarck at that time. I was anxious to get my first glimpse of the real West and eager to join the Seventh, whose name had become a household one the length and breadth of the land. I thought myself the luckiest young man alive, and even started a moustachio. Reaching Bismarck, where the railroad ended, I crossed the Missouri by ferry and reported for duty at Fort Abe the first week in November to Major Reno, commanding. I was assigned to I Troop, one of those which had been wiped out by the Sioux in the spring. It was commanded by Captain John C. Thomas, who was sent for to meet me and show me to my quarters. He came presently and we walked along the parade together. Captain Thomas was a man of medium height, powerfully built and clean-shaven. His hair was iron gray, a striking thing in a man no more than forty. He had little to say, showing in every respect the reserve which I was later to understand fully. But for that, I might have made the mistake of questioning him about the Little Bighorn.

Captain Thomas took me into the Custer house, saying I would be quartered here with seven other new lieutenants. Mrs. Custer had gone Back East and the house was bare of furniture. As I expressed curiosity, we strolled though the empty rooms in which had echoed only months before the clink of the general's saber and the sound of his voice calling "Libbie! Libbie!" to his wife. In the small study he had written those articles for *Galaxy Magazine* which had stirred the country's blood, while his beloved "Libbie" waited patiently outside, for he could not compose unless she sat near.

Then we went into the long drawing room. On the walls still hung trophies of the general's passion for hunting— the heads of grizzlies, black-tail deer, and antelope. On the mantel were a yellow fox, an owl, and a sandhill crane. But on the floor was a strange arrangement. At one end were four bedrolls, and at the other end three. I stood a moment, then asked what it meant.

"That's the way it is," said the captain. He was looking out a window. "I expect three of them have one set of ideas about Custer, all favorable, and four have another. You must decide for yourself."

I did not hesitate. "I've always been for a fair fight," I said, and put my bedroll down beside the three. Captain Thomas did not turn around to notice my decision.

•   •   •

That night at mess I met the other seven officers, all of my
rank, with whom I was to share quarters. My opposite number in I Troop turned out to be a Lieutenant Alvin Thadius.
He was short and chunked, with round red cheeks like apples, and he hailed from Ohio. I took a liking to him at
once, but I did not realize how deep the currents ran until
we returned to the Custer drawing room to bed down. When
Thadius saw where I had put my roll he said he hoped that
did not mean I had been taken in by Autie Custer the way
half the country had. I replied that I disliked passing judgment on a dead man.

"There are five troops dead," said Thadius. "And they
have passed judgment, wherever they are, on the man who
brought them to it!" In an instant he was as ruffled up as
a prairie chicken at mating. "He disobeyed orders, he
would not listen to his scouts—Bloody Knife told him they
would never see the set of the sun that day. But he took
six hundred men with him to the slaughter!"

The others were watching me as I sat with one boot
already drawn off. I was not on firm ground, for Thadius
had arrived two weeks before me and doubtless had more
of the facts. But he was not a year older than I, and I
resolved to be as stubborn as he was quick-tempered.

"Reno failed to support him," I said. "He heard firing
over the hill but he dug in. An officer may think first of
the safety of his own command, but not a gentleman."

I regretted this as soon as the words were out of my
mouth. Thadius came to his feet with his round cheeks red-
der than ever.

"A butcher is no gentleman!" he cried.

This stung me to the raw. I hauled off my other boot and
stood. "It takes a gentleman to recognize one," I said.

He started for me with a lunge and we would have had
a bobbery then and there had not Lieutenant Nokes, who
was a rather sentimental lad, come between us. The eight
of us went to bed in silence, four across from four. As I
lay accustoming my bones to the plank floor and my mind
to this inauspicious beginning, the glass eyes of the griz-

zlies gleamed down at me, reflecting the light of the dying fire. I tossed and turned for several hours, and I could hear Alvin Thadius doing likewise.

By the first blizzard I found what I had joined. It was not the Seventh Cavalry, nor a fighting force of any kind, but an unruly mass of men divided into two camps. Five hundred recruits and thirty green officers had come from the East too late in the season to train properly, and with them they had brought along the bitterness felt back home about the Little Bighorn. Every troop was split, I Troop included. There were five hundred remounts in the stables, too, and it was hard to tell which were the more cantankerous, animals or men. Only those who had been with Custer—officers such as Captains Benteen and Thomas, Lieutenants Varnum and DeRudio—held their peace. All the long howling winter matters worsened. Discipline became nearly impossible to maintain. The recruits would slip guard at night and cross the Missouri ice to Bismarck to drink and brawl among themselves. A patrol located a little lake near the fort in which warm springs melted the ice along the shore, and here the big pike lay so thick the men could heave them out in piles with pitchforks. But quarrels over dividing them soon stopped the "fishing."

Even Major Reno's attempt to divert the men only increased tensions. It had been General Custer's policy to permit "theatricals" now and then, in which the men dressed up and performed skits and dances and so on. But the theatricals that winter ended with the first. One of the pieces announced was a recitation by Tommy Gudge, our Troop I bugler, a boy of eighteen, and when Tommy stood onstage to recite, the Custer-haters had put him up to doing one of Mr. Henry Wadsworth Longfellow's latest poems, called "The Revenge of Rain-in-the-Face." This was based on the yarn that when the general lay fallen, his heart had been cut out of him by savages. Toward the end of the poem Tommy had worked up such a head of steam that his voice fairly cracked on these lines:

> *"Revenge!" cried Rain-in-the-Face,*
> *"Revenge upon all the race*
> *Of the White Chief with yellow hair!"*

At this point a sergeant in the rear rose up and shouted "Revenge!" himself, and in a flash the fists were flying. A riot was averted only by calling in the guard and banging a few heads with carbine butts.

Fort Lincoln that winter of '76–'77 was a haunted post. It seemed that all the dead were with us still, making up an unseen regiment, the old Seventh, the immortal Seventh, mocking the new one with the memory of its gallantry. It preyed on the mind.

I well recall poor Nokes, for instance. We eight lieutenants still lay separated on the floor of the Custer drawing room those endless nights with the wind helling down out of Canada across the plains and wailing at the eaves. One night we were awakened by Nokes, who jumped out of his roll and commenced to yell at us.

"Hear that singing? Hear it? That's the wives and Mrs. Custer singing as they did the day the news came, crying and singing in this room. I can't stand it. Tell them to stop. Tell them to stop!"

And he began to sing at the top of his voice, " 'E'en though a cross it be, nearer, my God, to Thee!' " It was a terrifying thing, of course, at such an hour, and Allenberry and I seized Nokes and tried to calm him, telling him it was only the wind.

"No, no, it's the wives of the dead. It's the widows singing." Nokes howled. "I can't stand it!"

We finally got the unfortunate lad back in his roll, but we had to hold him down all night, and in the morning took him to the surgeons because he still shook and did not seem to have control of his limbs. Nokes stayed with them and in the spring was shipped Back East to a hospital. I have not heard of him since.

One night in March I learned what lay behind Captain Thomas's reserve. I was officer of the guard, and while inspecting the various sentry boxes saw a light in the stables. Knowing the farriers were all asleep or carousing over in Bismarck, I went to investigate. To my surprise I found the captain currying a small bay horse by the light of a lantern. He told me it was General Custer's horse Dandy.

"How can that be, Captain?" I asked. "I understood that neither man nor horse escaped."

"He had two—Vic and this one," said the captain. "On the morning of the battle he took his choice of the two to ride that day. Vic was younger and he took him. That's how this one comes to be here."

I went around to the head and looked more closely at the bay. I must admit my flesh crawled, because though he should have been a ghost horse he was very much alive, with lots of spunk in his eyes and the way he carried his head. Though small for cavalry, he belonged at the head of a column. Captain Thomas went on currying and telling me about him. Dandy had been the general's favorite, and had been bought by the government in Kansas for one hundred forty dollars. He could run down a deer and no horse was better alongside the rump of a buffalo bull. When I asked why the captain felt he had to care for him, he replied that feelings were so high, even among the farriers, that most of them would not lay hands on a pet of Custer's.

I commented that that was pretty low, but he said such sympathies were not confined to the farriers. Last fall, before I came, there had been a subscription started among the officers to buy the horse from the government and ship him to Mrs. Custer as a memorial. All the old officers had paid in, but when most of the new arrivals refused, Major Reno returned the money. He would not send Dandy away unless commissioned names were listed, for he did not want the general's lady to suspect what a state the regiment was in.

It occurred to me that this might be a good time to ask Captain John Thomas about the Little Bighorn and his part in it. I knew nothing about the man except that he had been brevetted colonel during the war, having command of a regiment in Virginia after the cavalry fight at Brandy Station. He was one of those officers growing old in the service, with little to look forward to except gray hairs, which he already had, and retirement at major's rank.

"Captain," I said, "do you mind my asking you about the battle?"

"Ask if you like, Peddie," he said, working away with a comb. "But I have nothing to tell. I was not present. I should have been, since I had I Troop then, as now. But before we took the field an officer was needed to conduct some Cheyenne prisoners to Oklahoma and resettle them there. Custer happened to pick me, I do not know why. Captain Keogh took I Troop in my place, and was killed. I could not return to Fort Abe till July, and then it was all over. I met the wounded when they came down by steamer."

"Oh," I said. Then I asked what no man should ask of another under such circumstances, but I was only twenty-three years of age. "How do you feel about it, Captain?"

For a moment he was silent. Then he turned to me and his face betrayed a terrible look. It was as though his skin had been flayed to ribbons and I could see clear through to his vitals.

"How would you feel?" he asked.

I could not answer. I had no idea how I would feel. But I could see, as if by lightning, how the man must have been tormented.

On the one hand he must have hated Custer for sending him away and denying him the chance a soldier seldom has—the chance to die a hero. That part of him must have blamed the general for the disaster, despised him as much as did young Alvin Thadius and many of the recruits.

On the other hand, the instinct to survive is strong in every man, so he must have been grateful to his commander for having spared his life. And all that gratitude must have made him stand at times on the side of those who worshipped Custer for his daring and leadership. The awful struggle for allegiance in the regiment, which they could fight out among them, had been dueling on a year in John Thomas, and he bore it alone.

When he saw my confusion, the captain looked away and laid a gentle hand on Dandy's neck.

"I am just like this horse, Peddie," he said. "Another went in his place and he did not see that day, either. If he can stand it, then I can. And I can care for him if others will not."

I had to leave the stables and be by myself in the cold clear night. Sudden insight into the soul of a fellow human being often matures one in a minute as much as does a full year's campaign.

Spring came. The ice went out of the Missouri and Major Reno took the Seventh into the gumbo mud daily to train the spleen out of it. The Sioux had left the agencies now. Sitting Bull and Crazy Horse were north behind the mountains and sent word down they intended scalping every white man in North Dakota. So the Seventh trained, and at least learned how to get on and off a horse and which was the business end of a Colt and Springfield. We knew we would take the field, but no man could say when he would return or if. Not many of the old Seventh had, and this one was scarce its equal.

On 14 May 1877 we marched through the west gate of Fort Abe. I can still hear the leather slapping and gear clinking and fifes squealing a tune—not "Garry-owen," which was the regimental song when Autie Custer led it, but "The Girl I Left Behind Me." The last verses of that song I will never forget, for they took on that day a meaning far beyond their words:

> *Full many a name our banners bore*
> *Of former deeds of daring,*
> *But they were of the days of yore,*
> *In which we had no sharing;*
> *But now our laurels freshly won*
> *With the old ones shall entwined be,*
> *Still worthy of his sire each son,*
> *Sweet girl I left behind me.*

Few men have seen the plains and prairies, the mountains and rivers and spaces of the Dakota country as it was then, as God made it, and I thank Him for the privilege of admiring his handiwork.

We went up to Fort Buford, crossed the Missouri, and then went up the Yellowstone, taking four weeks at it. The ground had not yet started to thaw and the nights were cold. One day we encountered a hailstorm on Froze-to-Death Creek, with hailstones as big as hickory nuts, and the horses, hit on the hocks by them, thought they were being beaten and became frantic. Another day we went over a rise and before us were buffalo all the way to the horizon. We estimated the herd at thirteen thousand. After the first rains the prairie was covered with grass plover running in pairs. The sickle-billed curlew whistled all day, hovering overhead so still you could drop them with a shot. Little green and purple anemones were the first flowers to come out.

We camped a few days at Sunday Creek in an abandoned cantonment of logs with dirt roofs before heading north to seek Sitting Bull in the mountains. But here Major Reno sent for Captain Thomas, and when the latter returned he said I Troop was detached for special duty. We were to take our four wagons, with mules and drivers, and mount up at once. F. F. Gerard, the scout, would accompany us. He did not say what the duty would be, and neither Thadius nor I inquired. We left that afternoon and marched up the Yellowstone for a week.

The country here was wilder than could be imagined. We saw elk in bands as large as five hundred. We camped among cottonwoods six feet around the trunk. The men killed some beaver and Gerard showed them how to cook the tails. They were delicious, resembling cold roast pork in flavor. Since we saw no hostiles, the men enjoyed themselves as much as the rate of the march and their own cussedness allowed. It was discovered that the wagons were being hauled empty except for a collection of hammers, saws, planes, and nails.

We crossed the Yellowstone near the mouth of the Bighorn, and here an unpleasant incident showed that I Troop was still composed of boys, not men. The river being high, we slowed the horses behind a skiff, and the lariat of Thadius's came loose. The current wound it around the animal's legs and downstream he went. I dived in under him to cut him free with my knife but became tangled myself, and we would both have drowned had not Thadius come in and finished the job, so that the horse brought us ashore clinging to his headstall. But when, having swallowed my pride along with several gallons of snow-water, I tried to thank him for the rescue, he said he had been interested only in rescuing the citizens from the cost of a remount.

"Why, damn you!" I burst out.

"Why, damn you both!" Captain Thomas had come up, mad enough to eat snake. "I will have officers with me, not jabbering squaws. Whether you realize it or not, Sitting Bull has scouts down here, I know he has, and he will have our heads up on a lodge if we don't soldier."

He saw some of the troopers grinning like apes.

"And that applies to you men," he said. "Now get those mules and wagons over—if Crazy Horse doesn't make a troop out of this one, I will!"

There was considerable settling down after that. Not that those for Custer were friendlier toward those against, but each was more considerate of his own skin. We were three hundred miles from Fort Abe by then and half that from the regiment. The earth might have swallowed all of I Troop up and not a living soul the wiser.

The next day, to prove the captain right, we saw our first hostiles, a party of three at a distance. F. F. Gerard asked to use the captain's glasses. He was a small, wizened man who wore buckskin and possessed a sense of humor despite the fact that his teeth caused him pain, doubtless due to his diet over many years on the plains. After a long look he said they were Oglala, and if he was not mistaken one was old Red Moon, a chief not overly fond of cavalry.

We marched another three days, sighting savages on each of them. Captain Thomas gave orders there would be no bugling or shooting or fires at night. We marched up a creek called the Rosebud and found wickiups with skins still tied on them. We also found warnings in Cheyenne scratched in sandstone on the bluffs along the creek. That night we learned from Sergeant Biersdorf where we were going. He had been that way the year before. We were going back to the Little Bighorn.

Midmorning of 25 June, a year to the very day after the battle, I Troop came up a hill in columns of twos, wagons to the rear, and Captain Thomas threw up his hand.

"There it is," he said simply.

I heard nothing in his voice, but I could not help conjecture what was in his mind.

Thadius and I looked down a valley. To the west it widened out in swells toward the Bighorns, high and blue. On three of the knolls, C, E, F, and I Troops had stood a year ago that day and given up their lives. Southward were the high bluffs and deep ravines where Reno fought cut off. Below, a stream sparkled in the sun. It was the Little Bighorn.

"We have come to meet Colonel Mike Sheridan, General Phil's brother, with Captain Nowland and a party of Ree scouts," the captain went on. "The dead could not be buried properly last year because there was no time. We are to rebury the men in one place and mark their graves. The officers are to be placed in caskets we must build. We will then take them in the wagons back to Fort Union, where the infantry will escort them on to Fort Abe and the railroad. In the East their families are awaiting them. We will then rejoin the regiment."

Thus I Troop learned why it had returned to the Little Bighorn. Camp was pitched near the stream. In the afternoon Colonel Sheridan and Captain Nowland arrived from Fort Miles, guided by two Rees—Horns-in-Front and Two Strikes—who had been with the Seventh the year before. They had sighted many Sioux in parties of various size, and asked Gerard's opinion. The scout replied he doubted they would trouble us while scattered, but if banded up they might get notions.

The duty was commenced at once, and sad duty it was.

The troopers had been laid to rest where they had fallen, scattered over a lot of ground and buried shallow under heaps of stones. The wolves had been their usual busy selves. And where the valley had been thick with dust from drought and hoofs a year before now the grass was stirrup-high and flowers were everywhere. The officers were easier to find. By each one a length of lodge pole had been driven in the earth, with a Roman numeral on it, and Captain Nowland had a chart showing the numbers and decorations. Autie Custer's grave was covered with a basket from a Sioux travois, pinned down with stakes. The general's heart may have broken when he saw his regiment was lost, but I can state positively it was not cut out of him.

It was a quiet camp that night, no fires, no calls, and guards out all around. In the morning my detail began digging graves near the Little Bighorn and bringing the departed comrades to them, while that under Thadius made roughboard coffins out of green willow for the officers. Human nature being what it is, the men got shorter with one another as the day dragged on. Relics found in the grass stuck under their hides like arrows—canteens, a ring, cartridges, knives, boots, guttapercha buttons from the sleeves of blouses. Once two troopers squared off with fists high until I stopped them. Like as not there would have been a general ruckus had it not been for the Sioux. There were fifty or more of them in evidence now, sitting their ponies out on the knolls a mile off like wooden Indians, not live ones. But they were live, all right.

In the afternoon Captain Thomas sent Gerard and the Rees out to circle. When they returned a parley was held. Gerard reported another hundred Sioux hiding in the hollows, and some Cheyenne.

"They're banding, Cap'n," he said. "When Red Moon gets enough parties in, he'll come for us. He was here last year and he knows how."

The scout talked some Ree and signed to Two Strikes, then pulled a blade of grass. "He claims this valley is medicine ground to the Sioux after what they did to Longhair. They ain't going to let anybody dig him up and take him away. Any buck who dies on this ground goes up there on a real fast pony." He pointed to the sky. "Can you follow that, Cap'n?"

"I can," Thomas said. "When will they be ready, Frank?"

"By tomorrow."

Meantime, Colonel Sheridan had been pacing. He was a tall man with a spade beard and had been personally sent from Washington by President Grant on this mission. Now he stared off at the Sioux.

"History repeating itself," he said, almost to himself. "Next year my brother can order a command to come for us as we have come for the others." He faced Captain Thomas. "I am no Indian fighter, Captain, I admit it frankly. But I do recognize odds if Custer did not, and it seems clear there may be another slaughter here tomorrow. If we abandon the wagons and leave during the night we can have a start on them by morning. What do you propose?"

John Thomas turned his face toward the Sioux and we could not see it. I believed I was the only man who understood his terrible position. In this very place a year before, the commander to whom he owed both gratitude and enmity, George Armstrong Custer, had made his decision. Now, under almost the same circumstances, John Thomas had to make his. Finally, he answered.

"I will do that if you order it, Colonel. But we came out here to take some brave men home. I would hate to lose this troop, but I would hate to leave the general and the others here again. If we truck our tails between our legs, the Sioux will think their medicine is stronger in this Territory than ours. I think we should leave here in good order with our duty done, or not at all."

No one had anything to say. But even Two Strikes and Horns-In-Front got the drift from Gerard's face.

Colonel Sheridan pulled off his gauntlets. "I have heard about you in St. Paul, Captain. Has the fact that you were not present here last year influenced your tactics now?"

I held my breath, but the captain met his eyes squarely.

"Sir, it has not," he said.

Colonel Sheridan nodded. "I have also heard rumors about the condition and morale of the Seventh, but I know nothing about this troop. Will they fight?"

"I don't know, Colonel," said Captain Thomas. "But they must find out sometime, as we all must."

Colonel Sheridan slapped his gauntlets together. "Very well. When can we be finished here?"

"By noon tomorrow."

The colonel turned his back as though to indicate the responsibility rested now on other shoulders, and the parley ended. Captain Thomas ordered the four wagons driven into a half circle so that we could make a stand behind them with our backs to the Little Bighorn. Seeing this, I Troop knew it was to stay.

That night Captain Thomas ordered as many fires built as the men wished, as if to show the Sioux we were not perturbed about them. The troopers gathered around each blaze to talk in low tones and calculate our chances on the morrow. We were five officers, three scouts, four skinners, and forty-eight men, a total of sixty against no one knew how many hostiles, but the odds were reckoned at more than six to one. The consensus was that Red Moon had kept the bulk of his band concealed to trap us, as Sitting Bull had done successfully. We might stand them off for several hours, but the outcome was assured. The Custer haters said we were to fight the second Battle of the Little Bighorn, and that Longhair had led us to it in death as surely as he had led the others in life. Many troopers, convinced they would not see another night, turned messages and valuables over to their comrades in the hope that some would survive.

I took no part in this grim vigil, but said my prayers as usual and turned in beside Thadius, who shared a tent with me. I may have expected he would make some peaceful overture, but he did not. The situation seemed unreal to me—being on this hallowed battlefield a year later, the presence of the enemy in overwhelming numbers, the preparations for a stand which must end in tragedy. I fell asleep thinking only that I would never have the chance to display my moustachio in Baltimore.

The day dawned clear. After a cooked breakfast tents were struck, canteens filled, men posted on guard between the wagons, and the skinners turned into horse holders at the rear. Captain Thomas ordered that the remainder complete the work we had been sent to do. At this there was muttering that he had gone mad, but my detail proceeded to bring in the last of the heroes and prepare graves while Thadius's finished the carpentry. Except for the scrape of shovel against stone and the bang of hammers, all was silence. There was no sign of Sioux. They would come when they were ready.

They came near noon, all at once, pouring out of the hollows by the hundreds, spreading out like a swarm. Still a mile away but riding toward us were the brightly painted Cheyenne, who were better horsemen, riding in wide circles and sliding under the necks of their ponies to show what we would have to shoot at. I estimate Red Moon had at least four hundred. And there were many waving carbines, weapons they had taken from our fallen.

We had just filled in the last place of honor, outside the perimeter of the wagons, and started running back to form up. I remember troopers' faces staring, figures in blue standing as though rooted. Then Alvin Thadius came on the run to meet me, holding something in his hand and crying like a child. He held up a dirt-stained triangle of cloth, which I recognized as a guidon he must have found with one of the officers.

"You see this, Peddie," he yelled. "This is what he did to them and what he'll do to us. And before I die, dear God, I'll have it out with you!"

And as I came up short, thunderstruck that this could happen now, Thadius was on me using his fists like clubs. My corporal came to pull him off and was pitched upon by someone else at once, and in seconds most of I Troop was battling it out beyond the wagons, standing and swinging or rolling in the grass among the markers at one another's throats, the line of defense gone and the Sioux not half a mile away. I do not recall an incident like it in the annals of the United States Cavalry. Had something even more unlooked-for not occurred we would have been massacred, every living one.

Thadius and I were at grips near the right front wagon and suddenly I heard the high-pitched yelp of Frank Gerard.

"Look, Cap'n—look yonder. They know that horse—blow the charge! Blow the charge!"

And all at once the bell of Tommy Gudge's bugle blew the charge, and the most stirring of all calls was carried above the desperate men and out over the valley. It was so unexpected that men stopped blows in midair or rose from the ground to see. The obstinate lad from Ohio crawled off me and we stood ourselves.

Over the knolls came a little bay horse upon the lope. When the notes of the bugle reached his ears, he pricked them up, then went into a gallop toward us, right across the front of the swarm of Sioux. And the whole four hundred of the savages stopped their ponies and their yelling. Gerard was right. They did know that horse. They could not believe their eyes any more than we. To them it was a spirit horse with a spirit rider on his back—more powerful medicine than mortal men, red or white, could ever make.

Right between the Sioux and us he galloped, with no sound but the drumming of his hoofs, and he came between the wagons to a halt, blowing and nickering. The Sioux forgotten, we gathered around him. He was all dirt and foam, his eyes sunken and his ribs nearly through his hide. In some way he had broken loose at Fort Abe, and trailing lariat and picket pin had come two hundred miles over mountains and rivers and prairies, had found his way back to the Little Bighorn where he was the year before and where his master now lay in a box of willow.

Captain Thomas leaped down from his wagon and stood beside him for a time. Then he took off his hat.

"Let there be no more fighting among us," he said at length. "I know what has been in your minds. Some men were picked a year ago to make history here. They made it and they will not be forgotten. But what you bear is a grudge against your luck. You came to the regiment too late and could not share their glory.''

He put his hand upon the mane of the little bay. I realized that what he had to say was for his own sake as well as ours.

''This horse was left behind the way you were. But he came two hundred miles to prove he bears no grudge. He missed one fight and he intends to see he does not miss another. If he can do as much, why, so can we. We will now harness these wagons and mount up and march out of here in good order.''

For a minute all stood, not a dry eye among us. Then a cheer rang out and troopers shook hands, as did Alvin Thadius and I. If the souls of the departed were present that day, looking down from the blue sky on that scene in the green valley, it must have lifted their hearts.

Mules were harnessed, Tommy Gudge blew boots and saddles, and I Troop came into column. While the Sioux still sat a quarter of a mile away, believing we had joined forces with the Great Beyond, which in a way we had, Captain Thomas threw his hand forward and we marched past them out of the valley as though on parade, our guidon fluttering and our heads high. At the head of the column stepped the little bay.

So there was a kind of Second Battle of the Little Big-horn after all, which was won without a shot being fired. Dandy was returned to Fort Abe with his master and the other heroes. When I Troop rejoined the regiment in the north and related the foregoing, the subscription for him was raised at once. One hundred forty dollars was paid the government, and the general's horse was shipped East to ''The Girl He'd Left Behind Him.'' From her home in Monroe, Michigan, Mrs. Custer sent a moving letter of thanks. It may interest the reader to know that Dandy became the horse of Autie Custer's old father, who was over seventy then, and together they headed up temperance processions and Fourth of July parades for many years.

As for the breach in the ranks of the Seventh Regiment,

it was wholly healed, as evidenced by ensuing victories at Wounded Knee and against the Nez Percé at Bear Paw.

Alexander Peddie was unable, in Dakota Days, *to describe the action at Bear Paw to which he alludes, since prior to it he was transferred to Fort Huachuca in Arizona. Nor does he mention Captain John Thomas again in his volume. Records of the Adjutant General disclose, however, that the captain, conducting himself gallantly at the head of I Troop, was killed in action against the Nez Percé. Subsequently a recommendation for the posthumous award of the Congressional Medal of Honor was made in his case, but the citation was never approved. Letters of the day reveal, ironically, that sentiment in both Congress and the War Department was against it and several others on the grounds that too-generous award of the medal had been made after the Battle of the Little Bighorn.*

THE FACE

⬇

Ed Gorman

The war was going badly. In the past month more than sixty men had disgraced the Confederacy by deserting, and now the order was to shoot deserters on sight. This was in other camps and other regiments. Fortunately, none of our men had deserted at all.

As a young doctor, I knew even better than our leaders just how hopeless our war had become. The public knew General Lee had been forced to cross the Potomac with ten thousand men who lacked shoes, hats, and who at night had to sleep on the ground without blankets. But I knew—in the first six months in this post—that our men suffered from influenza, diphtheria, smallpox, yellow fever, and even cholera; ravages from which they would never recover; ravages more costly than bullets and the advancing armies of the Yankees. Worse, because toilet and bathing facilities were practically nil, virtually every man suffered from ticks and mites and many suffered from scurvy, their bodies on fire. Occasionally, you would see a man go mad, do crazed dances in the moonlight trying to get the bugs off him. Soon enough he would be dead.

This was the war in the spring and while I have here referred to our troops as "men," in fact they were mostly boys, some as young as thirteen. In the night, freezing and sometimes wounded, they cried out for their mothers, and it was not uncommon to hear one or two of them sob while they prayed aloud.

I tell you this so you will have some idea of how horrible things had become for our beloved Confederacy. But even given the suffering and madness and despair I'd seen for the past two years as a military doctor, nothing had prepared me for the appearance of the Virginia man in our midst.

On the day he was brought in on a buckboard, I was working with some troops, teaching them how to garden. If we did not get vegetables and fruit into our diets soon, all of us would have scurvy. I also appreciated the respite that working in the warm sun gave me from surgery. In the past week alone, I'd amputated three legs, two arms, and numerous hands and fingers. None had gone well, conditions were so filthy.

Every amputation had ended in death except one, and this man—boy; he was fourteen—pleaded with me to kill him every time I checked on him. He'd suffered a head wound and I'd had to relieve the pressure by trepanning into his skull. Beneath the blood and pus in the hole I'd dug, I could see his brain squirming. There was no anesthetic, of course, except whiskey, and that provided little comfort against the violence of my bone saw. It was one of those periods when I could not get the tart odor of blood from my nostrils, nor its feel from my skin. Sometimes, standing at the surgery table, my boots would become soaked with it, and I would squish around in them all day.

The buckboard was parked in front of the general's tent. The driver jumped down, ground-tied the horses, and went quickly inside.

He returned a few moments later with General Sullivan, the commander. Three men in familiar gray uniforms followed the general.

The entourage walked around to the rear of the wagon.

The driver, an enlisted man, pointed to something in the buckboard. The general, a fleshy, bald man of fifty-some years, leaned over the wagon and peered downward.

Quickly, the general's head snapped back and then his whole body followed. It was as if he'd been stung by something coiled and waiting for him in the buckboard.

The general shook his head and said, "I want this man's entire face covered. Especially his face."

"But, General," the driver said. "He's not dead. We shouldn't cover his face."

"You heard what I said!" General Sullivan snapped. And with that, he strutted back into his tent, his men following.

I was curious, of course, about the man in the back of the wagon. I wondered what could have made the general start the way he had. He'd looked almost frightened.

I wasn't to know till later that night.

My rounds made me late for dinner in the vast tent used for the officers' mess. I always felt badly about the inequity of officers having beef stew while the men had, at best, hardtack and salt pork. Not so bad that I refused to eat it, of course, which made me feel hypocritical on top of being sorry for the enlisted men.

Not once in my time here had I ever dined with General Sullivan. I was told on my first day here that the general, an extremely superstitious man, considered doctors bad luck. Many people feel this way. Befriend a doctor and you'll soon enough find need of his services.

So I was surprised when General Sullivan, carrying a cup of steaming coffee in a huge, battered tin cup, sat down across from the table where I ate alone, my usual companions long ago gone back to their duties.

"Good evening, Doctor."

"Good evening, General."

"A little warmer tonight."

"Yes."

He smiled dourly. "Something's got to go our way, I suppose."

I returned his smile. "I suppose." I felt like a child trying to act properly for the sake of an adult. The general
frightened me.

The general took out a stogie, clipped off the end, sniffed
it, licked it, then put it between his lips and fired it up. He
did all this with a ritualistic satisfaction that made me think
of better times in my home city of Charleston, of my father
and uncles handling their smoking in just the same way.

"A man was brought into camp this afternoon," he said.

"Yes," I said. "In a buckboard."

He eyed me suspiciously. "You've seen him up close?"

"No. I just saw him delivered to your tent." I had to be
careful of how I put my next statement. I did not want the
general to think I was challenging his reasoning. "I'm told
he was not taken to any of the hospital tents."

"No, he wasn't." The general wasn't going to help me.

"I'm told he was put under quarantine in a tent of his
own."

"Yes."

"May I ask why?"

He blew two plump, white, perfect rings of smoke toward the ceiling. "Go have a look at him, then join me in
my tent."

"You're afraid he may have some contagious disease?"

The general considered the length of his cigar. "Just go
have a look at him, Doctor. Then we'll talk."

With that, the general stood up, his familiar brusque self
once again, and was gone.

The guard set down his rifle when he saw me. "Good eve-
nin', Doctor."

"Good evening."

He nodded to the tent behind him. "You seen him yet?"

"No, not yet."

He was young. He shook his head. "Never seen anything
like it. Neither has the priest. He's in there with him now."
In the chill, crimson dusk I tried to get a look at the guard's
face. I couldn't. My only clue to his mood was the tone of
his voice—one of great sorrow.

I lifted the tent flap and went in.

A lamp guttered in the far corner of the small tent, casting huge and playful shadows across the walls. A hospital cot took up most of the space. A man's body lay beneath the covers. A sheer cloth had been draped across his face. You could see it billowing with the man's faint breath. Next to the cot stood Father Lynott. He was silver-haired and chunky. His black cassock showed months of dust and grime. Like most of us, he was rarely able to get hot water for necessities.

At first, he didn't seem to hear me. He stood over the cot torturing black rosary beads through his fingers. He stared directly down at the cloth draped on the man's face.

Only when I stood next to him did Father Lynott look up. "Good evening, Father."

"Good evening, Doctor."

"The general wanted me to look at this man."

He stared at me. "You haven't seen him, then?"

"No."

"Nothing can prepare you."

"I'm afraid I don't understand."

He looked at me out of his tired cleric's face. "You'll see soon enough. Why don't you come over to the officers' tent afterwards? I'll be there drinking my nightly coffee."

He nodded, glanced down once more at the man on the cot, and then left, dropping the tent flap behind him.

I don't know how long I stood there before I could bring myself to remove the cloth from the man's face. By now, enough people had warned me of what I would see that I was both curious and apprehensive. There is a myth about doctors not being shocked by certain terrible wounds and injuries. Of course we are, but we must get past that shock—or, more honestly, put it aside for a time—so that we can help the patient.

Close by, I could hear the feet of the guard in the damp grass, pacing back and forth in front of the tent. A barn owl and then a distant dog joined the sounds the guard made. Even more distant, there was cannon fire, the war never ceasing. The sky would flare silver like summer lightning. Men would suffer and die.

I reached down and took the cloth from the man's face.

"What do you suppose could have done that to his face, Father?" I asked the priest twenty minutes later.

We were having coffee. I smoked a cigar. The guttering candles smelled sweet and waxy.

"I'm not sure," the priest said.

"Have you ever seen anything like it?"

"Never."

I knew what I was about to say would surprise the priest. "He has no wounds."

"What?"

"I examined him thoroughly. There are no wounds anywhere on his body."

"But his face—"

I drew on my cigar, watched the expelled smoke move like a storm cloud across the flickering candle flame. "That's why I asked you if you'd ever seen anything like it."

"My God," the priest said, as if speaking to himself. "No wounds."

In the dream I was back on the battlefield on that frosty March morning two years ago when all my medical training had deserted me. Hundreds of corpses covered the ground where the battle had gone on for two days and two nights. You could see cannons mired in mud, the horses unable to pull them out. You could see the grass littered with dishes and pans and kettles, and a blizzard of playing cards—all exploded across the battlefield when the Union Army had made its final advance. But mostly there were the bodies— so young and so many—and many of them with mutilated faces. During this time of the war, both sides had begun to commit atrocities. The Yankees favored disfiguring Confederate dead, and so they moved across the battlefield with Bowie knives that had been fashioned by sharpening with large files. They put deep gashes in the faces of the young men, tearing out eyes sometimes, even sawing off noses. In the woods that day, we'd found a group of our soldiers who'd been mortally wounded but who'd lived for a time after the Yankees had left. Each corpse held in its hand some memento of the loved ones they'd left behind—a photograph, a letter, a lock of blond hair. Their last sight had been of some homely yet profound endearment from the people they'd loved most.

This was the dream—nightmare, really—and I'd suffered it ever since I'd searched for survivors on that battlefield two years previous.

I was still in this dream-state when I heard the bugle announce the morning. I stumbled from my cot and went down to the creek to wash and shave. The day had begun.

Casualties were many that morning. I stood in the hospital tent watching as one stretcher after another bore man after man to the operating table. Most suffered from wounds inflicted by minié balls, fired from guns that could kill a man nearly a mile away.

By noon, my boots were again soaked with blood dripping from the table.

During the long day, I heard whispers of the man General Sullivan had quarantined from others. Apparently, the man had assumed the celebrity and fascination of a carnival sideshow. From the whispers, I gathered that guards were letting men in for quick looks at him, and the lookers came away shaken and frightened. These stories had the same impact as tales of specters told around midnight campfires. Except this was daylight and the men—even the youngest of them—hardened soldiers. They should not have been so afraid but they were.

I couldn't get the sight of the man out of my mind, either. It haunted me no less than the battlefield I'd seen two years earlier.

During the afternoon, I went down to the creek and washed. I then went to the officers' tent and had stew and coffee. My arms were weary from surgery but I knew I would be working long into the night.

The general surprised me once again by joining me.
"You've seen the soldier from Virginia?"

"Yes, sir."

"What do you make of him?"

I shrugged. "Shock, I suppose."

"But his face—"

"This is a war, General, and a damned bloody one. Not all men are like you. Not all men have iron constitutions."

He took my words as flattery, of course, as a military man would. I hadn't necessarily meant them that way. Military men could also be grossly vain and egotistical and insensitive beyond belief.

"Meaning what, exactly, Doctor?"

"Meaning that the soldier from Virginia may have become so horrified by what he saw that his face—" I shook my head. "You can see too much, too much death, General, and it can make you go insane."

"Are you saying he's insane?"

I shook my head. "I'm trying to find some explanation for his expression, General."

"You say there's no injury?"

"None that I can find."

"Yet he's not conscious."

"That's why I think of shock."

I was about to explain how shock works on the body— and how it could feasibly effect an expression like the one on the Virginia soldier's face—when a lieutenant rushed up to the general and breathlessly said, "You'd best come, sir. The tent where the soldier's quarantined— There's trouble!"

When we reached there, we found half the camp's soldiers surrounding the tent. Three and four deep, they were, and milling around idly. Not the sort of thing you wanted to see your men doing when there was a war going on. There were duties to perform and none of them were getting done.

A young soldier—thirteen or fourteen at most—stepped from the line and hurled his rifle at the general. The young soldier had tears running down his cheeks. "I don't want to fight anymore, General."

The general slammed the butt of the rifle into the soldier's stomach. "Get hold of yourself, young man. You seem to forget we're fighting to save the Confederacy."

We went on down the line of glowering faces, to where two armed guards struggled to keep soldiers from looking into the tent. I was reminded again of a sideshow—some irresistible spectacle everybody wanted to see.

The soldiers knew enough to open an avenue for the general. He strode inside the tent. The priest sat on a stool next to the cot. He had removed the cloth from the Virginia soldier's face and was staring fixedly at it.

The general pushed the priest aside, took up the cloth used as a covering, and started to drop it across the soldier's face—then stopped abruptly. Even General Sullivan, in his rage, was moved by what he saw. He jerked back momentarily, his eyes unable to lift from the soldier's face. He handed the cloth to the priest. "You cover his face now, Father. And you keep it covered. I hereby forbid any man in this camp to look at this soldier's face ever again. Do you understand?"

Then he stormed from the tent.

The priest reluctantly obliged.

Then he angled his head up to me. "It won't be the same anymore, Doctor."

"What won't?"

"The camp. Every man in here has now seen his face." He nodded back to the soldier on the cot. "They'll never be the same again. I promise you."

In the evening, I ate stew and biscuits, and sipped at a small glass of wine. I was, as usual, in the officers' tent when the priest came and found me.

For a time, he said nothing beyond his greeting. He simply watched me at my meal, and then stared out the open flap at the camp preparing for evening, the fires in the center of the encampment, the weary men bedding down.

Many of them, healed now, would be back in the battle within two days or less.

"I spent an hour with him this afternoon," the priest said.

"The quarantined man?"

"Yes." The priest nodded. "Do you know some of the men have visited him five or six times?"

The way the priest spoke, I sensed he was gloating over the fact that the men were disobeying the general's orders. "Why don't the guards stop them?"

"The guards are in visiting him, too."

"The man says nothing. How can it be a visit?"

"He says nothing with his tongue. He says a great deal with his face." He paused, eyed me levelly. "I need to tell you something. You're the only man in this camp who will believe me." He sounded frantic. I almost felt sorry for him.

"Tell me what?"

"The man—he's not what we think."

"No?"

"No; his face—" He shook his head. "It's God's face."

"I see."

The priest smiled. "I know how I must sound."

"You've seen a great deal of suffering, Father. It wears on a person."

"It's God's face. I had a dream last night. The man's face shows us God's displeasure with the war. That's why the men are so moved when they see the man." He sighed, seeing he was not convincing me. "You say yourself he hasn't been wounded."

"That's true."

"And that all his vital signs seem normal."

"True enough, Father."

"Yet he's in some kind of shock."

"That seems to be his problem, yes."

The priest shook his head. "No, his real problem is that he's become overwhelmed by the suffering he's seen in this war—what each side has done to the other. All the pain. That's why there's so much sorrow on his face—and that's what the men are responding to. The grief on his face is the same grief they feel in their hearts. God's face."

"Once we get him to a real field hospital—"

And it was then we heard the rifle shots.

As the periphery of the encampment was heavily protected, we'd never heard firing this close.

The priest and I ran outside.

General Sullivan stood next to a group of young men with weapons. Several yards ahead, near the edge of the camp, lay three bodies, shadowy in the light of the campfire. One of the fallen men moaned. All three men wore our own gray uniforms.

Sullivan glowered at me. "Deserters."

"But you shot them in the back," I said.

"Perhaps you didn't hear me, Doctor. The men were deserting. They'd packed their belongings and were heading out."

One of the young men who'd done the shooting said, "It was the man's face, sir."

Sullivan wheeled on him. "It was what?"

"The quarantined man, sir. His face. These men said it made them sad and they had to see families back in Missouri, and that they were just going to leave no matter what."

"Poppycock," Sullivan said. "They left because they were cowards."

I left to take care of the fallen man who was crying out for help.

In the middle of the night, I heard more guns being fired. I lay on my cot, knowing it wasn't Yankees being fired at. It was our own deserters.

I dressed and went over to the tent where the quarantined man lay. Two young farm boys in ill-fitting gray uniforms stood over him. They might have been mourners standing over a coffin. They said nothing. Just stared at the man.

In the dim lamplight, I knelt down next to him. His vitals still seemed good, his heartbeat especially. I stood up, next to the two boys, and looked down on him myself. There was nothing remarkable about his face. He could have been any one of thousands of men serving on either side.

Except for the grief.

This time I felt the tug of it myself, heard in my mind the cries of the dying I'd been unable to save, saw the families and farms and homes destroyed as the war moved across the countryside, heard children crying out for dead parents, and parents sobbing over the bodies of their dead children. It was all there in his face, perfectly reflected, and I thought then of what the priest had said, that this was God's face, God's sorrow and displeasure with us.

The explosion came, then.

While the two soldiers next to me didn't seem to hear it at all, I rushed from the tent to the center of camp.

Several young soldiers stood near the ammunition cache. Someone had set fire to it. Ammunition was exploding everywhere, flares of red and yellow and gas-jet blue against the night. Men everywhere ducked for cover behind wagons and trees and boulders.

Into this scene, seemingly unafraid and looking like the lead actor in a stage production of *King Lear* I'd once seen, strode General Sullivan, still tugging on his heavy uniform jacket.

He went over to two soldiers who stood, unfazed, before the ammunition cache. Between explosions I could hear him shouting, ''Did you set this fire?''

And they nodded.

Sullivan, as much in bafflement as anger, shook his head. He signaled for the guards to come and arrest these men.

As the soldiers were passing by me, I heard one of them say to a guard, ''After I saw his face, I knew I had to do this. I had to stop the war.''

Within an hour, the flames died and the explosions ceased. The night was almost ominously quiet. There were a few hours before dawn, so I tried to sleep some more.

I dreamed of Virginia, green Virginia in the spring, and the creek where I'd fished as a boy, and how the sun had felt on my back and arms and head. There was no surgical table in my dream, nor were my shoes soaked with blood.

Around dawn somebody began shaking me. It was Sullivan's personal lieutenant. "The priest has been shot. Come quickly, Doctor."

I didn't even dress fully, just pulled on my trousers over the legs of my long underwear.

A dozen soldiers stood outside the tent looking confused and defeated and sad. I went inside.

The priest lay in his tent. His cassock had been torn away. A bloody hole made a targetlike circle on his stomach.

Above his cot stood General Sullivan, a pistol in his hand.

I knelt next to the cot and examined the priest. His vital signs were faint and growing fainter. He had at most a few minutes to live.

I looked up at the general. "What happened?"

The general nodded for the lieutenant to leave. The man saluted and then went out into the gray dawn.

"I had to shoot him," General Sullivan said.

I stood up. "You had to shoot a priest?"

"He was trying to stop me."

"From what?"

Then I noticed for the first time the knife scabbard on the general's belt. Blood streaked its sides. The hilt of the knife was sticky with blood. So were the general's hands. I thought of how Yankee troops had begun disfiguring the faces of our dead on the battlefield.

He said, "I have a war to fight, Doctor. The men—the way they were reacting to the man's face—" He paused and touched the bloody hilt of the knife. "I took care of him. And the priest came in while I was doing it and went insane. He started hitting me, trying to stop me and—" He looked down at the priest. "I didn't have any choice, Doctor. I hope you believe me."

A few minutes later, the priest died.

I started to leave the tent. General Sullivan put a hand on my shoulder. "I know you don't care very much for me, Doctor, but I hope you understand me at least a little. I can't win a war when men desert and blow up ammunition dumps and start questioning the worthiness of the war itself. I had to do what I did. I hope someday you'll understand.''

I went out into the dawn. The air smelled of camp fires and coffee. Now the men were busy scurrying around, preparing for war. The way they had been before the man had been brought here in the buckboard.

I went over to the tent where he was kept and asked the guard to let me inside. ''The general said nobody's allowed inside, Doctor.''

I shoved the boy aside and strode into the tent.

The cloth was still over his face, only now it was soaked with blood. I raised the cloth and looked at him. Even for a doctor, the sight was horrible. The general had ripped out his eyes and sawed off his nose. His cheeks carried deep gullies where the knife had been dug in deep.

He was dead. The shock of the defacement had killed him.

Sickened, I looked away.

The flap was thrown back, then, and there stood General Sullivan. ''We're going to bury him now, Doctor.''

In minutes, the dead soldier was inside a pine box borne up a hill of long grass waving in a chill wind. The rains came, hard rains, before they'd turned even two shovelfuls of earth.

Then, from a distance over the hill, came the thunder of cannon and the cry of the dying.

The face that reminded us of what we were doing to each other was no more. It had been made ugly, robbed of its sorrowful beauty.

He was buried quickly and without benefit of clergy— the priest himself having been buried an hour earlier—and when the ceremony was finished, we returned to camp and war.

CANDLES IN THE BOTTOM OF THE POOL

▼

Max Evans

Joshua Stone III moved along the cool adobe corridor listening to the massive walls. They were over three feet thick, the mud and straw solidified hard as granite. He appeared the same.

The sounds came to him faintly at first, then stronger. He leaned against the smooth dirt plaster and heard the clanking of armor, the twanging of bows, the screams of falling men and horses. His chest rose as his lungs pumped the excited blood. His powerful hands were grabbing their own flesh at his sides. It was real. Then the struggles of the olive conquerors and the brown vanquished faded away like a weak wind.

He opened his eyes, relaxing slightly, and stepped back, staring intently at the wall. Where was she? Would she still come to him smiling, waiting, wanting? Maybe. There was silence now. Even the singing of the desert birds outside could not penetrate the mighty walls.

Then he heard the other song. The words were unintelligible, ancient, from forever back, back, back, but he felt and understood their meaning. She appeared from the unfathomable reaches of the wall, undulating like a black wisp ripped from a tornado cloud. She was whole now. Her black lace dress clung to her body, emphasizing the delicious smoothness of her face and hands. The comb of Spanish silver glistened like a halo in her hair. His blue eyes stared at her dark ones across the centuries. They knew. She smiled with much warmth, and more. One hand beckoned for him to come. He smiled back, whispering, "Soon. Very soon."

"YES, YES, YES," she said, and the words vibrated about, over, through, under, and around everything. He stood, still staring, but there was only the dry mud now.

He turned, as yet entranced, then shook it off and entered through the heavily timbered archway into the main room. The light shafted in from the patio windows, illuminating the big room not unlike a cathedral. In a way it was. *Santos* and *bultos* were all over. The darkly stained furniture was from another time, hand hewn and permanent like the house itself.

He absorbed the room for a moment, his eyes caressing the old Indian pots spotted about, the rich color of the paintings from Spain, the cochineal rugs dyed from kermes bugs. Yes, the house was old; older than America. He truly loved its feeling of history, glory, and power.

Then his gaze stopped on the only discord in the room. It was a wildly colored, exaggerated painting of himself. He didn't like the idea of his portrait hanging there. He didn't need that. He allowed it only because his niece, Aleta, had done it. He was fond of her.

Juanita, the aged servant, entered with a tray. It held guacamole salad, tostados, and the inevitable Bloody Marys. He asked her in perfect Spanish where his wife, Carole, was.

She answered in English, "On the patio, señor. I have your drinks." She moved out ahead of him, bony, stiff, bent, but with an almost girlish quickness about her. She'd been with them for decades. They'd expected her demise for years, then given up.

Carole lounged in the desert sun, dozing the liquor away. He couldn't remember when she started drinking so heavily. He had to admit that she had a tough constitution—

almost as much as his own. It was usually around midnight before alcohol dulled her to retire. She removed the over-sized sunglasses and sat up as Juanita placed the tray on a small table by her. The wrinkles showed around the eyes, but her figure was still as good as ever. She rubbed at the lotion on her golden legs and then reached for her drink. At her movement, he had a fleeting desire to take her to bed. Was that what had brought them together? Was that what had held them until it was too late? Maybe. She pushed the burnt blonde hair back and placed the edge of the glass against her glistening lips. He thought the red drink was going down her throat like weak blood to give her strength for the day. He gazed out across the green mass of trees, grass, and bushes in the formal garden beyond the patio. He heard the little brook that coursed through it, giving life to the oasis just as the Bloody Marys did his wife.

It was late morning, and already the clouds puffed up beyond the parched mountains, promising much, seldom giving. It was as if the desert of cacti, lizards, scorpions, and coyotes between the mountains and the *hacienda* was too forbidding to pass over. It took many clouds to give the necessary courage to one another. It rarely happened.

He picked up his drink, hypnotized by the rising heat waves of the harsh land.

"I've decided," he said.

"You've decided what?"

"It's time we held the gathering."

She took another sip, set it down, and reached for a cig-arette. "You've been talking about that for three years, Joshua."

"I know, but I've made up my mind."

"When?"

"Now."

"Now? Oh God, it'll take days to prepare." She took another swallow of the red drink. "I'm just not up to it. Besides, Lana and Joseph are in Bermuda. Sheila and Ralph are in Honolulu."

"They'll come."

"You can't just order people away from their vaca-

tions." She took another swallow, pulled the bra of her
bikini up, walked over and sat down on the edge of the
pool, and dangled her feet in it. Resentment showed in her
back. He still felt a little love for her, which surprised him.
There was no question that his money and power had been
part of her attraction to him. But at first, it had been good.
They'd gone just about everywhere in the world together.
The fun, the laughs, the adventure had been there even
though some part of his business empire was always in-
truding. What had happened? Hell, why didn't he admit it?
Why didn't she? It had worn out. It was that simple. Just
plain worn out from the heaviness of the burdens of empire
like an old draft horse or a tired underground coal miner.

She splashed the water over her body, knowing from his
silence there was no use. "Well, we might as well get on
with it. When do you call?"

He finished the drink, stood up, and moved towards the
house, saying, "As I said, now."

Joshua entered the study. His secretary for the past ten
years looked up, sensing something in his determined
movement.

"All right, Charlotte."

She picked up the pad without questioning. He paced
across the Navajo rugs, giving her a long list of names.
Occasionally he'd run his hands down a row of books, playing them like an accordion. He really didn't like organization, but when he decided, he could be almost magical
at it. There was no hesitation, no lost thought or confusion.
He was putting together the "gathering" just as he'd ex-
panded the small fortune his father had left him. It kept
growing, moving.

When he finished dictating the names, he said, "We'll
have food indigenous to the Southwest. Tons of it. I want
for entertainment the Russian dancer from Los Angeles,
Alfredo and his guitar from Juárez, the belly dancer what's-
her-name from San Francisco, the mariachis from Mexico
City, and the brass group from Denver."

His whole huge body was vibrating now. A force exuded

from Joshua—the same force that had swayed decisions on many oil field deals, land developments, cattle domains, and, on occasion, even the stock market—but never had Charlotte seen him as he was now. There was something more, something she could not explain. Then he was done. He pushed at his slightly graying mass of hair and walked around the hand-carved desk to her. He pulled her head over to him and held it a moment against his side. They had once been lovers, but when she came to work for him that was over. There was still a tenderness between them. She was one of those women who just missed being beautiful all the way around, but she had a sensual appeal and a soft strength that was so much more. She had his respect, too, and that was very hard for him to give.

He broke the mood with, "Call Aleta and Rob first."

She took the book of numbers and swiftly dialed, asking, "Are you sure they're in El Paso?"

"Yes. Aleta's painting. She's getting ready for her show in Dallas." He took the phone, "Rob, is Aleta there?"

In El Paso, Rob gave an affirmative answer and put his hand over the phone: "Your Uncle *God* is on the horn."

Aleta wiped the paint from her hands and reached for the receiver. "Don't be so sarcastic, darling; he might leave you out of his will."

The vibrations were instantaneous down the wire between the man and the girl. She would be delighted to come.

When the conversation was over and Aleta informed her husband, he said, "The old bastard! He's a dictator. I'd just love to kill him!"

He finished with Lana and Joseph Helstrom in the Bahamas with, "No kids. Do you understand? This is not for children."

The husband turned to his wife, saying, "We're ordered to attend a gathering at Aqua Dulce."

"A gathering?"

"A party. You know how he is about labeling things."

"Oh Christ, two days on vacation and he orders us to a party."

"I could happily murder the son of a bitch and laugh for years," Joseph said, throwing a beach towel across the room against a bamboo curtain.

Finally, Joshua was finished. Charlotte got up and mixed them a scotch on the rocks from the concealed bar behind the desk. They raised their glasses, and both said at the same time, "To the gathering." They laughed together as they worked together.

Suddenly Charlotte set her glass down and, not having heard the phone conversations, stated almost omnipotently, "Half of them would delight in doing away with you."

Joshua nodded, smiling lightly. "You're wrong, love, a good two-thirds would gladly blow me apart, and all but a few of the others would wish them well."

"Touché."

"They do have a tendency to forget how they arrived at their present positions. However, that's not what concerns me. All are free to leave whenever they wish, but most don't have the guts. They like cinches but never acknowledge that on this earth no such thing exists. Even the sun is slowly burning itself to death."

"Another drink?"

"Of course. This is a moment for great celebration."

She poured the drinks efficiently, enjoying this time with him. Sensing something very special happening. Thrilled to share with him again.

They touched glasses across the desk, and he said, almost jubilantly, "To the Gods, goddamn them!"

Carole instructed Juanita in the cleaning and preparing of the house. She put old Martin, the head caretaker and yard man, and his two younger sons, to trimming the garden. This last was unnecessary because old Martin loved the leisure and independence of his job. He kept everything in shape anyway. It did, however, serve its purpose. Carole felt like she was doing *something*. In fact, an excitement she hadn't felt for a long time came upon her. She remembered the first really important entertaining she'd done for Joshua after their marriage. He was on a crucial Middle East oil deal.

It was in their New York townhouse in the days they were commuting around the world to various homes and apartments. She had really pulled a coup. Carole had worked closely with the sheik's male secretary and found what to her were some surprising facts. At first she'd intended to have food catered native to the guests' own country and utilize local belly dancers of the same origin. But after much consultation she served hamburgers and had three glowing, local-born blondes as dancing girls. The sheiks raved over the Yankee food they'd heard so much about and were obviously taken with the yellow-topped, fair-skinned dancing girls. They were also highly captivated by Carole herself. The whole thing had been a rousing success. Joshua got his oil concessions, and she had felt an enormous sense of accomplishment.

Today, as she moved about the vast *hacienda*, she felt some of that old energy returning. There was something different though. Her excitement was mounting, but it was more like one must feel stalking a man-eating tiger and knowing that at the next parting of the bushes they would look into each other's eyes.

Joshua checked out the wine cellar. He loved the silence and the dank smell. He touched some of the ancient casks as he had the history books in the study. He was drawn to old things now, remembering, recalling, conjuring up the history of his land . . . the great Southwest. He lingered long after he knew the supply of fine wines was more than sufficient. He moved the lantern back and forth, watching the shadows hide from the moving light. Carole had long wanted him to have electricity installed down here, but he'd refused. Some things need to remain as they are, he felt. Many of the old ways were better. Many worse. He'd wondered uncounted times why men who could build computers and fly to distant planets were too blind, or stupid, to select the best of the old and the best of the new and weld them together. He knew that at least the moderate happiness of mankind was that simple. An idiot could see it if he opened up and looked. It would not happen during Joshua's brief encounter with this planet. He knew it and was disgusted by it.

He set the lantern on a shelf and stood gazing at the wall ending the cellar. It was awhile before the visions would begin coming to him. He didn't mind. Time was both nothing and everything. Then he heard the hoofs of many horses walking methodically forward. It was like the beat of countless drumsticks against the earth. A rhythm, a pattern, a definite purpose in the sound. Closer. Louder. The song came as a sigh at first, then a whisper; finally it was clear and hauntingly lovely. He felt thousands of years old, perhaps millions, perhaps ageless. Colors in circular and elongated patterns danced about in the wall. Slowly they took form as if just being born. Swiftly now, they melded into shape, and he saw Cortés majestically leading his men and horses in clothing of iron. From the left came Montezuma and his followers in dazzling costumes so wildly colored they appeared to be walking rainbows. They knelt and prostrated themselves to the gods with four legs. Beauty had bent to force.

Joshua was witnessing the beginning of the Americas. The vision dissolved like a panoramic movie, and the song seeped away.

Then Oñate appeared, splashing his column across the Rio Grande at the pueblo of Juárez, and headed north up the river. The cellar suddenly reverberated with the swish of a sword into red flesh, and there was a huge, moving collage of churning, charging horses, and arrows whistling into the cracks of armor, and many things fell to the earth and became still. Oñate sat astride his horse surveying the compound of a conquered pueblo.

The song came again suddenly, shatteringly, crescendoing as Joshua's Spanish princess stood on a hill looking down. She came towards him, appearing to walk just above the earth. As she neared, smiling, with both arms out, he moved to the wall. As they came closer, he reached the wall with his arms outspread, trying to physically feel into it, but she was gone. He stayed thusly for a while, his head turned sideways, pushing his whole body against the dirt.

For a moment he sagged and took a breath into his body that released him. He turned, picked up the lantern, and zombied his way up to the other world. The one here.

All was ready. The tables were filled with every delicacy of the land from which Joshua, his father, and grandfathers twice back had sprouted. The *hacienda* shined from repeated dusting and polishing. A *cantina* holding many bottles from many other lands was set up in the main room, and an even greater display was waiting for eager hands, dry throats, and tight emotions in the patio.

Carole moved about, checking over and over that which was already done. Joshua had one chore left.

"Martin, drain the pool."

Martin looked at his master, puzzled. "But sir, the guests will . . ."

"Just drain the pool."

"Well . . . yes sir."

When Carole saw this, she hurried to Martin and asked in agitated confusion what in hell's madness possessed him to do such a thing.

"It was on orders of Mr. Joshua, madam."

"Then he's mad! We cleaned the pool only yesterday!"

She found Joshua in the study and burst in just as Charlotte finished rechecking her own list and was saying, "Everything has been done, Joshua. The doctors are even releasing Grebbs from the hospital so he can make it."

"Of course, I knew you'd take care of . . ."

"Joshua!"

He turned slowly to her.

"Have you lost all your sanity? Why did you have Martin drain the pool?"

"It's simple, my dear. Pools can become hypnotic and distracting. We have far greater forms of entertainment coming up."

She stood there unable to speak momentarily. She pushed at her hair and rubbed her perspiring palms on her hips, walking in a small circle around the room, finally giving utterance, "*I* know you're crazy, but do you want everyone else to know it?"

"It will give them much pleasure to finally find this flaw in my nature they have so desperately been seeking."

She turned and cascaded from the room, hurling back, "Oh, my God!"

Forty-eight hours later they came from all around the world. They arrived in jets, Rolls-Royces, Cadillacs, Mercedes, and pickup trucks. They moved to the *hacienda* magnetized.

The greetings were both formal and friendly, fearful and cheerful. Carole was at her gracious best, only half-drunk, expertly suppressing their initial dread with her trained talk. But there was a difference in the hands and arms and bodies that floated in the air towards Joshua. These appurtenances involved a massive movement of trepidation, hate, and fatherhood.

Joshua took Aleta in his grand and strong arms and lifted her from the floor in teasing love and respect. Her husband, Rob, died a little bit right there. His impulse of murder to the being of this man was intensified and verified. Rob wanted *in* desperately. He craved to become part of the Stone domain; craved to be part of the prestige and power. Marrying the favorite niece had seemed the proper first step. It hadn't worked. Joshua had never asked him, and Aleta absolutely forbade Rob to even hint at it. His lean, handsome face had a pinched appearance about it from the hatred. He had dwelled on it so long now that it was an obsession—an obsession to destroy that which he felt had ignored and destroyed him. It was unjustified. Joshua simply didn't want to see Rob subservient to him—not the husband of his artist niece. Aleta had never asked Joshua for anything but his best wishes. He felt that Rob must be as independent as she or else they wouldn't be married. He was wrong. Being a junior partner in a local stock brokerage firm didn't do it for Rob. And their being simply ordered here to Aleta's obvious joy had tilted his rage until he could hardly contain it.

Others—who were *in*—felt just as passionately about

Joshua, but they all had their separate and different reasons.

Lana and Joseph Helstrom certainly had a different wish for Joshua. Joseph just hadn't moved as high in the organization as swiftly as he felt he should, and Lana had a hidden yen for Joshua. In fact, she often daydreamed of replacing Carole.

And there was the senior vice president, Grebbs, who wanted and believed that Joshua should step up to the position of chairman of the board and allow him his long overdue presidency. He had lately been entering hospitals for checkups, which repeatedly disclosed nothing wrong— but then x-rays do not show hatred or they would have been white with explosions all over his body.

None of these things bothered Joshua now. The gathering grew in momentum of sound, emotion, and color. The drinks were consumed along with the food, and the talk was of many things. People split up into ever-changing groups. Those who had been to the *hacienda* before remarked about this alteration or that. Those who were new to its centuries made many, many comments about all the priceless objects of art and craft. Whether they hated or loved the master of the house, they were somehow awed and honored to be in this museum of the spirit of man and Joshua himself.

Alfredo, the guitarist from Juárez, played. His dark head bent over his instrument, and the long delicate fingers stroked from the wood and steel the tenderness of love, the savagery of death. It seemed that these songs, too, came from the walls. Maybe somehow they did.

The music surged into the total system of Joshua. He felt stronger, truer than ever before. He was ready now to make his first move—the beginning of his final commitment. He looked about the room, observing with penetration his followers. His eyes settled on Charlotte. And then, as if knowing, unable to resist, she came to him. She handed him a new scotch and water, holding her own drink with practiced care. He turned, and she followed at his side. They wandered to the outer confines of the house—to his childhood room. She did not question. He turned on a small lamp that still left many shadows.

"My darling," he said softly, touching the walls with one hand, "this is where it all started."

She looked at him, puzzled, but with patience.

"I think I was five when I first heard the walls. It was gunfire and screams, and I knew it had once happened here. You see, this, in the days of the vast Spanish land grants, was a roadhouse, a *cantina*, an oasis where the dons and their ladies gathered to fight and fornicate. They are in the walls, you know, and I hear them. I even see them. I had just turned thirteen when I first *saw* into the walls."

Joshua's eyes gleamed like a coyote's in lantern light. His breath was growing, and there was an electricity charging through all his being. Charlotte was hypnotized at his voice and what was under it. His hand moved down the walls as he told her of some of the things he'd seen and heard. Then he turned to her and raised his glass for a toast.

"To you, dear loyal, wonderful Charlotte, my love and my thanks."

"It has all been a fine trip with you, Joshua. I could not have asked more from life than to have been a part of you and what you've done. Thank you, thank you."

He took the drink from her hand and set it on a dresser. Taking her gently by the arm, he pulled her to the wall. "Now lean against it and listen and you, too, will hear." She did so, straining with all her worth. "Listen! Listen," he whispered, and his powerful hands went around her neck. She struggled very little, and in a few moments she went limp. He held her a brief second longer, bending to kiss her on the back of the neck he'd just broken. Then with much care he picked her up, carried her to the closet, and placed her out of sight behind some luggage. He quietly closed the door, standing there a while looking at it. He moved, picked up his drink, and returned to his people.

In the patio, Misha, the Russian dancer from Kavkaz on Sunset Boulevard, was leaping wildly about, crouching, kicking. A circle formed around him, and the bulk of

Joshua Stone III dominated it all. He was enjoying himself to the fullest, clapping his hands and yelling encouragement. The dance had turned everyone on a few more kilocycles. They started drinking more, talking more and louder, even gaining a little courage.

The gray, fiftyish Grebbs tugged at Joshua, trying to get his true attention. He kept bringing up matters of far-flung business interests. He might remind one in attitude of a presidential campaign manager, just after a victory, wondering if he'd be needed now. He rubbed at his crew cut hair nervously, trying to figure an approach to Joshua. His gray eyes darted about slightly. His bone-edged nose presented certain signs of strength and character, but weakness around the mouth gave him away. He was clever and did everything that cleverness could give to keep all underlings out of touch with Joshua. He had hoped for a while that this gathering had been called to announce Joshua's chairmanship, and the fulfillment of his own desperate dream.

Joshua motioned to Lotus Flower, the belly dancer, and she moved gracefully out into the patio ahead of the music. Then the music caught up with her. The Oriental lady undulated and performed the moves that have always pleased men.

As Grebbs tugged at Joshua again, he said, without taking his eyes from the dancer, "Grebbs, go talk business to your dictaphone." Just that. Now Grebbs knew. He moved away, hurting.

Lana stood with Carole. They were both watching Joshua with far different emotions.

Lana spoke first, about their mutual interest. "Has Joshua put on some weight?"

"No, it's the same old stomach."

"He's always amazed everyone with his athletic abilities."

"Really?" This last had a flint edge to it.

"Well, for a man who appears so awkward, it is rather surprising to find how swiftly and strongly he can move when he decides to. Carole, you do remember the time he leaped into Spring Lake and swam all the way across it, and then just turned around and swam all the way back. You must remember that, darling. We all had such a good time.''

"Oh, I remember many things, *darling*."

Rob was saying to Joseph Helstrom, "There's something wrong here. I feel it. Here it's only September, and he's already drained the pool."

Joseph touched his heavy-rimmed glasses and let the hand slowly slide down his round face. "Yeah, he demanded we all come here on instant notice, and he's not really with us."

"The selfish bastard." Rob exhaled this like ridding himself of morning spittum.

The dancer swirled ever closer to Joshua, her head back, long black hair swishing across her shoulders. He smiled, absorbed in the movement of flesh as little beams of hatred were cast across the patio from Grebbs, Rob, Joseph—and others. Joshua didn't care—didn't even feel it. As the dance finished, Rob walked out into the garden and removed a small automatic pistol from the back of his belt under his jacket. He checked the breech and replaced the gun.

Joshua worked his way through the crowd, spoken to and speaking back in a distracted manner. His people looked puzzled after his broad back. He made his way slowly down the stairs towards the wine cellar, one hand caressing the wall. He stopped and waited. The song came from eternities away, soft, soothing, amidst the whispers of men planning daring moves.

The whole wall now spun with colors slowly forming into warriors. Then, there before Joshua's eyes was Esteban, the black man, standing amidst the Pueblo Indians. Joshua had always felt that Esteban was one of the most exciting and mysterious—even neglected—figures in the history of America. It has never been settled for sure how or why he arrived in the Southwest. However, his influence would always be there. He had started the legend of the Seven Golden Cities of Cíbola, which Coronado and many others searched for in vain. He was a major factor in the Pueblo Revolt of 1680, afterwards becoming the chief of several of these communities. He became a famous medicine man and was looked on as a god. But, like all earthly gods, he fell. A seven-year drought came upon the land of the Tewas, and when he could not dissipate it, he was blamed for it. They killed him, and the superstitious Zuñis skinned him like a deer to see if he was black all the way through.

Now, at last, Joshua was looking upon this man of dark skin and searing soul, as he spoke in the Indian tongue to his worshippers. He talked to them of survival without the rule of iron. They mumbled low in agreement. Maybe Joshua would learn some of the dark secrets before this apparition dissolved back to dried mud.

Joshua watched as up and down the river the Indians threw rock and wood at steel in savage dedication. Men died screaming in agony, sobbing their way painfully to the silence of death. The river flowed peacefully before him now, covering the entire wall and beyond. Then the feet splashed into his view, and he saw the remnants of the defeated Spanish straggle across the river back into Mexico.

Joshua's Spanish lady in black lace sat on a smooth, round rock staring across a valley dripping with the gold of autumn. She was in a land he'd never seen. She turned her head toward him and gave a smile that said so much he couldn't stand it. He reached towards the wall, and she nodded her head up and down and faded away with the music. Silence. More silence. Then, "Joshua."

He turned. It was Lana. She moved to him, putting her hands on his chest. "Joshua, what is it? You're acting so strangely."

"Did you see? Did you hear?" he asked, looking out over her head.

"I . . . I . . . don't know what you mean, darling. See what?"

"Nothing. Nothing." He sighed.

"Can I help? Is there *anything* I can do?"

He pulled her against him and kissed her with purpose. She was at first surprised and then gave back to him. He picked her up and shoved her violently against the wooden frame between two wine barrels.

"No, no, not here."

"There is no other time," he said. "No other place." As he reached under her, one elbow struck a spigot on a barrel. He loved her standing there while a thin stream of red wine poured out on the cellar floor, forming an immediate pool not unlike blood.

She uttered only one word, "Joshua," and the wine sound continued.

Both he and Lana were back among the people now. Carole came to him.

"Where've you been? Where is Charlotte? The phone is ringing constantly. Where is she?"

"She's on vacation."

"Today? I can't believe you, Joshua. You always bragged about how she was there when you needed her."

"We don't need her now."

"You really are mad. Mad! Today of all days we need her to answer the phone."

"Take the damned phone off the hook. No one ever calls good news on a phone, anyway. If they have anything good to say, they come and see you personally." He walked away and left her standing there looking after him in much confusion.

All afternoon he had been wanting to visit his old friend Chalo Gonzales from the Apache Reservation. They met when they were kids. Chalo's father had worked the nearby orchards and alfalfa fields for Joshua's father. He and Chalo hunted, fished, adventured together off and on for years. He'd gone with him to the reservation many times and learned much of nature and Indian ways. Chalo had given him as much as anyone—things of real value. He found him dressed in a regular business suit and tie, but he wore a band around his coarse, dark hair.

"Ah, amigo, let's walk in the garden away from this . . ." and he made a gesture with his arm to the scattered crowd. "How does it go with you and your people?"

"Slow, Joshua, but better. As always, there's conflict with the old and the young. The old want to stay with their own ways. The young want to rush into the outside world."

"It's the nature of youth to be impatient. It can't be helped."

"Oh, sure, that is the truth. But our young want to take the best of the old and good ways with them. They want both sides now. Now."

"That's good, Chalo. They're right."

"But nothing happens that fast. It has been too many centuries one way. You can't change it in a few years."

"It's a big problem I admit, but you will survive and finally win. You always have, you know."

"You've always given me encouragement. I feel better already."

They talked of hunts, and later adventures when they both came home for the summer from school. Chalo had been one of few to make it from his land to Bacone, the Indian college.

Joshua felt Chalo was his equal. He was comfortable with him. They stood together and talked in a far recess of the secluded garden where they could see the mountains they'd so often explored. Joshua felt a surge of love for his old friend. He knew what he must do. He'd spotted the root a few minutes back. He didn't dare risk it with his hands. Chalo was almost as strong as he was in both will and muscle.

He picked up the root and began drawing designs with it in a spot of loose ground, as men will do who are from the earth. Then, as his friend glanced away, Joshua swung it with much force, striking him just back of the ear. He heard the bone crunch and was greatly relieved to know he wouldn't have to do more. Without any wasted time, he dragged and pushed him into a thick clump of brush. He checked to see if the body was totally hidden, tossed the root in after it, walked to the wall, and looked out across the desert to the mountains again. He was very still; then he turned, smiling ineluctably, and proceeded to the party.

• • •

Dusk came swiftly and hung awhile, giving the party a sudden subdued quality. It was the time of day that Joshua liked best. He finally escaped the clutchers and went to his study, locking the door and grinning at the phone Carole had taken off the hook and deliberately dangled across the lamp.

He drew the shades back and sat there absorbed in the hiding sun, and watched the glowing oranges and reds turn to violet and then a soft blue above the desert to the west. He knew that life started stirring there with the death of the sun. The coyotes and bobcats were already moving, sniffing the ground and the air for other living creatures. Many mice, rabbits, and birds would die this night so they could live. The great owl would soon be swooping above them in direct competition. The next day the sun would be reborn, and the vultures would dine on any remains, keeping the desert clean and in balance.

Someone knocked on the door. It was Carole.

"Joshua, are you in there?" Then louder, "Joshua, I know you're there because the door is locked from the inside. What are you doing with the door locked anyway?" Silence. "At least you could come and mix with your guests. You did *invite* them, you know." She pounded on the door now. "My God, at least speak to me. I am your wife, you know." Silence. She turned in frustration and stamped off down the hall, mumbling about his madness.

Joshua turned his lounge chair away from the window and stared at the wall across the room. There were things he had to see before he made the final move. Pieces of the past that he must reconstruct properly in his mind before he took the last step.

It did come. As always he heard it first, then saw it form, whirling like pieces of an abstract world—a new world, an old world, being broken and born, falling together again. The Spanish returned. They came now with fresh men, armor, horses, and cannon. They marched and rode up the Rio Grande setting up the artillery, blasting the adobe walls to dust. Then they charged with sabers drawn and whittled the shell-shocked Indians into slavery. They mined the gold from the virgin mountains with the Indians as their tools. And then it all vanished inwardly.

There was quiet and darkness now until he heard his name. "Joshua, Joshua, Joshua." It came floating from afar as if elongated, closer, closer. She was there. He leaned forward in the chair, his body tense, anxious. She stood by a river of emerald green. It was so clear that he could see the separate grains of white sand on its bottom. The trees, trunks thicker than the *hacienda*, rose into the sky. They went up, up past his ability to see. The leaves were as thick as watermelons, and fifty people could stand in the shade of a single leaf. The air danced with the light of four suns shafting great golden beams down through the trees.

She moved towards him through one of the beams and for a moment vanished with its brilliance. Now she was whole again, standing there before him. He ached to touch her. He hurt. An endless string of silver fish swam up the river now. The four suns penetrated the pure water and made them appear to be parts of a metallic lava flow from a far-off volcano. But they were fish, moving relentlessly, with no hesitation whatsoever, knowing their destination and fate without doubt.

Again the word came from her as she turned and walked down the river, vanishing behind a tree. "Joshua."

For a fleeting moment he heard the song. He closed his eyes. When he opened them, there was just the darkness of the room. He didn't know how long he sat there before returning to the party.

He moved directly to the bar in the patio and ordered a double scotch and water. His people were scattered out now, having dined, and were back into the drinking and talking. The volume was beginning to rise again. It was second wind time. As the bartender served the drink, he felt something touch his hand. It was Maria Windsor.

She smiled like champagne pouring, her red lips pulling back over almost startling white teeth. She smiled with her blue eyes, too.

"It has been such a long time," she said.

"Maria, goddamn, it's good to see you." And he hugged

her, picking her off the floor without intending to. She was
very small and at first appeared to be delicate. But this was
a strong little lady. She was a barmaid in his favorite place
in El Paso when he first met her. He'd always deeply admired the polite and friendly smoothness with which she
did her job. One never had to wait for a drink, the ashtray
was emptied at the proper moment, and she knew when to
leave or when to stand and chat. Joshua had introduced her
to John Windsor, one of his junior vice presidents, and now
they were married.

"I love the portrait Aleta did of you."

"Well, I feel embarrassed hanging it there, but what
could I do after she worked so hard on it? How are you
and John getting along?" he asked.

"How do you mean? Personally or otherwise?"

"Oh, all around I suppose."

"Good," she said. "Like all wives, I think he works too
hard sometimes, but I suppose that's natural. Here he comes
now."

John shook hands and greeted his boss without showing
any apparent fear and revealing a genuine liking for him.
He once told Maria that he'd love Joshua to his death, just
for introducing her to him. He was about five eleven,
straight and well-muscled, and had thick brown hair that he
wore longer than anyone in the whole international organization. He, too, had a nice, white smile.

Joshua ordered a round for the three of them. He raised
his glass: "My friends, you'll be receiving a memo in the
next few days that I think you will enjoy. Here's to it."
Several days before the party, Joshua had made out a paper
giving John Windsor control of the company. It had not
been delivered yet.

He left them glowing in anticipation and went to find his
favorite kin, Aleta. As he moved, the eyes of hatred moved
with him . . . drunker now, braver. He walked into the garden, bowing, speaking here and there, but not stopping. The
moon, hung in place by galactic gravity, beamed back the
sun in a blue softness. The insects and night birds hummed
a song in the caressing desert breeze. The leaves on the

trees moved just enough to make love. There was a combination of warmth and coolness that only the desert can give.

Aleta had seen her uncle and somehow knew he was looking for her. She came to him from where she'd been sitting on a tree that was alive but bent to the ground. She'd been studying the light patterns throughout the garden for a painting she had in mind.

"Uncle Joshua, it's time we had a visit."

He took both her hands and stood back looking at her. "Yes, it's time, my dear. You are even more beautiful than the best of your paintings."

"Well, Uncle, that's not saying much," she said, being pleasingly flattered just the same.

He led her to an archway and opened the iron gate. They walked up a tiny, rutted wagon road into the desert. The sounds of the gathering became subdued. The yucca bushes and Joshua trees—that he'd been named after—speared the sky like frozen battalions of soldiers on guard duty forever.

"Remember when we used to ride up this trail?" she asked.

"Yes, it seems like yesterday."

"It seems like a hundred years ago to me."

He laughed. "Time has a way of telescoping in and out according to your own time. That's the way it should be. You were a tough little shit," he added with fondness. "You were the only one who could ride with me all day."

"That was simple bullheadedness. I knew I was going to be an artist someday, and you have to have a skull made of granite to be an artist."

He was amused by her even now. "But you also had a bottom made of rawhide."

They talked of some of her childhood adventures they'd shared. Then the coyotes howled off in a little draw. The strollers stood like the cacti, listening, absorbing the oldest cry left.

When the howls stopped, he spoke: "I love to hear them. I always have. I even get lonely to hear them. They're the only true survivors."

"That somehow frightens me," she said with a little shudder.

"It shouldn't. You should be encouraged. As long as they howl, people have a chance here on earth. No longer, no less. It is the final cry for freedom. It's hope."

They walked on silently for a spell. "You really are a romantic, Uncle. When I hear people say how cold you are, I laugh to myself."

"You know, Aleta darling, you're the only person who never asked me for anything."

"I didn't have to. You've always given me love and confidence. What more could you give?"

"I don't know. I wish I did."

"No, Uncle, there's no greater gift than that."

"Aleta, the world is strange. Mankind has forgotten what was always true—that a clean breath is worth more than the most elegant bank building. A new flower opening is more beautiful than a marble palace. All things rot. Michelangelo's sculpture is even now slowly breaking apart. All empires vanish. The largest buildings in the world will turn back to sand. The great paintings are cracking, the negatives of the best films ever made are right now losing their color and becoming brittle. The tallest mountains are coming down a rock at a time. Only thoughts live. You are only what you think."

"That's good," she said, "then I'm a painting, even if I am already beginning to crack."

He liked her words and added some of his own: "You know, honey, the worms favor the rich."

"Why?"

He rubbed his great belly. "Because they're usually fatter and more easily digestible."

"Do you speak of yourself?"

"Of course," he smiled. The coyotes howled again, and he said, "I love you, my dear Aleta."

"And I love you."

He stroked her hair and moved his hand downward. It had to be swift, clean. With all his strength, even more than he'd ever had before. He grabbed her long, graceful neck and twisted her head. He heard the bones rip apart. She gasped only once, and then a long sigh of her last breath exuded from her. He gathered her carefully in his arms and walked out through the brush to the little draw where the coyotes had so recently hunted. Then he stretched her out on the ground with her hands at her sides and gently brushed her hair back. She slept in the moonlight.

He walked swiftly back to the *hacienda*. As he left the garden for the patio, Rob stepped in front of him.

"Joshua, have you seen Aleta?"

"Of course, my boy, of course."

"Well, where is she?"

"Look, I don't follow your wife around. She's certainly more capable than most of taking care of herself." Joshua moved on. Rob followed him a few steps, looking at his back with glazed eyes.

Grebbs grabbed at him in one last desperate hope that Joshua was saving the announcement to the last.

"Joshua, I have to talk with you. Please."

Joshua stopped and looked at the man. He was drunk, and that was something Grebbs rarely allowed himself to be in public. He looked as if pieces of flesh were about to start dropping down into his clothing. His mouth was open, slack and watery.

Joshua said, with a certainty in his voice that settled Grebbs's question, "Grebbs, you're a bad drinker. I have no respect for bad drinkers." And he moved on.

Grebbs stared at the same back the same way Rob had. He muttered, actually having trouble keeping from openly crying, "The bastard. The dirty bastard. I'll kill you! You son of a bitch!"

The thing some of these people had been uttering about Joshua now possessed them. A madness hovered about, waiting for the right moment, and then swiftly moved into them. Now all the people of music started playing at once. The Russian was dancing even more wildly, if not so expertly. The belly dancer swished about from man to man, teasing. The mariachis walked about in dominance for a while, then the brass group would break through. It was a

cacophony of sound that entered the heads of all there . . .
throbbing like blood poison.

Carole started sobbing uncontrollably. Lana began cursing her husband, Joseph, in vile terms—bitterly, with total
malice. Joseph just reached out and slapped her down
across the chaise lounge, and a little blood oozed from the
corner of her mouth. He could only think of a weapon, any
weapon to use on the man who he felt was totally responsible for the matrix of doom echoing all around. We always
must have something to hate for our own failures and
smallness. But this did not occur to Joseph, or Lana, or
Carole, or the others. Only Alfredo, the guitarist, sat alone
on the same old bent tree that Aleta had cherished, touching
his guitar with love.

Maria took John aside and told him they were leaving,
that something terrible was happening. She was not—and
could not be—a part of it. He hesitated but listened. They
did finally drive away, confused, but feeling they were
right.

Grebbs dazedly shuffled to the kitchen looking for a
knife, but old Juanita and her two sisters were there. He
then remembered an East Indian dagger that lay on the
mantel in the library as a paperweight. In his few trips to
the *hacienda* he'd often studied it, thinking what a pleasure
it would be to drive it into the jerking heart of Joshua Stone
III.

He picked it up and pulled the arched blade from the
jeweled sheath. He touched the sharp unused point with
shaking fingers. At that precise instant, Rob felt in the back
of his belt and touched the automatic. He removed it and
put it in his jacket pocket. Joseph Helstrom looked about
the patio for an instrument to satisfy his own destructive
instincts.

Joshua entered the door to the cellar, shut it, and shoved
the heavy iron bolt into place. He called on all his resources
now in another direction. An implosion to the very core of
time struck Joshua. Now, right now, he must visualize all
the rest of the history of his land that occurred before his
first childish awareness. Then, and only then, could he

make his last destined move. It began to form. The long lines of Conestoga wagons tape-wormed across the prairies and struggled through the mountain passes, bringing goods and people from all over the world to settle this awesome land. They came in spite of flood, droughts, blizzards, Indian attacks, and disease. They were drawn here by the golden talk of dreamers, and promising facts.

The ruts of the Santa Fe Trail were cut so deep they would last a century. The mountain men took the last of the beaver from the sweet, churning waters of the mountains above Taos and came down to trade, to dance the wild fandangos, to drink and pursue the dark-eyed lovelies of that village of many flags.

A troop of cavalry charged over the horizon into a camp of Indians, and the battle splashed across the adobe valleys in crimson. Thousands of cattle and sheep were driven there and finally settled into their own territories. Cowboys strained to stay aboard bucking horses, and these same men roped and jerked steers, thumping them hard against the earth. They gambled and fought and raised hell in the villages of deserts and mountains, creating written and filmed legends that covered the world more thoroughly than Shakespeare.

The prospectors walked over the mountains searching for—and some finding—large deposits of gold, silver, and copper. And, as always, men of money took away the rewards of their labors and built themselves great palaces.

And Joshua saw the Italians, Chinese, and many other nationalities driving the spikes into the rail ties. The trains came like the covered wagons before them—faster, more powerful—hauling more people and goods than ever before. The double-bitted axes and two-man saws cut the majestic pines of the high places, taking away the shelter of the deer, lion, and bear.

Now Joshua closed his eyes, for he knew all the rest. When he opened them, he heard the song begin again. It was both older and newer each time he heard it. There was a massive adobe church, and his lady walked right through the walls and into the one he sat staring at. Now, as she spoke his name, he knew his final move was near. For the first time, he turned away from her and headed for the door. She smiled, somehow exactly like the song.

As he opened the door and pulled it shut, he felt a presence come at him. He was so keyed up, so full of his feelings, that he just stepped aside and let it hurtle past. It was Grebbs. He'd driven the dagger so deep into the door that he couldn't pull it out to strike again. Grebbs had missed all the way. Joshua gathered him up around the neck with one hand, jerked the dagger from the door with the other, and smashed him against the wall. He shoved the point of the dagger just barely under the skin of Grebbs's guts. Grebbs's eyes bulged, and he almost died of fright right there, but the hand of his master cut any words off. It was quite a long moment for the corporate vice president.

"What I should do, Grebbs, is cut your filthy entrails out and shove them down your dead throat. But that's far too easy for you."

Joshua dropped him to the floor and drove the knife to the hilt in the door. He then strode up the stairs three at a time, hearing only a low, broken sob below him.

As he entered the world of people again, Carole grabbed at him, visibly drunk and more. She said, "God! God! What are you doing?" He moved on from her as she shrieked, "You don't love me!" He ignored this, too, and when she raked her painted claws into the back of his neck, he ignored that as well. She stood looking at her fingers and the bits of bloody flesh clinging to her nails.

Rob blocked his way, again demanding attention. "I'm asking you for the last time! Do you hear me? Where is Aleta?"

He pushed the young man aside, saying as he went, "I'll tell you in a few minutes." This surprised and stopped Rob right where he stood.

Then Joshua raised his arms and shouted, "Music, you fools! Play and dance!" The drunken musicians all started up again, jerky, horrendously out of synchronization.

Joshua went to the kitchen and very tenderly lifted an exhausted and sleeping Juanita from her chair. He explained to her two sisters that he would take Juanita to her room on the other side of the *hacienda*. They were glad and went on cleaning up. He led her slowly out a side door. On the other side of many walls could be heard the so-called music sailing up, dissipating itself in the peaceful desert air.

As he walked the bent old woman along, he spoke to her softly, "It's time for you to rest, Juanita. You've been faithful all these decades. Your sisters can do the labors. You will have time of your own now. A long, long time that will belong just to you. You've served many people who did not even deserve your presence."

There was an old well near the working shed where her little house stood. They stopped here.

"Juanita, you are like this—this dried-up well. It gave so much for so long, it now has no water left."

He pulled the plank top off. Juanita was weary and still partially in the world of sleep. Joshua steadied the bony old shoulders with both his hands. He looked at her in the moonlight and said, "Juanita, you are a beautiful woman."

She twitched the tiniest of smiles across her worn face and tilted her head just a little in an almost girlish move.

Then he said, "Juanita, I love you." He slipped a handkerchief from his pocket, crammed it into her mouth, jerked her upside down, and hurled her head-first into the well. There was just a crumpled thud. No more.

In the patio, the music was beginning to die. A dullness had come over the area. A deadly dullness. But heads started turning, one, two, three at a time towards the *hacienda* door. Their center of attention, Joshua, strode amongst them. There were only whispers now. Joshua saw a movement and stopped. The heavy earthen vase smashed to bits in front of him. He looked up, and there on a low wall stood Helstrom like a clown without makeup. He, too, had missed.

Joshua grabbed him by both legs and jerked him down against the bricks of the patio floor. He hit, and his head bounced. Joshua gripped him by the neck and the side of one leg and tossed him over and beyond the wall.

He turned slowly around, his eyes covering all the crowd. No one moved. Not at all. He walked back through them to the house and in a few moments returned. He carried a huge silver candelabra, from the first Spanish days, with twenty lighted candles. He walked with it held high. None moved, except to get out of his way. Alfredo sat on the edge of the empty pool. His feet dangled down into its empty space. He tilted his head the way only he could do and softly, so very softly, strummed an old Spanish love song—a song older than the *hacienda*. Joshua walked to the steps of the pool and with absolute certainty of purpose stepped carefully down into it. It seemed a long time, but it was not. He placed the candelabra in the deepest part of the pool, stepped back, and looked into the flames. Then he raised his head and stared upwards at all the faces that now circled the pool to stare down at him. He turned in a complete circle so that he looked into the soft reflections in each of their eyes. He was all things in that small turn. None of them knew what *they* were seeing. He walked back up the steps, and there stood Rob.

Joshua said, "Come now, Rob, and I'll tell you what you really want to know."

Alfredo went on singing in Spanish as if he were making quiet love. The circle still looked downwards at the glowing candles.

Near the largest expanse of wall on the whole of the *hacienda*, Joshua said quietly to Rob, "I killed her. I took her into the desert and killed sweet Aleta."

Rob was momentarily paralyzed. Then a terrible cry and sound of murder burst from him as he ripped the edge of his pocket pulling out the gun. He fired right into the chest of Joshua, knocking him against the wall. He pulled at the trigger until there was nothing left. Joshua stayed upright for a moment, full of holes, and then fell forward, rolling over, face up. The crowd from the pool moved towards Rob, hesitantly, fearfully. They made a half-circle around the body.

Rob spoke, not looking away from Joshua's dead, smiling face as if afraid he'd rise up again, "He killed Aleta."

Grebbs, saying things unintelligible like a slavering idiot, pushed his way through the mass, stopping with his face above Joshua's. Then he vented a little stuttering laugh. It broke forth louder and louder, and haltingly the others were caught up with him. They laughed and cried at the same time, not knowing really which they were doing. None thought to look at the wall above the body. It didn't matter, though, for all those who might have seen were already there. On a thin-edged hill stood Charlotte the dedicated, Aleta the beloved, Chalo the companion, and old Juanita the faithful. They were in a row, smiling with contentment. Just below them, the lady in black lace walked forward to meet Joshua.

As he moved into the wall, there came from his throat another form of laughter that far, far transcended the hysterical cackling in the patio. He glanced back just once, and the song overcame his mirth. He took her into his arms and held her. They had waited so very long. It was over. They walked, holding hands, up the hill to join those he loved, and they all disappeared into a new world.

The wall turned back to dirt.

None could stay at the *hacienda* that night. Just before the sun announced the dawn, the last candle in the bottom of the pool flickered out. The light was gone.

THE SHAMING OF BROKEN HORN

▼
▼

Bill Gulick

Toward sundown of the second day after the train reached Fort Hall, Harlan Faber, elected wagon captain, called a meeting of the emigrant families, as was the custom when a question affecting them all had to be voted on. Well aware by now that this western land was a man's land in which a woman must keep silent, Mary Bailey told her pa she guessed she'd stay by their wagons and catch up on the mending. But her pa said, "You got a right to be there. I want you to help me make up my mind which way to vote."

"Your mind's already made up, isn't it, Pa?"

"I know what I'd like to do, sure. But I want you at that meeting. Since your ma left us, you've taken her place, seems like."

So Mary went along, carrying some mending with her to keep her hands busy, standing at the edge of the crowd with her lanky, gray-haired, slow-spoken pa, Jed, and her younger brother, Mike, who was slim, dark-eyed and, at fourteen, beginning to consider himself an adult. Mary, a pretty, black-haired, grave young lady of eighteen, had put away childish notions years ago.

Facing the crowd stood Harlan Faber. With him were Peter Kent, factor of Fort Hall; Broken Horn, the fierce-eyed Bannock chief whose imperious edict had brought on this present crisis; Tim Ramsey, guide for the wagon train; and a pair of American trappers who had drifted into the trading post the day before. Faber raised his hand for silence.

"You folks all know what this meeting's about. The trail forks here. What we got to decide is whether we want to go on to Oregon, like we'd planned, or change our plans and go to Californy."

As the wagon captain outlined the situation facing the emigrants, Mary studied the two American trappers curiously, for there were strange tales of these wild, rootless men. Both wore ragged, grease-stained buckskins and had an alert, almost savage look about them. To the stooped, older man, Charley Huff, she gave no more than a brief glance; but the younger man, Dave Allen, standing to tall and straight, was so handsome and had such nice gray eyes that she stared at him shamelessly.

"If we go to Oregon," Faber was saying, "we'll have to pass through Bannock country. The Bannocks are on the warpath against Americans, Broken Horn says, an' will fight us every step of the way. But if we turn south an' head fer Californy, stayin' clear of Bannock country, Broken Horn says his bucks won't pester us. That's how matters stand. Speak up, men, an' tell me how you feel."

One by one the men spoke their sentiments, while their womenfolk listened in silence. Jed whispered, "Well, Mary?"

"It's up to you, Pa. It's whatever you want to do."

"It's the seedlings I'm thinkin' about. To bring a whole wagonload of 'em this far, then give up—"

"Jed Bailey!" Faber called out. "You got anything to say?"

New England born and bred, Jed shifted his weight from one foot to the other, cocked his head at the sky as if looking for sign of rain, then said slowly, "Does it freeze in Californy, come winter?"

Tim Ramsey said no it didn't, normally. Peter Kent and the two trappers agreed. Faber let his eyes run over the crowd. "Any more questions 'fore we take a vote?"

"Get on with it!" a man shouted. "Call the roll!"

"All right." Faber took a sheet of paper out of his pocket. "Joshua Partridge."

"Here!"

"I know you're here, you blamed fool! How do you vote?"

"Californy!"

"Frank Lutcher."

"Californy!"

"Matthew Honleiker."

"Californy!"

And so it went, down through the list until forty-nine names had been called. Now, with only one name left, the wagon captain paused, looked at Jed, then said, "Jedidiah Bailey."

Jed studied the blue sky and the far reach of parched land to the west. At last he said, "A man can't grow decent apples in country where it don't freeze."

"That ain't an answer, Jed. How do you vote?"

"Oregon."

Mary heard a murmuring run through the crowd. "Stubborn old fool . . . Jed Bailey and his damned apple trees . . . Let him git scalped. . . ."

Faber tallied the list. "Results of the vote. Fer Californy, forty-nine. Fer Oregon, one. Majority rules, as agreed. We'll pull out first thing in the mornin' fer Californy." He looked angrily at Jed. "Forty-nine of us, anyhow. I wash my hands of you, Jed Bailey. Meetin's adjourned."

The Bailey family walked back to their wagons in silence, Mary feeling proud of her pa, but not knowing how to put it into words. Mike went out to check on the grazing mules. Jed took a pair of wooden buckets and headed for the creek to get water for the seedlings. Mary readied supper. It being early July, dark came late and though the sun had sunk by the time she called her menfolk to supper—a good meat stew filled with fresh vegetables grown in the Fort Hall garden, baked beans sweetened with molasses, hot biscuits and dried-apple pie—there was still plenty of twilight left when they finished eating. Because she loved her pa and knew how worried he was, Mary treated him extra good.

"More pie, Pa?"

"Thank you kindly, Mary, but I reckon not." He gave her a gentle smile. "You're a fine cook, girl, just like your ma was. The man that marries you will get a real prize."

"Fiddlesticks!" Mary said, but the praise pleased her just the same.

Lighting his pipe, Jed brooded into the fire while Mike got out cleaning stick, rag and oil and set to work cleaning his rifle. Busy with the dishes, Mary did not hear the visitors approach until Peter Kent said, "Good evening, Mr. Bailey. May I have a word with you?"

"Sure. What's on your mind?"

Turning around, Mary got the fright of her life, for standing an arm's reach away was that murderous-looking Indian, Broken Horn. Likely she would have screamed if she hadn't looked past him and seen Charley Huff and Dave Allen. Dave Allen was smiling at her with those nice gray eyes, and somehow she knew nothing bad could happen when he was around. But watching Broken Horn sniff animal-like at the stew simmering in the iron pot and the pie keeping warm in the open Dutch oven, she did feel a mite uneasy.

"You're set on going to Oregon, I take it," Kent said. "Do you plan to wait here until an Oregon-bound train willing to fight its way through Bannock country comes along?"

"Can't hardly do that. Ours was the last train due to leave Independence this season." A questioning look came into Jed's eyes. "You got a proposition, Mr. Kent?"

"Yes. Charley and Dave here also want to go to Oregon.

I'll vouch for their reliability, if you want to hire them as guides. I've talked to Chief Broken Horn, and he's agreed—for a reasonable consideration—to let you pass through his country.''

''How much?''

''One hundred dollars.''

''And these gents, how much do they want?''

''Two hundred dollars—apiece.''

Jed fiddled with his pipe. ''That's a sight of money.''

''It's a sight of a job takin' two wagons an' three greenhorns through bad Injun country,'' Charley grunted.

''There's one thing I must make clear,'' Dave said, looking first at Mary, then at Jed. ''If you do hire us, you've got to do exactly as we tell you at all times.''

That was a mighty bossy way for a mere guide to talk, Mary thought angrily. Finishing the dishes, she carried them to the wagon and put them away. As she turned back to the fire, her mouth flew open in horror. Chief Broken Horn, fascinated by the smell emanating from the stewpot, had lifted its lid and was plunging a dirty butcher knife into its depths. This time she did scream.

''Stop that, you heathen!''

The Indian gave no sign that he heard her. Seizing the first weapon handy—a broom leaning against the wagon wheel—she made for him. As she raised the broom to strike, Dave Allen leaped toward her and caught her wrists.

''Easy, ma'am!''

Paying no attention to the commotion, Chief Broken Horn sniffed at the piece of meat he had impaled on his knife, diagnosed it as edible and disposed of it at a single bite. Finding the sample good, he dipped his bare hand into the pot, gobbled down its contents, then, still masticating noisily, stooped and picked up the apple pie. Indignantly Mary struggled against the steel-like grip on her wrists.

''Let me go!''

The nice gray eyes weren't smiling now. ''Don't you want to go to Oregon?''

''Of course I do!''

''You won't get there by beating Indian chiefs on the

head with a broom. If you hit Broken Horn, he'd be so insulted he'd kill us all first chance he got!''

It was too late to save the pie anyway, so Mary let go of the broom. ''All right, Mr. Allen. I won't harm your precious Indian. Now let me go.''

The grin came back to his face, and he released her. ''That's better.'' He turned to Jed. ''Think you can control your daughter?''

Jed looked questioningly at Mary. Shamefaced, she dropped her gaze to the ground. She was still trembling with anger, not only at Chief Broken Horn but also at these two trappers who, to her way of thinking, were heartlessly taking advantage of her pa. Why, five hundred dollars was half of the family's lifetime savings! But this was a man's world, and it was not her place to object.

''I'll make no trouble, Pa. I promise.''

''That's sensible talk,'' Dave said. He nodded to Jed. ''It's set, then. We'll pull out first thing in the morning.''

West of Fort Hall the trail followed Snake River across flat, monotonous sagebrush desert, with mountains faint in the heat-hazed distance to the northwest and the green, swift-flowing river often lost deep in lava-walled canyons. Jed drove one wagon, Mary the other, except when the road got too bad, at which times Dave would tie his saddle horse to the tail gate, climb to the driver's seat and take the reins. He drove as he did everything else, with a casual skill which the mules recognized and responded to, though the stubborn brutes gave Mary all kinds of trouble.

''Good mules,'' he said, grinning at her as the wagon topped a particularly bad grade. ''How come Jed was smart enough to use mules instead of oxen?''

''Pa is a smart man.''

''What's he going to do with those seedlings?''

''Raise apples. Back home he had the finest apple orchard in the state.''

''Why did you leave?''

''Ma died a year ago, and it took the heart out of Pa. He got restless, hearing about the free land in Oregon and how scarce fresh fruit was out there. He kept talking about it, and I thought a change might do him good.''

The wagon was on a perfectly level stretch of trail now, and there was no reason why Dave shouldn't turn the reins over to her, but he lingered. ''Kind of hard on a woman, ain't it, leaving her friends and all?''

''Pa and Mike are all that matter to me.''

''Most girls your age think more of catching a husband than they do of their pa and brother.''

The way he put it exasperated her. ''You make getting married sound like trapping.''

He threw back his head and laughed heartily. ''I meant no offense. But judging from what I've seen of women, most of 'em do have men on their minds when they get to be your age.''

''I'll bet they pestered you no end when you lived in civilized country.''

''Well, they did, if you want the truth.''

''Is that why you ran away and turned trapper?''

''Nope. I just wanted to see what was on the other side of the hill.''

''Did you find out?''

''Sure. Another hill—with another side to it.'' He stopped the wagon, handed her the reins and climbed down. Mounting his horse, he said with a grin, ''Don't say anything to those mules, gal. Maybe they'll think I'm still driving and won't give you no trouble.''

Angrily she watched him gallop away. Then she gave the off-wheeler a lick with the whip that made him jump as if he'd been scalded.

For a week they traveled west without molestation, save for the torment of heat, dust and monotony. Dave said the fact that they saw no Indians didn't mean the Indians hadn't seen them. Chief Broken Horn had ridden ahead, he said, to warn his people that the party of whites was coming; and scouts watching from ridge tops likely were noting the progress of the wagons.

''We won't be safe,'' Dave said, ''till we're into the Blue Mountains. And we'll have company before we get out of

Bannock country, you can bet on that. When we do, Charley and I will tell you how to behave. Make sure you listen.''

The two trappers had brought along several extra horses to pack their gear, and when Charley suggested that one of the animals' loads be stowed in a wagon, freeing the horse for Mike to ride and accompany him on hunts for fresh meat, the old trapper made himself a friend for life.

From dawn till dusk, Mike tagged after Charley, listening with youthful awe to Charley's rambling tales of beaver trapping, Indian fighting and wilderness adventures. Mary was aware of the relationship that existed between boy and man, but she saw no harm in it.

One evening they camped in a grassy swale bare of trees, with the river five hundred feet below. It was quite a chore lugging up water for the seedlings; and by the time it was finished, Jed was done in. He lay down on the ground with a weary sigh.

''Jehoshaphat, I'm tired! Hungry too. What's for supper, Mary?''

Mary was exhausted; the fuel was scant, and what there was of it refused to burn. ''Nothing,'' she said shortly, ''unless somebody fetches me some decent firewood.''

''Mike,'' Jed said, ''cut your sister some wood. Hustle, now!''

Charley and Mike were squatting nearby, the old trapper rambling on while the boy listened intently. Mary gave her brother a sharp look. ''Mike!''

''Hmm?''

''Did you hear your pa?''

''What'd he say?''

''He told you to fetch me some firewood.''

''Aw, fetch it yourself. That's squaw work.''

Mary stared at her brother. Jed sat up with a scowl. ''What did you say, son?''

Mike flushed, gave Charley a sidelong glance and muttered, ''Cutting firewood is squaw work. Ain't it, Charley?''

''Why, yeah, boy,'' Charley answered, scratching his

ribs. "Amongst Injuns, that's how it is. The buck kills the game an' brings it home, an' his squaw skins an' cooks it."

Dave, who had just strolled up, looked at Mike and said, "Don't believe everything Charley tells you, son."

"But Charley knows all about squaws!" Mike said indignantly. "He's had dozens of 'em! . . . Haven't you, Charley?"

"Wal, not dozens—"

Mary put her hands on her hips. "I never heard the like! Stuffing a boy full of awful stories!"

"Mike, fetch Mary some wood," Dave said firmly. "Jump, now! . . . Charley, you help him."

Charley looked hurt. "Me? Me fetch wood?"

"If you want to eat, you'd better."

After supper, Mary strolled off into the twilight and sat down on a boulder overlooking the whispering river. Though she'd promised her pa she'd make no trouble, the chore of feeding four hungry, ungrateful men three times a day was getting on her nerves; and she knew if she had to listen to any more of their idle chatter, she'd likely bust loose and say something she'd regret. Hearing a quiet step behind her, she looked around. Dave had followed her.

"Nice night."

"Yes."

"You'd ought not to wander away from camp alone. Some Injun might see you and pack you home with him."

"Just let one try."

Sitting down beside her, he lighted his pipe. "Charley don't mean no harm. He just likes to tell big windies."

"Has he had many squaws?"

"Two or three."

"Did he—marry them?"

"Bought 'em."

She stared at him, not sure whether he was teasing her or telling the blunt truth. Deciding he was telling the truth, she exclaimed, "Do you mean to say Indian women are bought and sold like—like horses?"

"Sure. A man picks out a squaw he wants, dickers with

her pa and settles on a price. Some come higher than others, naturally. You take a young, healthy woman that's a good cook, she'll cost a man a sight more than a run-of-the-mill squaw would.''

"What if she doesn't like the man that buys her? What if she refuses to live with him?''

"Why, he beats her. That generally makes her behave.''

"I think that's horrible!''

His eyes were twinkling, and now the suspicion came to her that he hadn't been telling the truth. She was dying to ask him if he'd ever owned any squaws, but blessed if she'd give him a chance to tease her further. Grinning, he held out his hand and helped her up. "Come on, you'd better get back to camp. You're too good a cook to lose.''

The Bannocks appeared while they were nooning next day. Seeing the squaws and children in the band, Dave said their intentions likely were peaceable, for Indians didn't take their families along when they had war in mind. But watching the savages set up their tepees a quarter of a mile down the valley, Mary felt uneasy.

Chief Broken Horn, accompanied by half a dozen of the leaders of the tribe, rode into camp presently. Broken Horn made a long speech, emphasized by many dramatic gestures. The gist of it was, Dave said, that Broken Horn considered himself quite a great man. Had he not made forty-nine wagons turn aside from the Oregon trail because the American emigrants feared him? Was it not only through his generosity and by his consent that this small party was being permitted to cross his lands after paying the toll he demanded?

"Can't say as I like that kind of talk,'' Jed muttered.

"Let him brag,'' Dave said. "It don't hurt us a bit.''

When the chief finished his speech, Dave frowned, then came over to Mary and said, "We're going to have company for supper.''

"Chief Broken Horn?''

"Yeah. He and six of his headmen. You're to fix them

a big feed, he says, with lots of stew and pie like you cooked for him back at Fort Hall.''

"I didn't cook anything for him! He stole that food, and you know it.''

"Well, he tells it different. Anyhow he seems to like your cooking and wants more of it.''

"Do you mean to tell me I've got to feed seven of those heathen?''

"Afraid so. He says when he eats well, his dreams are good. He says if his dreams are good tonight, he'll let us go on in peace. But if his dreams are bad—''

"Now, look here!'' Jed cut in angrily. "The old thief made a bargain and he's got to stick to it, good dreams or bad!''

"We've got to humor him,'' Dave said, shaking his head. He looked at Mary. "Can you do it? Can you rustle up enough stew and pie to make them happy?''

Mary was tired and she was scared, but most of all, right now, she was mad. Seemed like all she'd done since she'd left home was cater to men, cooking for them, washing for them, mending for them. She hadn't minded doing those chores for her own family because that was her job. But if this was a man's land, why didn't the men out here act like men? Why had Harlan Faber and the other men back at Fort Hall let an arrogant old Indian turn them aside from their original destination? Why didn't Charley and Dave make Chief Broken Horn live up to his promise with no nonsense about dreams?

"All right,'' she said wearily. "I'll feed them. But you'll all have to help me.''

Charley and Mike had killed an antelope and two deer the evening before, so meat was no problem. There was still half a barrel of dried apples left in the wagon, plenty of beans, sugar and flour, fifty pounds of potatoes she'd bought at Fort Hall, and a few carefully hoarded onions, carrots and dried peas. While Charley chopped wood and Dave carried water, she had Mike stretch a large square of canvas on the ground beside one of the wagons—on this her guests would sit. Brushing aside her pa's objections that it was casting pearls before swine, she made him dig out the family's best china, silverware, glasses, pitcher and a white linen tablecloth, which she laid and set on the canvas ground cloth. Except for the fact that her banquet table had no legs, it looked as attractive as any she'd ever set back home.

How much food could a hungry Indian eat? She made a liberal estimate of what a normal man with a healthy appetite could do away with at one sitting and tripled it, just to be on the safe side. She took special care that there should be more apple pie than her guests could possibly consume.

After putting a quantity of dried apples to soak for several hours, she prepared two dozen pie shells. When the apples had soaked sufficiently, she filled the shells, covered them with thin strips of dough, coated them with brown sugar and baked them until they were almost done. One of her most precious culinary treasures was a square tin of grated cheese flakes, which time and the dry western air had long since drawn all moisture from, but which, when sprinkled generously over the top of an apple pie and heated for a few minutes, melted and blended with the sugar to give the pie a delightful flavor. The tin was kept in a wooden chest in the wagon, along with her spices, extracts and family medical supplies. She asked Mike to get it for her.

Climbing into the wagon, he rummaged around, then called, "Is it the red tin?"

"No, the blue one. Hurry, Mike!"

He clambered out of the wagon and handed her the tin. Taking a tablespoon, she hurriedly ladled a liberal layer of powdery flakes over the top of each pie, set them back in the Dutch ovens to bake and turned her attention to other tasks. Some minutes later she was exasperated to find Mike, whom she had told to return the tin to the chest, curiously staring down at what remained of its contents.

"Mike, will you please quit dawdling and put that away?"

"How come you sprinkled this stuff on the pies?"

"Because it's cheese, you idiot!"

"Don't smell like cheese." He dipped finger and thumb into the tin, took a tiny pinch, sampled it. "Don't taste like cheese either."

She stared at the tin in horror. It wasn't blue. It was green. And pasted on its side was a faded label. She read it and suddenly felt faint. "Oh, my goodness!"

She ran to one of the Dutch ovens, opened it and snatched out a pie. Heedless of scorched fingers, she tried a tiny sample of the browned, delicious-looking crust. Mike did the same. He made a face.

"You going to feed these pies to the Indians?"

She closed her eyes and tried to think. The stuff wouldn't kill them, of that she was sure. It was too late to bake more pies, certainly, for even now the guests were arriving. Dressed in their finest, followed at a respectful distance by a horde of curious squaws, children and uninvited braves, Chief Broken Horn and his subchiefs had dismounted from their horses and were walking into camp. Worn-out and nerve-ragged after her long afternoon of work, Mary felt like dropping to the ground and giving way to tears. Instead she got mad. She got so mad that she didn't care a hang what happened, just so long as those pies didn't go to waste. Opening her eyes, she gave her brother a grim look.

"I certainly am. Get me the sugar, Mike. Indians will eat anything if it's sweet enough."

Judging from the amount of food consumed and the rapidity with which it vanished, the feast was a huge success. The Indians were vastly fascinated by the plates, dishes and silverware, though they used their bare hands more than they did the knives, forks and spoons. The cold tea, liberally sugared, was a great hit, too, disappearing as fast as Mike could fill the glasses. And the pie brought forth approving grunts from all.

Mary had given her own menfolk strict orders not to partake of the pie, telling them that she feared there might not be enough to go round; but as the Indians one by one lapsed into glassy-eyed satiety, with half a dozen still uneaten pies before them, Dave gazed longingly at the beautiful

creation on the tablecloth between himself and Chief Broken Horn. He smiled up at Mary.

"Sure does look like fine pie. Can't I have a piece?"

"No," Mary said sharply.

"Not even a little one?" he persisted, picking up the pie.
"Why, if you knew how long it's been since I tasted—"

"I said 'no,' " Mary cut in, rudely snatching the pie out
of his hand. Pretending that she'd done it for the sake of
her guests, she turned to Chief Broken Horn and smiled.
"More pie, Mr. Broken Horn?"

The Indian made a sign indicating he was full up to his
chin. As he looked her over from head to toe, a greedy,
acquisitive light came into his black eyes. He turned and
grunted something to Dave. Dave laughed and winked at
Mary.

"He says you're a better cook than his own squaw is."

"That's very kind of him."

"He wants to know if your pa will sell you. He says
he'd pay a fancy price."

Mary was too tired to have much of a sense of humor
right then. From the way Jed's face froze, he wasn't in a
joking mood either. "I won't stand for that kind of talk in
front of Mary."

"He didn't mean it as an insult," Dave said. "He meant
it as a—"

Chief Broken Horn showed exactly how he had meant it
by reaching up, seizing Mary's left wrist and pulling her
toward him. Livid-faced, Jed leaped to his feet. Dave swore
and reached for the pistol in his belt. Charley drew his
knife. Mike ran and grabbed up his rifle. But Mary was too
angry to wait for help from her menfolk. Quick as a wink,
she drew back her right arm and plastered Chief Broken
Horn full in the face with the apple pie.

For a moment there wasn't a sound. The Indians were
all staring at their chief, who lay flat on his back—pawing
pie out of his eyes, kicking his heels in the air in a most
unchieftain-like manner.

Getting his feet under him, Chief Broken Horn gave
Mary a stunned, horrified glance, then wheeled and ran for

his horse as if all the hounds of hell were after him. The other Indians wasted no time in following.

Mary took a long, deep breath. Turning to look at Jed, she said in a voice filled with shame, "I'm sorry, Pa."

"Don't be," Dave said, and his nice gray eyes were hard as flint. "If you hadn't done what you did, I'd have killed him where he sat."

A body does queer things in time of stress. Suddenly becoming aware of the way her menfolk were staring at her, their weapons in their hands, their eyes filled with amazement, relief and admiration, she began to laugh. She laughed till tears ran out of her eyes, but for the life of her she couldn't stop. Dave put an arm around her shoulders and said gently, "Easy, Mary—easy."

She sighed and quietly fainted.

As dark came on and the fires burned low, they sat huddled together, their backs against a wagon for safety's sake, listening to the drums in the Indian village. Mary was frightened now, but looking around, seeing the grim looks on the faces of her menfolk as they balanced their rifles across their knees, she was sure of one thing—her men would act like men if the need arose, and she was proud of them all.

"What do you think they'll do?" Jed said.

"Hard to tell," Dave answered. "Broken Horn has lost considerable face, being made a fool of by a woman in public. If there's going to be an attack, it will likely come at dawn. He'll spend the night stirring up the young bucks. The war drums are going already."

Charley, who had been listening intently to the sounds coming from the village, interrupted, "Quiet, boy!"

"What's the matter?"

"Them drums. They don't sound like war drums to me. Sound more like medicine drums."

"What's the difference?" Mary asked.

Patiently Dave explained that when Bannocks prepared for battle, the drums were pounded in one fashion; but when there was sickness in the tribe and the medicine man was called in to recite his chants and attempt to heal the ill person, the drums were beaten in another manner. "But Charley's wrong," he added. "Chief Broken Horn isn't going to let his medicine man fool around curing sick people tonight."

"Maybe he's sick. Eating all that food—"

"He's got the stomach of a wolf. No, they're war drums, no question about that," Dave insisted.

In the faint glow of the dying fires Mary saw a bulky figure appear on the far side of camp. Dave called out a challenge in the Bannock tongue and was quickly answered by an Indian woman. He told her to approach the wagon, and she did so—her hesitant pace showing how frightened she was. She was fat, wrinkled and middle-aged. Dave asked her who she was and what she wanted. As she spoke, he translated.

"She says she's Broken Horn's squaw."

"Is he going to attack?" Jed said.

"She says no."

"So he's going to stick to his bargain after all?"

"But the young bucks might, she says, if they can work up nerve enough. They're arguing it out now."

"Can't he keep them in line?"

Mary saw Dave frown as the squaw spoke. "She says he ain't interested in anything right now except the mess of bad spirits that have crawled into his belly. She says he's sick as a dog—and so are all the other chiefs that ate with us." Dave turned and gave Mary a sharp look. "She thinks you poisoned 'em."

"I didn't!"

"How come they all took sick, then?"

Mary flushed. "Maybe it was the beans and all that cold tea they drank."

"It was the apple pie, wasn't it? You wouldn't let us eat any of it, but you made sure they stuffed themselves with it. What did you put in that pie, Mary?"

Defiantly Mary looked at Dave. "Epsom salts."

"What?"

"It won't hurt them. In fact, they made such pigs of themselves, it might even do them some good. Why, I wouldn't be surprised but what they all dream real nice dreams—when they finally get to sleep. That's what you wanted, wasn't it?''

Dave looked shaken. In fact, all her menfolk were staring at her, awe and respect in their eyes. Suddenly the squaw started gabbling furiously, pointing an accusing finger at Mary. Dave listened for a time, then he silenced her with a gesture.

''She says either you poisoned her man or cast an evil spell on him because he grabbed hold of you. Whichever it was you did, she's begging you to make him well. What shall I tell her?''

Mary smiled. ''Tell her I cast a spell.''

''Now, look here!''

''Tell her, please. Tell her that all white women have the power to cast spells over men when they get angry with them.''

Reluctantly Dave spoke to the Indian woman. Her black eyes grew wide with fright as she stared at Mary, then she grunted a question. Dave said, ''She wants to know how long the spell will last.''

''Tell her two days. Tell her if her husband and the other sick chiefs lie quietly for two days and nights, thinking nothing but peaceful thoughts, they will get well. But if they let their people attack us, they will die.''

An admiring grin spread over Dave's face. ''Now why didn't I think of that?''

As he spoke to the squaw, Mary saw the frightened look fade from the woman's face. The squaw nodded vigorously, turned to go, hesitated; then shyly walked up to Mary, touched Mary's breast, then her own, grunted something and ran off into the darkness. Mary looked at Dave.

''What did that mean?''

Dave didn't answer for a moment. Then, an uneasy light coming into his nice gray eyes, as if he were looking into the future, he answered, ''She says you know how to handle men and she's glad you hit her husband with that pie. She's been wanting to sock the old fool for years.''

NO ROOM AT THE INN

▼
▼

Bill Pronzini

When the snowstorm started, Quincannon was high up in a sparsely populated section of the Sierra Nevada—alone except for his rented horse, with not much idea of where he was and no idea at all of where Slick Henry Garber was.

And as if all of that wasn't enough, it was almost nightfall on Christmas Eve.

The storm had caught him by surprise. The winter sky had been clear when he'd set out from Big Creek in midmorning, and it had stayed clear until two hours ago; then the clouds had commenced piling up rapidly, the way they sometimes did in this high-mountain country, getting thicker and darker-veined until the whole sky was the color of moiling coal smoke. The wind had sharpened to an icy breath that buffeted both him and the ewe-necked strawberry roan. And now, at dusk, the snow flurries had begun—thick flakes driven and agitated by the wind so that the pine and spruce forests through which the trail climbed were a misty blur and he could see no more than forty or fifty feet ahead.

He rode huddled inside his fleece-lined long coat and

rabbit-fur mittens and cap, feeling sorry for himself and at the same time cursing himself for a rattlepate. If he had paid more mind to that buildup of clouds, he would have realized the need to find shelter much sooner than he had. As it was, he had begun looking too late. So far no cabin or mine shaft or cave or suitable geographical configuration had presented itself—not one place in all this vast wooded emptiness where he and the roan could escape the snapping teeth of the storm.

A man had no sense wandering around an unfamiliar mountain wilderness on the night before Christmas, even if he *was* a manhunter by trade and a greedy gloryhound by inclination. He ought to be home in front of a blazing fire, roasting chestnuts in the company of a good woman. Sabina, for instance. Dear, sweet Sabina, waiting for him back in San Francisco. Not by his hearth or in his bed, curse the luck, but at least in the Market Street offices of Carpenter and Quincannon, Professional Detective Services.

Well, it was his own fault that he was alone up here, freezing to death in a snowstorm. In the first place he could have refused the job of tracking down Slick Henry Garber when it was offered to him by the West Coast Banking Association two weeks ago. In the second place he could have decided not to come to Big Creek to investigate a report that Slick Henry and his satchel full of counterfeit mining stock were in the vicinity. And in the third place he could have remained in Big Creek this morning when Slick Henry managed to elude his clutches and flee even higher into these blasted mountains.

But no, Rattlepate John Quincannon had done none of those sensible things. Instead he had accepted the Banking Association's fat fee, thinking only of that *and* of the additional $5000 reward for Slick Henry's apprehension or demise being offered by a mining coalition in Colorado *and* of the glory of nabbing the most notorious—and the most dangerous—confidence trickster operating west of the Rockies in this year of 1894. Then, after tracing his quarry to Big Creek, he had not only bungled the arrest but made a second mistake in setting out on Slick Henry's trail with the sublime confidence of an unrepentent sinner looking for the Promised Land—only to lose that trail two hours ago, at a road fork, just before he made his *third* mistake of the day by underestimating the weather.

Christmas, he thought. 'Tis the season to be jolly. Bah. Humbug.

Ice particles now clung to his beard, his eyebrows; kept trying to freeze his eyelids shut. He had to continually rub his eyes clear in order to see where he was going. Which, now, in full darkness, was along the rim of a snow-skinned meadow that had opened up on his left. The wind was even fiercer here, without one wall of trees to deflect some of its force. Quincannon shivered and huddled and cursed and felt sorrier for himself by the minute.

He should never have decided to join forces with Sabina and open a detective agency. She had been happy with her position as a female operative with the Pinkerton Agency's Denver office; he had been more or less content working in the San Francisco office of the United States Secret Service. What had possessed him to suggest, not long after their first professional meeting, that they pool their talents? Well, he knew the answer to that well enough. *Sabina* had possessed him. Dear, sweet, unseducible, infuriating Sabina—

Was that light ahead?

He scrubbed at his eyes and leaned forward in the saddle, squinting. Yes, light—lamplight. He had just come around a jog in the trail, away from the open meadow, and there it was, ahead on his right: a faint glowing rectangle in the night's churning white-and-black. He could just make out the shapes of buildings, too, in what appeared to be a clearing before a sheer rock face.

The lamplight and the buildings changed Quincannon's bleak remonstrations into murmurs of thanksgiving. He urged the stiff-legged and balky roan into a quicker pace. The buildings took on shape and definition as he approached. There were three of them, grouped in a loose triangle; two appeared to be cabins, fashioned of rough-hewn logs and planks, each with a sloping roof, while the bulkiest structure had the look of a barn. The larger cabin, the one with the lighted window, was set between the other two and farther back near the base of the rock wall.

A lane led off the trail to the buildings. Quincannon couldn't see it under its covering of snow, but he knew it was there by a painted board sign nailed to one of the trees at the intersection. *TRAVELER'S REST*, the sign said, and below that, in smaller letters, *Meals and Lodging*. One of the tiny roadhouses, then, that dotted the Sierras and catered to prospectors, hunters, and foolish wilderness wayfarers such as himself.

It was possible, he thought as he turned past the sign, that Slick Henry Garber had come this way and likewise been drawn to the Traveler's Rest. Which would allow Quincannon to make amends today, after all, for his earlier bungling, and perhaps even permit him to spend Christmas Day in the relative comfort of the Big Creek Hotel. Given his recent run of foul luck, however, such a serendipitous turnabout was as likely to happen as Sabina presenting him, on his return to San Francisco, with the holiday gift he most desired.

Nevertheless, caution here was indicated. So despite the warmth promised by the lamplit window, he rode at an off-angle toward the barn. There was also the roan's welfare to consider. He would have to pay for the animal if it froze to death while in his charge.

If he was being observed from within the lighted cabin, it was covertly: no one came out and no one showed himself in the window. At the barn he dismounted, took himself and the roan inside, struggled to reshut the doors against the howling thrust of the wind. Blackness surrounded him, heavy with the smells of animals and hay and oiled leather. He stripped off both mittens, found a lucifer in one of his pockets and scraped it alight. The barn lantern hung from a hook near the doors; he reached up to light the wick. Now he could see that there were eight stalls, half of which were occupied: three saddle horses and one work horse, each nibbling a pile of hay. He didn't bother to examine the saddle horses because he had no idea what type of animal Slick Henry had been riding. He hadn't got close enough to his quarry all day to get a look at him or his transportation.

He led the roan into an empty stall, unsaddled it, left it there munching a hay supper of its own. Later, he would ask the owner of Traveler's Rest to come out and give the beast a proper rubdown. With his hands mittened again he braved the storm on foot, slogging through calf-deep snow to the lighted cabin.

Still no one came out or appeared at the window. He moved along the front wall, stopped to peer through the rimed window glass. What he could see of the big parlor inside was uninhabited. He plowed ahead to the door.

It was against his nature to walk unannounced into the home of a stranger, mainly because it was a fine way to get shot, but in this case he had no choice. He could have shouted himself hoarse in competition with the storm before anyone heard him. Thumping on the door would be just as futile; the wind was already doing that. Again he stripped off his right mitten, opened his coat for easy access to the Remington Navy revolver he carried at his waist, unlatched the door with his left hand, and cautiously let the wind push him inside.

The entire parlor was deserted. He leaned back hard against the door to get it closed again and then called out, "Hello the house! Company!" No one answered.

He stood scraping snowcake off his face, slapping it off his clothing. The room was warm: a log fire crackled merrily on the hearth, banking somewhat because it hadn't been fed in a while. Two lamps were lit in here, another in what looked to be a dining room adjacent. Near the hearth, a cut spruce reached almost to the raftered ceiling; it was festooned with Christmas decorations—strung popcorn and bright-colored beads, stubs of tallow candles in bent can tops, snippets of fleece from some old garment sprinkled on the branches to resemble snow, a five-pointed star atop the uppermost branch.

All very cozy and inviting, but where were the occupants? He called out again, and again received no response. He cocked his head to listen. Heard only the plaint of the storm and the snicking of flung snow against the window-pane—no sound at all within the cabin.

He crossed the parlor, entered the dining room. The puncheon table was set for two, and in fact two people had been eating there not so long ago. A clay pot of venison stew sat in the center of the table; when he touched it he found it and its contents still slightly warm. Ladlings of stew and slices of bread were on each of the two plates.

The hair began to pull along the nape of his neck, as it always did when he sensed a wrongness to things. Slick Henry? Or something else? With his hand now gripping the butt of his Navy, he eased his way through a doorway at the rear of the dining room.

Kitchen and larder. Stove still warm, a kettle atop it blackening smokily because all the water it had contained had boiled away. Quincannon transferred the kettle to the sink drainboard. Moved then to another closed door that must lead to a bedroom, the last of the cabin's rooms. He depressed the latch and pushed the door wide.

Bedroom, indeed. And as empty as the other three rooms. But there were two odd things here: The sash of a window in the far wall was raised a few inches; and on the floor was the base of a lamp that had been dropped or knocked off the bedside table. Snow coated the window sill and there was a sifting of it on the floor and on the lamp base.

Quincannon stood puzzled and scowling in the icy draft. No room at the inn? he thought ironically. On the contrary, there was plenty of room at this inn on Christmas Eve. It didn't seem to have *any* people in it.

On a table near the bed he spied a well-worn family Bible. Impulse took him to it; he opened it at the front, where such vital statistics as marriages, births, and deaths were customarily recorded. Two names were written there in a fine woman's hand: Martha and Adam Keene. And a wedding date: July 17, 1893. That was all.

Well, now he knew the identity of the missing occupants. But what had happened to them? He hadn't seen them in the barn. And the other, smaller cabin—guest accommodations, he judged—had also been in darkness upon his arrival. It made no sense that a man and his wife would suddenly quit the warmth of their home in the middle of a Christmas Eve supper, to lurk about in a darkened outbuilding. It also made no sense that they would voluntarily decide to rush off into a snowstorm on foot or on horseback. Forced out of here, then? By Slick Henry Garber or someone else? If so, *why*?

Quincannon returned to the parlor. He had no desire to go out again into the wind and swirling snow, but he was not the sort of man who could allow a confounding mystery to go uninvestigated—particularly a mystery that might involve a criminal with a handsome price on his head. So, grumbling a little, his unmittened hands deep in the pockets of his coat, he bent his body into what was swiftly becoming a full-scale blizzard.

He fought his way to the barn first, because it was closer and to satisfy himself that it really *was* occupied only by horses. The wind had blown out the lantern when he'd left earlier; he relighted it, but not until he had first drawn his revolver. One of the animals—not the rented roan—moved restlessly in its stall as he walked toward the far end. There were good-sized piles of hay in each of the empty stalls as well, he noticed. He leaned into those stalls with the lantern. If anyone were hiding in a haypile it would have to be close to the surface to avoid the risk of suffocation; he poked at each pile in turn with the Navy's barrel. Hay and nothing but hay.

In one corner of the back wall was an enclosure that he took to be a harness room. Carefully he opened the door with his gun hand. Buckles and bit chains gleamed in the narrow space within; he saw the shapes of saddles, bridles, hackamores. Something made a scurrying noise among the floor shadows and he lowered the lantern in time to see the tail end of a packrat disappear behind a loose board. Dust was the only other thing on the floor.

He went back toward the front, stopped again when he was abreast of the loft ladder. He climbed it with the lantern lifted above his head. But the loft contained nothing more than several tightly stacked bales of hay and a thin scattering of straw that wouldn't have concealed the packrat, much less a man or a woman.

No one in the main cabin, no one in the barn. That left only the guest cabin. And if that, too, was deserted? Well, then, he thought irascibly, he would sit down in the main cabin and gorge himself on venison stew while he waited for somebody—the Keenes, Slick Henry, the Ghost of Christmas Past—to put in an appearance. He was cold and tired and hungry, and mystery or no mystery he was not about to wander around in a blizzard hunting for clues.

Out once more into the white fury. By the time he worked his way through what were now thigh-deep drifts to the door of the guest cabin, his legs and arms were stiff and his beard was caked with frozen snow. He wasted no time getting the door open, but he didn't enter right away. Instead he let the wind hurl the door inward, so that it cracked audibly against the wall, while he hung back and to one side with his revolver drawn.

Nothing happened inside.

He waited another few seconds, but already the icebound night was beginning to numb his bare hand; another minute or two of exposure and the skin would freeze to the gunmetal. He entered the cabin in a sideways crouch, caught hold of the door and crowded it shut until it latched. Chill, clotted black encased him now, so thick that he was virtually blind. Should he risk lighting a match? Well, if he wanted to see who or what this cabin might contain, he would *have* to risk it. Floundering around in the dark would no doubt mean a broken limb, his luck being what it was these days.

He fumbled in his pocket for another lucifer, struck it on his left thumbnail, ducked down and away from the flare of light. Still nothing happened. But the light revealed that this cabin was divided into two sparsely furnished bedrooms with an open door in the dividing wall; and it also revealed some sort of huddled mass on the floor of the rear bedroom.

In slow strides, holding the match up and away from his body, he moved toward the doorway. The flame died just as he reached it—just as he recognized the huddled mass as the motionless body of a man. He thumbed another match alight, went through the doorway, leaned down for a closer look. The man lay drawn up on his back, and on one temple blood from a bullet furrow glistened blackly in the wavering flame. Young man, sandy-haired, wearing an old vicuna cloth suit and a clean white shirt now spotted with blood. A man Quincannon had never seen before—

Something moved behind him.

Something else slashed the air, grazed the side of Quincannon's head as he started to turn and dodge, drove him sideways to the floor.

The lucifer went out as he was struck; he lost his grip on the Navy and it went clattering away into blackness as thick as the inside of Old Scratch's fundament. The blow had been sharp enough to set up a ringing in his ears, but the thick rabbit-fur cap had cushioned it enough so that he wasn't stunned. He pulled around onto his knees, lunged back toward the doorway with both hands reaching. Above him he heard again that slashing of the air, only this time the swung object missed him entirely. Which threw the man who had swung off balance, at the same instant Quincannon's right hand found a grip on sheepskin material not unlike that of his own coat. He yanked hard, heard a grunt, and then the heavy weight of his assailant came squirming and cursing down on top of him.

The floor of an unfamiliar, black-dark room was the last place Quincannon would have chosen for hand-to-hand combat. But he was a veteran of any number of skirmishes, and had learned ways to do grievous damage to an opponent that would have shocked the Marquis of Queensbury. (Sabina, too, no doubt.) Besides which, this particular opponent, whoever he was, was laboring under the same disadvantages as he was.

There were a few seconds of scrambling and bumping about, some close-quarters pummeling on both sides, a blow that split Quincannon's lip and made his Scot's blood boil even more furiously, a brief and violent struggle for possession of what felt like a long-barreled revolver, and then, finally, an opportunity for Quincannon to use a mean and scurrilous trick he had learned in a free-for-all on the Baltimore docks. His assailant screamed, quit fighting, began to twitch instead; and to groan and wail and curse feebly. This vocal combination made Quincannon's head hurt all the more, and led him, since he now had possession of the long-barreled revolver, to thump the man on top of the head with the weapon. The groaning and wailing and cursing ceased apruptly. So did the twitching.

Quincannon got to his feet, stood shakily wiping blood from his torn lip. He made the mistake then of taking a blind step and almost fell over one or the other of the two men now lying motionless on the floor. He produced another lucifer from his dwindling supply. In its flare he spied a lamp, and managed to get to it in time to light the wick before the flame died. He located his Navy, holstered it, then carried the lamp to where the men lay and peered at the face of the one who had tried to brain him.

"Well, well," he said aloud, with considerable relish. "A serendipitous turnabout after all. Just what I wanted for Christmas—Slick Henry Garber."

Slick Henry Garber said nothing, nor would he be able to for a good while.

The young, sandy-haired lad—Adam Keene, no doubt—was also unconscious. The bullet wound on his head didn't seem to be serious, but he would need attention. *He* wouldn't be saying anything, either, for a good while. Quincannon would just have to wait for the full story of what had happened here before his arrival. Unless, of course, he got it from Adam Keene's wife . . .

Where *was* Adam Keene's wife?

Carrying the lamp, he searched the two bedrooms. No sign of Martha Keene. He did find Slick Henry's leather satchel, in a corner of the rear room; it contained several thousand shares of bogus mining stock and nine thousand dollars in greenbacks. He also found evidence of a struggle, and not one but two bullet holes in the back wall.

These things, plus a few others, plus a belated application of imagination and logic, allowed him to make a reasonably accurate guess as to tonight's sequence of events. Slick Henry had arrived just before the snowstorm and just as the Keenes were sitting down to supper. He had either put his horse in the barn himself or Adam Keene had done it; that explained why there had been *three* saddle horses present when only *two* people lived at Traveler's Rest. Most likely Slick Henry had then thrown down on the Keenes: he must have been aware that Quincannon was still close behind him, even if Quincannon hadn't known it, and must have realized that with the impending storm it was a good bet his pursuer would also stop at Traveler's Rest. And what better place for an ambush than one of these three buildings? Perhaps he'd chosen the guest cabin on the theory that Quincannon would be less on his guard there than at the other two. To ensure that, Slick Henry had taken Adam Keene with him at gunpoint, leaving Mrs. Keene in the main cabin with instructions to tell Quincannon that no other travelers had appeared today and to then send him to the guest cabin.

But while the two men were in that cabin Adam Keene had heroically attempted to disarm Slick Henry, there had been a struggle, and Keene had unheroically received a bullet wound for his efforts. Martha Keene must have heard at least one of the shots, and fearing the worst she had left the main cabin through the bedroom window and hidden herself somewhere. Had Slick Henry found her? Not likely. But it seemed reasonable to suppose he had been out hunting for her when Quincannon came. The violence of the storm had kept him from springing his trap at that point; he had decided instead to return to the guest cabin as per his original plan. And this was where he had been ever since, waiting in the dark for his nemesis to walk in like a damned fool—which was just what Quincannon had done.

This day's business, Quincannon thought ruefully, had been one long, grim comedy of errors on all sides. Slick Henry's actions were at least half doltish and so were his own. Especially his own—blundering in half a dozen different ways, including not even once considering the possibility of a planned ambush. Relentless manhunter, intrepid detective. Bah. It was a wonder he hadn't been shot dead. Sabina would chide him mercilessly if he told her the entire story of his capture of Slick Henry Garber. Which, of course, he had no intention of doing.

Well, he could redeem himself somewhat by finding Martha Keene. Almost certainly she had to be in one of the three buildings. She wouldn't have remained in the open, exposed, in a raging mountain storm. She would not have come anywhere near the guest cabin because of Slick Henry. And she hadn't stayed in the main cabin; the open bedroom window proved that. Ergo, she was in the barn. But he had searched the barn, even gone up into the hayloft. No place to hide up there, or in the harness enclosure, or in one of the stalls, or—

The lamp base on the bedroom floor, he thought.

No room at the inn, he thought.

"Well, of course, you blasted rattlepate," he said aloud. "It's the only place she *can* be."

Out once more into the whipping snow and freezing wind (after first taking the precaution of binding Slick Henry's hands with the man's own belt). Slog, slog, slog, and finally into the darkened barn. He lighted the lantern, took it to the approximate middle of the building, and then called out, "Mrs. Keene! My name is John Quincannon, I am a detective from San Francisco, and I have just cracked the skull of the man who terrorized you and your husband tonight. You have nothing more to fear."

No response.

"I know you're here, and approximately where. Won't you save both of us the embarrassment of my poking around with a pitchfork?"

Silence.

"Mrs. Keene, your husband is unconscious with a head wound and he needs you. Please believe me."

More silence. Then, just as he was about to issue another plea, there was a rustling and stirring in one of the empty stalls to his left. He moved over that way in time to see

Martha Keene rise up slowly from her hiding place deep under the pile of hay.

She was young, attractive, as fair-haired as her husband, and wrapped warmly in a heavy fleece-lined coat. She was also, Quincannon noted with surprise, quite obviously with child.

What didn't surprise him was the length of round, hollow glass she held in one hand—the chimney that belonged to the lamp base on the bedroom floor. She had had the presence of mind to snatch it up before climbing out of the window, in her haste dislodging the base from the bedside table. The chimney was the reason neither he nor Slick Henry had found her; by using it as a breathing tube, she had been able to burrow deep enough into the haypile to escape a superficial search.

For a space she stared at Quincannon out of wide, anxious eyes. What she saw seemed to reassure her. She released a thin, sighing breath and said tremulously, "My husband . . . you're sure he's not—?"

"No, no. Wounded I said and wounded I meant. He'll soon be good as new."

"Thank God!"

"And you, my dear? Are you all right?"

"Yes, I . . . yes. Just frightened. I've been lying here imagining all sorts of dreadful things." Mrs. Keene sighed again, plucked clinging straw from her face and hair. "I didn't *want* to run and hide, but I thought Adam must be dead and I was afraid for my baby . . . oh!" She winced as if with a sudden sharp pain, dropped the lamp chimney and placed both hands over the swell of her abdomen. "All the excitement . . . I believe the baby will arrive sooner than expected."

Quincannon gave her a horrified look. "Right here? *Now?*"

"No, not that soon." A wan smile. "Tomorrow . . ."

It was his turn to put forth a relieved sigh as he moved into the stall to help her up. Tomorrow. Christmas Day. Appropriate that she should have her baby then. But it wasn't the only thing about this situation that was appropriate to the season. This was a stable, and what was the stall where she had lain with her unborn child but a manger? There were animals in attendance, too. And at least one wise man (wise in *some* things, surely) who had come bearing a gift without even knowing it, a gift of a third—no, a half—of the $5000 reward for the capture of Slick Henry Garber.

Peace on earth, good will to men.

Quincannon smiled; of a sudden he felt very jolly and very much in a holiday spirit. This was, he thought, going to be a fine Christmas after all.

GERANIUM HOUSE

▼

Peggy Simson Curry

We heard about them long before we saw them. News traveled fast in those days even though we didn't have telephones in the valley. Old Gus, the mailman, gave us the full report. "They come in from Laramie in a two-wheeled cart," he said, "him ridin' and her walkin' beside the cart and the old sway-bellied horse pullin' it. That cart was mostly filled with plants, and she was carrying one in her arms, just like most women carry a baby."

"Where they going to live?" my uncle Rolfe asked.

"They moved into that old homestead shack on the flats," Gus said. "Been there since the Indians fired the west range, that shack. Used to belong to a man named Matt but he died a spell ago, and I guess they're welcome to it." He sucked on the end of his drooping brown mustache and added, "Him now, he don't look like he'd be much—his pants hangin' slack and his shoulders humped worse'n my granddad's. But her! You'd have to see her, Rolfe. What she's got ain't anything a man could put words to."

As soon as Gus finished his coffee and started back to

town in his buggy, my mother mixed a batch of bread. "We'll take over a couple of loaves and a cake," she said. "A woman deserves better than that dirt-roofed cabin on the flats."

My uncle Rolfe stood looking out the kitchen window. He was big and handsome in a wild, blackheaded way. He was always splitting his shirts and popping off buttons, and he never cared what he had on or how it fitted. Uncle Rolfe came to live with us and take over part of the ranch when my father died, and you'd never have thought he was my mother's brother, for she was small and neat and had pale brown hair.

"Anne," Uncle Rolfe said, "I wouldn't be in a hurry to rush over and welcome a couple of squatters. We don't know anything about them and they don't come from much when they have to put up in a dead man's shack on the flats. What's more, they won't stay long."

The color flew high in my mother's cheeks. "You don't understand about a woman," she said. "You don't know how much it helps to have a friend of her own kind in this big lonesome country. You've been a bachelor too long to see a woman's side of things, Rolfe Annister."

"Well," he said, "I aim to leave them alone."

But the next morning when we were ready to go, Uncle Rolfe got in the buggy. "Won't hurt me to meet them, I guess." Then he turned to me and smiled. "Billy, you want to drive this morning?"

I was thirteen that spring morning in the mountain country, and nothing ever sounded better than the clop-clop of the horses' hoofs and the singing sound of the buggy wheels turning along the dirt road. The meadowlarks were whistling and Uncle Rolfe began humming under his breath, the way he did sometimes when the sky was soft and the grass coming green.

It was six miles to the homesteader's cabin and we were almost there before we saw it, for it sat low on the flat land among the sagebrush and was the same silver-gray color. The river ran past it but there weren't any trees along the water, only a few scrubby willows still purple from the fall, for they hadn't leafed out yet.

First thing we noticed was the color in the windows of the old cabin, big blossoms of red and pink and white. My mother stepped out of the buggy and stared. "Geraniums!" she exclaimed. "I never saw anything so beautiful!"

The two-wheeled cart was beside the door and so old and bleached it might have been part of the land. And we saw the horse picketed in the sagebrush. Like Gus had said, he was a pack of bones with a belly slung down like a hammock.

My mother carefully carried her box with the cake and bread to the front door and knocked. She was wearing her new gloves, the ones Uncle Rolfe had bought her in Denver when he shipped the cattle.

The door opened slowly and all I saw that first moment was the woman's eyes, big and dark and shining. She was young and her hair was so blond it looked almost white and was drawn back tight until it made her eyes seem larger and blacker. She was brown-skinned and tall and she looked strong. Her dress was clean but so worn my mother would have used it for a rag.

"I'm Anne Studer," my mother said. "We're your neighbors. This is my brother, Rolfe, and my son, Billy."

The woman seemed to forget my mother and Uncle Rolfe. She bent over and put her hand on my head and smiled down into my face. "Billy," she said, and her hand stroked my head and I could feel she loved me, for the warmth came right out of her hand.

She asked us to come in and then I saw the bed on the floor near the stove and the man there in the blankets. His face was thin and gray and he sat up, coughing. "Sam," she said, "we've got company—our neighbors."

He didn't try to get up but just lay there, and I thought how terrible it was he didn't have any bunk or bedstead, only the floor under him. Then he smiled at us and said, "The trip was too much for me, I guess. We've come a long way. Melora, will you put on the coffee?"

The woman went to the old stove that had pools of velvety-looking rust on the lids and she set a small black pot on it and filled the pot with water from the bucket. Her arms were soft and rounded but strong lifting the bucket.

No one said anything for a few moments and I could hear a rustling that seemed to come from all the corners of the room.

"You've got lots of mice," my uncle Rolfe said.

Melora smiled at him. "I know. And we forgot to bring traps."

Mother looked around and drew her skirts close to her, her mouth pinching into a thin line. I saw her touch the shiny lid of a tin can with her toe. The can lid was nailed over a hole in the rotting wooden floor.

Melora cut the cake, saying what a beautiful cake it was, and glancing at my mother, who still had that tight look on her face. Then she poured coffee into two battered tin cups and three jelly glasses. "Billy," she said to me, "if I'd been expecting you, I'd surely have fixed lemonade and put it in the river to cool." She stroked my head again and then walked over to one of the geraniums and I could see her fingers busy among the leaves. Her hands moved so softly and quietly in the plant that I knew she was loving it just as she had loved me when she touched me.

We didn't stay long and Melora walked to the buggy with us. She shook my mother's hand and said, "You were good to come. Please come back soon—and please bring Billy."

Driving home, my mother was silent. Uncle Rolfe finally said, "I knew we shouldn't go there. Makes a man feel low in his mind to see that. He's half dead, and how are they going to live?"

"I'm going to ride over with mousetraps," I said. "I'll set them for her."

My mother gave me a strange look. "You're not going alone," she said firmly.

"No," my uncle Rolfe said. "I'll go with him."

A few nights later we rode to the house on the flats and Uncle Rolfe set twelve mousetraps. Sam was in bed and Melora sat on an old spike keg, her hands folded in her lap. We'd just get started talking when a trap would go off and Uncle Rolfe would take it outside, empty it, and set it again.

"Sam's asleep now," Melora said. "He sleeps so much—and it's just as well. The mice bother him."

"Isn't there any other place you can go?" Uncle Rolfe asked, a roughness in his voice. "You can't live off this land. It won't grow anything but sagebrush."

"No, we haven't any other place to go," Melora replied, and her strong shoulders sagged. "We've no kin and Sam needs this climate. I've got more plants coming from Missouri—that's where we used to live. I'll sell my geraniums. We'll manage—we always have."

She walked out in the night with us when we were leaving. She put her arm around me and held me hard against her. "So young," she said, "so alive—I've been around death a long time. Sam—look at Sam. And our babies died. We had two. And now, now I'll never have another child— only the geraniums." Her voice broke and I knew she was crying. Her arms swept me closer and there was something about the way she clung to me that made me hurt inside.

"Come on, Billy," Uncle Rolfe said gruffly. I pulled away from Melora and got my horse. I could still hear her sobbing as we rode away.

We were riding quietly in the dark when my uncle Rolfe began to talk to himself, as though he'd forgotten I was there. "Beautiful," he said, "and needing a strong red-blooded man to love her. Needing a child to hold in her arms—and there she is, tied to *him*. Oh Lord, is it right?"

A week later my uncle Rolfe wrapped a piece of fresh beef in a white sack and rode off toward the flats. My mother watched him go, a frown on her forehead. Then she said to me, "Billy, you bring in the milk cows at five o'clock. I don't think your uncle Rolfe will be back by then."

The next morning I saw a pink geranium on the kitchen table and a piece of brown wrapping paper beside it. On the paper was written in strong sloping letters, "For Anne from Melora."

It wasn't long till everybody in the valley spoke of the cabin on the flats as "Geranium House." On Sundays, before the haying season started, the ranchers drove out in their buggies and they always went past the cabin on the flats. The women stopped to admire the flowers and usually bought one or two plants. They told my mother how beautiful Melora was and how kind—especially to the children.

"Yes," my mother would say and get that pinched look about her mouth.

One morning in early August when Gus brought the mail, he told us Melora had been driving all over the valley in the cart, selling geraniums and visiting with the women. "And she's got a new horse to pull the cart," he said, "a big black one."

That afternoon my mother saddled her horse and taking me with her went riding through the horse pasture. "I'm looking for the black gelding," she said. "Seems to me I haven't noticed him around lately."

We rode until sundown but we didn't find the gelding. I said he might have jumped the fence and gotten out on the range or into one of the neighbor's pastures.

"Yes," she said, frowning, "I suppose he could have."

She asked Uncle Rolfe about the black gelding and Uncle Rolfe let on like he didn't hear her. "Well," my mother said tartly, "there's such a thing as carrying goodwill toward your neighbors too far."

"You haven't," he said angrily. "You never bothered to go back. And she must be lonely and tired of looking at a sick man every day."

"She hasn't returned my call," my mother said, her chin in the air. "I'm not obligated to go there again. Besides, there's something about her—the way she looks at Billy—"

"You've forgotten, Anne, what it is to hunger for love, for a child to be part of you—for a man's arms around you in the night."

Tears came into my mother's eyes. "No, Rolfe! I haven't forgotten. But I've got Billy—and when I saw her eyes and her hands on the geraniums——Rolfe, it isn't that I don't like her. It's—it hurts me to be around her.''

Uncle Rolfe put his hand on her shoulder. "I'm sorry, Anne. I shouldn't have said a word.''

"If she comes here," my mother said, "I'll make her welcome, Rolfe.''

And then one warm morning I saw the two-wheeled cart driving up in front of the house, and I saw that the horse pulling it was our black gelding.

"Billy!" Melora called to me. "How are you, Billy?" And she got out of the cart and put her arms around me and I could feel the warmth coming from her body and covering me like a wool blanket in winter.

My mother came to the door and asked Melora in. "How's Sam?" she said.

Melora put her hand to her eyes as though she wanted to brush something away. She was thinner than when I'd last seen her and her eyes burned bigger and brighter in her face that now had the bones showing under the fine tanned skin. But still she looked strong, the way a wire is tight and strong before it breaks. "Sam," she said, "Sam's all right. As good as he'll ever be. It's a weakness, a sickness born in him—as it was in our babies. Anne, I didn't know Sam was a sick man when I married him. He never told me.''

Uncle Rolfe came in with his black hair looking wilder than usual. The color burned in Melora's cheeks and her eyes lighted. "Hello, Rolfe," she said, "and thank you for being so kind to Sam.''

"That's all right," Uncle Rolfe said gruffly.

"I went to town to see the minister," Melora said, still looking at Uncle Rolfe. "I asked him to find me a baby I could adopt—like you suggested. He said 'no.' ''

"He did!" Uncle Rolfe sounded shocked.

"He said I had nothing to take care of a baby," Melora went on. "He said I had my hands full now. I begged him to help me, but he just sat there with a face like stone and said it wasn't my lot in life to have a child.''

"The fool!" Uncle Rolfe muttered.

My mother set food on the table and asked Melora to stay and eat with us.

Melora shook her head. "I'm going home and fix something for Sam. He can't eat much this hot weather but I tell him he must try. And he gets so lonesome when I'm gone."

My uncle Rolfe went out and helped her into the cart. He stood for a long time looking down the road after she left.

Two weeks later we saw the buggy of Gus, the mailman, coming up the road. It wasn't the day for bringing mail. The horses were running and a big cloud of dust rose behind the buggy. My mother and I stepped onto the porch just as Uncle Rolfe rode in from the haying field with a piece of machinery across the saddle in front of him. My uncle Rolfe dismounted and waited for Gus. The buggy rattled to a stop. The horses were panting and sweating, for it was a hot morning.

"Melora's taken Sadie Willard's baby," Gus said, "and drove off with it."

"Oh no!" My mother twisted her hands.

"Happened a little while ago," Gus said. "Sadie went to feed the chickens and when she came back she saw Melora's cart going over the hill in front of the house. She thought that was strange. She went in the house and looked everywhere and the baby was gone. She sent the sickle grinder to the hay field after Jim and just as I left Jim come in and said he'd get the neighbors and they'd go after Melora. It's a terrible thing and Jim's about crazy and Sadie sittin' cryin' like her heart would break."

Uncle Rolfe looked at my mother. "Anne, you take the lunch to the meadow at noon for our hay hands. Billy, you come with me." He jammed his big hat lower on his black head and we started for the barn.

The heat waves shimmered all around us on the prairie as we rode toward Geranium House. When we got there our horses were covered with lather, but there wasn't any sign of the cart or Melora. Everything looked still and quiet and gray except for the flowers blooming in the windows and around the outside of the cabin.

Uncle Rolfe pushed the door open and Sam was propped up on some pillows, reading an old newspaper. There were two bright spots of color in his thin cheeks. "Hello, Rolfe," he said. "Thought you'd be making hay."

"Where's Melora?" Uncle Rolfe asked.

"Melora? She left me a lunch and said she was going to drive up to the timber and get some water lilies. A lily pond she found a while ago, I guess. I don't know where it is, though."

"I do," Uncle Rolfe said.

"Folks are lookin' for her," I said, my voice rising with excitement. "I bet they're goin' to——" Uncle Rolfe's big hand covered my mouth and he shoved me toward the door.

"What's wrong?" Sam said. "Has something happened to Melora?" And his face twisted like he was going to cry.

"No," Uncle Rolfe said gently, "nothing's wrong with Melora. You just take it easy, Sam."

It took us a while to reach the timber, for it was so hot we couldn't crowd the horses and there was no wind moving to cool things off. The smell of pines was thick, almost clogging my nose, and I could see big thunderclouds building up behind the mountains.

I didn't know where the pond was but Uncle Rolfe rode right to it. It was a small pond and very smooth, with the blue dragonflies hanging over the yellow lilies. Uncle Rolfe got off his horse and I followed. He took a few steps and stopped, staring.

There sat Melora under an aspen tree, holding the baby against her breast and her eyes closed and her mouth smiling. She didn't look like any ordinary woman sitting there. She looked like the pictures of saints they have in Sunday school books.

Uncle Rolfe said, "Melora——"

She opened her eyes and looked at us. Then she said in a small frightened voice, "I only wanted to have him a little while to myself—to feel him in my arms. I meant no harm to him." She got up then, holding the baby carefully. "He's asleep and don't you bother him."

"They're looking for you," Uncle Rolfe said. "Melora,

you shouldn't have done this. The women will never be your friends again.''

Melora bowed her head and began to cry. The sun came through the trees and made her hair shine until it looked like a halo. ''I only wanted to hold him,'' she said. ''I only wanted to have him in my arms a little while.''

''Hush!'' Uncle Rolfe said roughly. ''Where's the cart?''

''I hid it in the trees.''

Then Uncle Rolfe took hold of her arm and said to me, ''You bring the horses, Billy.''

Melora cried all the way through the timber until we reached the cart. Then she sat stiff and quiet, holding the baby. I rode along behind, leading Uncle Rolfe's horse.

When we got to the cabin on the flats there were several buggies and saddle horses there, and men were standing by the front door, their faces dark and angry. Inside the cabin I could hear Sam shouting hoarsely, ''She meant no harm, I tell you! She's good, a good woman with no mean thing in her!''

Uncle Rolfe took the baby and gave it to Sadie's husband, Jim Willard, and the baby wakened and started to cry. Jim Willard stared at Melora, his face ugly. ''You get outta this country!'' he shouted. ''We've got no place for baby stealers in the valley. If you ain't gone by tomorrow night, I'll burn this shack to the ground!''

Melora shrank back, pressed against the wheel of the cart, her eyes filled with a terrible look of pain and her lips moving but no word coming out. The men began to mutter and shift restlessly and someone said, ''Why don't we load their stuff and start 'em out of the valley now?''

Jim Willard kicked at one of the geranium plants that sat beside the cabin door. His big boot ground the blossom into the dirt. Melora gave a little cry and covered her face with her hands.

''That's enough, Jim!'' Uncle Rolfe's voice was cold. He moved to stand close to Melora, his shaggy black head lifted, his fists clenched. ''You men go home and leave her be. She's got no other place to go and her man's sick. I'll take care of things. I'll be responsible for her—and for him, too.''

One of the men moved forward toward Melora, and Uncle Rolfe's big hand grabbed him and shoved him aside, spinning him away like a toy man. There was some arguing then but Uncle Rolfe stood silent with that fierce look in his eyes. After a while the men got on their horses and in their buggies and went away. Melora walked slowly into the house and we could hear Sam half crying as he spoke her name, and then her voice, soft and warm, ''I'm here, Sam. Now don't you fret. Sleep now, and when you waken I'll have supper ready.''

''Come on, Billy,'' Uncle Rolfe said. His voice sounded old and tired. We rode slowly toward home.

It was black that night in the mountain country, black and sultry, the window curtains hanging motionless. When I went to bed it was too hot to sleep and I could hear thunder rumbling in the distance. Lightning began to play through the house, flashing streaks of blue and red, and I heard my uncle Rolfe moving in the bedroom next to mine. I heard his boots on the floor and then his steps going to the kitchen and a door closing. I got out of bed and ran through the dark house and when the lightning flared again, I saw my uncle Rolfe walking toward the barn. A little later, when the lightning glowed so bright it made me shiver, I saw my uncle Rolfe ride past the window, his hat pulled low on his black head. He was headed toward the flats.

I was awake a long time, for it was hard to sleep with the thunder getting close and loud and the lightning popping all around. When the storm broke I got up again and closed the door of Uncle Rolfe's room. A little later my mother came into the kitchen and lighted the lamp and heated some milk for us to drink. We sat close together in the kitchen until the storm went over and a cool wet wind began to blow through the house.

I never knew when Uncle Rolfe got home that night but the next morning he was at the breakfast table. And all the rest of the summer he didn't ride toward the flats again.

It was far into fall and I was going to country school when Gus came one Saturday morning and brought my mother two large red geranium plants with the penciled message on brown wrapping paper, "To Anne with love, from Melora."

"Pretty," Gus said. "Never did see such geraniums as are in that house now. And Melora, she's bloomin' like the flowers."

Uncle Rolfe put down the local paper he'd just started to open and turned to look at Gus.

"Yes sir," Gus went on, "she always was a woman a man had to look at more than once, but now she's downright beautiful. Sam, he's not much better. Might be he'd die tomorrow and might be he'd live a few years yet. Never can tell about things like that. And I guess if he did die, somebody'd look out for a woman like Melora."

"I expect so," my mother said, pouring coffee for Gus.

"The Lord's favored her, make no mistake about that," Gus went on, "for she's going to have that baby she's been hankerin' for. The women, they've all forgive her for what she did and been up there with baby clothes and buyin' her geraniums again." Gus sighed and sucked at the end of his drooping brown mustache. "Only the Lord's doing would give a woman a baby when she needed it so bad and didn't have but a shell of a man to love her."

My mother lifted her head and stared at my uncle Rolfe, a strange softness in her eyes and around her mouth. My uncle Rolfe looked back at my mother and it seemed to me they said a lot of things to each other without speaking a word. Then my uncle Rolfe opened the local paper and began to read the news.

THREE-TEN TO YUMA

▼

Elmore Leonard

He had picked up his prisoner at Fort Huachuca shortly after midnight and now, in a silent early morning mist, they approached Contention. The two riders moved slowly, one behind the other.

Entering Stockman Street, Paul Scallen glanced back at the open country with the wet haze blanketing its flatness, thinking of the long night ride from Huachuca, relieved that this much was over. When his body turned again, his hand moved over the sawed-off shotgun that was across his lap and he kept his eyes on the man ahead of him until they were near the end of the second block, opposite the side entrance of the Republic Hotel.

He said just above a whisper, though it was clear in the silence, "End of the line."

The man turned in his saddle, looking at Scallen curiously, "The jail's around on Commercial."

"I want you to be comfortable."

Scallen stepped out of the saddle, lifting a Winchester from the boot, and walked toward the hotel's side door. A figure stood in the gloom of the doorway, behind the screen, and as Scallen reached the steps the screen door opened.

"Are you the marshal?"

"Yes, sir." Scallen's voice was soft and without emotion. "Deputy, from Bisbee."

"We're ready for you. Two-oh-seven. A corner... fronts on Commercial." He sounded proud of the accommodation.

"You're Mr. Timpey?"

The man in the doorway looked surprised. "Yeah, Wells Fargo. Who'd you expect?"

"You might have got a back room, Mr. Timpey. One with no windows." He swung the shotgun on the man still mounted. "Step down easy, Jim."

The man, who was in his early twenties, a few years younger than Scallen, sat with one hand over the other on the saddle horn. Now he gripped the horn and swung down. When he was on the ground his hands were still close together, iron manacles holding them three chain lengths apart. Scallen motioned him toward the door with the stubby barrel of the shotgun.

"Anyone in the lobby?"

"The desk clerk," Timpey answered him, "and a man in a chair by the front door."

"Who is he?"

"I don't know. He's asleep... got his brim down over his eyes."

"Did you see anyone out on Commercial?"

"No... I haven't been out there." At first he had seemed nervous, but now he was irritated, and a frown made his face pout childishly.

Scallen said calmly, "Mr. Timpey, it was your line this man robbed. You want to see him go all the way to Yuma, don't you?"

"Certainly I do." His eyes went to the outlaw, Jim Kidd, then back to Scallen hurriedly. "But why all the melodrama? The man's under arrest—already been sentenced."

"But he's not in jail till he walks through the gates at

Yuma," Scallen said. "I'm only one man, Mr. Timpey, and I've got to get him there."

"Well, dammit . . . I'm not the law! Why didn't you bring men with you? All I know is I got a wire from our Bisbee office to get a hotel room and meet you here the morning of November third. There weren't any instructions that I had to get myself deputized a marshal. That's your job."

"I know it is, Mr. Timpey," Scallen said, and smiled, though it was an effort. "But I want to make sure no one knows Jim Kidd's in Contention until after train time this afternoon."

Jim Kidd had been looking from one to the other with a faintly amused grin. Now he said to Timpey, "He means he's afraid somebody's going to jump him." He smiled at Scallen. "That marshal must've really sold you a bill of goods."

"What's he talking about?" Timpey said.

Kidd went on before Scallen could answer. "They hid me in the Huachuca lock-up 'cause they knew nobody could get at me there . . . and finally the Bisbee marshal gets a plan. He and some others hopped the train in Benson last night, heading for Yuma with an army prisoner passed off as me." Kidd laughed, as if the idea were ridiculous.

"Is that right?" Timpey said.

Scallen nodded. "Pretty much right."

"How does he know all about it?"

"He's got ears and ten fingers to add with."

"I don't like it. Why just one man?"

"Every deputy from here down to Bisbee is out trying to scare up the rest of them. Jim here's the only one we caught," Scallen explained—then added, "Alive."

Timpey shot a glance at the outlaw. "Is he the one who killed Dick Moons?"

"One of the passengers swears he saw who did it . . . and he didn't identify Kidd at the trial."

Timpey shook his head. "Dick drove for us a long time. You know his brother lives here in Contention. When he heard about it he almost went crazy." He hesitated, and then said again, "I don't like it."

Scallen felt his patience wearing away, but he kept his voice even when he said, "Maybe I don't either . . . but what you like and what I like aren't going to matter a whole lot, with the marshal past Tucson by now. You can grumble about it all you want, Mr. Timpey, as long as you keep it under your breath. Jim's got friends . . . and since I have to haul him clear across the territory, I'd just as soon they didn't know about it."

Timpey fidgeted nervously. "I don't see why I have to get dragged into this. My job's got nothing to do with law enforcement . . ."

"You have the room key?"

"In the door. All I'm responsible for is the stage run between here and Tucson—"

Scallen shoved the Winchester at him. "If you'll take care of this and the horses till I get back, I'll be obliged to you . . . and I know I don't have to ask you not to mention we're at the hotel."

He waved the shotgun and nodded and Jim Kidd went ahead of him through the side door into the hotel lobby. Scallen was a stride behind him, holding the stubby shotgun close to his leg. "Up the stairs on the right, Jim."

Kidd started up, but Scallen paused to glance at the figure in the arm chair near the front. He was sitting on his spine with limp hands folded on his stomach and, as Timpey had described, his hat low over the upper part of his face. *You've seen people sleeping in hotel lobbies before,* Scallen told himself, and followed Kidd up the stairs. He couldn't stand and wonder about it.

Room 207 was narrow and high-ceilinged, with a single window looking down on Commercial Street. An iron bed was placed the long way against one wall and extended to the right side of the window, and along the opposite wall was a dresser with wash basin and pitcher and next to it a rough-board wardrobe. An unpainted table and two straight chairs took up most of the remaining space.

"Lay down on the bed if you want to," Scallen said.

"Why don't you sleep?" Kidd asked. "I'll hold the shotgun."

The deputy moved one of the straight chairs near to the door and the other to the side of the table opposite the bed. Then he sat down, resting the shotgun on the table so that it pointed directly at Jim Kidd sitting on the edge of the bed near the window.

He gazed vacantly outside. A patch of dismal sky showed above the frame buildings across the way, but he was not sitting close enough to look directly down onto the street. He said, indifferently, "I think it's going to rain."

There was a silence, and then Scallen said, "Jim, I don't have anything against you personally . . . this is what I get paid for, but I just want it understood that if you start across the seven feet between us, I'm going to pull both triggers at once—without first asking you to stop. That clear?"

Kidd looked at the deputy marshal, then his eyes drifted out the window again. "It's kinda cold, too." He rubbed his hands together and the three chain links rattled against each other. "The window's open a crack. Can I close it?"

Scallen's grip tightened on the shotgun and he brought the barrel up, though he wasn't aware of it. "If you can reach it from where you're sitting."

Kidd looked at the window sill and said without reaching toward it, "Too far."

"All right," Scallen said, rising. "Lay back on the bed." He worked his gun belt around so that now the Colt was on his left hip.

Kidd went back slowly, smiling. "You don't take any chances, do you? Where's your sporting blood?"

"Down in Bisbee with my wife and three youngsters," Scallen told him without smiling, and moved around the table.

There were no grips on the window frame. Standing with his side to the window, facing the man on the bed, he put the heel of his hand on the bottom ledge of the frame and shoved down hard. The window banged shut and with the slam he saw Jim Kidd kicking up off of his back, his body straining to rise without his hands to help. Momentarily,

Scallen hesitated and his finger tensed on the trigger. Kidd's feet were on the floor, his body swinging up and his head down to lunge from the bed. Scallen took one step and brought his knee up hard against Kidd's face.

The outlaw went back across the bed, his head striking the wall. He lay there with his eyes open looking at Scallen.

"Feel better now, Jim?"

Kidd brought his hands up to his mouth, working the jaw around. "Well, I had to try you out," he said. "I didn't think you'd shoot."

"But you know I will the next time."

For a few minutes Kidd remained motionless. Then he began to pull himself straight. "I just want to sit up."

Behind the table, Scallen said, "Help yourself." He watched Kidd stare out the window.

Then, "How much do you make, Marshal?" Kidd asked the question abruptly.

"I don't think it's any of your business."

"What difference does it make?"

Scallen hesitated. "A hundred and fifty a month," he said, finally, "some expenses, and a dollar bounty for every arrest against a Bisbee ordinance in the town limits."

Kidd shook his head sympathetically. "And you got a wife and three kids."

"Well, it's more than a cowhand makes."

"But you're not a cowhand."

"I've worked my share of beef."

"Forty a month and keep, huh?" Kidd laughed.

"That's right, forty a month," Scallen said. He felt awkward. "How much do you make?"

Kidd grinned. When he smiled he looked very young, hardly out of his teens. "Name a month," he said. "It varies."

"But you've made a lot of money."

"Enough. I can buy what I want."

"What are you going to be wanting the next five years?"

"You're pretty sure we're going to Yuma."

"And you're pretty sure we're not," Scallen said.

"Well, I've got two train passes and a shotgun that says we are. What've you got?"

Kidd smiled. "You'll see." Then he said right after it, his tone changing, "What made you join the law?"

"The money," Scallen answered, and felt foolish as he said it. But he went on, "I was working for a spread over by the Pantano Wash when Old Nana broke loose and raised hell up the Santa Rosa Valley. The army was going around in circles, so the Pima County marshal got up a bunch to help out and we tracked Apaches almost all spring. The marshal and I got along fine, so he offered me a deputy job if I wanted it." He wanted to say that he started for seventy-five and worked up to the one hundred and fifty, but he didn't.

"And then someday you'll get to be marshal and make two hundred."

"Maybe."

"And then one night a drunk cowhand you've never seen will be tearing up somebody's saloon and you'll go in to arrest him and he'll drill you with a lucky shot before you get your gun out."

"So you're telling me I'm crazy."

"If you don't already know it."

Scallen took his hand off the shotgun and pulled tobacco and paper from his shirt pocket and began rolling a cigarette. "Have you figured out yet what my price is?"

Kidd looked startled, momentarily, but the grin returned. "No, I haven't. Maybe you come higher than I thought."

Scallen scratched a match across the table, lighted the cigarette, then threw it to the floor, between Kidd's boots. "You don't have enough money, Jim."

Kidd shrugged, then reached down for the cigarette. "You've treated me pretty good. I just wanted to make it easy on you."

The sun came into the room after a while. Weakly at first, cold and hazy. Then it warmed and brightened and cast an oblong patch of light between the bed and the table. The morning wore on slowly because there was nothing to do and each man sat restlessly thinking about somewhere else, though it was a restlessness within and it showed on neither of them.

The deputy rolled cigarettes for the outlaw and himself and most of the time they smoked in silence. Once Kidd asked him what time the train left. He told him shortly after three, but Kidd made no comment.

Scallen went to the window and looked out at the narrow rutted road that was Commercial Street. He pulled a watch from his vest pocket and looked at it. It was almost noon, yet there were few people about. He wondered about this and asked himself if it was unnaturally quiet for a Saturday noon in Contention . . . or if it were just his nerves . . .

He studied the man standing under the wooden awning across the street, leaning idly against a support post with his thumbs hooked in his belt and his flat-crowned hat on the back of his head. There was something familiar about him. And each time Scallen had gone to the window—a few times during the past hour—the man had been there.

He glanced at Jim Kidd lying across the bed, then looked out the window in time to see another man moving up next to the one at the post. They stood together for the space of a minute before the second man turned a horse from the tie rail, swung up and rode off down the street.

The man at the post watched him go and tilted his hat against the sun glare. And then it registered. With the hat low on his forehead Scallen saw him again as he had that morning. The man lying in the arm chair . . . as if asleep.

He saw his wife, then, and the three youngsters and he could almost feel the little girl sitting on his lap where she had climbed up to kiss him good-bye, and he had promised to bring her something from Tucson. He didn't know why they had come to him all of a sudden. And after he had put them out of his mind, since there was no room now, there was an upset feeling inside as if he had swallowed something that would not go down all the way. It made his heart beat a little faster.

Jim Kidd was smiling up at him. "Anybody I know?"

"I didn't think it showed."

"Like the sun going down."

Scallen glanced at the man across the street and then to Jim Kidd. "Come here." He nodded to the window. "Tell me who your friend is over there."

Kidd half rose and leaned over looking out the window, then sat down again. "Charlie Prince."

"Somebody else just went for help."

"Charlie doesn't need help."

"How did you know you were going to be in Contention?"

"You told that Wells Fargo man I had friends . . . and about the posses chasing around in the hills. Figure it out for yourself. You could be looking out a window in Benson and seeing the same thing."

"They're not going to do you any good."

"I don't know any man who'd get himself killed for a hundred and fifty dollars." Kidd paused. "Especially a man with a wife and young ones . . ."

Men rode to town in something less than an hour later. Scallen heard the horses coming up Commercial, and went to the window to see the six riders pull to a stop and range themselves in a line in the middle of the street facing the hotel. Charlie Prince stood behind them, leaning against the post.

Then he moved away from it, leisurely, and stepped down into the street. He walked between the horses and stopped in front of them just below the window. He cupped his hands to his mouth and shouted, *"Jim!"*

In the quiet street it was like a pistol shot.

Scallen looked at Kidd, seeing the smile that softened his face and was even in his eyes. Confidence. It was all over him. And even with the manacles on, you would believe that it was Jim Kidd who was holding the shotgun.

"What do you want me to tell him?" Kidd said.

"Tell him you'll write every day."

Kidd laughed and went to the window, pushing it up by the top of the frame. It raised a few inches. Then he moved his hands under the window and it slid up all the way.

"Charlie, you go buy the boys a drink. We'll be down shortly."

"Are you all right?"

"Sure I'm all right."

Charlie Prince hesitated. "What if you don't come down? He could kill you and say you tried to break ... Jim, you tell him what'll happen if we hear a gun go off."

"He knows," Kidd said, and closed the window. He looked at Scallen standing motionless with the shotgun under his arm. "Your turn, Marshal."

"What do you expect me to say?"

"Something that makes sense. You said before I didn't mean a thing to you personally—what you're doing is just a job. Well, you figure out if it's worth getting killed for. All you have to do is throw your guns on the bed and let me walk out the door and you can go back to Bisbee and arrest all the drunks you want. Nobody's going to blame you with the odds stacked seven to one. You know your wife's not going to complain ..."

"You should have been a lawyer, Jim."

The smile began to fade from Kidd's face. "Come on—what's it going to be?"

The door rattled with three knocks in quick succession. Abruptly the room was silent. The two men looked at each other and now the smile disappeared from Kidd's face completely.

Scallen moved to the side of the door, tiptoeing in his high-heeled boots, then pointed his shotgun toward the bed. Kidd sat down.

"Who is it?"

For a moment there was no answer. Then he heard, "Timpey."

He glanced at Kidd who was watching him. "What do you want?"

"I've got a pot of coffee for you."

Scallen hesitated. "You alone?"

"Of course I am. Hurry up, it's hot!"

He drew the key from his coat pocket, then held the shotgun in the crook of his arm as he inserted the key with one hand and turned the knob with the other. The door opened—and slammed against him, knocking him back against the dresser. He went off balance, sliding into the wardrobe, going down on his hands and knees, and the shotgun clattered across the floor to the window. He saw Jim Kidd drop to the floor for the gun . . .

"Hold it!"

A heavyset man stood in the doorway with a Colt pointing out past the thick bulge of his stomach. "Leave that shotgun where it is." Timpey stood next to him with the coffeepot in his hand. There was coffee down the front of his suit, on the door and on the flooring. He brushed at the front of his coat feebly, looking from Scallen to the man with the pistol.

"I couldn't help it, Marshal—he made me do it. He threatened to do something to me if I didn't."

"Who is he?"

"Bob Moons . . . you know, Dick's brother . . ."

The heavyset man glanced at Timpey angrily. "Shut your damn whining." His eyes went to Jim Kidd and held there. "You know who I am, don't you?"

Kidd looked uninterested. "You don't resemble anybody I know."

"You didn't have to know Dick to shoot him!"

"I didn't shoot that messenger."

Scallen got to his feet, looking at Timpey. "What the hell's wrong with you?"

"I couldn't help it. He forced me."

"How did he know we were here?"

"He came in this morning talking about Dick and I felt he needed some cheering up, so I told him Jim Kidd had been tried and was being taken to Yuma and was here in town . . . on his way. Bob didn't say anything and went out, and a little later he came back with the gun."

"You damn fool." Scallen shook his head wearily.

"Never mind all the talk." Moons kept the pistol on Kidd. "I would've found him sooner or later. This way, everybody gets saved a long train ride."

"You pull that trigger," Scallen said, "and you'll hang for murder."

"Like he did for killing Dick . . ."

"A jury said he didn't do it." Scallen took a step toward the big man. "And I'm damned if I'm going to let you pass another sentence."

"You stay put or I'll pass sentence on you!"

Scallen moved a slow step nearer. "Hand me the gun, Bob."

"I'm warning you—get the hell out of the way and let me do what I came for."

"Bob, hand me the gun or I swear I'll beat you through that wall."

Scallen tensed to take another step, another slow one. He saw Moons' eyes dart from him to Kidd and in that instant he knew it would be his only chance. He lunged, swinging his coat aside with his hand and when the hand came up it was holding a Colt. All in one motion. The pistol went up and chopped an arc across Moons' head before the big man could bring his own gun around. His hat flew off as the barrel swiped his skull and he went back against the wall heavily, then sank to the floor.

Scallen wheeled to face the window, thumbing the hammer back. But Kidd was still sitting on the edge of the bed with the shotgun at his feet.

The deputy relaxed, letting the hammer ease down. "You might have made it, that time."

Kidd shook his head. "I wouldn't have got off the bed." There was a note of surprise in his voice. "You know, you're pretty good . . ."

At two-fifteen Scallen looked at his watch, then stood up, pushing the chair back. The shotgun was under his arm. In less than an hour they would leave the hotel, walk over Commercial to Stockman and then up Stockman to the station. Three blocks. He wanted to go all the way. He wanted to get Jim Kidd on that train . . . but he was afraid.

He was afraid of what he might do once they were on the street. Even now his breath was short and occasionally he would inhale and let the air out slowly to calm himself. And he kept asking himself if it was worth it.

People would be in the windows and the doors though you wouldn't see them. They'd have their own feelings and

most of their hearts would be pounding . . . and they'd edge
back of the door frames a little more. The man out on the
street was something without a human nature or a person-
ality of its own. He was on a stage. The street was another
world.

Timpey sat on the chair in front of the door and next to
him, squatting on the floor with his back against the wall,
was Moons. Scallen had unloaded Moons' pistol and placed
it in the pitcher behind him. Kidd was on the bed.

Most of the time he stared at Scallen. His face bore a
puzzled expression, making his eyes frown, and sometimes
he would cock his head as if studying the deputy from a
different angle.

Scallen stepped to the window now. Charlie Prince and
another man were under the awning. The others were not
in sight.

"You haven't changed your mind?" Kidd asked him seriously.

Scallen shook his head.

"I don't understand you. You risk your neck to save my
life, now you'll risk it again to send me to prison."

Scallen looked at Kidd and suddenly felt closer to him
than any man he knew. "Don't ask me, Jim," he said, and
sat down again.

After that he looked at his watch every few minutes.

At five minutes to three he walked to the door, motioning
Timpey aside, and turned the key in the lock. "Let's go,
Jim." When Kidd was next to him he prodded Moons with
the gun barrel. "Over on the bed. Mister, if I see or hear
about you on the street before train time, you'll face an
attempted murder charge." He motioned Kidd past him,
then stepped into the hall and locked the door.

They went down the stairs and crossed the lobby to the
front door, Scallen a stride behind with the shotgun barrel
almost touching Kidd's back. Passing through the doorway
he said as calmly as he could, "Turn left on Stockman and
keep walking. No matter what you hear, keep walking."

As they stepped out into Commercial, Scallen glanced at
the ramada where Charlie Prince had been standing, but

now the saloon porch was an empty shadow. Near the corner, two horses stood under a sign that said *Eat*, in red letters; and on the other side of Stockman the signs continued, lining the rutted main street to make it seem narrower. And beneath the signs, in the shadows, nothing moved. There was a whisper of wind along the ramadas. It whipped sand specks from the street and rattled them against clapboard, and the sound was hollow and lifeless. Somewhere a screen door banged, far away.

They passed the cafe, turning onto Stockman. Ahead, the deserted street narrowed with distance to a dead end at the rail station—a single-story building standing by itself, low and sprawling with most of the platform in shadow. The westbound was there, along the platform, but the engine and most of the cars were hidden by the station house. White steam lifted above the roof to be lost in the sun's glare.

They were almost to the platform when Kidd said over his shoulder, "Run like hell while you're still able."

"Where are they?"

Kidd grinned, because he knew Scallen was afraid. "How should I know?"

"Tell them to come out in the open!"

"Tell them yourself."

"Dammit, *tell* them!" Scallen clenched his jaw and jabbed the short barrel into Kidd's back. "I'm not fooling. If they don't come out, I'll kill you!"

Kidd felt the gun barrel hard against his spine and suddenly he shouted, "Charlie!"

It echoed in the street, but after there was only the silence. Kidd's eyes darted over the shadowed porches. "Dammit, Charlie—hold on!"

Scallen prodded him up the warped plank steps to the shade of the platform and suddenly he could feel them near. "Tell him again!"

"Don't shoot, Charlie!" Kidd screamed the words.

From the other side of the station they heard the trainman's call trailing off, ". . . Gila Bend. Sentinel, Yuma!"

The whistle sounded loud, wailing, as they passed into

the shade of the platform, then out again to the naked glare of the open side. Scallen squinted, glancing toward the station office, but the train dispatcher was not in sight. Nor was anyone. "It's the mail car," he said to Kidd. "The second to last one." Steam hissed from the iron cylinder of the engine, clouding that end of the platform. "Hurry it up!" he snapped, pushing Kidd along.

Then, from behind, hurried footsteps sounded on the planking, and, as the hiss of steam died away—"Stand where you are!"

The locomotive's main rods strained back, rising like the legs of a grotesque grasshopper, and the wheels moved. The connecting rods stopped on an upward swing and couplings clanged down the line of cars.

"Throw the gun away, brother!"

Charlie Prince stood at the corner of the station house with a pistol in each hand. Then he moved around carefully between the two men and the train. "Throw it far away, and unhitch your belt," he said.

"Do what he says," Kidd said. "They've got you."

The others, six of them, were strung out in the dimness of the platform shed. Grim-faced, stubbles of beard, hat brims low. The man nearest Prince spat tobacco lazily.

Scallen knew fear at that moment as fear had never gripped him before; but he kept the shotgun hard against Kidd's spine. He said, just above a whisper, "Jim—I'll cut you in half!"

Kidd's body was stiff, his shoulders drawn up tightly. "Wait a minute . . ." he said. He held his palms out to Charlie Prince, though he could have been speaking to Scallen.

Suddenly Prince shouted, "Go down!"

There was a fraction of a moment of dead silence that seemed longer. Kidd hesitated. Scallen was looking at the gunman over Kidd's shoulder, seeing the two pistols. Then Kidd was gone, rolling on the planking, and the pistols were coming up, one ahead of the other. Without moving, Scallen squeezed both triggers of the scatter gun.

Charlie Prince was going down, holding his hands tight

to his chest, as Scallen dropped the shotgun and swung around drawing his Colt. He fired hurriedly. *Wait for a target!* Words in his mind. He saw the men under the platform shed, three of them breaking for the station office, two going full length to the planks ... one crouched, his pistol up. *That one! Get him quick!* Scallen aimed and squeezed the heavy revolver and the man went down. *Now get the hell out!*

Charlie Prince was facedown. Kidd was crawling, crawling frantically and coming to his feet when Scallen reached him. He grabbed Kidd by the collar savagely, pushing him on and dug the pistol into his back. "Run, damn you!"

Gunfire erupted from the shed and thudded into the wooden caboose as they ran past it. The train was moving slowly. Just in front of them a bullet smashed a window of the mail car. Someone screamed, "You'll hit Jim!" There was another shot, then it was too late. Scallen and Kidd leaped up on the car platform and were in the mail car as it rumbled past the end of the station platform.

Kidd was on the floor, stretched out along a row of mail sacks. He rubbed his shoulder awkwardly with his manacled hands and watched Scallen who stood against the wall next to the open door.

Kidd studied the deputy for some minutes. Finally he said, "You know, you really earn your hundred and a half."

Scallen heard him, though the iron rhythm of the train wheels and his breathing were loud in his temples. He felt as if all his strength had been sapped, but he couldn't help smiling at Jim Kidd. He was thinking pretty much the same thing.

THE TIN STAR

▼▼

John M. Cunningham

Sheriff Doane looked at his deputy and then down at the daisies he had picked for his weekly visit, lying wrapped in newspaper on his desk. "I'm sorry to hear you say that, Toby. I was kind of counting on you to take over after me."

"Don't get me wrong, Doane," Toby said, looking through the front window. "I'm not afraid. I'll see you through this shindig. I'm not afraid of Jordan or young Jordan or any of them. But I want to tell you now. I'll wait till Jordan's train gets in. I'll wait to see what he does. I'll see you through whatever happens. After that, I'm quitting."

Doane began kneading his knuckles, his face set against the pain as he gently rubbed the arthritic, twisted bones. He said nothing.

Toby looked around, his brown eyes troubled in his round, olive-skinned face. "What's the use of holding down a job like this? Look at you. What'd you ever get out of it? Enough to keep you eating. And what for?"

Doane stopped kneading his arthritic hands and looked

down at the star on his shirt front. He looked from it to the smaller one on Toby's. "That's right," he said. "They don't even hang the right ones. You risk your life catching somebody, and the damned juries let them go so they can come back and shoot at you. You're poor all your life, you got to do everything twice, and in the end they pay you off in lead. So you can wear a tin star. It's a job for a dog, son."

Toby's voice did not rise, but his eyes were a little wider in his round, gentle face. "Then why keep on with it? What for? I been working for you for two years—trying to keep the law so sharp-nosed money-grabbers can get rich, while we piddle along on what the county pays us. I've seen men I used to bust playing marbles going up and down this street on four-hundred-dollar saddles, and what've I got? Nothing. Not a damned thing."

There was a little smile around Doane's wide mouth. "That's right, Toby. It's all for free. The headaches, the bullets and everything, all for free. I found that out long ago." The mock-grave look vanished. "But somebody's got to be around and take care of things." He looked out of the window at the people walking up and down the crazy boardwalks. "I like it free. You know what I mean? You don't get a thing for it. You've got to risk everything. And you're free inside. Like the larks. You know the larks? How they get up in the sky and sing when they want to? A pretty bird. A very pretty bird. That's the way I like to feel inside."

Toby looked at him without expression. "That's the way you look at it. I don't see it. I've only got one life. You talk about doing it all for nothing, and that gives you something. What? What've you got now, waiting for Jordan to come?"

"I don't know yet. We'll have to wait and see."

Toby turned back to the window. "All right, but I'm through. I don't see any sense in risking your neck for nothing."

"Maybe you will," Doane said, beginning to work on his hands again.

"Here comes Mettrick. I guess he don't give up so easy. He's still got that resignation in his hand."

"I guess he doesn't," Doane said. "But I'm through listening. Has young Jordan come out of the saloon yet?"

"No," Toby said, and stepped aside as the door opened. Mettrick came in. "Now listen, Doane," he burst out, "for the last time—"

"Shut up, Percy," Doane said. "Sit down over there and shut up or get out."

The flare went out of the mayor's eyes. "Doane," he moaned, "you are the biggest—"

"Shut up," Doane said. "Toby, has he come out yet?"

Toby stood a little back from the window, where the slant of golden sunlight, swarming with dust, wouldn't strike his white shirt.

"Yes. He's got a chair. He's looking this way, Doane. He's still drinking. I can see a bottle on the porch beside him."

"I expected that. Not that it makes much difference." He looked down at the bunch of flowers.

Mettrick, in the straight chair against the wall, looked up at him, his black eyes scornful in his long, hopeless face.

"Don't make much difference? Who the hell do you think you are, Doane? God? It just means he'll start the trouble without waiting for his stinking brother, that's all it means." His hand was shaking, and the white paper hanging listlessly from his fingers fluttered slightly. He looked at it angrily and stuck it out at Doane. "I gave it to you. I did the best I could. Whatever happens, don't be blaming me, Doane. I gave you a chance to resign, and if—" He left off and sat looking at the paper in his hand as though it were a dead puppy of his that somebody had run a buggy over.

Doane, standing with the square, almost chisel-pointed tips of his fingers just touching the flowers, turned slowly, with the care of movement he would have used around a crazy horse. "I know you're my friend, Percy. Just take it easy, Percy. If I don't resign, it's not because I'm ungrateful."

"Here comes Staley with the news," Toby said from the window. "He looks like somebody just shot his grandma."

Percy Mettrick laid his paper on the desk and began smoothing it out ruefully. "It's not as though it were dishonorable, Doane. You should have quit two years ago, when your hands went bad. It's not dishonorable now. You've still got time."

He glanced up at the wall clock. "It's only three. You've got an hour before he gets in . . . you can take your horse . . ." As he talked to himself, Doane looking slantwise at him with his little smile, he grew more cheerful. "Here." He jabbed a pen out at Doane. "Sign it and get out of town."

The smile left Doane's mouth. "This is an elective office. I don't have to take orders, even if you are mayor." His face softened. "It's simpler than you think, Percy. When they didn't hang Jordan, I knew this day would come. Five years ago, I knew it was coming, when they gave him that silly sentence. I've been waiting for it."

"But not to commit suicide," Mettrick said in a low voice, his eyes going down to Doane's gouty hands. Doane's knobby, twisted fingers closed slowly into fists, as though hiding themselves; his face flushed slightly. "I may be slow, but I can still shoot."

The mayor stood up and went slowly over to the door.

"Goodbye, Doane."

"I'm not saying goodbye, Percy. Not yet."

"Goodbye," Mettrick repeated, and went out of the door.

Toby turned from the window. His face was tight around the mouth. "You should have resigned like he said, Doane. You ain't a match for one of them alone, much less two of them together. And if Pierce and Frank Colby come, too, like they was all together before—"

"Shut up, shut up," Doane said. "For God's sake, shut up." He sat down suddenly at the desk and covered his face with his hands. "Maybe the pen changes a man." He was sitting stiff, hardly breathing.

"What are you going to do, Doane?"

"Nothing. I can't do anything until they start something.

I can't do a thing. . . . Maybe the pen changes a man. Sometimes it does. I remember—''

"Listen, Doane," Toby said, his voice, for the first time, urgent. "It maybe changes some men, but not Jordan. It's already planned, what they're going to do. Why else would young Jordan be over there, watching? He's come three hundred miles for this."

"I've seen men go in the pen hard as rock and come out peaceful and settle down. Maybe Jordan—''

Toby's face relapsed into dullness. He turned back to the window listlessly. Doane's hands dropped.

"You don't think that's true, Toby?"

Toby sighed. "You know it isn't so, Doane. He swore he'd get you. That's the truth."

Doane's hands came up again in front of his face, but this time he was looking at them, his big gray eyes going quickly from one to the other, almost as though he were afraid of them. He curled his fingers slowly into fists, and uncurled them slowly, pulling with all his might, yet slowly. A thin sheen on his face reflected the sunlight from the floor. He got up.

"Is he still there?" he asked.

"Sure, he's still there."

"Maybe he'll get drunk. Dead drunk."

"You can't get a Jordan that drunk."

Doane stood with feet apart, looking at the floor, staring back and forth along one of the cracks. "Why didn't they hang him?" he asked the silence in the room.

"Why didn't they hang him?" he repeated, his voice louder.

Toby kept his post by the window, not moving a muscle in his face, staring out at the man across the street. "I don't know," he said. "For murder, they should. I guess they should, but they didn't."

Doane's eyes came again to the flowers, and some of the strain went out of his face. Then suddenly his eyes closed and he gave a long sigh, and then, luxuriously, stretched his arms. "Good God!" he said, his voice easy again. "It's funny how it comes over you like that." He shook his head violently. "I don't know why it should. It's not the first time. But it always does."

"I know," Toby said.

"It just builds up and then it busts."

"I know."

"The train may be late."

Toby said nothing.

"You never can tell," Doane said, buckling on his gun belt. "Things may have changed with Jordan. Maybe won't even come. You never can tell. I'm going up to the cemetery as soon as we hear from Staley."

"I wouldn't. You'd just tempt young Jordan to start something."

"I've been going up there every Sunday since she died."

"We'd best both just stay in here. Let them make the first move."

Feet sounded on the steps outside and Doane stopped breathing for a second. Staley came in, his face pinched, tight and dead, his eyes on the floor. Doane looked him over carefully.

"Is it on time?" he asked steadily.

Staley looked up, his faded blue eyes distant, pointed somewhere over Doane's head. "Mr. Doane, you ain't handled this thing right. You should of drove young Jordan out of town." His hand went to his chest and he took off the deputy's badge.

"What are you doing?" Doane asked sharply.

"If you'd of handled it right, we could have beat this," Staley said, his voice louder.

"You know nobody's done nothing yet," Toby said softly, his gentle brown eyes on Staley. "There's nothing we can do until they start something."

"I'm quitting, Mr. Doane," Staley said. He looked around for someplace to put the star. He started for the desk, hesitated, and then awkwardly, with a peculiar diffidence, laid the star gently on the window sill.

Doane's jaw began to jut a little. "You still haven't answered my question. Is the train on time?"

"Yes. Four ten. Just on time." Staley stood staring at

Doane, then swallowed. "I saw Frank Colby. He was in the livery putting up his horse. He'd had a long ride on that horse. I asked him what he was doing in town—friendly like." He ducked his head and swallowed again. "He didn't know I was a deputy, I had my star off." He looked up again. "They're all meeting together, Mr. Doane. Young Jordan, and Colby and Pierce. They're going to meet Jordan when he comes in. The same four."

"So you're quitting," Doane said.

"Yes, sir. It ain't been handled right."

Toby stood looking at him, his gentle eyes dull. "Get out," he said, his voice low and tight.

Staley looked at him, nodded and tried to smile, which was too weak to last. "Sure."

Toby took a step toward him. Staley's eyes were wild as he stood against the door. He tried to back out of Toby's way.

"Get out," Toby said again, and his small brown fist flashed out. Staley stepped backward and fell down the steps in a sprawling heap, scrambled to his feet and hobbled away. Toby closed the door slowly. He stood rubbing his knuckles, his face red and tight.

"That didn't do any good," Doane said softly.

Toby turned on him. "It couldn't do no harm," he said acidly, throwing the words into Doane's face.

"You want to quit, too?" Doane asked, smiling.

"Sure, I want to quit," Toby shot out. "Sure. Go on to your blasted cemetery, go on with your flowers, old man—" He sat down suddenly on the straight chair. "Put a flower up there for me, too."

Doane went to the door. "Put some water on the heater, Toby. Set out the liniment that the vet gave me. I'll try it again when I get back. It might do some good yet."

He let himself out and stood in the sunlight on the porch, the flowers drooping in his hand, looking against the sun across the street at the dim figure under the shaded porch.

Then he saw the two other shapes hunkered against the front of the saloon in the shade of the porch, one on each side of young Jordan, who sat tilted back in a chair. Colby and Pierce. The glare of the sun beat back from the blinding white dust and fought shimmering in the air.

Doane pulled the brim of his hat farther down in front and stepped slowly down to the board sidewalk, observing carefully from squinted eyes, and just as carefully avoiding any pause which might be interpreted as a challenge.

Young Jordan had the bottle to his lips as Doane came out. He held it there for a moment motionless, and then, as Doane reached the walk, he passed the bottle slowly sideward to Colby and leaned forward, away from the wall, so that the chair came down softly. He sat there, leaning forward slightly, watching while Doane untied his horse. As Doane mounted, Jordan got up. Colby's hand grabbed one of his arms. He shook it off and untied his own horse from the rail.

Doane's mouth tightened and his eyes looked a little sad. He turned his horse, and holding the flowers so the jog would not rattle off the petals, headed up the street, looking straight ahead.

The hoofs of his horse made soft, almost inaudible little plops in the deep dust. Behind him he heard a sudden stamping of hoofs and then the harsh splitting and crash of wood. He looked back. Young Jordan's horse was up on the sidewalk, wild-eyed and snorting, with young Jordan leaning forward half out of the saddle, pushing himself back from the horse's neck, back off the horn into the saddle, swaying insecurely. And as Jordan managed the horse off the sidewalk Doane looked quickly forward again, his eyes fixed distantly ahead and blank.

He passed men he knew, and out of the corner of his eye he saw their glances slowly follow him, calm, or gloomy, or shrewdly speculative. As he passed, he knew their glances were shifting to the man whose horse was softly coming behind him. It was like that all the way up the street. The flowers were drooping markedly now.

The town petered out with a few Mexican shacks, the road dwindled to broad ruts, and the sage was suddenly on all sides of him, stretching away toward the heat-obscured mountains like an infinite multitude of gray-green sheep.

He turned off the road and began the slight ascent up the little hill whereon the cemetery lay. Grasshoppers shrilled invisibly in the sparse, dried grass along the track, silent as he came by, and shrill again as he passed, only to become silent again as the other rider came.

He swung off at the rusty barbed wire Missouri gate and slipped the loop from the post, and the shadow of the other slid tall across his path and stopped. Doane licked his lips quickly and looked up, his grasp tightening on the now sweat-wilted newspaper. Young Jordan was sitting his horse, open-mouthed, leaning forward with his hands on the pommel to support himself, his eyes vague and dull. His lips were wet and red, and hung in a slight smile.

A lark made the air sweet over to the left, and then Doane saw it, rising into the air. It hung in the sun, over the cemetery. Moving steadily and avoiding all suddenness, Doane hung his reins over the post.

"You don't like me, do you?" young Jordan said. A long thread of saliva descended from the corner of his slackly smiling mouth.

Doane's face set into a sort of blank preparedness. He turned and started slowly through the gate, his shoulders hunched up and pulled backward.

Jordan got down from the saddle, and Doane turned toward him slowly. Jordan came forward straight enough, with his feet apart, braced against staggering. He stopped three feet from Doane, bent forward, his mouth slightly open.

"You got any objections to me being in town?"

"No," Doane said, and stood still.

Jordan thought that over, his eyes drifting idly sideways for a moment. Then they came back, to a finer focus this time, and he said, "Why not?" hunching forward again, his hands open and held away from the holsters at his hips.

Doane looked at the point of his nose. "You haven't done anything, Jordan. Except get drunk. Nothing to break the law."

"I haven't done nothing," Jordan said, his eyes squinting away at one of the small, tilting tombstones. "By God,

I'll do something. Whadda I got to do?'' He drew his head back, as though he were farsighted, and squinted. ''Whadda I got to do to make you fight, huh?''

''Don't do anything,'' Doane said quietly, keeping his voice even. ''Just go back and have another drink. Have a good time.''

''You think I ain't sober enough to fight?'' Jordan slipped his right gun out of its holster, turning away from Doane. Doane stiffened. ''Wait, mister,'' Jordan said.

He cocked the gun. ''See that bird?'' He raised the gun into the air, squinting along the barrel. The bright nickel of its finish gleamed in the sun. The lark wheeled and fluttered. Jordan's arm swung unsteadily in a small circle.

He pulled the trigger and the gun blasted. The lark jumped in the air, flew away about twenty feet, and began circling again, catching insects.

''Missed 'im,'' Jordan mumbled, lowering his arm and wiping sweat off his forehead. ''Damn it, I can't see!'' He raised his arm again. Again the heavy blast cracked Doane's ears. Down in the town, near the Mexican huts, he could see tiny figures run out into the street.

The bird didn't jump this time, but darted away out of sight over the hill.

''Got him,'' Jordan said, scanning the sky. His eyes wandered over the graveyard for a moment, looking for the bird's body. ''Now you see?'' he said, turning to Doane, his eyes blurred and watering with the sun's glare. ''I'm going down and shoot up the damned town. Come down and stop me, you old—''

He turned and lurched sideways a step, straightened himself out and walked more steadily toward his horse, laughing to himself. Doane turned away, his face sick, and trudged slowly up the hill, his eyes on the ground.

He stopped at one of the newer graves. The headstone was straight on this one. He looked at it, his face changing expression. ''Here lies Cecelia Doane, born 1837, died 1885, the loyal wife . . .''

He stooped and pulled a weed from the side of the grave, then pulled a bunch of withered stems from a small green funnel by the headstone, and awkwardly took the fresh flowers out of the newspaper. He put the flowers into the funnel, wedging them firmly down into the bottom, and set it down again. He stood up and moved back, wiping sweat from his eyes.

A sudden shout came from the gate, and the sharp crack of a quirt. Doane turned with a befuddled look.

Jordan was back on his horse, beating Doane's. He had looped the reins over its neck so that it would run free. It was tearing away down the slope headed back for town.

Doane stood with his hat in his hand, his face suddenly beet red. He took a step after Jordan, and then stood still, shaking a little. He stared fixedly after him, watching him turn into the main road and toward the main street again. Then, sighing deeply, he turned back to the grave. Folding the newspaper, he began dusting off the heavy slab, whispering to himself. "No, Cissie. I could have gone. But, you know—it's my town."

He straightened up, his face flushed, put on his hat, and slapping the folded paper against his knee, started down the path. He got to the Missouri gate, closed it, and started down the ruts again.

A shot came from the town, and he stopped. Then there were two more, sharp spurts of sound coming clear and definite across the sage. He made out a tiny figure in a blue shirt running along a sidewalk.

He stood stock-still, the grasshoppers singing in a contented chorus all around him in the bright yellow glare. A train whistle came faint from off the plain, and he looked far across it. He made out the tiny trailed plume of smoke.

His knees began to quiver very slightly and he began to walk, very slowly, down the road.

Then suddenly there was a splatter of shots from below. The train whistle came again, louder, a crying wail of despair in the burning, brilliant, dancing air.

He began to hurry, stumbling a little in the ruts. And then he stopped short, his face open in fear. "My God, my empty horse, those shots— Toby, no!" He began to run, shambling, awkward and stumbling, his face ashen.

From the end of the street, as he hobbled panting past the tight-shut Mexican shanties, he could see a blue patch in the dust in front of the saloon, and shambled to a halt. It wasn't Toby, whoever it was, lying there facedown: face buried in the deep, pillowing dust, feet still on the board sidewalk where the man had been standing.

The street was empty. None of the faces he knew looked at him now. He drew one of his guns and cocked it and walked fast up the walk, on the saloon side.

A shot smashed ahead of him and he stopped, shrinking against a store front. Inside, through the glass door, he could see two pale faces in the murk. Blue powder smoke curled out from under the saloon porch ahead of him.

Another shot smashed, this time from his office. The spurt of smoke, almost invisible in the sunlight, was low down in the doorway. Two horses were loose in the street now, his own, standing alert up past the saloon, and young Jordan's, half up on the boardwalk under one of the porches.

He walked forward, past young Jordan's horse, to the corner of the saloon building. Another shot slammed out of his office door, the bullet smacking the window ahead of him. A small, slow smile grew on his mouth. He looked sideways at the body in the street. Young Jordan lay with the back of his head open to the sun, crimson and brilliant, his bright nickel gun still in his right hand, its hammer still cocked, unfired.

The train whistle moaned again, closer.

"Doane," Toby called from the office door, invisible. "Get out of town." There was a surge of effort in the voice, a strain that made it almost a squeal. "I'm shot in the leg. Get out before they get together."

A door slammed somewhere. Doane glanced down between the saloon and the store beside it. Then he saw, fifty yards down the street, a figure come out of another side alley and hurry away down the walk toward the station. From the saloon door another shot slammed across the street. Toby held his fire.

Doane peered after the running figure, his eyes squinting thoughtfully. The train's whistle shrieked again like the ultimatum of an approaching conqueror at the edge of town, and in a moment the ground under his feet began to vibrate slightly and the hoarse roar of braking wheels came up the street.

He turned back to young Jordan's horse, petted it around the head a moment and then took it by the reins close to the bit. He guided it across the street, keeping its body between him and the front of the saloon, without drawing fire, and went on down the alley beside his office. At the rear door he hitched the horse and went inside.

Toby was on the floor, a gun in his hand, his hat beside him, peering out across the sill. Doane kept low, beneath the level of the window, and crawled up to him. Toby's left leg was twisted peculiarly and blood leaked steadily out from the boot top onto the floor. His face was sweating and very pale, and his lips were tight.

"I thought he got you," Toby said, keeping his eyes on the saloon across the street. "I heard those shots and then your horse came bucketing back down the street. I got Jordan. Colby got me in the leg before I got back inside."

"Never mind about that. Come on, get on your feet if you can and I'll help you on the horse in back. You can get out of town and I'll shift for myself."

"I think I'm going to pass out. I don't want to move. It won't hurt no worse getting killed than it does now. The hell with the horse! Take it yourself."

Doane looked across the street, his eyes moving over the door and the windows carefully, inch by inch.

"I'm sorry I shot him," Toby said. "It's my fault. And it's my fight now, Doane. Clear out."

Doane turned and scuttled out of the back. He mounted the horse and rode down behind four stores. He turned up another alley, dashed across the main street, down another alley, then back up behind the saloon.

He dismounted, his gun cocked in his hand. The back door of the place was open and he got through it quickly, the sound of his boot heels dimmed under the blast of a shot from the front of the saloon. From the dark rear of the room, he could see Pierce, crouched behind the bar, squinting through a bullet hole in the stained-glass bottom half of the front window.

There was a bottle of whisky standing on the bar beside Pierce; he reached out a hand and tilted the bottle up to his mouth, half turning toward Doane as he did so. Pierce kept the bottle to his lips, pretending to drink, and, with his right hand invisible behind the bar, brought his gun into line with Doane.

The tip of Pierce's gun came over the edge of the bar, the rest of him not moving a hair, and Doane, gritting his teeth, squeezed slowly and painfully on his gun trigger. The gun flamed and bucked in his hand, and he dropped it, his face twisting in agony. The bottle fell out of Pierce's hand and spun slowly on the bar. Pierce sat there for a moment before his head fell forward and he crashed against the edge of the bar and slipped down out of sight.

Doane picked up his gun with his left hand and walked forward to the bar, holding his right hand like a crippled paw in front of him. The bottle had stopped revolving. Whisky inside it, moving back and forth, rocked it gently. He righted it and took a short pull at the neck, and in a moment the pain lines relaxed in his face. He went to the batwing doors and pushed one of them partly open.

"Toby!" he called.

There was no answer from across the street, and then he saw the barrel of a revolver sticking out of his office door, lying flat, and behind it one hand, curled loosely and uselessly around the butt.

He looked down the street. The train stood across it. A brakeman moved along the cars slowly, his head down. There was nobody else in sight.

He started to step out, and saw then two men coming up the opposite walk, running fast. Suddenly one of them stopped, grabbing the other by the arm, and pointed at him. He stared back for a moment, seeing Jordan clearly now, the square, hard face unchanged except for its pallor, bleak and bony as before.

Doane let the door swing to and continued to watch them over the top of it. They talked for a moment. Then Colby ran back down the street—well out of effective range—sprinted across it and disappeared. Down the street the engine, hidden by some buildings, chuffed angrily, and the cars began to move again. Jordan stood still, leaning against the front of a building, fully exposed, a hard smile on his face.

Doane turned and hurried to the back door. It opened outward. He slammed and bolted it, then hurried back to the front and waited, his gun ready. He smiled as the back door rattled, turned, fired a shot at it and listened. For a moment there was no sound. Then something solid hit it, bumped a couple of times and silence came again.

From the side of the building, just beyond the corner where Pierce's body lay, a shot crashed. The gun in the office door jumped out of the hand and spun wildly. The hand lay still.

He heard Jordan's voice from down the street, calling, the words formed slowly, slightly spaced.

"Is he dead?"

"Passed out," Colby called back.

"I'm going around back to get him. Keep Doane inside." Jordan turned and disappeared down an alley.

Doane leaned across the bar, knocked bottles off the shelves of the back bar and held his pistol on the corner of the wall, about a foot above the floor.

"Pierce," he said.

"Throw out your guns," Pierce answered.

Doane squinted at the corner, moved his gun slightly and fired. He heard a cry of pain, then curses; saw the batwing doors swing slightly. Then he turned and ran for the back door. He threw back the bolt and pushed on the door. It wouldn't give. He threw himself against it. It gave a little at the bottom. Colby had thrown a stake up against it to keep him locked in.

He ran back to the front.

Across the street, he could see somebody moving in his

office, dimly, beyond the window. Suddenly the hand on the floor disappeared.

"Come on out, you old ——," Pierce said, panting. "You only skinned me." His voice was closer than before, somewhere between the door and the corner of the building, below the level of the stained glass.

Then Doane saw Toby's white shirt beyond the window opposite. Jordan was holding him up, and moving toward the door. Jordan came out on the porch, hugging Toby around the chest, protecting himself with the limp body. With a heave he sent Toby flying down the steps, and jumped back out of sight. Toby rolled across the sidewalk and fell into the street, where he lay motionless.

Doane looked stupidly at Toby, then at young Jordan, still lying with his feet cocked up on the sidewalk.

"He ain't dead, Doane," Jordan called. "Come and get him if you want him alive." He fired through the window. Dust jumped six inches from Toby's head. "Come on out, Doane, and shoot it out. You got a chance to save him." The gun roared again, and dust jumped a second time beside Toby's head, almost in the same spot.

"Leave the kid alone," Doane called. "This fight's between you and me."

"The next shot kills him, Doane."

Doane's face sagged white and he leaned against the side of the door. He could hear Pierce breathing heavily in the silence, just outside. He pushed himself away from the door and drew a breath through clenched teeth. He cocked his pistol and strode out, swinging around. Pierce fired from the sidewalk, and Doane aimed straight into the blast and pulled as he felt himself flung violently around by Pierce's bullet.

Pierce came up from the sidewalk and took two steps toward him, opening and shutting a mouth that was suddenly full of blood, his eyes wide and wild, and then pitched down at his feet.

Doane's right arm hung useless, his gun at his feet. With his left hand he drew his other gun and stepped out from the walk, his mouth wide open, as though he were gasping for breath or were about to scream, and took two steps toward Toby as Jordan came out of the office door, firing. The slug caught Doane along the side of his neck, cutting the shoulder muscle, and his head fell over to one side. He staggered on, firing. He saw Toby trying to get up, saw Jordan fall back against the building, red running down the front of his shirt, and the smile gone.

Jordan stood braced against the building, holding his gun in both hands, firing as he slid slowly down. One bullet took Doane in the stomach, another in the knee. He went down, flopped forward and dragged himself up to where Toby lay trying to prop himself up on one elbow. Doane knelt there like a dog, puking blood into the dust, blood running out of his nose, but his gray eyes almost indifferent, as though there were one man dying and another watching.

He saw Jordan lift his gun with both hands and aim it toward Toby, and as the hammer fell, he threw himself across Toby's head and took it in the back. He rolled off onto his back and lay staring into the sky.

Upside down, he saw Toby take his gun and get up on one elbow, level it at Jordan and fire, and then saw Toby's face, over his, looking down at him as the deputy knelt in the street.

They stayed that way for a long moment, while Doane's eyes grew more and more dull and the dark of his blood in the white dust grew broader. His breath was coming hard, in small sharp gasps.

"There's nothing in it, kid," he whispered. "Only a tin star. They don't hang the right ones. You got to fight everything twice. It's a job for a dog."

"Thank you, Doane."

"It's all for free. You going to quit, Toby?"

Toby looked down at the gray face, the mouth and chin and neck crimson, the gray eyes dull. Toby shook his head. His face was hard as a rock.

Doane's face suddenly looked a little surprised, his eyes went past Toby to the sky. Toby looked up. A lark was high above them, circling and fluttering, directly overhead.

"A pretty bird," Doane mumbled. "A very pretty bird."

His head turned slowly to one side, and Toby looked down at him and saw him as though fast asleep.

He took Doane's gun in his hand, and took off Doane's star, and sat there in the street while men slowly came out of stores and circled about them. He sat there unmoving, looking at Doane's half-averted face, holding the two things tightly, one in each hand, like a child with a broken toy, his face soft and blurred, his eyes unwet.

After a while the lark went away. He looked up at the men, and saw Mettrick.

"I told him he should have resigned," Mettrick said, his voice high. "He could have taken his horse—"

"Shut up," Toby said. "Shut up or get out." His eyes were sharp and his face placid and set. He turned to another of the men. "Get the doc," he said. "I've got a busted leg. And I've got a lot to do."

The man looked at him, a little startled, and then ran.

PERMISSIONS